Also by Bernadette Strachan

THE RELUCTANT LANDLADY

About the Author

Bernadette Strachan was born in Fulham, London. Before becoming an author she ran a wool shop, produced radio commercials and was a voice-over agent representing many household names including Stephen Fry, Hugh Laurie and Johnny Vegas. Bernadette is married to Matthew. They have one daughter, Niamh, and live in the shadow of Twickenham's rugby stadium. *Handbags and Halos* is her second novel.

Bernadette Strachan

Handbags and Halos

HODDER

Copyright © 2005 by StrawnyGawn Words and Music

First published in Great Britain in 2005 by Hodder and Stoughton
A division of Hodder Headline

The right of Bernadette Strachan to be identified as the Author
of the Work has been asserted by her in accordance with the
Copyright, Designs and Patents Act 1988

A Hodder paperback

7

A CIP catalogue record for this title is
available from the British Library

ISBN 0 340 83198 7

Typeset in Sabon by Palimpsest Book Production Limited,
Polmont, Stirlingshire

Printed and bound by
Mackays of Chatham Ltd, Chatham, Kent

Hodder Headline's policy is to use papers that are natural, renewable
and recyclable products and made from wood grown in sustainable
forests. The logging and manufacturing processes are expected to
conform to the environmental regulations of the country of origin.

Hodder and Stoughton Ltd
A division of Hodder Headline
338 Euston Road
London NW1 3BH

This book is for
Niamh Strachan
and for
Lily and Jim Gaughan

They never met, but I suspect
they'd like each other an awful lot.

Acknowledgements

Thank you, each and every person who bought *The Reluctant Landlady* – if I could I'd buy every one of you a hot chocolate or a vodkatini, depending on personal preference. Thank you, Jenna Strachan, for baby minding over and above the call of duty while I was writing this book. Thank you, Annette Green, for your wise agenting. Thank you, Julia Tyrell, for introducing me to Annette. Thank you, Sara Kinsella, for your patience and for your skilful editing. Thank you, Hazel Orme, for your precision. Thank you, Stuart Mills and Marie Benton from the Downs Syndrome Association, for ensuring that Clover is true to life. Thank you, Kate Haldane and Penny Warnes-Killick, for your brave reading of the first rough manuscript. And, finally, thank you, Matthew Strachan for the inspired ideas, the ruthless criticism, the cups of tea, as well as all the good stuff that Niamh and I get from you every day.

Nell Fitzgerald had been worried for some time now that she was shallow, but had fended off such thoughts with a bag of Chipstix and a soap opera. She had reassured herself that a shallow person wouldn't worry about being shallow; they'd be too shallow to notice their own essential shallowness.

Ipso facto she was deep.

This thought pleased her, but then she would look down at the Chipstix and up at the screen and conclude that no truly deep person would be enjoying these activities quite so much.

Ergo, Nell was shallow.

One

Her big mistake, that rat-coloured dawn, was to spend so long on the note. Nell wanted it to say everything that was in her head, to translate the flounderings of her heart. Somehow she'd spent the small hours distilling two poetic sides of A4 into 'I don't love you any more. Sorry. And please don't sleep with that permed girl from the off-licence for revenge.'

It would have to do. Daylight was rudely insinuating itself through the wonky Ikea blind. As she crept about the Arctic bedroom, she endeavoured to be stealthy. She was not designed for stealth, and the room wouldn't co-operate. The floorboards creaked a jaunty tune under her clumsy feet and the cupboard doors squealed like persecuted cats.

At every squeak, Nell threw a paranoid glance at the figure in the bed. Spreadeagled in the rumpled sheets, Gareth remained asleep but was eerily quiet. He could usually be relied on to snore the 'Hallelujah Chorus', but this morning he slept like a vestal virgin. His silence added considerably to the tension of dismantling three years of her life.

If Nell was honest Gareth was already firmly in the past. Long ago her heart had fled this stuffy flat, shoehorned into the eaves. Now her less impulsive, far noisier body was following. Clutching an archive of greying knickers to her chest, she gazed down at the face that had once fascinated her. Frowning and purplish, it radiated anger even in sleep. A rugby-player's mug, it bore the stud marks of every boot that had trodden it into the mud, and was attached to a rugby-player's body without the customary conduit of a neck.

Suddenly Gareth shuddered, and smacked his lips like a

camel. Nell panicked and dropped her knickers – hardly a first. Gareth's eyelids creased and he dragged a leaden hand across his brow.

Nell willed him not to wake up. She badly needed a few hours' start. His anger could only be dealt with at a distance. During arguments he had two volumes, Loud and Even Louder, and a habit of positioning his face an inch from hers. He was opinionated, lacked emotional brakes, and fighting with him made Nell feel as if she'd been run over by a tank.

He nestled further into the duvet. Nell's lungs rebooted.

For somebody who never had anything to wear, Nell had an awful lot of clothes. Disregarding time-consuming niceties like folding, she waded through the multicoloured swamp of her wardrobe and had soon filled a rucksack.

Underfoot a tiny white teddy, holding a scarlet heart embroidered with 'I LOVE YOU!' in gold thread, stared up at her, accusation shining from its button eyes. She was paralysed. She didn't want it: she *knew* that Gareth had bought it at a garage on St Valentine's Day, despite his insistence that he'd sent away for it and had it specially embroidered. To leave it behind seemed callous, though . . . She tutted and stuffed it head-first into the rucksack.

A faint whir from the bedside table sent her tiptoeing crazily across the floorboards to slap the clock radio before it burst into life. A wilful creature, it woke them when it wanted to. Despite much fiddling with its innards, they'd grown used to being startled into yelping wakefulness by Fat Boy Slim at all hours.

Under the covers Gareth muttered something and farted extravagantly. He was coming to. Nell dragged on her jean jacket, wincing at the noise as it slid over her bangles. Then she propped up the flimsy note in front of the bedside photo of their Cretan holiday, with the kind of care usually afforded to fragments of nuclear waste.

Two sunburned foreheads peeped over the top of the note and unexpected pain sang through her. Once, those foreheads had been happy together. She shook herself. The room was brightening and so was Gareth. It was time to go before the knocking of her heart woke him up.

She stole over to the door like a jewel thief, picked up her bag and slunk out. No lingering last looks, no tearful kiss on the brow. Nell didn't feel like a romantic figure in a touching scene, more like a lifer who had stumbled on the keys to the main gate.

She negotiated the stairs silently and efficiently, executing the turns on the landings like a figure-skater. At the front door she stood with her hand on the latch, her mind speeding. She was almost free. Still as a waxwork, she frowned at the greasy cord carpet the landlord had promised to replace. 'I really am sorry, Gareth,' she whispered.

As she slipped through the front door, like a ghost, Nell took a last view of the 1920s semis opposite and breathed in the west London early-morning air for the last time. Then she eased the rusty garden gate shut behind her.

She was out.

Across the way, she saw the tousled mongrel from two doors down, his raggedy ears pricked. She was used to his attentions – she was the kind of girl who always had a square of chocolate in her handbag. She blew him a kiss and he darted across the street to greet her, blind to the milk float lumbering round the corner.

As Nell bent to tighten the strap on her rucksack, the mongrel speeded up, the milkman's life flashed before his eyes, and the float careered into Gareth's garden wall. Four hundred milk bottles leaped into the air. The ones that didn't break made as much noise as the ones that did. Even without the hollering of the milkman and the ecstatic barking of the dog, it was easily the noisiest event Nell had witnessed outside a surround-sound Multiplex.

With dread she peered at the tiny window high under the roof. The blind flew up. Gareth glowered down. She watched as he took in the irate milkie, his partly demolished wall, the

Gold Top tidal wave and his runaway girlfriend, who was as white as the milk that lapped at her feet.

Gareth's considerable jaw dropped. Then he disappeared. Nell reckoned she had two minutes. He would scan the note, locate something to throw on, then take the stairs in a series of leaps.

Two minutes tops. She sank, dejected, on to what was left of the wall to await the inevitable scene, then did the traditional thing and burst into tears.

Luckily for Nell, the milkman was an unusual man. 'I don't like to see a woman cry,' he said firmly, then asked her what was wrong.

When he heard her gurgled, damp reply, his overall and peaked cap transformed into shining armour. 'Hop on.' He started up the milk float. 'I'll get you out of here. No big bully's having a go at you if I've got anything to do with it.'

So on Nell hopped, tears stemmed by the surrealism of making her escape in a milk float. The battered vehicle coughed, then reversed bumpily over the remains of the wall. The milkman's eyes were two slivers of blue steel as he set his chin towards the high street. Testosterone rolled off him in waves: this was how Clint Eastwood would deliver yoghurt.

The front door burst open.

'It's him!' squeaked Nell – a signal for her getaway driver to put his foot down and burn rubber.

But he was already burning rubber. Nell felt . . . Stupid is the best word to describe how it feels to flee for one's life in a vehicle with a top speed of eight miles an hour.

Burly legs akimbo, Gareth stood at the gate, radiating rage and confusion. He had on one of Nell's extensive collection of short cheap dressing-gowns (a particularly short cheap fuchsia nylon one) and it wasn't quite up to the job.

Nell saw him bend down to retrieve something from the milky rubble, then turned to stare resolutely ahead. She willed him, just this once, to decide against confrontation.

Beside her, the milkman was hunched over the wheel, his face a poem of determination. Behind her she heard the slap-thwap-thwap of large flat feet running through milk.

Gareth drew level with Nell, who was perched in the tiny cab. It was vaguely humiliating that he was walking only moderately fast to keep up but, worse, he was silent. He simply glared at her as he kept pace with the milk float, pink garment flapping pornographically.

Her gaze fixed ahead, Nell's face crumpled. This was so much more painful than it had to be.

The pounding of Gareth's feet slowed and stopped. The milk float turned the corner of the street and the milkman uttered a triumphant 'Ha!'

It was safe for Nell to risk a peek over her shoulder.

Gareth stood in the middle of the road. Now she could she what he'd picked up from the pavement. That wretched little bear, still insisting 'I LOVE YOU!', was in his hand. As she watched he brought it to his face.

In the three years they'd spent together, Nell had never seen Gareth make a gesture like that.

Nell was bad at planning. She was bad at lots of things – maths, lying, icing cakes – but this failing was particularly relevant on that early morning. It was obvious now: she should have called her grandmother to check that she could stay with her *before* she'd left Gareth.

'Posh,' the cab driver had commented, when she'd asked him to take her to Hans Place, Knightsbridge. Nell had squirmed. Claudette de Montrachet was indeed posh: she was wealthy, elegant, cultured, and she considered the Queen to be Teutonic trailer-trash.

Nell had run speedily through the options open to her, and discounted her mother immediately. The tiny terraced house in Fulham was already bursting with half-brothers and -sister, not to mention a stepfather with a belly for every day of the week. Nell had struck out on her own ten years ago, and didn't feel able to go back. It was as if the family had healed round the tiny hole she had left.

A trawl through her friends had ruled them out too. It's one thing to turn up expectedly, quite another to knock on the door at sunrise, asking to monopolise the sofa-bed for the foreseeable future.

Obviously, her Official Best Friend would take her in without hesitation, but Nell could imagine the look on Tina's boyfriend's face when he was confronted before breakfast with a lovelorn refugee and it didn't translate as 'Do come in'.

As for a hotel, Nell's purse ruled that out. Rather firmly.

So, Claudette's it would have to be.

It was a tiny round brass doorbell. It would take little or no effort to push it, but Nell hesitated on the wide stone step.

It shouldn't be like this, she thought. It's a known fact that a grandmother is a plump apron-wearer with bad legs, a bingo habit, flour on the end of her nose and a noisy welcome for any passing prodigal grandchild.

But there was no guarantee of a welcome from Claudette. Her sense of family loyalty was as slender as her waist. How Nell envied her friends their cosy, dumpy grans, who could be relied upon to go about their business in M&S separates, the ensemble daringly complemented with Clarks slip-ons. She felt underprivileged to have a grandmother who wore Chanel to defrost the fridge and was on first-name terms with Manolo Blahnik (*'Darling* Mano!').

To be fair to Claudette, this description was unjust – she would never have been caught dead defrosting a fridge.

The red-brick mansion block gleamed damply in the drizzle, perfect, smug, expensive. It made Nell want to run off and set up home in a cardboard box. She pressed the bell marked 'de Montrachet'.

With disconcerting speed a faintly aggrieved male voice wafted out of the grille. 'Yes?'

'Hi, Fergus. It's Nell.'

The slightest pause, like a hummingbird missing a beat, then, 'Nell who, Miss?'

Fergus was the only butler Nell had ever encountered outside the pages of P. G. Wodehouse. If they were all like him she wasn't surprised they were an endangered species. '*Nell*, Fergus. Nell Fitzgerald.' He'd known her since she was a teenager and still opened the door to her on the first Sunday of every month when she paid a dutiful visit to her grandmother.

'Good morning, Miss. Are we expecting you?'

'No. Just a spur-of-the-moment thing.' Another pause. Fergus was good at them. 'Is it OK if I come in? It's ever so slightly raining on me down here.'

Fergus watched impassively as Nell manhandled her unwieldy rucksack across the threshold of the penthouse. He was immaculate in pinstripe trousers and a frock coat. To Nell, who always dressed as if she were fleeing from a burning building, he was abnormally neat. It just wasn't right.

'A pleasant surprise, Miss.' Fergus's all-purpose monotone might as easily have conveyed, 'Your hair is on fire' or 'I have two hours to live'. He was displaying neither pleasure nor surprise.

Uncomfortably aware that her Reeboks – surely the first ever to enter this address – were seeping proletarian crud into the Wilton, Nell asked, 'Is my grandmother up?'

'Madame does not rise until eight.' Then, with an eloquent glance at an ormolu clock on an inlaid side-table, Fergus pointed out, as if to a slow-on-the-uptake toddler, 'It is now six twenty, Miss.'

Nell itched to pick up the clock and beat Fergus insensible, but she explained evenly, 'I need somewhere to crash. *Stay*, I mean. Just for a while. Could I dump my stuff in a spare room and work it out with Grand – Madame when I get back from work?'

With a tilt of his Brylcreemed head, Fergus agreed. He was

a professional and emitted only the tiniest mew of distaste as he picked up the rucksack with a white-gloved hand. 'Follow me to the Heliotrope Room, Miss,' he whispered, and sashayed – he was the only person Nell knew who really did sashay – down the endless hall ahead of her.

The Heliotrope Room was large and luxurious, with lavender walls. Later the office dictionary would enlighten Nell: 'heliotrope' meant 'lavender' – she'd half expected to find an Edwardian time-machine by the bed.

'Ring if you need anything, Miss.' Fergus closed the door noiselessly behind him. He did everything noiselessly, as if his personal soundtrack had been muted. It was almost as disconcerting as the Brylcreem.

Marooned on a Persian rug worth more than a Barratt starter home, Nell felt overwhelmed by the style in which Claudette chose to live. Silk curtains draped the windows and crystal scent bottles glittered in strict formation on the antique dressing-table. The taste displayed was faultless but, as usual in this penthouse, Claudette's granddaughter felt as if she'd ordered a bacon sarnie but was being force-fed *pâté de foie gras*.

In her unironed, milk-splattered combats Nell was a blot on the elegant landscape. She decided to shower and change before she went into the office. She was trembling, she noticed. It had been a big day already and she wasn't usually up yet.

As she tugged at the rucksack's recalcitrant zip, Nell tried to imagine what her mother would say when she heard where her eldest child was staying. There would be a sustained blast of Dublin-style bad language, followed by an eloquent attempt to talk her out of it.

Nell was the fragile link between the two sides of her family. When Patsy Fitzgerald – freckled, lively and with legs that might have made a pope reconsider – had stepped off the ferry into Philippe de Montrachet's life thirty years ago, she had been catnip to the bored, spoilt young man raised on a bland diet of debs.

With hindsight, maybe he should have introduced his girl-friend to his mother *before* he realised she was pregnant. He was cut out of Claudette's life – and purse – on the spot. It was only later, after Philippe had released himself into the wild and Patsy was struggling as a single parent to bring up Nell, that Claudette had reappeared.

Now, as Nell pulled the first of her tangled clothes out of her rucksack, she felt a reprise of the feelings she'd had as a teenager when she'd visited her grandmother. Guilt at leaving her overworked, exhausted mum at home in their bare flat had always floated in the scented air of this apartment. The two women never spoke: Claudette had always sent her chauffeur to Patsy's door. Nell cringed at the memory, then squashed it by piling her current woes on top. They covered it nicely.

She continued to unpack her things. And, by gum, what things they were. As useless crumpled item followed useless crumpled item on to the satin eiderdown, Nell despaired of finding two useless crumpled items that went together. A sarong in March? And as for this floppy jumper, it had been sitting in its H&M bag, waiting patiently to go back to the shop since Gareth had mentioned casually that it made her look ever so slightly pregnant. Did she really need eighteen thongs? Bras were mysteriously absent but at least she'd remembered to pack her fabulous green suede boots.

Well, one of them.

Showering in the en-suite bathroom, which was large enough to host a bar mitzvah, Nell basted her bottom with Dior shower gel. Later, when she was dressed, the mirror confirmed she looked every bit as dishevelled as usual, but underneath the sarong and the pregnancy jumper her skin was as smooth as a (very wealthy) newborn baby's.

Fergus held open the front door for her as she bustled out of the apartment. 'Might I enquire what time you intend to return, Miss?' he asked.

'I'm going for a drink after work, so lateish. What time does Claudette go to bed?'

'Madame retires at ten.' Fergus always made Nell feel that she'd chosen her words clumsily. 'Might I suggest that you breakfast with her tomorrow morning? I'm sure she will be most interested to hear your plans.'

The subtitles were clear. She'd only just arrived but this smarmy throwback was rabid to know when she was leaving. 'Me too,' she muttered.

Two

It was a very long morning at Morgan Theatrical Management. Zoë, the receptionist, had been ordered not to put Gareth through, but couldn't be trusted for the twin reasons of inefficiency and sadism, so every time the phone rang on Nell's desk, she leaped like a cricket. Finding it impossible to concentrate, she pushed urgent memos around her blotter. Despite the tempting array of superstar cellulite on the cover she didn't even feel up to a covert flick through *heat*. She needed to talk to Tina, bring her up to date. By this late stage of the morning they should have exchanged a dozen or so stupid emails and had a couple of long chats in the loo. But Tina had been cloistered with her boss all morning: when Nell finally got her on the phone, she grumbled, 'It's like having a bloody normal job.'

'I need to speak to you,' said Nell, injecting dark meaning into her delivery.

'Can't,' whined Tina. 'We've got a new client arriving any minute. His nibs is very excited, reckons she'll add some class to the list. She's the new pet astrologer on breakfast telly. Will it keep?'

'I suppose it'll have to.'

Tina and Nell had worked together at Morgan's for five years. They were PAs, a catch-all title that meant they were humble enough to make coffee but confident enough to negotiate contracts. Tina's boss was the senior agent, and answerable only to Nell's boss, the eponymous Louis Morgan. Nell and Tina's friendship had rapidly outstripped the standard banal office relationship and they knew everything about each other's likes, dislikes, fears and hopes. Nell often had to sieve her life through Tina before she was quite sure what to make of it. This latest development would thrill her friend: Tina had lobbied long and hard for Gareth's removal and it felt strange to withhold such vital information.

That morning a momentous step for Nell-kind had been taken in a loft extension, but all around her the pale-wood and glass-brick fiefdom of Morgan Theatrical Management carried on as normal.

Dean, the post-boy, trundled past with his little cart, giving his myriad spots a tender, surreptitious feel. In Accounts, Jean's lilac perm was bent low over Nell's petty-cash receipts, which made their usual sensational reading. Behind her monumental reception desk Zoë carried on with her meticulous manicure, occasionally pressing the wrong button on the high-tech switchboard.

None of them knew about Nell's troubled thoughts as she doodled little houses on a letter marked 'EXTREMELY URGENT'. Surely, she reasoned, Gareth should have come looking for her by now with a baseball bat or, worse, flowers? Where were the venomous/pathetic phone calls damning her bitch arse to hell/begging her to come home? His silence was articulate. Was it possible she could have lived with a man for three years and had no effect on him whatsoever? If this was true, it pushed her shallowness to new heights. As it were.

With a deft mental back-flip, Nell switched from dreading the sound of Gareth's voice to dreading not hearing it.

A mug of coffee appeared on her blotter. 'Dean!' she said, glad of the distraction. 'How did you know that that was what I wanted most in the world just now?'

'Dunno.' Never eloquent, Dean was always tongue-tied in Nell's vicinity. His mute adoration was a major source of amusement to the thrill-hungry staff at Morgan Theatrical Management. An awkward, shuffling bundle of loose-fitting sweat-clothes, he was an innocent under the streetwise gear. This made him perfect for teasing.

But not today: today Nell appreciated him. 'Mmm. Now, that's what I call a good cup of coffee.'

Dean made an embarrassed noise that might have been 'Thank you', 'Kiss me' or 'Disestablishmentarianism' and stumbled out, tripping over his laces.

It was then that Nell noticed the lone Twix lounging in her in-tray. Never keen on the idea of Prozac, she self-prescribed chocolate at times of stress. Today certainly qualified, so Nell undressed the Twix as greedily as if it was a boy-band member full of cider.

'Two hundred and forty calories, and fourteen grams of fat!' trilled a crystal clear voice from the doorway.

'And almost as enjoyable as sexual intercourse. Good morning, Linda.'

For it was she: Linda, the office manager, in all her colour-co-ordinated glory. Not a pleat out of place and not a heart beneath her chainstore silk-effect tie-neck blouse.

'You look tired,' chirruped Linda, in the sweet tone that only the truly evil can achieve. She was the Mozart of passive aggression. 'Thursday already! Can you believe it? Anything planned for the weekend?'

'Fear. Anxiety. Some dread,' answered Nell, candidly. 'You?'

'Mum's coming down so we're taking in a needlework exhibition and she's going to look for a cardigan in the sales.'

Nell hadn't expected lesbian orgies but this sounded dull even by Linda's standards. 'Have you ever wondered why people in offices do that?'

'Do what? Buy cardigans?' Linda's faultlessly powdered nose wrinkled with puzzlement.

'Ask each other what they do at the weekend.'

'Some of us are genuinely interested in our colleagues' well-being,' said Linda, like a melodious Sunday-school teacher. 'For example, I'm honoured that the temp trusted me with the information that she needs this afternoon off to visit a sexually transmitted diseases clinic.' Across the open-plan outer office a muffled sob was heard as a peroxide head hit a desk. The rest of the staff swivelled to look at Barry, the security guard, who went pale.

Linda jangled an old Nescafé jar full of coins. 'I'm collecting!' she announced.

'You're expecting?' Nell misheard wickedly. Linda's front bottom was famously unexplored – like the Congo Basin, but less interesting.

'*Collecting*,' stressed Linda, slightly pink. 'The cleaner's having another baby.'

'Are we super-fertile in this company or what?' asked Nell, dropping in two tenpence pieces as heavily as she could in the hope that they might sound like fifties. 'We're always collecting for babies. Or birthdays. Or retirements. Or weddings.'

'I'm always collecting, you mean.' Linda liked to feel that she wore the immense burden of her duty lightly. 'Somehow I've got to make time to slip out to Mothercare, even though I have a mountain of typing to get through.'

Death threats, presumably, or long memos about how the misuse of company paperclips would bring about a nuclear holocaust. 'How's the Watergate investigation coming along?'

'Watergate? Oh, you're referring to the petty-cash discrepancies.' Linda's face took on a closed look: she was a sphinx in man-made fibres. 'There have been developments.' And with that she was gone, in a cloud of Tweed by Lenthéric.

The staggering sum of eight pounds ten had been unaccounted for when the petty cash had last been reconciled and scandal had rocked the office. Although this was roughly a twentieth of what Louis Morgan regularly spent on lunch, Linda was as implacable as the Witch-finder General.

Along with scaring juniors, allocating blame was one of Linda's favourite pastimes. It was generally believed that Jean, who had been in Accounts since God was in nappies, had hushed up a rogue taxi fare but so far, despite many 'little chats' with Linda over milky tea and thinly disguised threats, she hadn't cracked.

'COFFEE, DARLING!' came a roar from Louis's office. He had woken up.

'No, thanks, just had one,' Nell called back.

'VERY FUCKING FUNNY!'

Nell scuttled the length of his Serengeti-proportioned office, holding a china cup like a sacrificial offering. Louis was already barking dictation at her as she folded herself into an uncomfortable chrome and leather designer chair. Knees tucked behind her ears, she started to scribble.

Louis Morgan, half Welsh and half French, saw himself as a benign paterfamilias to his respectful staff, wise beyond his years and, indeed, his height. His staff saw him as a bearded despot who was prone to tantrums that would shame a toddler high on E numbers, and unable to pass a female posterior without offering loud, expert analysis. They didn't appreciate his efforts to bond with them by pretending they were sacked. However, Louis was a happy man: he was immensely wealthy and on first-name terms with Liz Hurley, which was all his scant spirituality demanded.

'Book me a table for two at nine p.m., the Ivy. A discreet corner,' he said.

Hunched like a stick insect, Nell wrote, 'IVY.9. DISC.' She had never mastered shorthand, and had devised a baroque system of her own that rivalled ancient runes for intricacy and, unfortunately, clarity. She was always booking Louis into the wrong restaurant opposite the wrong slapper. 'I'll do my best. It's short notice.'

'Tell them who it's for,' advised Louis, complacently.

'Oh, I see. You *want* to sit by the bogs.'

'They apologised.' When Louis growled from behind his beard like that, Nell was reminded of a Jack Russell she had known as a child: it had had a tumour on its back and a habit of urinating on sleeping babies. 'Tell Hildegard I have a late meeting and will be staying in town.'

'HILD MEET,' doodled Nell desperately. 'Claridges? Or is she a Travelodge kind of gal?'

'Claridges will do nicely, thank you.'

'CLARG' wrote Nell, decisively. 'Anything else?'

'Of course there's some-fucking-thing else,' fizzed Louis. 'What do you think I pay you for? There's more to being my PA than booking restaurants and putting laxatives in Linda's herbal tea. Yes,' he nodded, 'I know about that.'

'They were organic.' Nell bent over her pad.

She knew there was more to her job. There was lying to Louis's wife. There was smiling at the clients, mostly actors with egos as unwieldy as an elephant on a string. There was making appointments for starry-eyed young actresses, secure in the knowledge that their only audition would be a personal one in a hotel room during which Louis would call them 'Mummy' and after which he would never call them again. Oh, yes, there was much more to Nell's job.

'Read that back to me, darling,' ordered Louis, having dictated for the best part of an hour.

Stalling, Nell queried, 'Read? Back? *To* you, as it were?'

'GETONWITHIT!' roared Louis, dislodging antique Hobnob fragments from his beard.

'Right.' Nell squinted at the worm trails on her pad. 'Yes. *Okaaaaaaaay.* Here we go.' She limped through an approximation of what Louis had said, hoping he hadn't been paying attention to what he was saying.

'I suppose that will have to do,' he said wearily, when she'd finished. 'Now fuck off, darling.'

As Nell rose, like a winkle extracting itself from its shell, Louis asked suddenly, 'Are you, you know, all right?'

Nell was surprised by this question from such an unexpected quarter. 'Why do you ask?'

'You don't seem your usual self.'

'I split up with my boyfriend.' She had an urge to say it out loud, just to make it real. She shrugged.

'Really? I'm sorry to hear that.' Louis raised his unruly

eyebrows. 'Plenty more fish in the sea, darling,' he added. 'Go on now. Fuck off. Quicker rather than slower, there's a love.'

When Nell reached the door she stopped. Emboldened by Louis's uncharacteristic flash of compassion, she asked tentatively, 'Louis, do you ever, you know, find this business . . .' She hesitated, then spoke the word that had been bothering her recently: *'Shallow?'*

'Shallow?' Louis frowned, nonplussed. 'Showbusiness *shallow*?' He examined this novel idea. 'Darling, you are standing in a cathedral of light entertainment. You are the handmaiden of the high priest. Can it be shallow to bring the likes of Ant and Dec to the masses?' He studied Nell as if he were seeing her clearly for the first time. As she backed out, he said, 'Don't forget to book my primal-scream session, will you?'

'Don't people usually ring their mothers at times like this?' Nell stared, mystified, at her shorthand, fingers poised above the Mac keyboard. Maybe, on such an unsettling day she should peek over the emotional parapet and really *talk* to Patsy. She looked at the clock: would her mum be home or would she be out at one of her umpteen cleaning jobs?

Patsy Fitzgerald had always had a capacity for hard work, which, along with good legs and obedient hair, she hadn't passed on to her daughter. All through Nell's childhood, Patsy had held down a medley of menial jobs to keep their home together. Nell had been a 'good' child, quiet and undemanding as she was shuttled between kind or resentful neighbours who'd been press-ganged into helping keep the Fitzgerald ship afloat.

Patsy's sparkling looks had remained intact, and her cheerfulness almost never faltered, but her little girl had seen the lines of anxiety that crept into her face as they ate their tinned spaghetti in the evenings.

Then Ringo had appeared.

He wasn't cut from a Mills and Boon template – romantic heroes tend to have lots of hair and no belly, rather than the other way round – but he had transformed Patsy's life. His nickname was testimony to his fanatical devotion to the Beatles and the impressive dimensions of his nose. Nell was introduced to him in McDonald's on her tenth birthday, six months before he became her stepfather.

Then everything had changed. Their lifestyle, although still modest, was secure in the little terraced house in pre-gentrification Fulham. Ringo adored his Irish princess and looked after her little girl as lovingly as if she were his own. But that little girl still hoped childishly that the handsome daddy she knew only from blurred snapshots might come back for her. Ringo's booming London laugh drove her further into the daydreams that had sustained her through her early years.

Babies had come along. The twins, John and Paul (of course), and then Georgina (naturally) seemed to fill the house to bursting point. At seventeen Nell had found a flat share. She loved them all, she knew she did, but she felt out of place. They were loud, raucous and funny, with a self-confidence Nell lacked after a childhood spent tiptoeing round a snoozing, harassed mum. They were the salt of the earth, but . . .

Tina's sleek head came round a door at the other side of the office and distracted Nell from her gloomy analysis of family life. She snatched up the phone and dialled her friend's internal number. 'Meet me in the kitchenette.'

'Can't.'

'You have to.'

'Can't!'

'I've left Gareth.'

The line went dead. Tina was already half-way to the kettle.

Nell sped towards the rendezvous and realised too late that she was on a collision course with Linda. She tried to manoeuvre herself out of the woman's path by circling Jean twice, but Linda knew the routes through Morgan Theatrical Management like a gamekeeper knows his woods and bobbed up in front of Nell by the photocopier.

'Do you like it?' She was holding up a limp beige Babygro. 'For the cleaner's baby?'

Without breaking step Nell said, 'It's by far the most stunning and wantable Babygro I have ever seen in all my days,' hoping that hyperbole might shorten their exchange.

'Is that a stye on your left eye?' asked Linda, but Nell was already two desks away, bottom stuck out like a tea-tray as she zoomed along.

The kitchenette was a whitewashed windowless rectangle lit by a merciless fluorescent tube. Had it not been for the rows of novelty mugs it might have been an interrogation cell. Day-Glo cards were attached to the fingermarked walls with messages that read, in language that betrayed Linda's authorship, 'WASH THAT MUG', 'USE YOUR OWN MILK' and 'CRUMBS = MICE = DISEASE = DEATH or DAYS OFF'. On entering this haven, Nell was dismayed to discover that Tina was not alone.

Jane From Accounts was demurely preparing a Pot Noodle. 'Hiya!' she sang.

'Hiya!' Nell tried not to look crestfallen. She liked Jane From Accounts, who was quiet, easy-going and, helpfully, heavier than Nell. They often chatted inconsequentially while they waited for a frozen pizza to realise its destiny in the microwave.

Jane From Accounts lived with her mother somewhere beginning with R (Nell wasn't good on detail) and Nell found her banal interchanges with Jane a reassuring tile in the mosaic of office life. Now she plunged in without preamble: 'Did the whole home-help-elasticated-bandage thing work itself out?'

'Ho-ho, yes!' Jane From Accounts's novelty earrings trembled with pleasure as she recalled the hilarity of her mother's predicament. 'Turned out it was a medium and, of course, Mum is an XXL! Must be where I get it from!'

Nell recognised a cue when she heard one. She snorted loyally. 'I think you've lost a couple of pounds, actually.'

'Really? No!' Jane From Accounts's face shone as she

plucked at the homemade corduroy culottes that Nell itched to steal and burn. She was stirring her Pot Noodle with the kind of assiduous care normally lavished on an ancient family recipe. 'Nice, erm, sarong,' she said.

'Jesus!' Tina, glowering impatiently in the corner, noticed Nell's outfit. 'A sarong?'

'Yes. A sarong.' Nell was rather tired of today. 'I need a Cup-a-soup,' she said baldly, and without shame.

In a sad small baby voice that might be used to talk of dead kittens, Jane From Accounts said, 'They've all gone.'

'There *are* one or two left . . .' Tina paused for effect. 'They're Linda's.'

Struck dumb by the enormity of what was being suggested, the three stared at each other. Then, as if at some secret signal, Tina switched on the kettle, Jane From Accounts went to the photocopier on lookout, and Nell reached a shaking hand to the highest shelf in the cupboard and snatched the nearest sachet. *Damn!* Tomato and basil. It had none of the pizzazz of minestrone, or the elegance of asparagus with croûtons, but it would have to do.

'Quickly!' hissed Tina, holding out a mug with 'World's Best Uncle' on it.

Nell tipped in the powdery granules, freaking out mutedly when some drifted down to the chequered lino. She rubbed at it with a frantic toe: it wasn't out of the question for Linda to have a mini forensics lab in her filing cabinet. '*Go! Go!*' she barked and Tina poured in the boiling water.

Hardly daring to breathe, Nell slammed the cupboard door with one hand and stirred briskly with the other.

It was done.

She raised the steaming mug. When her eyes met Tina's the gleam of triumph was mutual.

At the photocopier, ignored by her partners in crime, Jane From Accounts was coughing and stamping like a toddler with a cigar.

Suddenly, unaccountably, Linda was among them. 'There

you are,' she rebuked Nell. 'I've got everybody looking for you.'

Mug aloft, Nell said, 'Uh?' in Neanderthal tones. She felt like one of the Great Train Robbers caught scratching his head with a gold ingot.

'There's a stack of publicity photos to be signed. Come on. Bring your soup.'

So Nell came on and brought her soup, leaving Jane From Accounts mouthing, *'Sorry!'* and Tina bent double with silent laughter.

Three

Writing 'Best regards, Lydia Chambers' over and over again was boring but therapeutic. Nell had ensconced herself in the post room with a hundred photographs of this ancient actress to autograph them for the fan club. It was a fraudulent aspect of her job that sometimes made her pause for thought. It was hard to resist the urge to sign the odd one 'With best regards, I am a hopeless alcoholic who can't fasten my bra in the mornings without a double vodka, Lydia Chambers', but Nell was a pro and didn't succumb.

The door opened and Tina sidled in with the air of a secret agent. 'He thinks I'm out getting him a granary bap. Tell me what's been going on,' she hissed, squatting down beside Nell and her stack of ten-by-fours.

'Well . . .' began Nell, and launched into an account of that morning's events. She left out no detail, either of emotion or incident: the rules forbade holding back.

Tina listened attentively, neat head nodding as the story rolled out. She was, as ever, frighteningly fashionable. Never knowingly under-funky, and always impeccably groomed, she formed an interesting counterpoint to Nell, who had come late to colour co-ordination. She paid the same attention to *Vogue* as Nell did to wine-boxes, and this difference in priorities showed.

As the saga continued to unfold Tina did an awful lot of stifled giggling – rather too much for Nell's liking. She was painfully aware that her love life read like an episode of *The Goodies*, but just now she needed careful handling.

'If this was a Richard Curtis film you'd marry that milkman,' said Tina, when Nell had finished.

'Well, it's not a film, it's my life,' Nell pointed out.

'So,' said Tina, somehow managing to sustain her squat – all that time at the gym obviously paid off, 'what now?' It was a typical Tina response to emotional upheaval. A doer rather than a thinker, she believed that introspection was worse for your health than cigarettes, that Tori Amos albums merited a government health warning. She habitually moved at a hundred miles an hour, while Nell favoured a more leisurely pace, with lots of nice sit-downs for cake.

'Dunno.' Nell borrowed Dean's word.

'That's not much of an answer. You sound as if some-body's pulled your plug out.'

'They have!' protested Nell. 'Give me a break, Teen. Eight hours ago I was living with Gareth.'

'And now you've got the future back. You've got to grab it with both hands!' She sounded unsettlingly like a motivational speaker. 'The best thing is to get back on the bike straight away.'

'The bike?' Nell didn't own one. They smacked of exercise and health.

'Or the horse.'

'You've lost me.'

'We need to set you up with a bloke. Pronto.'

Nell's felt-tip gave Lydia a Frankenstein scar across her forehead. '*No!*' she growled, and wrote it in large letters on Lydia's lifted cheeks. 'Promise me on Marti's life.'

Tina pulled a sulky face and nodded. She believed that love made the world go round. Failing that, lust made the world go round. Failing that, being taken out for a posh dinner by anybody with a penis made the world go round.

Nell struggled to explain how the world looked to her that drizzly morning. 'Look,' she said, 'Gareth has been there, right at the forefront of everything, blocking out all the light, for three years. Suddenly he's gone and there's a big blank space. Quite a scary blank space, if I'm honest.' She sighed. There was more to say but she wasn't sure how to describe the creeping feelings of futility that were being drip-fed into her consciousness. There was no guarantee that Tina would understand her paranoia about being shallow. If she started ranting about how vacuous her life and job were, Tina would presumably suggest that things were the same as they'd always been: why did it suddenly matter?

And Nell would have no answer.

'First things first.' Tina changed tack. 'You've got to have somewhere to stay. Obviously you'll crash with me and Marti for now.'

'Well . . .'

'We'll have a great laugh!'

Nell didn't share her certainty. She'd never had a great laugh with Marti. Or even a medium-sized one. In fact, there'd been times she'd considered feigning a stroke to get off home early. 'Actually I'm staying with Claudette,' she said.

'That old – your grandmother?'

'She's not so bad.'

'"Not so bad"?' parroted Tina. 'You've always described her as a head-fuck of the highest order.'

'It's for the best. She's got plenty of room.'

'But there's a jacuzzi in the basement at Marti's. And a plasma screen. And there's a rumour going round that George Michael's bought the loft across the hall!' She scrabbled for inducements. 'You needn't get up all weekend. I'll bed-bath you!'

'Tempting though that is, I've already made arrangements with Claudette,' lied Nell.

'Marti's coming in tomorrow. He'll persuade you.' Tina straightened up lithely.

Nell smiled to herself. Marti Goode couldn't have persuaded her that sugar was sweet.

Working in a theatrical agency, Nell was used to actors. She was used to their vanity, their charisma, their miserliness, their quick-wittedness, their inability to change their knickers without round-the-clock emotional support, but she'd never got used to the sheer *noise* some of them could generate.

As a rule, the smaller the talent the greater the commotion. Blair Taylor burst through Morgan Theatrical Management's double glass doors as if he was a helicopter making an emergency landing. 'Zoë! My angel!' he bellowed, his satin-lined coat flapping as he swooped to bestow air kisses on her. 'Mwah! Mwah! Did your nan like the photo?' he enquired, loud enough to be heard in the suburbs. He swivelled round. 'The nans love me,' he howed at the rodent-featured teenager who had slunk in in his wake. 'Don't they, Carlos?'

'Fnhh,' mumbled Carlos, shoulders hunched.

'I've just kitted him out top to toe in Bond Street.' Blair's tangerine face beamed with pride. 'Whaddayathink?'

'Lovely.' Zoë admired Carlos, while surreptitiously removing stealable items from the reception desk.

Blair looked about for others to greet. As befitted Britain's best-loved quizmaster, he was perpetually in host mode. Six foot four of fake tan and *chutzpah*, he had a Saturday-evening show, a recording contract, a ghost-written autobiography, his own coffee mug in Richard and Judy's makeup room and no discernible talent. 'And here's the lovely Linda!' He spotted his next quarry. 'Give us a snog, love!' He kissed her extravagantly, leaving a neat brown smudge on each cheek.

'You smell nice,' said Linda, daintily, as she fought to recover her equilibrium.

'Paco Rabanne and spunk, darling. Oh, here's gorgeous Nell. Isn't she gorgeous? She always looks gorgeous!'

Nell endured the mandatory embrace. At this proximity, Blair's aftershave was toxic. She told him that Louis was ready to see him.

'Behave yourselves while I'm gone, girls.' Blair delivered a resounding slap to Linda's bottom. It was possibly the only time that a male hand had achieved contact without the threat of a court case. 'Keep your hands off my Carlos, d'you hear?'

'I'll try,' promised Linda, the curl of her lip betraying that she would only touch Carlos in an emergency, with some-body else's bargepole.

Blair was always loquacious on his favourite subject – himself – but this meeting was unusually long. Nell had a stack of paperwork to do, but decided it would be a foolish waste of effort to tackle it if Louis wasn't around to notice so instead she applied herself to a copy of *Hello!* and tried to puzzle out how Prince Charles's hair worked.

Earwigging on Zoë's efforts to entertain the sulky Carlos in Reception helped pass the time. 'Do you think it's going to rain again?' asked Zoë, conversationally.

'I ain't a pouf, right?' he snarled.

Zoë gave up.

'*Hai carramba*!' Jane From Accounts appeared. She was twitching and seemed over-excited.

'You what?' said Nell.

'*Arriba arriba*!' She rolled her Rs recklessly and mimed castanets. 'The leaving party!' she gushed. 'For Sue, the secre-tary! You can't have forgotten! It's Friday fortnight!' She ran out of steam and exclamation marks as she registered Nell's blank look. 'Don't tell me you're not coming! Me and Sue have arranged it all. It's at that authentic salsa bar under W. H. Smith's.' She yelped like a dog that had been trodden on and did a deeply unsensuous wiggle.

Nell pulled an expressive face.

'You don't like salsa.' The imaginary castanets clattered to the floor. 'But I thought everybody liked salsa,' she said, in a small, disappointed voice.

Writhing Englishmen in bad suits who imagined that a glass of room-temperature rioja had transformed them into Antonio Banderas. Yum, thought Nell, what's not to like? But she *did* like Jane From Accounts and as, in the absence of a royal wedding, this party was obviously the biggest thing in her life, she grinned and said, 'Only messing about. I love salsa. I'll be there.'

'Ai! Ai! Ai!' shrieked Jane From Accounts into her face and undulated to the post room.

Perhaps, Nell consoled herself, by this time next week she'd be over the worst of the fallout from breaking up with Gareth. She would no longer be both dreading, and desperate for, the sound of his voice: she would be ready to face the basement under W. H. Smith's without terror.

Perhaps.

The door to Louis's office flew open and Blair staggered out, real pain etched on his face, which was ashen under his slap. He was walking as if under a spell – a spell that broke when he saw Nell's surprised face.

'No,' he whispered, leaning over her desk. '*No!*' he bayed, casting his kohl-rimmed eyes heavenwards. 'Carlos! Get me to my colonic irrigation!' He gave Nell another lingering, harrowed look. 'I can honestly say I've never needed one so much.'

'*What* was all that about?' Zoë was at Nell's desk before the doors had slammed behind him.

'Dunno,' said Nell, who was finding Dean's vocabulary useful today.

'Did you see the way he looked at you?' Jane From Accounts had stopped trying to teach Dean the rudiments of salsa – for which Dean was grateful – and was back.

'Yeah.' Nell felt uneasy, as all her colleagues turned like meerkats to peer at her. 'Get off, everyone,' she said limply.

'DARLING!' Her master's voice summoned her.

Nell picked up her pad and headed for Louis's door. 'He wants *me*, Linda,' she said, as that erect figure made for the door alongside her.

'This involves me too,' said, Linda, with a smile of such heartbreaking beauty that it had to signal disaster for Nell.

Nell glanced at the meerkats, who now looked as if a chill wind had blown over them. Jean gave a covert thumbs-up and Jane From Accounts made her gonk wave a furry hand.

In a strange way, it helped.

*   *   *

'So,' said Nell, folding herself into the low-slung leather chair and anxious to break the heavy silence, 'what sort of cardi are you after, Linda?'

'Never mind her fucking cardi,' snorted Louis. 'What have you got to say about *this?*' He motioned to Linda, who had stationed herself behind him, Gestapo-like in her pleats.

With demure, and entirely synthetic, reluctance, Linda put a slip of yellow paper on to the desk.

'Looks like a taxi receipt.' Nell had a hideous sinking feeling.

'One of *your* taxi receipts, Nell,' corrected Louis. His chubby fingers were laced together under his chin and he gazed at her sternly from beneath his ragged brows. It was a trick he'd picked up at the School for Horrid Bosses. 'Care to read out the fare?'

Nell would have much preferred to stuff it up Linda's skirt with some energy, but she picked it up and read out, 'Eight pounds and tenpence,' in what she hoped was a profoundly not-guilty-as-hell voice. She turned wide, questioning blue eyes on Louis.

'Can you see my initials or Linda's initials anywhere on it?'

'Er, let's see . . . Actually, I can't actually.' Nell managed to inject into the words a hint of surprise. She even turned over the hateful little bastard piece of paper to make sure. 'Now that you mention it.'

'So – correct me if I've got this wrong – that means it wasn't authorised?'

God, how she longed to tweeze out that beard hair by hair. 'Yes.' His theatricality was so unnecessary. Why didn't the old sod just sack her and be done with it? Then she could lose her relationship, her home and her job, all in one action-packed morning.

'Interesting, then, that the petty cash is short by exactly that amount. It's almost as if you'd been reimbursed, despite the lack of authorisation.'

'It is, isn't it?' agreed Nell, in a high voice she didn't quite recognise. She realised she was nodding over-vigorously, and stopped herself.

'What do you make of this, Linda?' Louis asked his hench-woman, with mock-solemnity.

Linda cleared her throat, like a policeman about to give evidence in an old movie, then said clearly, 'After extensive investigation I believe that on the twenty-eighth of February Miss Jean Pinkerton made a cash payment of eight pounds ten from company funds to Miss Eleanor Fitzgerald without logging this transaction. This transaction was therefore . . .' she paused to savour the word, a favourite of hers '. . . *illegal*.'

'It's a fair cop, Guv.' Nell had always wanted to say this, and hoped now that it might lighten the atmosphere.

It didn't. Louis continued to glare at her. This was very bad indeed: Nell relied on joking her way out of trouble with her boss. Suddenly she was staring unemployment in the face.

Behind Louis, Linda battled to remain impassive and profes-sional but she was evidently longing to perform a lap of honour.

'Tell me why I should continue to employ you,' grunted Louis.

The question startled Nell. Her mind raced. None of the traditional answers seemed appropriate. Or true. 'Er, I'm clean?'

'OK, you can't think of anything. Neither can I. Let's make this easier.' Not without difficulty, Louis lifted his legs on to his desk. 'Let's come up with reasons why I *shouldn't* employ you.'

Nell pretended to think hard, as if this was a real toughie.

Smoothly Louis reeled off a list. 'Lateness. Laziness. Epic personal phone calls. Post-lunch tipsiness. Two separate days off each month for girls' problems. Shall I go on?'

'You left out going home early.'

'So I did.'

Get it over with, Nell urged silently.

'But there is one thing that keeps me persevering with you.'

Nell was agog to hear what it was. Her ability to swear in Greek? The occasional low-cut top?

'The clients love you.'

'They do?'

'Yes, they tell me you're warm and funny and . . .' he stumbled over a word he didn't use much '. . . caring.'

Nell risked a small smile. She was starting to like this.

'No, don't smile,' warned Louis. 'I'm not praising you. I'm telling you that I don't want to employ you any more.'

Nell's face crumpled. She saw her mother crying. She heard her headmistress hollering, 'I told you so!' She foresaw having to fabricate yet another credible CV. The fight went out of her. 'OK,' she whispered.

'Unless you do one simple thing for me.'

'What?' Nell felt like a yo-yo. 'Am I sacked or not, Louis?'

'That depends. I need a favour. A small thing – you might even enjoy it if you approach it in the right spirit. And you'll get to keep your job.'

Nell didn't like his Cheshire Cat grin.

'Let me put you out of your misery.' Louis stood up and strode, a little lumpenly, round his domain. 'Morgan Theatrical Management has a problem. Blair Taylor.'

'What's wrong with him? Well, that's a long list – I mean, what's the problem?'

What could be seen of Louis's face behind his beard was drawn. 'There's a price on his head. The redtops want to out him.'

'*Out* him? You mean he's still in?' asked Nell, incredulously.

'Believe it or not, for large sections of the viewing community an air of mystery shrouds Blair's sexual preferences.'

'He wears purple mascara,' Nell pointed out. 'He's gay – very obviously. How can they out somebody who tried to buy Judy Garland's ashes?'

'*We* know he's gay, darling, and every male hairdresser in the land knows he's gay, but Middle England doesn't. They're more innocent than us media types and they think he hasn't found the right girl yet. They're the ones who buy the things that are sold in the ad breaks, so their opinions matter. His cosy little fan club will spontaneously combust if they discover, with graphic photographs and frank interviews, that he's Martha, not Arthur.'

'Why not come out before he's outed? He's allowed to be gay, you know.' Nell felt it was time to state the bleeding obvious. She was uneasy having such a conversation in the twenty-first century.

'Because he has a mews house, a Ferrari and a rent-boy habit to support.'

'Plenty of other celebs are gay,' protested Nell doggedly. 'It doesn't make any difference to their careers. Elton John's not short of a few bob, is he?'

'Elton John doesn't have a cookery slot on Midlands Radio to protect.' Louis stopped striding and leaned over his victim. Nell drew back. Her head was level with his groin, which didn't help an already awkward situation. 'Look, darling, for every Elt there's a dozen closet cases in sterile marriages. It's a fact of showbiz life. Blair needs a beard.'

'Eh? Why?' Nell lifted her eyes from Louis's zip to his furry face, and added hastily, 'Not that a beard isn't a wonderful, manly addition to any chin.'

'Don't you know anything?' asked Louis, kindly. 'A beard is a biz term for a girl who poses as a gay man's totty to preserve his heterosexual image. Throw a stone at a Beeb cocktail party and you'll hit a dozen. We need somebody to go to celebrity bashes on Blair's arm and be his girlfriend for the media.'

'What kind of fool would agree to that?' As she spoke Nell knew exactly what kind of fool Louis had in mind. 'No way!' She leaped out of the chair, missing his groin by inches.

'Not if it means keeping your job?'

Nell folded, then unfolded her arms. Then she folded them again. 'This is blackmail,' she said breathlessly.

'Yes. It's an ugly word, as they say, but it's a lovely feeling.'

'You understand what you're asking?'

'Perfectly.'

'It would be humiliating.'

'It would be *fun*.'

'It would be hell with knobs on.'

'I have to insist that you don't date anybody else, so it's perfect that you've just been dumped.' He ignored the outburst of spluttering this unleashed, and skated smoothly through Nell's squeaks of '*I dumped him!*' 'It'll probably be the next ice age before you get another boyfriend anyway. A lot of girls would give their eye teeth to go out with a celebrity.'

'There are celebrities and celebrities. You're asking me to be the arm-candy of the cheesiest man on television.'

'If you prefer we can prepare your P45.'

'Louis, this is horrible.'

'Yes, yes. Now, stop arsing about and give me your answer.'

'It's really this or the sack?' Nell felt sick. If she'd suspected her life was trivial before . . . There was only one possible answer: she wouldn't be able to live with herself if she prostituted herself in this way. This was wading too far in to the shallow end. She couldn't believe it but she was about to give up her job.

Then Louis sighed and shrugged. 'Maybe Jean has some savings. It won't be easy to find another job at her time of life. Especially without a reference.'

Nell stiffened. 'What's this got to do with her?'

'Everything. She gave you unauthorised funds.'

'We can file that under stealing,' Linda added, with a look of regret.

'You can't sack Jean! She's been here since you started the business. She's devoted her life to this company. Everybody loves her. *You* love her!'

'I didn't say I *wanted* to sack her. I'll have to – unless you let me buy you a sparkly frock and send you to a few parties with Blair. What do you say, darling?'

What could darling say, except yes?

*   *   *

It took Nell a while to compose herself after this spiritual mugging. The shallow quotient of her life had just been neatly squared. A day that she had thought couldn't get worse had spiralled into tragi-comedy.

'We all deserve a second chance,' Linda simpered. 'Now you can put the past behind you and start again. I, for one, won't hold it against you.'

'Thank you,' said Nell.

Four

The strict instructions not to tell a living soul didn't apply to her best friend, Nell decided. 'You're doing it again,' she shouted, over the babble of the trendy crowd at the achingly hip bar where they were sharing overpriced house white after work.

'Doing what?' Tina shouted back, her face lit spookily from beneath by the green neon that ringed their tiny table.

'Laughing at me.'

'But it's funny!' Tina defended herself.

Nell sighed. 'I thought we were going somewhere we could have a quiet chat.' The throng of Hoxton Fins and National Healthesque glasses were throwing up an impenetrable wall of sound as they loudly discussed whatever people who think that much about their hair discuss. 'Why don't we ever go to a nice, ordinary pub?'

Tina was scathing. 'Oh, right. A nice, ordinary pub with beer lakes on the tables, ancient roll-ups in the ashtrays and penicillin between the toilet tiles? If we're lucky we might get chatted up by BNP voters who're so drunk they'll think we're two sets of twins. Let's rush to one as soon as we've finished our drinks.'

Nell thought it sounded quite attractive, compared to the claustrophobic room they were in, which was as crowded as a containerload of illegal immigrants. Now that she was single again, she would be spending a disproportionate amount of her time in terrifyingly hip bars like this, all chosen by Tina.

During long nights of lying awake beside Gareth she had longed for the day when she would be free to go where she liked when she liked. Now that she was and she was here, in this uncomfortable and noisy dungeon, she felt as if she'd swapped one treadmill for another. Was there, she wondered as she knocked back the dregs, any *point* to this?

Tina was cupping Nell's ear. 'I'm very proud of you, you know.' The words cut warmly through the din.

'Are you?' she shouted back.

'Yes.' Tina squeezed her arm.

Nell went pink. Nobody ever said they were proud of her. Her mother was too distracted, and her grandmother could never be proud of somebody in high-street clothes. 'I'll get another bottle.'

She struggled to her feet, marvelling at how people managed to pull in places like this. She was horribly aware of what the green light must be doing to her complexion. Then she spotted the items in the glass cabinet behind her and jumped back, knocking a stranger's drink over the pregnancy jumper. 'What the hell are *they*?' she squawked.

'Antiquated gynaecological instruments,' Tina said, as if she often spent a convivial evening inches from a Victorian speculum.

Thank goodness Fergus had given her a key. I can let myself in and tiptoe off to bed, quiet as a mouse, without disturbing anybody, she thought, as she charged drunkenly down the hall like the Elephant Man, banging into various antiques, eventually tripping over a Chippendale side-table and rolling to the door of the Heliotrope Room.

Where had all her clothes gone? She located them at last in a Louis Quinze armoire. Padded silk hangers supported her sorry selection of faded garments, and lavender sachets had been inserted in her clogs. The reality of Nell's life had collided with the luxury of Claudette's.

For some reason Nell found the knot of her sarong as taxing as a Rubik's cube. By the time she'd pulled it, rather violently, over her head she was too dazed to contemplate the cleanse-tone-moisturise thing. Instead she crawled naked between linen sheets and gratefully closed her eyes to embark on a long dream involving Gareth, a white teddy and a pair of antique forceps.

Like Frankenstein in flip-flops Nell plodded down the hall behind Fergus. He opened the door to the breakfast room, and the bright sunshine almost made her scream in pain.

'Good morning, Nell.' Her grandmother's voice was as crisp as the sunlight. 'Do sit down.'

'Good morning.' Nell shuffled in and sat opposite her at the tiny, exquisitely laid round table. She raised a hand sheepishly to the tangled bathmat that was her hair.

'You look like a street person, dear,' Claudette noted calmly. 'Is that deliberate? One never knows with current fashions.'

'No, I'm just . . . tired.' Nell tried to smooth the lap of her scarlet PVC shortie mac, and wished she had packed a dressing-gown.

'The young are always tired.' Claudette looked as if she had never been tired. Flawless as a diamond, and about as hard, there was little to suggest that she was in her late seventies. Her slender frame was improbably erect – as if she was suspended from the ceiling by an invisible wire. Her pure white hair floated in a chic bob around cheekbones sharp enough to slice bread. A casual observer could not have guessed that she was related to the slumped bag of washing opposite.

Unless they had looked at their eyes. It wasn't the colour or the shape: something indefinable was common to both pairs. The romantic might have called it a spark.

Nell's eyes were puffy now, but she could see well enough to be cowed by her grandmother's formidable presence. 'How are you, Claudette?' she asked, with the formality the other's demeanour seemed to demand.

'Quite well, thank you.' Claudette eyed her granddaughter searchingly. 'Should I ask how you are, or defer the question until you are a little less . . . tired?'

'Oh, I'm really well, thank you.' A more honest answer

would have been that her mouth had been pebbledashed overnight, and mice had broken into her skull to play house anthems on tiny anvils.

Disapproval emanated from Claudette as unmistakably as her Chanel No. 5. 'Tea?' She made an unnecessary racket with spoons and bone china, then handed Nell a cup of a highly scented Chinese blend that stripped an inch of rancid felt from her tongue. She felt a nostalgic ache for the PG Tips in their cracked jar in Gareth's kitchen.

'I know that you girls' – Claudette pronounced it 'gels' – 'don't eat fried food so I thought you might join me in a fruit salad.'

'Might be a tight squeeze!' Claudette didn't laugh. 'I could murder some toast.'

'Fergus.' The butler stood, statue-like, by the door. 'My guest could murder some toast. Please instruct Carita accordingly.'

Off went Fergus to instruct the housekeeper, who lived behind the green baize door to the kitchen.

'Nell.'

The word sounded like the start of a speech. Nell sat up a little straighter, which sent pain zigzagging behind her eyebrows.

'Why were you crying last night?'

Jolted, Nell opened her eyes properly for the first time since her alarm clock had gone off. 'Crying?' she queried weakly.

Claudette nodded. Her unwavering hazel gaze fixed on her granddaughter's throbbing face.

'Was I?' Nell groped back through sticky clouds of drunken sleep and tried to remember. There *had* been a horrible groaning noise in her dreams. Shame flooded over her. 'I was.'

'Nell, I know you were.' A note of irritation had entered Claudette's tone. 'I'm endeavouring to discover why.'

This was the first direct personal question Nell had ever heard from her grandmother. It was, very possibly, the first sign of real interest Claudette had ever shown in a fellow human being. Nell plucked at her lapel, uncertain what to say. It wasn't easy to open up to a creature governed by etiquette rather than emotion.

And, besides, why *had* she been crying last night? Nell wondered. She could tell that an honest answer was expected. 'I suppose . . .'

The door opened and Fergus glided in with a plate of crustless brown toast.

'Thank you. That will be all.'

His exit sashay held a hint of huff.

'Go on.' Those bright, eerily young eyes were fixed on Nell.

'I left Gareth yesterday morning,' said Nell. 'We were together for three years, and although I don't regret it, I do feel kind of lonely.' She glanced at Claudette to see how this was going down.

Claudette had met Gareth two or three times and never commented on him: her silence had spoken volumes. She seemed to be waiting for more.

And there *was* more. Nell knew her heart was intact. Leaving Gareth was an overdue move that couldn't have been responsible for such an orgy of tears. There was a lot more.

Knotted feelings that Nell hadn't voiced before, not even to Tina, began to unravel themselves in the face of Claudette's expectancy. She had certainly never talked like this to Gareth, who came out in a rash if tricked into discussing emotions.

Nell started off slowly. 'I can't help feeling my life is a bit pointless.' She giggled uneasily. 'I'm not sure what I'm *for*.' Then, as she warmed to her theme she speeded up. 'I don't know where I fit in. Mum's remarried. Dad's missing-believed-drunk. I stayed far too long with a man I don't love. I work with actors who think they're gifted because they can look sincere in a dog-food commercial. To top it all,' she was gabbling now, 'I've been – yes, there's only one word for it, *blackmailed* into making a complete schmuck of myself.' She stopped dead. Many disparate thoughts had gelled in her hung-over brain.

As if she had been mesmerised into telling the truth by that intense gaze from across the table, Nell said clearly, 'I pay more attention to buying shoes than I do to the state of my soul. I want to matter. I want to make a difference. I don't want to be this shallow for the rest of my life. I want to do good.' Aware of how loud her rant had grown she repeated herself quietly. 'I really do. I want to do good.'

To be stared at is always unnerving but to be stared at by Claudette would have had an SAS man blurting secrets. Nell buttered toast with a tiny knife she hoped was the correct one and a virulent blush crept up her neck. *I want to do good!* So fucking lame – like a Miss World contestant. A woman like Claudette would never understand what she was getting at. She should have kept it to herself and carried on being shallow and brainless. It was what she was good at, after all.

'Do good, then.' Claudette broke the silence, like a silver spoon hitting a boiled egg. 'Might one ask what's stopping you?'

'Gazillions of things,' blurted Nell.

'Such as?'

'I do have a full-time job, you know.'

'A somewhat unrewarding one that doesn't sound *too* taxing.'

'I don't have the time.'

'What did you do last evening?'

'I had an urgent social engagement.' Which included accepting a dare to drink the entire cocktail menu in alphabetical order. 'And I've got to find somewhere to live,' she said triumphantly. This was a trump card. 'That means trawling through the small ads, finding a deposit, viewing dozens of poky little holes priced like mansions—'

'Stay here.'

'Here? Stay?' This stopped Nell in her tracks.

'There's plenty of room and it would remove one of the hurdles you seem so determined to erect for yourself. Stay as my guest for as long as you care to.'

Claudette made the offer with her trademark nonchalance, but it stunned Nell. She was accustomed to grand acts of generosity from her grandmother, but this was different: it was practical, even *kind*, unlike the chauffeur-driven jaunts of Nell's childhood. 'Oh,' she ventured, stupefied.

'I don't generally dispense advice.' Claudette dabbed her lips with a monogrammed napkin. 'It's patronising and almost invariably useless. I'm making an exception to suggest that if there is something you really want to do and you won't feel fulfilled unless you do it, then *do it*, my dear child.' She stood up with an elasticity that was beyond her much younger companion. 'You are, after all, part de Montrachet. You can achieve whatever you set your mind to.'

Left alone with her disappointingly dainty toast, Nell examined this new idea. Nobody had ever suggested to her that she could achieve whatever she wanted. And she had never thought very hard about what she did want – beyond what to have for dinner.

What sort of good can I do? wondered Nell, and rested her hot forehead on the cool table. And will those mice ever put their anvils away?

Freedom is a dangerous place, big and littered with mantraps. There is no comforting map.

Nell had no housing problem, no man problem, and a challenge to prod her into action. While she was making a decaff for 'the next Gloria Hunniford', Louis's words, Nell thought hard about the nature of doing good.

Of making a difference. Of being some use.

Most of the obvious notions were too fantastical. She couldn't see herself wiping the sores of lepers or clearing minefields while holding down a job in W1. Besides, in a few weeks she would have to pursue a bogus love affair. Their first date had been pencilled in during a break in Blair's punishing schedule recording his 'live' quiz shows. She would have to think small, local. Not too small, obviously:

emptying her pockets of change for street-corner beggars wasn't enough.

Tina entered the kitchenette and did a comedy double-take. 'Rugby shirt and flowery skirt? Come back, sarong, we miss you.'

'It's Gareth's.' Nell plucked at the emerald-green and yolk-yellow hooped top. 'I took it by mistake. All my nice bits are still at his.'

'Go and get them. Quickly.' A sartorial crime to Tina was a hanging offence.

'Yeah, yeah.' Nell didn't want to be the first to make contact.

A strangled voice behind them said, 'I think you look nice.' At the sink Dean, astonished by his daring, rinsed his mug and sped out.

'Thanks!' Nell called after him.

'He's wrong. You look like a street person.' Tina had echoed Claudette. 'Had enough of darling Granny's hospitality yet?'

'She said I could stay for as long as I liked.'

Tina pulled a face. 'That would be about twelve minutes, would it?'

'She *is* my flesh and blood, you know,' Nell reminded her.

'You used to say she was like Cruella de Vil only not so lovable.'

'Yeah. Well.' Claudette's encouragement – or was it a dare? – to follow her dream of doing good had changed the way Nell felt about her grandmother. She wondered how Tina would react when she heard about her new direction. Badly, Nell guessed. Tina lived emphatically in the here and now. Abstract notions of making a difference would probably send her to the nearest designer outlet in a cold sweat.

Surfing the Net can look like work to a passing boss, a fact Nell often exploited. Avidly plucking Rolos from her top drawer, she searched under 'volunteer' and 'London'. She reckoned she could fit in quite a lot of tea-making for elderly ladies – even help the homeless, as long as she didn't have to touch them.

Dozens of sites rolled over her screen. Volunteers were needed for loads of things. Most of it made dull reading: she soon knew far more than she had ever hoped to about clearing canals. 'Nah . . . nah . . . nah . . .' She scrolled though a handful of worthy causes before HelpingHands.com flickered to life in front of her.

This site was bright and modern and was asking the right questions. 'Do you have a few hours a week to visit vulnerable people in their own homes?'; 'Could you provide occasional support for isolated people?'; 'Could you help us help homeless people off the streets and off benefits?'

Yes, I could! thought Nell, excited.

'What are you looking so happy about?' Louis eyed her with distrust as she hit the escape button.

'I'm pleased with the filing I've been doing,' bluffed Nell, inexpertly. Her habit of filing everything under M for Miscellaneous regularly incurred torrents of creative abuse from her boss.

Louis frowned. 'I'm an old-fashioned boss. I don't like it when you're happy. Looking forward to your first date with Lover-boy?' He smiled as pain registered in her eyes. 'That's better. I'm having lunch with that bald imbecile from the Beeb. I'll have to get him drunk if I'm to have any hope of selling him my penguin sitcom so I'll see you tomorrow.'

By the time Louis reached Reception the website had reappeared. According to the address, Helping Hands' headquarters was ten minutes away. She could visit them during her lunch-hour.

Tina was buttoning up her sharply tailored coat. 'How are you feeling?' she asked.

'OK-ish.' There was no point in trying to fool Tina. 'You know.'

'I know.' Only two words, but their emotional shorthand

43

meant that Nell felt duly sympathised with for being love-lorn and forced to be the girlfriend of the most irritating man in the land. 'Fancy trawling the shops?'

'I'm broke.'

'You could help me look for something to wear to the party after my sister's reception.'

This wasn't very tempting. Tina's forthcoming brides-maidhood had been discussed more than Kennedy's assassination. Her thrifty sister had nursed hopes of second-hand peach taffeta with puffed sleeves; Tina had insisted on made-to-measure satin the colour of a dove's underbelly, and now she had decided to change into something even more glam for the party afterwards. Nell didn't feel like watching Tina shimmy into glamorous outfits that she wouldn't be able to persuade past her calves. 'I've got calls to make.'

'Work calls?'

'What do you think I am?'

Reassured, Tina went out, leaving Nell feeling guilty: she'd just lied to her best friend in the world.

Five

March was living up to its bad press and London was slick with sooty puddles. Camerton Street was a cul-de-sac of impressive buildings that had once bellowed the status of Society families but now housed corporate HQs and banks.

An ornate church hall, built in the days before they looked like rabbit hutches, straddled the end of the short street and Nell approached it slowly, strangely nervous. It was a moment-ous occasion. She felt like grabbing the lapels of a passer-by and saying, 'Guess what! I'm about to save my soul.' The short woman scuttling along in front of her probably wouldn't appreciate the significance of the news: the tall, dark, kind of handsome bloke trying to control a scampering child looked preoccupied. Despite her own preoccupation, Nell noticed he had a decent bum.

So this is Helping Hands, Nell thought. She climbed the steps and pushed open an arched oak door. She blinked in the fluo-rescent light, which was blinding after the dour afternoon she had left outside. The hall was large and bare, with lino under-foot and stark whitewashed walls. A chilly Victorian atmosphere pervaded it, despite the modern reception desk at the far end.

Nell went over to it. It was unmanned and she looked in vain for a bell.

Where was the hustle and bustle of good-doing? She had expected warmth, a cluster of pink-cheeked virtuous types, bursting with humility. But there were no stoic angels helping crippled children to walk. In fact, there were just two people on the banks of moulded-plastic orange chairs: a scrawny woman in a thin jacket hunched over a malodorous roll-up directly beneath a no-smoking sign, and a magnificently filthy man whose age was unguessable. He sprawled over three chairs in a donkey jacket that had evidently been buried at some point in its history. He was cradling a can of Special Brew in blackened fingers.

Feeling as conspicuously clean and respectable as a Waitrose sandwich, Nell stood at the desk expectantly, wearing her waiting face: alert, patient, ever-so-nice.

A blast of cold air ushered in a small girl, travelling at some speed, followed by a man. She was about seven, togged up in matching bobble hat and scarf. She braked beside Nell and smiled up at her unselfconsciously, showcasing an incomplete set of small teeth. 'My nose is cold.'

Nell rubbed it with a gloved hand. 'Is that better?'

'Your hand smells of ladybirds.' Whether this was a good or bad thing wasn't clear. 'He's my daddy,' she added helpfully, as a tall man with thick brown hair and a rather cross expression caught her up. Nell recognised him as the owner of the decent bum.

'Nobody on Reception?' he asked curtly. He had a distracted air and seemed perturbed. Chill air floated from his overcoat.

'Nope.' Nell was cheered by the innocent presence of the non-smoking, non-drinking, non-filthy child. Beneath the blonde fringe, which stick out crazily from the hat, the little girl's nose was gently flattened and her blue eyes, bright as a winter river, were tilted and surrounded by curled lashes.

'My name's Clover.' The child was a mine of information. 'My daddy's thirty-seven.'

'Somebody should be on duty.' Patience didn't seem to be Daddy's strong point: he looked about irritably.

'Shouldn't be long.' Nell tried to sound reassuring. It couldn't be easy living with a child with Down's, she thought. Soon she might be part of the team helping him, making the difference between coping and climbing the walls. She felt a premature twinge of pride.

'How old are you?' The lack of a receptionist didn't bother the child.

'Older than you,' Nell told her. The man had stepped round to the other side of the desk. 'Er, should you be doing that?' she asked. Then she lowered her voice. 'Look, you're obviously under a lot of strain.' She pointed exaggeratedly behind the back of his oblivious offspring. 'Try to hang on. I'm sure somebody will be along soon. It'll be OK.' That hit the right note, she thought. Understanding without being patronising. She patted his arm.

The man looked quizzically at her woolly glove, then at her face.

Beyond the desk a portholed door burst open and a girl, slender as a Twiglet with an abundant Afro, bounded out. She exuded brightness and energy. 'Sorry! Sorry, everybody! When you've gotta go, you've gotta go!' The smile was dazzlingly wide. 'Right. How can I help you?' The full wattage was turned on Nell.

'Why don't you look after this family first?' suggested Nell, with dark emphasis. Cheekily, the man had stayed put on the far side of the desk. He was even fingering a pile of post in a nosy way. Just a few minutes into doing good Nell had encountered a *situation*.

The receptionist giggled. 'Eh?' She looked from Nell to the man and back again. 'I don't think he needs my help.'

'I wouldn't say that, Joy. Come on, Clover.' He held out his hand to his daughter, then pushed open the portholed door. 'I'll be in my office if you need me.' He didn't look at Nell before he disappeared.

'I thought—' began Nell.

'He's my boss!' Joy thought it was very funny, which wasn't comforting. 'Let's start again. What can I do for you?'

Only partially recovered from a near-terminal cringe, Nell took another bite of macaroon and reread the application form she was filling in at a tiny table in the nearest café to Helping Hands. Something had told her that if she didn't go straight back with it, she never would.

Nell hoped he wouldn't hold it against her. OK, he ran the place and she had somehow mistaken him for a desperate, needy creature out of a Greek tragedy but there was no need to hold it against her.

And, no doubt, one day she'd be able to think of it without experiencing tension in her buttocks fierce enough to smash a conker. She scanned the form: she was using her best curly handwriting in the hope that an italic nib might compensate for a startling lack of substance.

After name, address and phone number, things got tough. Under 'Most Recent Voluntary Work' she considered putting 'Helping in school library', but that had been seventeen years ago. Besides, she'd only lasted half an afternoon before she was sent back to class for looking up 'willy' in the *OED*. 'None,' she had finally written. In her best handwriting.

'How Would You Like to Help?' had been easy. She'd simply ticked everything – 'Community Outreach', 'Personal Mentoring', 'Practical On-site'. Not knowing what they meant made it easy.

'Do You Have Skills That May Be of Use to Us?' stumped her. None of the boxes – DIY, gardening, counselling, translating – were tickable. *I must be able to do something useful.* Nell had stared at the box marked 'Other' until her brain hurt. Evidently her education had been different from that of those paragons who could build a garden shed while advising a foreigner on their emotional problems. Where did people get the time to learn *skills*? Didn't they know about television?

All Nell's talents – a loose definition – were useless. She could gossip; she could sleep till noon; she could do a brilliant impression of Bob Geldof. Even the most ornate calligraphy couldn't disguise their innate worthlessness. With a fit of bravado she ticked gardening and DIY and added 'Walking dogs, chatting to old ladies, rudimentary tap'.

Helping Hands needed the names of two referees before they would unleash her on unsuspecting disadvantaged people.

Claudette was an obvious choice: the swanky address might carry some weight. She would 'forget' to mention that they were related. It disturbed Nell that she didn't know anybody else remotely responsible. Tina wouldn't take it seriously, and Louis might fabricate a criminal record for her. None of her friends had sensible jobs: she knew a DJ and a children's entertainer, and she had lunch once a month with a girl who made plaster casts of babies' feet. She scribbled Zoë's name. Zoë would give Nell an *excellent* reference. She knew this because Nell would write it herself. She coughed as she described Zoë as a 'customer interface executive'.

Joy showed Nell into a tiny office and sat her down on another of those orange plastic chairs in front of a cluttered desk. 'He won't be a minute,' she said, and withdrew. Giggling.

Clover sat at a tiny desk in the corner, diligently colouring a picture of Snow White. She was absorbed, and as quiet as the proverbial mouse. Nell felt a hot wave of shame for having contemplated Clover as a handful: her little half-brother would have decorated the entire room with crayon and snot by now.

Her interviewer entered the room, moving quickly as if he had ten warring things on his mind. 'Hello,' he said, without glancing at her. 'You are . . . ?' He sat down and faced her. 'Ah. You.' There was no clue as to what the 'Ah' meant but Nell had her suspicions. He pointed to the small nameplate at the front of the overwhelmed desk, which read 'Phred Marchmain'. 'That's me. And I know it's a silly spelling,' he said, 'but you can blame my wife for that. It made her laugh and it stuck. Now . . .'

'I filled in my form,' she said brightly, and handed it over.

'Yes. I can see that.' Phred studied the form and its flimsy detail. 'Hmm,' he said, more than once as he rubbed the back of his dark head with one hand, then, 'Right,' and finally, 'I see.' His eyes reminded Nell of Irish coffee, but she experienced none of the pleasure she usually associated with

that intoxicating liquid. This version seemed vaguely to disap-
prove of her.

'I'm concerned,' he said baldly.

At least he was frank. 'What about?'

'You're promising us unlimited amounts of time. You do
have a private life, er . . . Eleanor?'

'Of course I do.' It stank, but she had one. 'I want to show
how willing I am. And it's Nell, by the way.'

'Well, Nell, it's not much use to us if you over-promise
yourself, then drop out because you can't keep it up.' That
frankness again.

'Maybe I was a bit impulsive,' conceded Nell, squirming.

'Maybe you were.' Phred looked at her for slightly longer
than the moment merited, then resumed scrutinising the form.

Silence hung between them like wet knitting as Phred
frowned and thought. 'DIY and gardening are good. We can
always use them,' he said eventually.

'Yup.' They weren't entirely false claims: Nell had once
handed Gareth a hammer.

'Your other skills are . . . interesting,' Phred deadpanned.
'Walking dogs.'

Nell nodded. She was going to bluff this out. 'It's a particular
strength.' She had to make him take her seriously. Recklessly,
she had made her acceptance at Helping Hands the corner-
stone of a whole new way of life: her tattered self-esteem
depended on it. 'People think all dogs are the same, *vis-à-vis*
walking,' she said.

'I take it they're not.' The ghost of a smirk hovered at the
edges of Phred's mouth.

'Never make the mistake of thinking they are,' advised
Nell. 'I can tell you that when a dog is walked by me, it
knows it's been walked.'

'It knows it's been walked,' repeated Phred, solemnly.

There was a pause, which Nell filled by willing herself not
to come up with any more dog-walking bullshit.

'"Chatting to old ladies". That would be different, I

suppose, from chatting to me or to Joy, for example?' The smirk threatened again. At least it lightened up his face.

'I'd be careful to employ very different topics.' Nell scrambled for one. 'The Second World War, maybe. I would definitely avoid talking about hip-hop or, er, abortions. And I'd offer them a nice cup of tea.'

'"Rudimentary tap".' To his credit, Phred said this with no emphasis. He turned the form over. 'OK, Nell Fitzgerald, what made you interested in volunteer work?'

That was easy. Nell answered without thinking, ignoring a lifetime's evidence that this was poor strategy: 'I want to do good.'

Phred's eyebrows leaped efficiently into his hair. Nell wished she could snatch the phrase and cram it back into her mouth.

'I don't know . . . I suspect you don't quite understand the nature of the work we try to do here.' All traces of a smile had disappeared. 'We get involved with people at their lowest ebb. We need to offer practical support. We can't indulge angel-of-mercy fantasies.'

She bridled at this (which was all the more insulting for being spot-on), but hesitated before she answered. This was important. Then her sensible side – sighted as rarely as the yeti – asserted itself and she said, 'Look, you're absolutely right. I don't understand what Helping Hands does, but I want to learn. I'm not the most practical person you'll ever meet but I care and I'm sincere and I really, really want to get involved. Can't you give me a break? I promise I won't let you down.' She was bristling with anticipation, just like the family mongrel used to when he was waiting for his evening tin of Chum. She had made a proper promise. Recent ones, along the lines of 'I promise I'll call back in ten minutes' to impatient clients, or 'I promise I'll only have one drink on the way home, two at the most' to Gareth, had been written on water. Nell needed a vote of confidence from this man.

Phred took his time. Nell wanted to shake him by his broad shoulders but she guessed that this was his habitual pace. At last he said, 'You can do a month with us, and then we'll see how you're faring.'

'Oh, yes! That's perfect! I love months!' gushed Nell, her bottom executing a swift tango on the chair.

'And you're sure about promising this much time?'

'Yes. Certain. Sure. Definite.'

'Right. Then as soon as I've had your references in, I'll find you your first assignment.'

'Assignment?' Nell found the word thrilling. 'Like James Bond?' Another phrase she wanted to snatch back. 'I mean, like . . .'

'OK, OK! Thank you – you can go now,' said Phred, gently, as words failed his interviewee.

Nell rose to leave. 'Thank you,' she said, and meant it.

The walk back to the office might have been on rose petals. Nell hadn't been so elated since her boyfriend in the fourth year had told her she was the world's best French-kisser. So what if Phred hadn't stuck to the script her overheated imagination had written, filled with lines like, 'If only there were more people like you this old world would be a better place'? So what if he hadn't seemed particularly grateful? Her new life had begun: soon she would be officially *deep*.

Six

Morgan Theatrical Management's lunch-hour had come and gone, but as Louis was still out of the office a relaxed – some might say indolent – air lingered. Zoë was giving her nails a final buff; Jane From Accounts was fretting over the calorie content of the sandwich she had wolfed while checking out the fitness equipment in John Lewis; Len, the nylon-shirted chief accountant, was enjoying a damned good Frederick Forsyth.

A wheel had come off Nell's adjustable chair long ago, so she sat down warily. It was capable of setting off, with her in it, at great speed across her tiny office. This made Zoë's day, but was less fun for Nell.

She grasped the phone. It was time to call her mum. There was so much to tell her, and she'd be glad to hear her daughter's news. Wouldn't she? At times like these the gap between Nell and her family swelled into a chasm.

Sometimes Nell fretted that her grandmother's snobbery ran in her own veins. She cringed at the stone cladding that Ringo was so proud of, at her mother's devotion to bingo and at the memory of her youngest half-brother's christening five years ago.

Patsy had explained to the priest how they'd chosen the unusual name Canvey. 'We ran out of Beatles,' she'd said, 'so we copied Posh and Becks and named him after where he was conceived. Canvey *Island*,' she'd enlarged.

'It was that or Back Seat!' Ringo had butted in.

Patsy, Ringo, John, Paul, Georgina and even little Canvey had been helpless with laughter around the font. Nell had tried to muster a giggle as she shot a nervous glance at the horrified priest.

That little tableau illustrated neatly how marginal Nell could feel when she was with her family. Consequently she wasn't with them that often.

The ringing ended abruptly, and a bright Dublin voice trilled, 'Hellooo!'

'Mum? It's Nell.'

'My darlin'!' No recriminations, no 'Hello, stranger'. Secretly, Nell hankered after them as proof of maternal affection, but her mother was congenitally cheerful. 'Are you at work, love?' Suddenly Patsy sounded anxious. 'Will you get into trouble for using the phone?' Patsy had a morbid dread of hearing that her kids were unemployed, which was puzzling as Nell was the only one with a proper job. The seventeen-year-old twins would only admit to doing 'this and that' and Georgina was 'looking around'.

'Don't worry. It's fine. How are things?'

'Mental!' laughed Patsy. 'That cat's on heat and Canvey's been sent home from nursery for biting the other kids. Ringo calls him Hannibal!' Patsy and Ringo weren't big on child psychology. 'The extension's coming away from the house but we're grand. How's Gavin?'

Nell didn't correct her. She'd only exposed Gareth to her folks once or twice. (He'd had a ball: Nell had spent the whole time wincing.) 'That's why I'm calling. I've got something to tell you.'

'You're pregnant?' The note of Catholic dread could be excused: Georgina had conceived as the school gates clanged shut behind her.

'God, no. I've left him.'

'Aw, you haven't? He seemed a decent fella.'

Patsy didn't know about Gareth's towering shortcomings because Nell had always presumed she wouldn't have the time to listen. 'It was right to move on.'

Patsy sighed. 'If you say so, love.' Thanks to her brush with Philippe de Montrachet, Patsy was conservative about men: if you found a half-way decent specimen, you hung on like a pit-bull terrier.

There was a pause while Nell gripped the receiver and prayed silently for proof that Patsy's mind followed traditional maternal lines. *Ask me where I'm staying. Ask me where I'm staying.*

'Hang on a minute. If you've left him where are you living, Eleanor?'

Patsy's slightly cross tone delighted Nell: for a moment she had sounded like any other mother. 'I'm at Claudette's.'

'*Whaaat?* Have you had a blow to the head or something?'

'Mum, she *is* my grandmother.'

'Don't I fecking know it. The auld witch has haunted me since the day I married your father. She spoiled him, then dropped him, and then she tried to interfere with how I brought you up. She's unnatural, a she-devil. You'll get out as soon as you can, won't you?'

Nell was saved having to confess her plans by a massive clatter at the other end of the line. Here it came: the shift of her mother's focus after a brief oasis when Nell had had her all to herself.

'Jaysus! That Canvey's after pulling every dish I own off the shelves. Oh, before I go and tidy up, Georgina's chosen a name for her baby.'

'What is it?' Nell braced herself. After all the Beatles and Canvey, anything was possible. Particularly if you factored in Georgina's devotion to Heavy Metal. Nell might well be a proud auntie to little Megaslaya.

'Annie.'

'Just Annie?'

'Don't you like it?'

'I love it!' Nell was relieved. 'I'll let you go, Mum.' There wasn't time to tell her about Helping Hands and how excited she was.

'It's great to hear from you, love. Look after yourself.'

Of course she would. She always had.

Marti Goode, loitering in Reception, was not half as famous as he wanted to be, and less famous than he thought he was.

His passport and his bald spot acknowledged that he was forty but his website insisted he was thirty-three. It also informed the curious that he was single, which made uneasy reading for Tina.

They had met in this very office, over a tepid Nescafé Tina had brought him. Ever since their first furtive snog, Marti had been looking over his shoulder, terrified that his agent, Tina's boss, would find out about them. His years in children's television heightened his natural paranoia: he was convinced that his career would be nobbled if the public discovered his live-in lover was a younger girl from the office. And Marti's career was everything to him.

Tina, so plain-spoken about everybody else's problems, was in deep denial about Marti. Nell could – and did – point out his many failings as a boyfriend. She reminded Tina that he would rather put his hand in a mangle than talk about their future; that he went to laughable lengths to keep their relationship secret, as though it were shameful in some way; that he had never used the word 'love'.

None of this mattered: Tina had convinced herself that if she hung on and 'proved' herself – as if she was on some sort of emotional assault course – her prize would be a happy-ever-after as Mrs Goode.

To the naked eye, especially Nell's, this wasn't much of a prize. By now, Nell had given up trying to work out why a funny, clever, strong-minded girl would knock herself out to win the miserly hand of an emotionally constipated has-been. She just listened, sympathised and administered medicinal rioja.

Sometimes, after an overdose of this magical liquid, Tina would stumble home and burp out the forbidden question, 'But you do love me, don't you, Marti?'

The answer, accompanied by a meaningful stare into the middle distance, was invariably a riff on 'Who really knows what love means?'

Marti, you see, was deep.

'I *love* your gadget show on ShopAtHome,' Zoë was telling him animatedly. 'You make everything sound so useful. I just ordered a combination fridge-cleaner-tampon-holder.'

'Good. Good.' Despite his wide smile, Marti winced. That slight tic in his left eye was getting worse. The only thing that eased it was half an hour listening to his agent assure him that this shopping-channel job was a stop-gap until he charged back into the mainstream where he belonged.

'We're ready for you now.' Tina collected Marti from Zoë's care in professional mode. As she led the way towards Nell's office she surreptitiously stroked the front of his jeans, a risky manoeuvre that always infuriated him. So he was a little flushed when she said loudly, 'We need to speak to Louis's PA about those, er, schedules.'

'Schedules?' Marti was sometimes slow to catch on.

Tina snatched up a clipboard, which held a list of Louis's dietary allergies – those he suffered from and those he aspired to – and said, out of the side of her mouth, 'Nell's dumped Gareth. She has to stay with us, yes?'

'Yes,' muttered Marti, as if he was sucking an OAP's toe.

'Really, I—' began Nell.

Tina cut her short. 'We insist, don't we, darling?'

Convulsing at the inflammatory endearment, Marti managed, 'Of course we do. How long would you be staying?'

'As long as she wants.' Tina was firm. 'Obviously.'

'We've got those people coming.'

'What people?'

'And I hope she doesn't mind that uncomfortable bed.'

Tina was puzzled. 'The spare bed's fine.'

'And we all know I'm allergic to cat hair.'

'She's not a cat, Marti,' Tina pointed out, with a *soupçon* of irritation, as Nell glanced down at herself to check.

'Of course she's not a cat,' hissed Marti, eyes darting to Louis's door, 'but Gareth has a cat.' He turned to Nell and whispered, 'Would you object to being Hoovered?'

'*Marti!*' snapped Tina.

'Honestly, folks, I'll be fine at Claudette's,' said Nell.

'Ah, well, if you're sure . . .' Marti didn't sound disappointed.

Nell had rarely been surer.

Seven

'Tonight?' It was Friday, a mere week since Nell had first visited Helping Hands and Phred was already on the phone.

'I only got your references this morning, but I thought you'd like to start your month as soon as possible. That customer interface executive friend of yours thinks you're a star, by the way.'

At the other end of the phone, Nell blushed.

Evidently Phred mistook shame for reluctance. 'Look, if it's too short notice . . .'

'No, absolutely not.' Mentally Nell stood to attention. 'Just give me the address and I'll be there.' She took down the details with a shaky hand. Her first assignment. 'And I'm babysitting?'

'Yes, for Carol. She's been in rehab for crack addiction. She needs someone to watch the kids while she goes to her NA meeting.'

Nell guessed that NA stood for something Anonymous, but couldn't think what. Was there a Naughtiness Anonymous? 'NA?'

'Narcotics Anonymous,' Phred clarified. 'She's doing pretty well, but her ex is a dealer and he wants her back, so we're supporting her in getting by on her own.'

'Right.' Nell's mind was reeling. A real live junkie. As somebody who was helpless in the face of her addiction to Rolos, Nell couldn't imagine what it would be like to fight crack cravings. 'Any special instructions?' she asked nervously.

'Be on time. Apart from that, be yourself. You'll be fine.'

He sounded as if he believed it.

Friday afternoons got a little ropy at Morgan Theatrical Management. Senior staff usually left early, which left juniors wrestling with the temptation to send Dean out for the cheapest, coldest white wine he could source.

They weren't great wrestlers so by five p.m. Tina, Nell, Jean, Jane From Accounts and Dean were all in Reception clustered round Zoë as she poured wine into mugs.

'I shouldn't, really,' said Jean, without conviction.

'No, you shouldn't.' Linda reared up behind her, like the bad fairy in a cut-price panto. 'You won't be insured if you injure yourself while you're drunk on company premises.'

'But I don't . . . I'm not drunk.' Jean's myopic eyes were troubled behind thick lenses.

'Of course you aren't,' Nell butted in. 'Listen, Linda, if Jean does somehow get her head stuck in a DVD player she promises not to sue. Glass of wine?'

'It's working hours,' said Linda, tartly, and stalked away.

Tina rolled her eyes. 'Why doesn't she go and get a job running a small South American republic and leave us in peace?' she hissed. Tina's self-possession was in no way compromised by the halter-necked evening dress she was wearing over her trouser suit: Zoë had asked to see what she'd finally bought for her sister's wedding party. 'Nellini, are you on for a glasseen or two after work?'

'Can't.'

'What do you mean?' Tina knew Nell's diary intimately. 'Yes, you can.'

'I'm going somewhere.'

'Eh?' Irritation had seeped into Tina's voice as she stepped out of the dress and smoothed the pristine folds of her trousers. 'Somewhere where? I don't know about this.'

'Could it involve a young man?' simpered Jean, who was incurably romantic although untouched by male hands since flares were in fashion the first time round.

'Already?' Zoë, a sensual pragmatist – or woeful slapper, depending on your viewpoint – was impressed. 'Blimey. You don't hang about.'

'It's not a man. It's just . . . an appointment.' Nell didn't want to share Helping Hands with everybody. Not yet. It felt too fragile.

'An appointment I don't know about. Charming.'

Nell realised, with a start, that Tina's annoyance wasn't ironic. 'Yeah. You must have missed my memo detailing my every thought and move.' She laughed.

Conspicuously, Tina didn't. 'Seriously,' she said seriously, 'where are you going?'

'I'm not being unfaithful to you with another girl, if that's what you're worried about.'

As Dean slipped out to apply something cold to his temples – he had a particularly visual imagination – Tina persisted: 'Where are you going on your own on a Friday night?'

'All right, m'lud, if you must know, and evidently you must, I'm going to help out at a volunteer centre.'

Blank looks all round. Zoë wrinkled her nose narkily. 'What's that when it's at home?' Deftly she cancelled an incoming call so she could hear Nell's answer.

'Is it like the Territorial Army?' asked Jean, urgently. She was a dab hand at derailing conversations.

'What? No. It . . . does good in the community.' There was that phrase again. 'Helping the elderly and the homeless, that kind of thing.' Nell waved her hands vaguely.

Zoë stared at her as if she had been speaking Esperanto, while Jean bared her dentures approvingly. Dean, who had returned, gazed at Nell as if she was Mother Teresa. A sexually attractive Mother Teresa.

'Awwww,' said Jane From Accounts, in the baby voice she used to express extreme approval. 'What a wovely thing to do. Don't you think it's wovely, Tina?'

Tina grimaced as if she'd just been shown an operation scar. Tina didn't seem to think it was wovely. 'The *elderly*?' she asked incredulously. Slowly and carefully, she enunciated, 'It's the weekend,' as if Nell might have forgotten.

'I'm only babysitting.' Nell was defensive.

'I think it's wovely,' beamed Jane From Accounts.

'Yeah. You said,' snapped Tina, then stomped away *à la* Linda.

'Pre-menstrual,' mouthed Nell to Jane From Accounts, to forestall any wobbling lips and tearful eyes.

As they pulled on their coats and drifted out into the London murk at six o'clock, Tina breezed past Nell with an acidic, 'Give my regards to the housebound.'

The lift smelt of various vintages of wee, but otherwise the high-rise block in Euston was in pretty good nick. The communal parts had recently been painted a hospital green and so far only a few graffiti artists had felt moved to decorate it. 'Dave G is a cnut,' claimed one orange scrawl.

Resisting the urge to write 'Sp. Must try harder' beside it, Nell knocked on a door that bore the ragged scars of a good kicking. The ex? she wondered. Her lurid imagination had no off switch.

The recovering addict answered the door. She didn't look the part, with her healthy complexion and shiny bob. 'You from HH? Come in. S'cuse the mess.'

There was no mess to s'cuse. Obviously one junkie and three under-fives made less mess than one rugby-player in his thirties.

'They're all asleep.' Carol nodded at a door with a *Teletubbies* poster tacked to it. 'There's our Hayley, our Leonardo and our Carly. If they wake up just read them a story. Don't listen if they say they're hungry. They're stuffed.' She pulled on a parka. She had a crisp, deft way of doing things. 'I'll be straight back after the meeting. Two hours at the most. And thanks . . . I don't know your name.'

'Nell.'

'Thanks, Nell. This is a lifeline for me.'

And she was gone, leaving Nell alone in her home with the warm glow of her thanks.

*   *   *

It was humiliating to be outwitted by a black-and-white tele-vision, but Nell had never been much good with remotes. She was a strange mixture of bored and tense as she sat on a sagging armchair watching a documentary on Cornish tin mines, powerless to change the channel.

The room was very, very clean. The wallpaper had been stripped but the DIY had stopped there and the walls were naked, unfinished. A few pieces of chipboard furniture were lit by a single unforgiving bulb overhead. There were no books or CDs, but a laundry basket overflowed with games and soft toys.

From that room Nell learned a lot about the people who lived in the flat. She learned how little Carol had, and how determined she was to hang on to it. Her hard-won respectability was obviously vital to her.

The only decoration in the entire spotless room was a large framed photo of three tiny, startlingly blond children.

'*Jesus!*' yelped Nell, as one of those heads materialised at her shoulder and lisped the words no babysitter wants to hear.

'He's wet the bed.'

How could little Leonardo have produced so much wee? He was only three, but from the condition of his mattress he hadn't been to the loo since he was born. He threatened defi-antly to kick Nell up her bumhole as she struggled to flannel him down in the minuscule bathroom.

'He's bad, isn't he?' Hayley was a grave little mother figure, standing with the baby in her arms.

'We'll soon have him nice and clean,' said Nell, optimisti-cally, as she wrestled with the little boy and a bar of soap.

'I'll shoot you!' he screamed, wriggling like a bag of ferrets.

Nell dried him hastily and patchily. Hayley pointed out the clean pyjamas. 'Thank you,' said Nell.

''S all right.'

A bribe of milk and biscuits was necessary before anybody was willing to go back to bed. After she'd read a quick story and tucked them in, Nell noticed that an orange street-lamp was glowering in through the window. She tugged at the curtain and discovered it was too small for the job.

'It doesn't close,' said Hayley, without complaint.

'Sleep tight.' Nell kissed Hayley's forehead – she didn't risk it with Leonardo as she didn't fancy a kick up her bumhole – then left them and closed the door.

Shivering, she retreated to the kitchen. There was no washing-machine so she ran cold water on to the soaked sheets in the sink. Nosily, she peeked into the cupboards.

Carol shopped carefully. Own-brand supermarket corn-flakes, soup and baked beans all jostled for space. Nell, who believed in the restorative power of junk food, slavered at the sight of potato granules. She closed the door firmly. Surely she was above stealing an addict's Smash.

The Cornish tin mines had given way to an interview with a politician whose manner was as oily as his hair. She could have switched off the television and just sat with her own thoughts, but they centred on the Doomsday countdown to the date with Blair, which crept nearer each day. Eventually, boredom reduced her to going through her bag: she had resigned herself to filling in the 'Personal Information' page in last year's pocket diary when she realised it had gone half nine.

Carol had been out for nearly three hours. Unease nibbled. Could be the buses, she reasoned. Or maybe the meeting had started late. She was resisting more colourful scenarios when she heard Hayley call, 'Lady! C'mere!'

Leonardo had been sick. On Hayley. And, rather ingeniously, on the baby who was on the other side of the room. 'Oh, noooo!' Nell didn't know where to start. Everybody except her was crying.

Nell shepherded them all back to the Arctic bathroom and held baby Carly while she supervised the sponging-down of the other two. Poor Hayley was sobbing hysterically as she tugged at gobbets of God-knew-what in her fringe. 'It's all right, it's all right,' repeated Nell, gently, like a mantra.

The click of the front door sounded like all the choirs of heaven. Giddy with relief, Nell shouted, 'Carol! We're in the bathroom.'

'Muuuummmmmmeeee!' howled Leonardo and Hayley together.

It took Carol a few moments to join them. Nell peered into her face. It bore no expression. She was quite blank, like a doll. 'Carol?' Nell held the baby a little tighter.

'Hello, my little darlings,' said Carol, in a small voice from the other end of the universe. Her eyes were all pupil and looked straight through Nell.

'Are you OK?' It was a stupid question but Nell couldn't think of a better one. She had never felt so uncomfortable or so inadequate in her life. She hesitated to give up the baby.

'What?' asked Carol absently.

'I said, are you all right?'

A male voice, like sandpaper, answered from the doorway: 'She's fine. We'll take it from here. Door's over there.'

'Dad!' Hayley looked delighted to see the scrawny bloke with the weasel face.

'Erm . . .' Nell knew she had to hand over Carly but her arms wouldn't work. Carol was leaking strangeness into the atmosphere.

'Come to Mummy.' Carol held out her arms.

The night seemed darker, the traffic louder and the bus conductor more bad-tempered than he needed to be. Nell phoned Helping Hands from the back of the top deck and wangled Phred's mobile number out of the evening receptionist. She forgot to apologise for disturbing him at home and instead spluttered, 'I think Carol's back on the you-know-what,' as soon as he answered. 'I didn't want to give the kids back but what could I do? She was all kind of weird and not there. Her ex was with her. Should I go back?'

It took Phred a while to calm her down and explain that Helping Hands had its limits. 'You did the right thing. There's a process to go through. I'll speak to her social worker tomorrow. Carol's relapsed before and it may happen again.' He sounded calm. 'It's a fact of life.'

Nell stepped off the bus. There were no high-rises in Knightsbridge. Had she really achieved anything that night except ensure that a young woman could abuse herself in comfort?

Had she done any bloody good at all?

Eight

It was the weekend, which meant no work. More than that, it meant no nothing. Nell's diary was as clear as a Quaker's conscience.

Ignoring the Saturday-morning glare that intruded through the heavy silk curtains, she rolled over and snuggled deeper under the covers.

By now on a 'normal' Saturday, Gareth would be sitting up in bed cradling an overflowing bowl of Rice Krispies, with kids' TV turned up good and loud. It had always bewildered Nell how a large, hairy man, complete with a degree and a mortgage, could find so much to laugh at in Saturday-morning telly. But laugh he did, until there couldn't be any hope of sleeping beside him and Nell dragged herself off to tackle the housework – which she put off as long as possible with a long shower, and as many rounds of toast as the inevitably mouldy loaf would allow. She had tried to work out why their bread was *always* mouldy: was it possible that they bought it that way?

The word 'housework' had specific connotations for Nell. For most people it involved the snap of rubber gloves, the smell of the strangely named Cif, dusters and elbow grease. For Nell, it involved moving piles of stuff behind or under things: the sofa, the bed, the curtains or, in a crisis, other larger piles of stuff. If there was an X in the month, the Hoover might be coaxed from its lair, and she would thunder round the flat with it, swearing inventively over its grouchy roar. 'How come you never Hoover?' she would ask Gareth, whose favourite theory was that you needed breasts to vacuum safely.

After the housework came the dreaded ritual of the Sainsbury's list. The procedure began with Nell asking Gareth what he wanted to eat in the coming week, and Gareth's reply of how-would-he-know. Reasonably, Nell would counter this by asking if *he* didn't know, how the sodding hell was *she* supposed to know? At this point there might be a hint of disrespect in her voice. Gareth would cordially invite her to get what she bloody liked and she would assure him that she bloody would and doors would be slammed.

Today there would be no housework and no shopping. Fergus and the invisible Carita ran the apartment perfectly without her help. Nell stretched her arms and legs like a starfish because she could. The bed was immense and she was accustomed to clinging to one side of a wonky divan, like a shipwreck survivor, as she cooked up crazy plans to snatch back the duvet next time Gareth moved. Now she luxuriated under a properly tucked-in sheet, soft blankets and a satin eiderdown. Claudette might be short on cuddles but she was big on creature comforts.

Odd, then, that Nell couldn't get back to sleep. She pummelled the pillows. She nipped to the loo. She lay on her tummy, then flipped on to her back. Eventually, at the crack of ten, she admitted defeat and went to the shower.

She had discovered a cunning knob that targeted forceful sprays of water all over her. As she trembled with delight at the warm jets that massaged her body, Gareth popped into her head. As soon as he located the shower in a hotel he would bundle her into it and attempt immediate sex. She smiled at visions of their soapy absurdities. Nell wasn't a dextrous girl, and on a slippery surface she became positively Norman Wisdom-like. Gareth would attempt heroically to maintain his erection and Nell's vertical status with varying success. Llandudno, she recalled dreamily, had been particularly memorable . . .

She turned off the shower and began energetically to towel herself dry, like a nun caught entertaining impure thoughts about Terry Wogan. Her face in the mirror was flushed.

Where had those thoughts come from? It was weeks since she and Gareth had made love. Her list of excuses had stretched as far as it would go – period, headache, post-traumatic stress disorder after seeing a woman faint on a bus – and she had resorted to sitting up watching television until his snores had sounded the all-clear.

Desire had fled, to be replaced by boredom and intolerance. Even the way he ate crisps made her want to murder him with a blunt instrument.

It hadn't always been like that, though, and now Nell indulged the amnesia of the newly separated. Gareth turned up in her head as he used to be – fresh, new, eager to please. And sexy. She could recall when the zip on his fly had been more engrossing than Linda's private emails. Nell had guffawed at his weak jokes and happily agreed with his ill-thought-out sexist notions – 'Yes, it *is* a waste of time teaching girls maths when they just go off and become beauty therapists' – to get to the tearing-off-his-boxers-with-her-teeth part of the evening all the quicker.

Of course, in those halcyon days his boxers had been clean.

'Am I missing him?' The question astonished her, but not as much as the answer: an inescapable *yes*. For ages Nell had ached for a Garethless weekend. She had fantasised feverishly about ways to maim herself so she could go to hospital and miss the spectacle of him stretched out on the sofa in a prehistoric tracksuit, toying with his tackle.

I've been conditioned, she thought. Like a rare chimp in a zoo, she'd grown so used to the other (frankly unsavoury) rare chimp who'd been bussed in to mate with her that without him she was pining.

'It's pride,' asserted Tina, with typical certainly when Nell called her. 'You're thinking about Gareth because you're insulted he hasn't called you.'

'I'm glad he hasn't,' lied Nell, valiantly.

'No, you're not.' Tina was having none of it. 'Not unless you're from the planet Zarg where hearts have been replaced by colanders. It must be really humiliating to spend three years with a man and discover he's not even curious about where you are, if you're with someone else, if you're alive or dead, if you—'

'I think I get the drift.' Tina's candour sometimes caused her to miss signs of bruising, but Nell was relieved that her friend was talking to her after yesterday evening's uncharacteristic coldness. Pointedly, Tina made no mention of Helping Hands and Nell didn't feel up to mentioning the subject. She was disturbed by her evening at Carol's and the questions it had raised about the nature of good-doing. 'Do you fancy going out tonight?' she asked hopefully.

'Marti and I are having a nice couply night in.' Ouch. That candour again. 'At least, we will be if the dog's diarrhoea clears up. Poor old Paddy, but it's hard to be romantic when a Labrador is producing pints of own-brand oxtail soup in the corner.'

'Okey-doke,' said Nell, breezily. 'It was just a thought. I'll have a quiet night in. Claudette and I can . . .' What, exactly? Take pot-shots at passing working-class folk? '. . . get to know each other better.'

'Yuck. In that case, you'd better come to lunch tomorrow.'

'Yes,' agreed Nell, emphatically. 'I'd better.'

'Ah! I see you're up and about, Miss Nell.' Fergus managed to imply that he had given up all hope of seeing her alive again. 'I will instruct Carita immediately.'

'Don't go to any trouble,' said Nell, weakly, to his retreating back. She had a disturbing vision of Carita being hauled down from a chimney she was sweeping to make a late breakfast.

A steely voice summoned her to her grandmother's study. 'Join me for a moment, child.'

Nell peered round the door. Claudette was setting delicate gold glasses on her elegant nose. 'In, in,' she instructed briskly, as if she were training a dim poodle. 'Ah. I see.' She looked Nell up and down.

'I'm casual today.' Nell tried to defend the baggy-kneed leggings and a tie-dye T-shirt she couldn't remember having seen before when it had emerged from her rucksack.

'Do you intend to leave the premises in that attire?'

'No. I'm not going anywhere until tomorrow.'

'An engagement?'

Carefully Nell said, 'I'm visiting my friends Martin and Christine for Sunday lunch-*eon*.'

'Delightful. Young marrieds?'

'Very much indeed so.' Grammatically clumsy *and* inaccurate. 'What have you got planned, Grand—' A lizard look flicked over the gold glasses and Nell corrected herself hastily, 'Claudette. I thought we might spend the evening together.'

'Impossible, unfortunately. I lunch with the Patterson-Urquharts, then to André of Mayfair for a blow-dry, on to the colonel for cocktails and, finally, dinner at my club with my MP, and dear Lady Cloake.'

Where, Nell marvelled, did she get her energy? And could she siphon some off for her granddaughter? Nell was already looking forward to getting back to bed.

As if she'd read her mind – and with those eyes it wasn't out of the question – Claudette said, 'I believe in leading a full life. In our native Paris, the de Montrachets were active in public works.'

Our native Paris. Nell felt about as Gallic as a pork scratching. She suspected that her forebears' chic French genes had taken one look at her in her mother's one hundred per cent Irish womb and pleaded prior engagements. 'I can't see any French in me at all,' she said wistfully.

'Nonsense.' Claudette snorted genteelly. 'Half of you is pure de Montrachet. Blood will out. Perhaps . . .' She cocked her head to one side and half smiled – twenty years fell away. 'Yes, perhaps a sprinkling of French dressing might help. We could call it your *Parisianisation. Bon.*'

Their quality time was over.

*   *   *

In the quiet of the breakfast room, Nell made a hunched, arthritic origami swan with the starched napkin. She was perturbed by talk of 'blood will out'. She didn't feel French and she never had. If she really had to, she was fairly confident she could smell of garlic, and being rude to foreigners might be fun, but matching her shoes to her handbag was beyond her.

'Brrrrreakfast!' A cheerful voice with exotically trilled Rs announced Carita's arrival with a large tray.

It was the first time Nell had seen her and she liked what she saw: an outrageously Latin shape barely tamed by a sky blue uniform, and merry black eyes.

'It ees so nice to have a young person in the house!' Her plump hands flew as she fussed round Nell, arranging plate, cutlery and tea-things just so. 'You are 'appy 'ere, yes?'

'Oh, yes, thank you very much.' Overwhelmed, Nell smiled shyly at this ball of fire.

'Good.' Carita draped a napkin round Nell's neck with easy familiarity. 'It ees good for families to be together at tough times. *Eat!*' she roared, then whisked out of the room, singing.

Nell watched the well-cushioned behind sway back to the kitchen. Why couldn't her grandmother be that sort of woman – all easy warmth?

She looked down at her plate. Egg-white omelette *aux fines herbes*. It looked good, but it would have looked even better snuggled up to an All-day Breakfast with Extra Beans.

Navy blue night was draped over Knightsbridge. The penthouse felt very empty. Claudette was at her club, Carita had gone out and Fergus had presumably folded himself up and tidied himself into the appropriate drawer. Saturday nights alone weren't much fun: Nell was almost looking forward to the advent of her counterfeit relationship.

The usual bland Saturday-night fare blared out of a tinny black-and-white television at the foot of Nell's bed. Last weekend she'd been puzzled by the apparent lack of televisions in the flat: wasn't it illegal not to have one or, at the very least, a health risk? Finally, Fergus had shown her, rather condescendingly, a colour set, which huddled, ignored, behind a fake bookshelf in the drawing room. Then he had rooted out this ancient portable for her. 'Madame only cares for BBC news and documentaries,' he'd explained, with the clear innuendo that Nell would be tuning in to wrestling, soft porn and *The Teletubbies*.

'Me too, me too.' Nell had shooed him out, anxious to catch a rerun of *Hollyoaks*. However, today had proved to her that even she had limits where television was concerned.

Her mobile phone lolled within reach. The first number in the memory was Gareth's. Why not just see how he was getting on? It might be nice to hear him say he'd missed her.

She thrust the phone under the covers. Gareth would rather eat his own legs than admit it. There would be no comfort from that quarter and she was bonkers to expect it.

Various scenarios of what might be going on back at his flat had been unfolding in her head all day . . . Gareth snoring in a filthy dressing-gown, an Everest of bottles beside him and stubble blooming on his chin. Gareth playing naked tag with the kind of big-breasted, accommodating girls last seen on *The Benny Hill Show*. Gareth slumped at the bottom of the stairs, the cat feasting disloyally on his rotting bones.

There was another alternative, even more grisly than the others: Gareth getting up, having a shower, going to work, getting home, enjoying a takeaway, watching a video, shuffling off, with a contented yawn, to bed.

How could she live with somebody for years and leave no trace? The waters had closed over her head. Gareth wasn't even *angry*, which was incredible in a man who swore at OAPs for not moving up the post-office queue fast enough.

Nell was surprised to discover that she *cared* about how Gareth was feeling. After all the arguing, sulking, shouting and daydreaming about how to kill him and get away with it, she still worried about him. It hurt, in a deep sore way, that he wasn't worried about her.

Raindrops blotted the pavement as Nell emerged from the tube station. Rain plus her hair equalled comedy, so she raced the short distance to Marti's loft as fast as she could.

Her mobile trilled. It was Tina. 'Could you please, please pick up a couple of bottles of fizzy water?'

'Sure.' Nell pirouetted abruptly.

'Oh, and Marti thinks you're mad.'

'Eh?'

'This visiting-the-poor thing. He says you don't know what you're doing and he gives it a month, tops.'

Nell frowned, baffled as to why Tina had reacted so drastically to something that had had very little impact on her so far. 'That's nice. Thank him for me,' she said flatly.

'He says—'

'He *says*,' interjected Nell tartly, '"Call the number on your screen to take advantage of an amazing special offer on these gold-plated ear-wax vacuum pens." That,' she finished, throat tight, 'is what he *says*.' But it felt wrong to flash her claws at Tina.

They both knew that Marti's home-shopping programme was a humiliating step backwards for him. His last terrestrial TV project, *Marti At Large*, had been axed not so much by popular demand as by popular indifference. The format relied on letters from polite, keen as mustard, BBC-style children, who preferred biographies of Isambard Kingdom Brunel to R'n'B videos, and wrote in to suggest daring yet instructive stunts for Marti to do, accompanied by the intrepid Paddy.

Paddy had been Marti's dog on *Show Me How*, the *Blue Peter* rip-off in which he'd started his career. Large, amiable, photogenic and happy to do anything for a marrowbone, Paddy was the nation's favourite Labrador. TV chiefs had made it clear: no Paddy, no *Marti At Large*. So Marti, whose antiseptic approach to life didn't make him much of an animal lover, was saddled with a canine sidekick he bitterly resented. 'Oi, Marti! Where's Paddy?' builders would shout from scaffolds. Not only did Paddy spell his name sensibly, he had also captured the hearts of the public in a way that was beyond Marti.

Marti At Large never took off. For some reason, possibly Marti's holier-than-thou persona, it attracted a high proportion of scoffing, cynical grown-up viewers. The polite, carefully written letters requesting that he visit the Crown jewels were heavily outnumbered by drunken adult suggestions that he stroll along the live rail of the Northern Line. The producers pulled the plug when the sole letter to arrive one week was a request for Marti to dress as the Pope and try to kiss Ian Paisley.

Nell did not relish life advice from Marti Goode.

Neither, however, did she relish a snappy argument with her best friend – even if she was being a bit of a twat. 'Sorry. That was below the belt.'

'And I'm sorry too,' mumbled Tina.

'What was that? Could you speak up, please, caller?'

'Shut your face and hurry up and get here.'

Which was about as elegant an apology as Nell would get from somebody as proud as Tina.

The block where Marti lived bristled with modern must-haves. It had CCTV, a concierge, underground parking, a gym, neighbours who read the *Independent* and a monthly service charge that would have sent Nell's extended family to Torremolinos for a year. Privately Nell thought it looked like a hi-tech prison, with its acres of chrome and steel.

Tina opened the floor-to-ceiling door, holding back the bouncing, barking Paddy with one leg.

'Have the shits cleared up?' asked Nell, before she stepped inside.

'Honestly, a simple "hello" is fine. Yes, he's been bunged up, thank you for asking.'

Nell still didn't move. 'I'm waiting to be Hoovered.'

Tina yanked her in. 'What are you wearing?' she asked, in a way that suggested she didn't quite approve.

'I came as I was.'

'Don't they have irons in Knightsbridge?'

Beside one of Tina's vast collection of perfect little black dresses, Nell had to concede that her milk-stained combats and Snoopy sweatshirt looked a tad grungy. 'It's only us three, so who cares?'

If Nell hadn't been busy withstanding Paddy's welcome she might have noticed that Tina didn't answer. A warning bell might have rung and she might have turned and run.

But no bell pealed and she strolled into the cavernous living area to see Marti handing a glass of something cold to a *man*.

Nell scowled accusingly at Tina, who was walking purposefully towards the kitchen area.

'Nell, meet Nic.' Marti's smile was professionally wide. 'With a C.'

'Nell.'

Oh, God. The man had said only one word, but it had told her plenty about himself and it was all bad. He had tried to imbue the one bare syllable of her name with dripping sensuality.

'Nic,' she answered, with no attempt at a smile. 'With a C.'

'I've heard a lot about you.' Nic embroidered this banal opener with a leer.

'Really? Well, I've heard absolutely *zilch* about *you*.' Nell's voice carried to her shamefaced hostess, who was faffing about with a bowl of hummus.

'Vodka and cranberry?' Mart smirked.

'In a pint glass.' Nell let her denim jacket drop to the floor so that she could relish Marti's cringe as the metal buttons hit reclaimed-oak boards.

Two endless black leather sofas flanked a large coffee-table fashioned from the crushed bodywork of a Mini. Deliberately, Nell sat at one end of the opposite sofa to Nic's.

But Nic was not the sort of man to let a car wreck keep him away from the ladies. He stood up and strode round it, resplendent in skin-tight patchwork suede trousers, to recline splay-legged beside her. Considering how long the sofa was, he sat awfully close.

'I see you're looking at my trousers,' he drawled.

'It's hard not to.' Best to be honest, thought Nell.

'They do get a lot of compliments.' He stretched out what there was of his legs. 'The boots are real alligator.'

'Gosh. Even the heels? That's an awful lot of alligator.' She *had* to mention the heels. They were high enough to get him a job in the circus.

Nic tucked his feet in sharply.

Marti returned with Nell's drink. 'This loony and I go back a long way.' He gestured at Nic with his mineral water. 'We could tell her a tale or two, couldn't we, mate?'

Nell had never heard Marti call anybody 'mate' before. It sounded wrong from his lips, like a Tory politician trying to relate to the yoof.

'Certainly could, Maestro, certainly could.' Nic winked at Nell. 'But then we'd have to kill her.'

'How about you just kill me and we skip the tales?'

Nic assumed a grave expression, which sat uneasily with his perm. 'I hear you've got a broken heart, Nell.'

Bridling, Nell took a healthy slug of vodka. It was none of his business.

'I've been there. It's hard, man.' Nic's voice was soft now, as if he was a vet with a cold rectal thermometer and Nell was a nervous tabby. She sensed Marti's admiration, as if he was in the presence of a master. 'Are you being good to yourself, babe? Plenty of long candlelit bubble baths with a glass of champagne?'

'And a sad song on the radio,' Nell said dreamily as she out-cliché-ed him. 'I've been walking in the rain and listening to the laughter of children, too.'

Nic was impressed. 'I knew you had soul,' he told her.

Marti was crunching ice with glee, knees pressed together in his excitement at the success of his matchmaking.

Nic was practically purring now, and leaning towards Nell as if he planned to undress her. 'I know those biological clocks tick very loud, babe, but I wouldn't worry if I were you. Such a beautiful lady won't be on her own for long.'

'But I'm not on my own.' Nell gestured to the front of her rumpled sweatshirt. 'I've got Snoopy. S'cuse me.' She jumped to her feet and made for the kitchen area.

'She's funny.' It was evident that Nic meant the exact opposite.

'Need any help?' she barked, as she marched towards Tina, who was marooned behind a marble-topped island unit.

'I've hidden the knives,' whispered Tina.

'Oh, I won't need a knife.' Nell snatched up an artichoke. 'I'm so furious I could maim you with this.' She backed Tina up against the Smeg fridge.

'I'm sorry,' hissed Tina, eyeing the artichoke, which was now at her throat, as if it was a grenade. 'Marti swore he was nice. Maybe when you get to know him . . . ?'

'Why would I get to know him? He's a lecher. On stilts. With a perm.'

'Ssh. He'll hear you.'

'No, he won't. His ears are full of styling gel.' Nell lowered her weapon. 'If I had a proper home to go to, I'd go to it right now.'

Tina's face twisted. 'Don't say that.'

'And you know I hate bloody artichokes.'

The food matched the surroundings: there wasn't enough of it and it was more concerned with style than fun. As Nell tried to secrete slivers of some exotic fish under a banana leaf, she realised with a pang that it was years since she'd sat down to one of her mum's roasts.

The monolithic basalt dining-table put plenty of space between her and Nic, but it still wasn't enough. He raved about the food, apparently the best fish he'd tasted outside Thailand. 'Have you been there?' he asked Nell.

'No.' She had reached the stage of one-word answers. She scowled at her mango salsa: she didn't approve of fruit in her dinner.

'You should go. In*cred*ible place.' His face lit up like an evangelist's. 'It's where I learned to express myself through sex.'

Tina coughed and a tiny chunk of mango hit the basalt.

Nell couldn't look at her.

'Sex, after all, is our purest form of communication,' he went on. 'There are so many pointless hang-ups in the West. We need to relax. Or, let's be honest, guys,' and here he pointed his Conran fork at Nell and Tina in turn, 'Western *women* need to relax.'

Nell still couldn't look at Tina so she stared at Nic. At least he had taken her mind off the salsa.

He carried on, leaning back in his chair: 'I mean, I must have had sex with, ooooh – thirty? Forty? Probably fifty stunning Thai ladies over there.'

Nell felt queasy. Something told her that the 'stunning Thai ladies' might not have enjoyed Nic's way of expressing himself quite as much as he had.

'Plus one ladyboy, don't forget!' put in Marti.

'That was a mix-up,' Nic snapped, suddenly grim-faced.

'You said it blew your mind, mate,' Marti reminded him cheerfully.

Now Nell just *had* to look at Tina and they shared a satisfying psychic smirk.

'Actually I had him beaten up.' Nic's tone was casual. 'Don't look at me like that, girlies. That's how it is with these people.'

'*These people?*' Nell was shocked out of her monosyllables. Her face felt hot. Nic had turned out to be much worse than your average permed creep: he was a sex tourist travelling thousands of miles to pay underprivileged foreign girls for the attention that no sane British woman would give him. 'Whaddaya mean "these people"?'

'Listen to this, everyone!' Marti, who was as allergic to confrontation as he was to cat hair, changed the CD in the hope of changing the atmosphere. 'Isn't it fantastic?' His grin was so wide his wisdom teeth showed.

'Isn't it the theme to *Show Me How*?' asked Tina.

'Nic composed it.' Marti closed his eyes as if a mighty symphony was crashing over him. 'Christ, you were ahead of your time,' he murmured, as a synthetic harmonica played a manic hornpipe.

'Hmm. Wasn't that music about forty seconds long, though?' asked Tina doubtfully, as the tune droned on, like a wasp trapped in the hi-fi.

'It's the twelve-inch. Fourteen minutes of this genius,' said Marti dreamily.

'I'm going outside for some fresh air.' Nell got up and slid open the large glass door to the terrace.

Tina followed and they leaned on the metal handrail and stared out at the silvery rooftops.

Nell broke the silence. 'Well, I'm getting to know him. And guess what? He's *really nice*.'

Tina didn't laugh: she seemed to be thinking hard. 'Marti thinks he's great . . .'

'What was all that sex bollocks about? *We*'re all uptight so *he* has to get on a plane and fly half-way around the world to abuse Thai girls? Promise me this is the last time you'll set me up, Teen.'

'Oh, God, I promise,' said Tina, fervently. Her hair was less immaculate than usual.

Must be the strain of preparing parrot fish for four, thought Nell. 'I know you couldn't stand Gareth,' she said, 'but he was important to me. I need to get over him, not just bounce on to the next guy. This is my life, not a sitcom. Do you know what I mean?' It was a tricky speech but Nell had had to make it.

Poor Tina looked guilt-stricken. 'I do, I really do. It was a crap idea, even if Nic hadn't turned out to be the Official

Worst Man In History.' Then she asked, sounding uncharac-
teristically shy, 'How can I help you get over Gareth?'

'Just be you,' said Nell, and added, 'You daft old slag.'
Things had been in danger of turning sentimental.

When they returned Marti was dishing out green-tea ice-cream.
It was his own recipe. Nell had moaned long and hard about
Gareth's ineptitude in the kitchen – he expected a round of applause
if he buttered some toast – but Marti's womanly expertise was
worse. She knew she could never contemplate sex with a man
who made mouthwatering meringues. 'Can I let Paddy lick my
bowl?' she asked evilly, knowing how Marti would feel about a
canine tongue anywhere near one of his earthenware platters.

Nic tittered. 'Careful he doesn't choke. You know how
accident prone our little doggy friend is!'

He was laughing immoderately, which puzzled Nell. As she
turned to ask him what he meant, Marti almost shouted, '*Yes!*
Give him the bowl!' then prattled on, with the desperation
of a drowning man, 'So, Nell, how's your eczema?'

'Marti!' Tina was outraged. 'For God's sake! Nell doesn't
want to bring her eczema to the table.'

'No. Sorry. Of course not. Stupid.' Clearly rattled, Marti
suggested they had their coffee in the sitting area.

The girls barely had time to exchange a puzzled glance before
Nic seated himself beside Nell. Closer than a Siamese twin,
with one arm draped casually along the back of the sofa, he
seemed to believe he was in with a chance. Legs spread wide,
he asked, 'Do you get out much?' in a sultry voice.

'Very, very seldom.'

'She's practically a recluse,' corroborated Tina.

Nic persisted: 'Do you like bikes? I've got a classic Harley.'

'My brother was killed on one,' Nell told him.

'And her sister.' Tina couldn't resist it.

'That is *tragic*.' But not tragic enough to derail a chatting-up.
'Do you like the sea? I've got this little place on the coast
where I go to recharge my soul. Long walks on the beach.
An open fire. A special lady.'

'LA?' queried Nell innocently.

'Well, no. Littlehampton.'

'Ah. L.*H*.'

A rattle of cups announced the coffee. 'My own special blend,' said Marti, modestly.

And almost as nice as Nescafé, in Nell's opinion.

Nic tried to recruit Marti in his effort to impress Nell. 'You've been to my place on the coast. Remember? You came down in the car with Paddy a year or so ago. Not *that* Paddy, obviously.' Interestingly, when he smiled Nic looked disfigured, rather than improved.

'How do you mean?' Tina frowned.

Marti was flapping again. The desperation was back. 'He doesn't mean anything. Yes, yes, your place on the coast is gorgeous. You should go there, Nell, you really should. In fact, why don't you both go now?'

'Marti!' squeaked Nell. 'What's wrong with you?'

Nic stroked his chin. 'You old bastard,' he said to Marti. 'They don't know, do they?' He seemed kind of impressed.

'What don't we know?' Tina was frowning. 'What don't I know?' she asked Marti, directly.

'Nothing. Let's talk about something else. Sex. Or feet,' he gabbled wildly.

'Babe,' Nic drawled to Tina, 'this might surprise you but *that* is not Paddy.' He pointed at the snoozing dog on the other side of the vast room.

'Of course it's Paddy,' scoffed Tina. 'Here, Paddy!' Paddy rose and ambled over, bringing his distinctive smell with him. 'See?'

'Oh, it's *a* Paddy. It's just not *the* Paddy.' He turned to Marti. 'Is he, mate?'

Marti, whose head was in his hands, muttered, 'No.'

'In fact, he's number . . . ?' Nic pushed.

'Three.' The word flew out on a sigh.

'I don't understand.' Tina jerked her eyes down to Paddy, who was licking her knee absentmindedly. 'Marti?'

There seemed to be no way of prising Marti's head out of his hands. Nic was only too pleased to fill in the gaps in their knowledge. 'The original Paddy was bought by the Beeb for *Show Me How*. He was an instant hit. Remember, mate?' He poked Marti in the ribs. 'Remember how they used to say that for every request for a signed photo of you there were three for one of Paddy?'

Marti groaned and Nic carried on: 'And one day they did a special on circuses. *Not* pretty, a Labrador getting sat on by a dancing elephant. Thank God it happened off camera.' He seemed to be having trouble keeping a straight face, but Tina and Nell were so shell-shocked they couldn't see the joke. He told them how, rather than confess to the kiddies and trigger nationwide mourning, the producers had found a replacement dog and nobody had noticed. Paddy number two was a natural. He even made the transition to *Marti At Large*. Thanks to the eager letters sent in by swotty no-mates kiddies, Paddy went to the top of the Eiffel Tower in a harness, hang-glided off the White Cliffs of Dover, even ventured up Nelson's Column in a basket. 'In fact,' said Nic, enjoying himself hugely, 'he was the picture of doggy health until his first day at ShopAtHome when the producer wheeled in the Automatic Electronic Dog-drying Towelette.'

Tina, who had been fondling the Labrador's head, pulled her hand away sharply. 'But that was only six months ago! I knew you then!'

'You didn't know *him*, darling,' sniggered Nic.

Tina was on her feet. 'How could you come home with a different dog and not tell me?' she yelled at Marti.

'You don't know what I've been through,' Marti replied morosely. 'I had to meet a cameraman under Blackfriars Bridge and give him five grand for the footage of Paddy exploding.'

Tina put a fist into her mouth and stared down at the dog, still unable to take it in. 'I wondered why you'd stopped letting me put headscarves round your neck,' she said sadly to him.

'I was only trying to protect you,' insisted Marti.

'Christ. A simple "sorry" is completely beyond you, isn't it?' Tina stormed off to the sleeping area, soon to become the shouting, sobbing and hitting your boyfriend area. Paddy trailed after her loyally, until she shouted, 'Oh, go away, whoever you are!'

The dog whined softly, heartbreakingly. Nell picked up her jacket, chastened by the unusual betrayal that had unfolded in front of her. 'Thanks for lunch!' she said, with unconvincing brightness. 'We'd better go and leave you to – well, you know.'

Nic seemed shocked when Marti refused to shake his hand. 'It was only a dog, man.'

'Like it was only a ladyboy?' suggested Nell.

He didn't ask for her number.

Nine

'Blimey!' said Zoë.

'Oh, my goodness!' said Jane From Accounts.

'Fuck me!' said the new bought-ledger clerk, whose name nobody could be bothered to remember.

Dean was speechless.

'Chanel?' cooed Tina, when Nell made her first trip of the day to the kitchenette.

'Yes,' admitted Nell, uneasily. It was only a suit – she hadn't expected such a reaction.

'It's beauuuuutiful,' Tina moaned, like a soft-porn starlet, as she caressed the nubbly cream fabric. She studied it reverently. 'The cut. Those buttons.' If fashion was Tina's religion then Chanel was her god. 'Do you know how much work went into what you're wearing?'

'It's only a skirt and jacket.'

'Get over there, you Philistine!' demanded the girl who had only ever entered a museum once in her life, to use the loo. 'Don't you dare attempt a Cup-a-soup in that work of art. I'll do it for you.'

'I can't keep it.' Nell, banished to the other side of the room under a sign that read 'DO NOT SMOKE IN HERE: I DON'T WANT YOUR CANCER', was starting to feel that the outfit was wearing her rather than the other way round. 'Claudette ambushed me with it this morning. She said it was to bring out my French blood. I think she's instructed Fergus to give my sarong a lethal injection.'

'If I borrowed my gran's clothes I'd be standing here in an acrylic polo-neck and elasticated slacks.'

'But she tells you she loves you and bakes a cake when you visit her.'

85

'Swings and roundabouts,' said Tina, reprovingly. 'She doesn't put me up in her fabulous penthouse apartment.'

Len, the accountant, wandered in, grasping his personal stash of Hermesetas. 'Hello, hello, hello! What have we here? A mothers' meeting?' He laughed immoderately, revealing an expanse of dazzling dentures. By far the most interesting thing about him was his maroon tie, but there was no harm in him. Nell always laughed at his weak jokes, but to Tina he didn't exist: he was simply beneath her radar with his chain-store shirts and his devotion to Shirley Bassey. 'Are we off somewhere special?' He'd noticed the suit too. 'You look a right cracker in that get-up.'

Pleased with the compliment, Nell thanked him.

'My wife has a similar rig-out. Marks and Spencer. She doesn't have your figure, of course.' Again, a ringside seat for the magnificent dentures.

'Do you know the price of this rig-out?' Tina addressed him directly for the first time ever.

'Not a clue,' he admitted happily. 'That's ladies' business.'

'Between ten and twelve thousand pounds.'

Nell thrust her Cup-a-soup out to arm's length and Len paled. 'I'll kill her,' he muttered.

Nell fought the urge to tear off the suit, which now felt as heavy as armour. 'How's life in the loft?' she asked Tina. 'You know, after the three Paddys thing.'

'Shush!' Tina prodded her out of the room. 'Don't mention that! If it ever gets out Marti will be all over the papers.'

'OK, OK, keep your hair on. This might come as a surprise but your boyfriend's dog's health is not a huge conversational topic with me. Did he ever get round to apologising?'

'Oh, I calmed down. He was only trying to protect me, after all. I felt terrible for shouting at him like that.'

Without a degree in psychology it was impossible to work out why Tina kept making excuses for the morally elastic Marti, so Nell didn't bother trying. 'I'd better go and look busy,' she said.

*   *   *

It had been over a week, she reminded herself, as she dialled, so he'd had ample time to cool down. Besides, she had to collect the rest of her stuff or she'd be stuck in this strange world of Snoopy sweatshirts and *haute couture* for the rest of her days. He couldn't still be angry, she reasoned, nimbly forgetting his vendetta against the man in the 7/11: it had lasted a year, triggered by a Crunchie's sell-by date.

They would be civilised and mature. They would ask how the other was. Her throat felt as narrow as a shrew's ankle.

'Hel*lo*,' said Gareth, in the way he always did.

'Hi. It's me.' She added, 'Nell,' helpfully, in case he didn't recognise her new mouse voice. She braced herself for a string of free-association expletives.

'Oh. Right.' Gareth was calm.

This was unusual and not to be trusted. 'I don't want an argument, Gareth.' She was talking very fast, something she'd had to resort to many times when she was trying to get through to him. 'I hope we can be grown-up about this. It doesn't have to be painful. Surely we both saw it coming. Can't we talk in a rational way? Keep it amicable?' She was breathless, as if she'd run for a bus in stilettos.

'Whatever.'

'Oh.' Nell hadn't thought past this bit. 'How are you?' she ventured.

'Nell, what do you want?' He was still calm, slightly bored even.

Nell's heart was thumping like a trapped bat. 'I need to pick up my things. If you haven't set fire to them.' She giggled nervously: it wasn't out of the question.

'Sure. When? I'll arrange to be out.'

Had Gareth been replaced by alien body-snatchers? Maybe she should throw in a question only the real Gareth could answer, like 'What's your favourite sexual fantasy?' This substitute would never guess that it involved Felicity Kendal and a faulty bathroom lock. 'I thought maybe tomorrow, Tuesday, during my lunch-hour?'

'Fine. Anything else?'

'Yes.' Suddenly she wanted to cry. 'I asked you how you are.' Her voice wobbled.

'For God's sake, Nell! Goodbye.'

'Goodbye,' she squeaked.

'Hang on!' he said, in a rush.

'Yes?' she said warmly, a tiny smile breaking through.

'Leave the keys.'

A fresh box of tissues in one hand, Tina held her friend with the other until the caterwauling stopped. The only possible venue for this kind of behaviour was the ladies': Nell had long associated personal trauma with the smell of Toilet Duck, but usually she was the one doling out platitudes and back rubs. 'I'm sorry. I don't know what's wrong with me.'

'Don't dare apologise to me. This is all part of my job description as best friend. Was he horrible to you?'

That started her off again. If only he had been, she could have felt angry and vindicated and relieved, and get over him by playing 'I Will Survive' very loudly while she was drunk. 'He wasn't horrible. He was nothing. He doesn't ca-a-a-are!' she howled into Tina's shoulder.

'He's a pig.' Tina patted Nell's back. 'Try not to get snot on the Chanel.'

'Hildegard has one of those.' Louis, too, had noticed the wondersuit. 'Of course, she looks like a bag of spanners in hers.' He sighed. 'When are you interviewing for the new secretary?'

'I'm not. Linda is. Thursday morning.'

'Bugger. I'm playing golf with various boring sods from Broadcasting House. Can it be rearranged?'

'Shouldn't think so. There are loads of them coming in.'

'Then I'll just have to trust you.'

'No, Louis, I told you. Linda's interviewing.' Nell had no wish to encroach on the office manager's territory.

Louis perched awkwardly on the edge of her desk, squashing a tube of Rolos beyond redemption. 'I'd rather you did it, darling. I trust your judgement more. I suspect that Linda has never . . . How can I put this without being offensive? She's never been shagged rotten. And I want somebody sexy this time. Not like the last dreadful little frump.'

'You're not bothered about typing speeds, experience, any of that stuff?'

'Nope. Slim. Attractive. Decorative. In a word, fuckable. It's non-negotiable.' Off he stalked, a confident man, certain of his powers. Unaware of the flattened Rolo clinging to his bum.

Zoë sounded sheepish. 'I'm putting Hildegard Morgan through. Sorry.'

Nell groaned and held the phone a few inches from her ear. Hildegard dealt alike with children, animals, foreigners and her husband's wage slaves: by talking VERY LOUDLY. Politeness was an indulgence she didn't have time for.

'Hire an ugly secretary. Got that?'

'I was going to hire the best person for the job.'

'No. She has to be ugly,' Hildegard insisted. 'At first I even thought you were too pretty but luckily Louis found you about as sexy as a chair leg so that worked out all right. I'm not taking any chances this time. Flat-chested. Scarred, if possible. A dwarf would be nice.' Her impressive offensiveness was neatly tied up with a threat: 'If Louis ends up having sex, Clintonesque or otherwise, with the new girl, I shall find you and I shall, well, let's work the details out later, but it won't be nice.'

'I enjoy our little chats, Hildegard.'

But she was gone.

The number calling her mobile was unfamiliar. 'Hello?' asked Nell quietly. The bus was crowded.

It was Phred. 'I thought you might like an update on Carol.'

'They haven't taken the kids away, have they?' Nell was

plunged back into that chilly, empty, spotless flat. She gripped the phone tightly.

'They're staying with their mum for the time being,' said Phred, in his calm, measured way. 'Social services weren't unanimous about it but her case-worker has faith in her. It's her last chance, though.'

For all the emotion in his voice Phred might have been discussing a frozen chicken, thought Nell. She saw the world in bright primary colours and mistrusted people who were too rational, who didn't get involved. 'Oh, thank God!'

'She's going to need practical support.'

Practical support. Maybe the poor woman needed the occasional hug as well. 'Yes, of course.'

'Ready for your next assignment?'

'Extremely ready.'

'Right. We call it "the soup kitchen", but it's much more than that. It's basically the late shift at Helping Hands. We serve a hot meal to whoever turns up and give them a bed if we can fit them in. Can you handle that?'

'I think so.'

When Phred had hung up, Nell added, 'And don't forget to polish your horns for the Satanic ritual later,' for the benefit of a large woman with a moustache, who was trying hard to look as if she wasn't listening.

'What is it?' Nell peered at her plate. A tiny bird was trussed up in the middle of it, in an artfully sploshed puddle of gravy.

'It's a quail, Nell.' At least the 'Miss' had atrophied. Fergus placed some matchsticks of carrot alongside it.

'Is it fully grown?'

'I believe it's dead.'

'Fer-gus.' Nell sighed. 'You know what I mean. Is it – was it – a chick?'

'It's a fully grown quail. Potato?'

'Yes, please. Be as heavy-handed as you like.' A dollop of mash improved just about anything, Nell found.

Fergus carefully placed a new potato dusted with chervil in the gravy. 'Another?' he asked.

Nell nodded. 'Go mad.'

Claudette deconstructed her quail expertly. The bird fell off its tiny bones.

Nell found it more of a challenge, and chased it round the gravy a couple of times before she conceded defeat and picked it up in her hands. 'Kentucky Fried Quail!' she said to her grandmother, who shuddered.

Over coffee, in tiny Sèvres cups in the drawing room, Claudette said, unexpectedly, 'I've been planning a party.'

Nell, who had downed her coffee in one and was marvelling at how minuscule each component of a truly posh meal could be, said, 'Lovely,' absentmindedly.

'It's time you met some truly eligible young chaps.'

That caught Nell's attention. Claudette's notion of an eligible chap was likely to be as wide of the mark as Marti's had been. 'I'm not really eligible myself right now,' she said cautiously. 'I'm about to embark on a pretend romance with Blair Taylor, remember?'

'I remember perfectly,' Claudette said reprovingly. 'The young men I have in mind are from ancient families who could buy and sell your wretched employer a dozen times over. If you make a good marriage, Nell, you can step right out of your little job, and out of your *pretend romance*. One must take the long view. Let's see. A week on Saturday would be an ideal date for me. How does that sound to you?'

'I happen to be free . . .' Nell didn't defend her 'little job', or point out that she didn't consider a robust bank balance and a pedigree as essential criteria for a life partner. She just hoovered up the microscopic *petits fours*.

'This is a strategy meeting.' Louis was attempting a Churchillian tone. 'We need to ensure that Operation Beard is a success.'

'Operation Beard?' queried Nell, with a raised eyebrow, from her perch near the floor. She was on that designer chair again.

'Operation Beard,' repeated Louis, menacingly, quelling any idea she might have had of giggling. 'This is a serious business. The media run this country. They're not to be under-estimated.'

Behind him, Linda nodded. She was already taking copious notes. Nell wondered why she didn't just order herself a nice dry-clean-only SS uniform and be done with it.

Louis turned to Blair, who was lounging on the sofa – usually the venue for Louis's 'discussions' with actresses. 'Most importantly we have to be confident that you can go sexual cold turkey for a month or two, Blair. It cost three grand to get those negatives off Carlos.'

'I really thought he was different,' Blair intoned sadly.

'He *was* different, if the photos are anything to go by,' said Louis, wryly.

'Ah. Yes.' Blair drifted off into a reverie.

'Can we get on?' Louis reeled him in. 'Blair, we have to insist that you keep your nose clean, sexually speaking. And talking of noses, don't buy or use any drugs. Tone down the clothes if you can – a little less satin. And absolutely no all-night getting-down-with-your-bad-self at gay clubs.'

Blair looked like a sulky schoolboy. 'At this rate I might as well be bleeding straight.'

'It's not as bad as you think,' said Louis, self-righteously.

'Oh, it is,' insisted Blair darkly, and shuddered. 'I tried it once. Never again. It was like early closing in Bury St Edmunds.'

After everyone had absorbed this inscrutable comment, Louis turned his hairy face to his underling. 'As for you, Nell, no men for the foreseeable future. Got that?'

'Shouldn't be too difficult,' she muttered.

'No,' agreed Louis, ungallantly. 'By the way, once the press get on to you, you could be papped at any moment so try to make a bit of an effort, darling. No more sarongs, for God's sake.'

'Papped?' Nell didn't like the sound of that. It sounded vaguely medical.

Linda was pleased to enlighten her: 'The paparazzi might take an off-guard photograph of you.'

'Oh.' Nell thought they were all overreacting and didn't believe the press or public were half as interested in Blair as Louis, in his paranoia, assumed. She felt safe from pappage.

'Linda will take you shopping for a few decent outfits. There's no point in dragging Blair out of the closet just so he can romance a bag-lady.'

'Please. Don't mince your words to spare my feelings.'

Louis ignored her, then told them how to behave when they were out at what he called 'PR opportunities'. 'I want big smiles, adoring glances, bottom squeezes, sexy body language, the lot.'

'Whose bottom are we talking about?' This seemed important to Blair.

After some thought, Louis answered, 'In these days of equality you can squeeze each other's.'

'I'm sorry,' said Blair, firmly. 'I cannot allow Nell's hand on my behind until the implants settle in.'

For which Nell's hand was grateful.

At least eighteen times Tina had asked, 'Now are you *sure* you don't want me to come with you?' and each time Nell had replied that she was sure, thank you very much. Now, standing on Gareth's doorstep, she wished she'd given in.

As always, the hallway smelt of the burnt onions on which the ground-floor tenant seemed to subsist. Up the stairs she went, past the stain on the first floor from when she'd missed Gareth's head with a hail of pork balls during a fierce argument about 'women's problems'. '*I am not pre-menstrual!*' she'd roared, like Boudicca riding into battle.

Fearfully, Nell opened her former front door and peered round it. The special stillness of an empty flat told her that Gareth had kept his word.

Everything looked the same. She was a visitor to the museum of her life. The bowl they'd bought together in Morocco still sat on the hall table, offering a jumble of junk-mail and minicab cards. Through the open sitting room door she could see the battered sofa huddling under a crumpled chenille throw. Nell remembered buying that throw, a cheaper copy of something she'd seen in *Elle Interiors*. She'd imagined that the room would have been transformed, that it would suddenly look as if people who read long books lived there. It had obstinately remained the sitting room of people who put snacking before housework.

The bedroom was tidy. Gareth had made the bed. How ironic, thought Nell, that he should make the effort now that she was gone, after three whole years of him asking, 'What's the point? We're only going to get back in and mess it up again.'

Two nylon flight-bags, self-consciously new, stood in the centre of the floor. Nell peeked into one and saw her clothes, neatly folded. The other bag contained her CDs, books and oddities. She could imagine the sneer on Gareth's face as he bade a heartfelt farewell to *Men Are From Mars, Women Are From Venus*, *Wuthering Heights* and her disco compilations.

The donkey work had been done for her. There was no reason to tarry, but it felt wrong to dash in and out. Nell sat down on the bed, and the mattress sagged beneath her in its idiosyncratic way. She lay back and the smell of the ylang-ylang fabric-conditioner Gareth had mocked filled her nostrils. She felt tired suddenly, and the bed was so comfortable, so *familiar*.

She glanced at the bedside table and noticed that the photo of their holiday in Crete had disappeared from its frame. Instead there was a picture of Gareth's brother. Gareth couldn't stand his brother.

Handbags and Halos

It was time to go. There was no place for her here. It was no longer her home. She left the key in the Moroccan bowl and pulled the door shut behind her. The waters closed over her head and she left no trace in Twickenham.

Ten

There was an entirely different vibe about Helping Hands when Nell presented herself for duty the next night. The cavernous entrance hall was crowded. The thirty beds available on a night-to-night basis were always heavily over-subscribed, and by ten p.m. all Joy could ever do was hand out photocopied lists of other shelters. She also invited people to take advantage of the hot meal that would be served down in the basement. 'Entrance is round the back,' she said over and over again, that strobe-like smile never wilting.

By her side, doling out lists and trying to match her good humour, Nell was surprised by the calm acceptance of the men and women who were turned down. There was the odd drunken complaint but, by and large, they seemed to accept, or even expect, the disappointment and simply went away, presumably to trudge on to the next address on the list.

Most of the faces were grubby, some were 'normal', to use an adjective that made Nell blush when it popped into her head. She reminded herself that they were all normal. Except, perhaps, the man with a knitted duck tied to his top hat. Joy greeted him with a cheerful 'Just the weather for Corky tonight!' and told him lasagne was on the menu – 'Your favourite'.

Nell would have loved to deal with the crowd the way Joy did. She was so sunny and friendly, dealing with the smallest, filthiest scrap of humanity as if they were royalty. Beside her, Nell felt awkward and lumbering. She couldn't stop her inner knee-jerk reactions. The broken noses made her nervous, and the yeasty smell of stale alcohol repelled her. Hating herself, she shrank from the fingers, stained darkest yellow with nicotine, that reached for the photocopied lists.

Of course, the Chanel suit didn't help. When Nell had put it on that morning in response to her grandmother's request (*'Un peu Parisienne aujourd'hui, pour moi?'*) she had completely forgotten about the soup kitchen. Encased in ten thousand pounds' worth of wool, Nell felt even more out of place.

She had caught Joy giving her a puzzled once-over. Joy's outfit of outrageous flares and a one-shouldered turquoise Lycra top contrasted sharply with Nell's visiting-duchess clobber, which was better suited to handing out rosettes at a gymkhana than helping the homeless.

Phred appeared through the slightly smelly throng, damp curls flopping on the raised collar of his sopping overcoat. 'God, it's a shitty night out there,' he said, as he came round the desk. 'Let's get as many of this lot into a warm bed as we can.'

Nell noticed that his gaze also loitered on her outfit, before he asked, 'Fancy a quick tour of the dorms?'

'Is that a come-on?' She laughed, then said quickly, 'Sorry. Yes. That would be a very good idea.' Phred looked mildly shocked. Working for Louis had given Nell a rather twisted notion of how to behave with people in authority – she plastered on a grave, interested expression.

The rooms upstairs were long and betrayed their Victorian origins. High-ceilinged, high-windowed and rather austere, they were whitewashed and lined with identical iron beds. A small cabinet stood beside each.

'Basic, isn't it?' said Nell, hugging her expensive arms round herself. 'Not much privacy.'

Phred nodded, with a resigned smile. 'It all comes down to money. We're trying to budget for rewiring, to get more power sockets fitted. My dream is to see a lamp by every bed.' He blinked, then said, with a wry smile, 'God, I sound like a cut-price Gandhi. Actually, my dream is world peace and a Porsche – but I'd like a lamp by every bed too.'

Nell giggled. She felt like applauding and saying, 'See? You *can* make a joke!' He reminded her of the younger teachers at school, who were so busy keeping order they forgot to be popular. 'Where are the kitchens?' she asked.

Phred led the way down to the basement. There was a separate entrance to this part of the building, but for now it was locked. Nell could make out shadowy outlines through the frosted door as a queue formed in the fog outside.

'Do you think we deserve a cup of tea?' asked Phred.

Nell always thought she deserved a cup of tea, so they sat opposite each other at one of the Formica tables that dotted the large room. Their large mugs were poured from an urn big enough to house a horse by a lady of comfortable proportions named Edith. She 'was' the kitchen, according to Phred. Edith tried unsuccessfully to look modest at this and asked Nell if she was a medium.

'In what way?' asked Nell, uncertainly.

'Overalls. Medium? Large?' Edith seemed to dislike full sentences, although she didn't shy from potential insult.

'Medium,' said Nell, emphatically, hoping they were largish mediums, and not those bastard smallish ones that Top Shop peddled.

Phred was quiet, which wasn't unusual, but so was Nell, which was. He made her nervous, she realised. It was important to her that he didn't decide she was daft, and the best way to ensure that he didn't was to say as little as possible.

Phred broke the silence: 'Be prepared to have ladle elbow tomorrow morning.'

'What's that?'

'You get it from dishing out lasagne to a hundred and fifty people. Edith and her ladies prepare the food but you and I are going to serve it.'

Flexing a non-existent muscle in her arm, Nell declared herself ready. It was warm down in the basement, and cosy, despite the towering chrome fridges and the past-it Formica. Enticing smells escaped from the massive ovens. Edith, dwarfed by the cooking equipment, was stirring something mushy in a pan large enough to bath Paddy in.

Phred glanced at his watch. 'We'd better assume the position,' he said. The crowd silhouetted outside the doors had grown. 'By the way,' he said, 'I've chosen your next assignment. It just might be tailor-made for you. A lady by the name of Maggie. Older, doesn't get out much, needs a bit of company. Nothing glamorous or remotely *secret agent* about it, I'm afraid. You up for it?'

'I'm so up I'm . . . down,' ended Nell lamely, wondering idly where her sense of humour, her common sense – in fact her personality – went when she was anywhere near Phred.

He smiled, then ambled off to unbolt the doors.

There had been something about his smile that Nell didn't like. It seemed to say all sorts of things, and none of them madly complimentary. In fact, it verged on a smirk. And it appeared a little too often.

An overall flew across the kitchen and hit her in the face. 'Get that on!' advised Edith. 'The hordes have arrived.'

Ladling is a skill. Phred was dolloping out neat piles of lasagne without any slips or drops. He had neat hands, Nell noticed.

She, however, had the hands of a chimp. She decorated a few cuffs with abstract splashes before she got the hang of things. Admittedly, the cuffs weren't pristine to start with, but they were attached to what might have been the wearer's only outfit. She tried to be more careful.

She gave the smaller, thinner, younger diners larger portions. It was the girls who broke her heart: bundled up in grimy layers, with tough, closed expressions, their fear was as evident as their hunger. Nell had never been so close to such vulnerability.

The line shuffled along. People carried everything they owned with them as they balanced a tray in one hand. Rotten blankets that Nell wouldn't have let a dog sleep on were draped carefully over shoulders. The distaste that Nell didn't like to admit to lingered, but as the evening wore on her attitude to the diners became more complex. She was surprised by an ache to rush round the counter and hug them. Some looked as if they might stab her for her trouble, but her antennae picked up their underlying loneliness. They seemed a distillation of the city's unhappiness.

Nell repressed her hugging urge in favour of becoming a really, really good ladler.

Phred hadn't been joking about the pain: within an hour her right arm was shrieking. 'Half-way through!' he said, with such chirpiness that she would have pushed him into one of Edith's vats if she'd had the strength.

Yet the second hour flew by. She was astonished when Phred announced it was time to lock up and started to usher out the stragglers, like a sheep-dog in Levi's. 'Goodnight, Lottie, see you, Bill.' He knew all the regulars and chatted with them as he stood with one hand on the bolt. Nell noticed that the conversation was strenuously 'ordinary' on both sides, not related to benefits or sleeping rough.

Despite her stiff arm, Nell felt she should offer to help clean the kitchen, but Edith and the other ladies shooed her out, once they'd stopped marvelling at the amount of lasagne she'd dripped down the front of her overall.

'Well done,' said Phred, in his low-key way, as they shrugged on their coats.

So she'd done well, Nell mused, as she slumped on the back seat of the bus. That was nice to hear. Would he have praised her if he'd known that she had been ever so slightly *afraid* of some of the people to whom she'd served dinner? She rubbed her tender right arm. Sore and tired, she didn't feel up to dissecting her feelings about the dinner queue; she already knew that this doing good business was more complicated than she'd imagined.

The bus was warm and dry and Nell was speeding home to comfort and safety. She was glad of it – and glad of Claudette for maybe the first time ever. She wondered if she should tell her grandmother about the eligible men who had asked for her hand in marriage that evening. The older the suitor and the fewer the teeth, the more romantic the language. One octogenarian, boasting just one black tooth, had been so eloquent she'd almost said yes.

'This is the kitchen.' Fergus stood up abruptly, nonplussed by Nell's sudden appearance at such a late hour on the wrong side of the green baize door.

'Yup. Cooker. Fridge. Sink. The clues are all there.' Nell dumped a plastic carrier-bag on the kitchen table, which was kept in an unimpeachably hygienic condition by Carita. She'd hoped that Fergus would be in bed by now. Perhaps he sat up all night, guarding his mistress from common people. Perhaps he was an android – it was not out of the question. 'I've been shopping. For food,' she elucidated, as Fergus frowned, '*proper* food.'

Out of the 7/11 bag tumbled a white-sliced loaf, tins of Heinz baked beans, Jammie Dodgers, Ginster's pasties and a selection of luridly flavoured crisps. '*Haute cuisine* is all very well, and I'm very grateful to Carita for all the trouble she goes to,' Nell explained, 'but I've been craving rubbish. Girl can't exist on quail alone,' she told Fergus.

'There's no room for these items in the cupboards.' Fergus had backed away, but he wasn't going down without a fight.

'I'll make room.' Nell opened the nearest door with determination. 'I OKed it with Madame,' she lied fluently.

'Very well.' Fergus nodded. There was something in his demeanour that suggested he had lost a battle, but not the war.

'It's only food, Fergus,' Nell reminded him.

'*Food*,' said Fergus, contemplatively, holding up a bag of Monster Munch between thumb and forefinger.

'How were your winos?' asked Tina, getting the wrong side of a tuna bap. 'Did the witty badinage flow as freely as the soup?'

They had colonised the corner table of Mario's with their usual ploy of strategic placing of bags on chairs. When this failed they would resort to loud discussion of problems related to the menstrual cycle. 'It was fine.' Nell didn't dare 'share': she knew intuitively that Tina would rip her story to sarcastic shreds and she didn't like to provoke that side of her personality. Instead she asked, for the billionth time, 'Why aren't you fat? You eat like a fat person but you look like a vegan.'

This was true. The relentless march of calories into Tina's hipless body made no difference to its boyish outline. They presumably found an exit that Nell's more pneumatic frame lacked.

'So, your ovaries swelled to the size of a London bus, you say?' replied Tina, which baffled Nell until she noticed the small man in a tan blouson executing a sharp about-turn with a tray. He found a place at the counter and ate his soup-of-the-day in safety.

'If I tell you about something that's worrying me, will you promise to help me and not tell me off?' asked Nell.

'I don't ever tell you off! I don't know how you can say such a thing!' Tina paused. 'I'm telling you off, aren't I?' she asked.

Nell nodded.

'Shit. Am I horrible? Don't answer that.' Tina shook her neat head. 'Tell me what you're worried about.'

'And you won't judge me? You'll just listen and give me an honest opinion?'

'Of course,' said Tina, with a pained expression.

All in a rush, Nell said, 'I'm worried that Gareth has a new girlfriend.'

Tina went pink and bit into her bap with a little too much venom.

'I know what you're thinking,' claimed Nell, with some justification. 'You're wondering why I'm so interested if I don't want him back. And that it's none of my business. Or it's the first step to a reunion. And you'd like to push me into that giant vat of pre-war mayonnaise we suspect Mario keeps out the back.'

Tina nodded energetically but remained silent.

'But this is about pride,' Nell explained. 'I mean, how *could* he? The bed isn't even cool yet.'

Tina's colour had calmed down. 'Before you ask how could he, surely we should find out if he really has? What are you basing this on?'

'The bed was made.' Nell hung her head miserably. 'Gareth would never, ever make the bed on his own. The more I think about it, the more certain I am. He'd rather be put to death than shake out a duvet.'

'This wouldn't stand up in court.' Tina was almost smiling, as if she felt sorry for Nell. 'You're beating yourself up over nothing. It's paranoia, Nelliphant.'

Nell sighed. They weren't dealing with a court room: they were dealing with the inside of her head, a far more messy and undisciplined place. 'Is it?' she pleaded.

'Yes, it is. Forget it,' said Tina, airily. 'See? I didn't judge you or tell you off.' She looked pleased with herself. As she pulled a sizeable helping of lemon mousse towards her she muttered, 'But if you do go back to him I'll—'

'You won't do anything, because I'm not going back to him.' Nell tutted at Tina's lack of sympathy. 'I'm allowed to miss him, you know.'

'Oh, yes. Of course you are. There's a lot to miss.' Tina looked nostalgically into the middle distance. 'Not many people can fart the national anthem. I can see how that would be hard to leave behind. And references to your breasts as funbags – so endearing. You'll miss him at every birthday when you remember all the lovely gifts he used to surprise you with. No, hang on . . .' Tina narrowed her eyes and pretended to concentrate. 'Now that I come to think of it, he always forgot your birthday. Although he did buy you that *lovely* Boots gift voucher last year. What fun you had spending that five pounds.'

Evidently Tina didn't understand what was going on in Nell's head. But, then, neither did Nell.

It was an unusual sensation, but Nell felt as if she'd earned her day's pay. She'd peered through her specially bought reading-glasses and fired incisive questions at the job applicants. 'Where do you see yourself in five years' time?' she'd asked, and 'Could you cope with a boss who considers large breasts a formal qualification?'

'I've earned a nice relaxing drink somewhere posh,' Nell congratulated herself, having offered the position to a delighted woman named Davina. Then the phone rang and Phred asked if she could help an elderly council tenant clear out his flat before he moved to a care home. 'No problem,' she said brightly.

Nell had a choice. She could lie to Tina about why she couldn't go for a drink or she could tell her the truth and face the consequences. Although she was a committed coward, even Nell could see that it was important to assert her own freedom to do what she wanted with her spare time so she took the deepest of breaths and told the truth.

'You're blowing me out so you can clean some loser's flat?'

'Apparently he has mobility problems and—'

'Oh, do shut up. As if you know what that means,' Tina snapped impatiently.

Nell bridled. She bloody well did know what it meant. Phred had explained. 'It's you who doesn't understand.'

'*I* don't understand why my best mate is suddenly unavailable whenever I want to see her.'

'God, Teen, you could exaggerate for a living. Why don't you have a nice *couply* evening with Marti?'

'He's going out with his bosses.'

'Invite yourself along.'

'Yeah, well, I kind of did, but he's worried that I'd just be bored.' Tina stuck out her chin. 'And I would. It'd be shit.'

'Yeah. Shit,' agreed Nell, who could read the subtitles. '*Love Actually*?'

'Yup. *Love Actually*.' Whenever Marti froze Nell out of his life she consoled herself with the DVD of *Love Actually*. She knew the script by heart.

Linda's crystal clear tones carried a long way as she asked, through the changing-room curtains, 'What are you? A sixteen?'

'I'm a ten,' hissed Nell, cowering in her greying bra and Mr Men knickers. 'Possibly a twelve on the hips.' She sighed. 'Well, a fourteen if it's cut tightly.'

It had been Linda's idea to spend Friday morning on the formal-wear floor of a large department store, where the stuffy, *Dynasty*-style clothes were a couple of decades too old for Nell. The staff scared her and the price tags terrified her. 'We could buy the whole of H&M, including the staff, for the price of one of these sequin-encrusted monstrosities!' she had pointed out.

Linda's answer was succinct. 'We want Blair to date a lady, not a slapper,' she'd said, with one of her best Mary Poppins smiles. Now she was whipping aside the curtain and thrusting an armful of heavy, dowdy, expensive dresses at Nell.

'Oi!' Nell grabbed the curtain and wrapped it round herself. Now that she was single her legs languished unshaved. Her body was *not* for public consumption.

'These are all quite slimming,' Linda reassured her.

Nell struggled into one alarmingly unflattering frock (that was the only word for them) after another, and performed a heavy-footed, bad-tempered fashion display for Linda, who said things like 'That disguises your upper arms well', and 'Oh dear, no, not with your bottom.'

Eventually Nell stood in front of the mirror in a full-length white creation covered with bugle beads, and said, 'Fabulous. Brilliant. I love it. We'll take it.' Silently she apologised to her red-faced reflection and ripped at the teeny tiny buttons down the back.

* * *

Friday was Sue's last day and the new secretary was following her around to learn the ropes. That had been Nell's idea and she was proud of it: it smacked of practicality, common sense and even, perhaps, the depth that would be the hallmark of the new, improved Nell Fitzgerald.

Somehow, wherever Davina happened to be most of the male staff were as well. They travelled behind her in a pack, each holding a blank fax sheet or an empty box file in an effort to validate their meanderings.

'So what are we? Chopped liver?' moaned Zoë, huffily, as she watched her colleagues stalk Davina through Reception. 'They wouldn't notice if I came in stark naked.'

'Would you *want* Len to notice?' asked Nell.

'S'pose not,' Zoë had to agree.

Louis arrived late, fizzing with ill-humour. 'DARLING!' he bellowed at Nell. 'Any chance of you not gossiping for a few minutes and doing some actual fucking work for an actual fucking change?' The door to his office slammed behind him, rattling Zoë's fillings.

There was a sure-fire way to change his mood. Nell put her head round his door and asked if he'd like to meet the new secretary.

'If I must.' He sighed. Then he saw Davina in the doorway and some of his hair straightened.

A tall brunette, Davina went in and out prodigiously at the traditional intervals. Her legs had evidently never been told when to stop. 'Good morning, Louis.' She sounded like a playful tiger.

'Davina has excellent typing speeds,' Nell informed him. 'She does shorthand and audio. She speaks fluent French, Italian and Russian, and has conversational Japanese.'

'Get out.'

Nell got out. Linda was hovering, cleverly positioned between the water-cooler and Jean's knitting-bag. There was no way for Nell to avoid her.

Disturbingly, Linda broke into one of her sweetest smiles,

the one she employed when she was delivering really bad news, perhaps 'Your salary's been halved,' or 'I know you had sex in the stationery cupboard and I have a Polaroid to prove it,' but today it was 'Hildegard's here to meet the new secretary. Shall I send her over to you?'

'It's always a pleasure to see Hildegard.' Nell's smile mirrored Linda's.

'Right. Good.' That didn't seem to be the reaction Linda had been hoping for.

Hildegard approached, and the water in the cooler trembled and jumped. She was a large woman who was in perpetual motion. Her untidy hair dripped from many clips, her large, mobile mouth was never still and her ungainly figure, mainly composed of suspect lumps, seemed to be trying to escape from her overwhelmed underwear.

Hellos, thank-yous – all the nonsense with which human society embroiders its intercourse – were meaningless to Hildegard. She greeted Nell with a hearty 'I hope she's a dog.'

'See for yourself.' Linda pointed to the oblong glass panel in Louis's door.

Hildegard peered through to see her husband seated on the sofa beside the Amazonian Davina, his abbreviated legs lifting as he laughed immoderately at something she'd said. He was eyeing her like an Atkins dieter in a chip shop. 'Fiend! Snake!' hissed Hildegard, into Nell's face. 'She's stunning! I'll deal with you after I've thrown her out on the street!' Her hand flew to the handle.

'Hildegard, wait.' Nell restrained her.

'Look at the breasts!' wailed Hildegard. 'Forty D at least!'

'Forty-two E, to be precise.' Nell put her hands on Hildegard's shoulders. 'But she's taken this job to pay for them and to have her penis renovated. On Davina's birth certificate, she's David.'

'You mean . . .'

They snatched another glance at Louis, who was wrinkling his nose playfully over his fluted glass. Hildegard's laughter was worse than her fury: it sounded like hamsters being mashed.

Nell might have added that Davina knew all about her new boss's peccadilloes and had assured her that she had handled oafs like him before, but that didn't seem important right now.

Eleven

Jane From Accounts was a different person after the application of tequila. As she shook her profuse booty, she stamped her heels with gusto on the salsa bar's tiny dance-floor. One novelty earring had disappeared but a tiny sombrero jiggled manically on her other lobe.

Sitting at the bar nursing a spritzer, Nell felt like Samuel Pepys in a mini-skirt: she was a reporter, an onlooker. The civilised, neatly dressed people she'd come in with a couple of hours ago had all been replaced by wild-eyed hedonists with guacamole down their fronts.

Nell was no stranger to bad behaviour on licensed premises but, God, she hated office parties. People who refused a sip of alcohol all year turned into lager louts. Venues like this tiny underground bar seemed to survive solely on work dos. All around her bank staff were flirting with each other as if they'd just been released from ten years in solitary confinement.

Len sat in a dark corner near to the dance-floor, oblivious to Jane From Accounts's bravura performance. He looked as if he'd been through the spin-cycle of a washing machine. A row of empty shot glasses accounted for his cheeks' rosy tinge. A dozing temp dribbled on his shoulder.

A handful of men had approached Nell through the evening, some almost sober. She had shaken her head with a smile in answer to their requests for a dance, grateful that the deafening volume of the throbbing Latin music rendered chatting-up impossible.

It had been some time since she had been in such a pulling palace without the guarantee of a warm boyfriend waiting at home. She reminded herself not to judge her own allure by the calibre of the swains that approached her – particularly the very thin one who had obviously been crying. Was she, she wondered, the only sober person there?

No: Linda was at the other end of the bar, sipping Britvic orange and scribbling on a small pad. Evidence, probably, for later use against her colleagues. Some particularly fervent scrawling was going on, so Nell followed her line of sight to where Tina was performing a tabletop lambada for an appreciative audience of blokes in damp suits who had no idea what their own names were.

Before they'd left the office Tina had had a brief, tense and very typical phone quarrel with Marti that had left her near to tears. Now she seemed to be recovering: maybe taking off her top had helped her get things straight in her mind. It was certainly proving a distraction for her spectators, who were spilling most of their expensive beer into their laps.

'Avvashot!' yelped a voice from table height.

'Zoë?' Nell waved away the proffered bottle. 'Why are you on your knees?'

'Am I?'

'Are you all right?' Nell asked the question traditionally put to people who are categorically not all right, and won't be for quite some time. Zoë's eyes were like pink liquorice allsorts and she seemed to have borrowed somebody else's hair.

'Yeah. It's great, innit?'

'Deeply fantabulous,' agreed Nell.

'Cworrrr,' said Zoë, doing a praiseworthy Sid James. 'Look at him over there. He's gorgeous!' The leer was replaced by a troubled frown. 'Oh, no. I've lost it. I'm seeing double. He's coming over, though, both of him.'

Zoë wasn't quite as drunk as she had thought. Two identical, breathtakingly handsome boys were shouldering their way through the heaving crowd. They seemed a foot taller than the mere mortals around them and their peroxide heads glowed like halos. The gurgling noises coming from Zoë were perfectly understandable.

'Paul! John!' Nell was shocked to see her half-brothers suddenly materialise in the throng of baying office workers. She hadn't seen them for six months: the spiky blond haircuts were new to her. 'What? How? Where?' she yelled, over the music.

'I rang you at work,' shouted John, who was distinguishable from his brother by the mole artfully positioned by his sensually full lips. 'The bird on the phone said you were busy but that you'd be here tonight.'

'That was meeee!' gushed Zoë, flinging up her hand as if answering a question at primary school. 'I'm the bird on the phone!'

'She's not really that small,' explained Nell, as the twins peered down. They helped Zoë to her feet. It took some doing but she seemed to enjoy it. While they draped her over a chair, Nell asked, 'What on earth are you doing here?' She'd never socialised with the twins: part of her had an inexplicable urge to hustle them away under blankets, like childkillers.

'We're inviting you to little Annie's christening.' Paul's accent was as profoundly sarf-London as his brother's. 'Next Saturday round at St Thomas's. Will you come?'

'Of course. She's my first niece.' Then Nell corrected herself: 'Half-niece.'

'Great.' Paul beamed.

John beamed.

Nell beamed.

It was one of the longest conversations she'd ever had with them.

The drunk on the bus sat beside her. This was to be expected. The drunk on the bus always sat beside Nell.

Getting out of the smoke-filled, noisy bar had been tricky. The rest of the Morgan staff had been incredulous that anybody could willingly leave such a beautiful place. Tina had clambered down from her tabletop stage and accused her point-blank of being sober. 'Why?' Tina had pleaded, like the disappointed mother of a teenage hooker. 'For God's sake, why?'

'Early start tomorrow.'

'I see. Fucking Helping fucking Hands. Great.' Tina's self-righteousness was in no way impaired by that fact that she was in her bra. 'Go. See if I care.'

Nell's excuse was partly true: her next assignment was at nine the next morning. However, she knew that a subtle shift in her priorities was also to blame for the shameful sobriety.

The drunk beside Nell was sharing with her a complex tale of woe: it was his birthday and none of those bastards cared.

Nell sighed. She was single and it was Friday, a lonely Friday night with just the babblings of a crumpled man spattered with kebab for diversion.

It wasn't all that different from a Friday night with Gareth.

The thin Saturday sunshine glinted on the glossy blue front door, which was open just wide enough to reveal a pair of sparkling eyes of the same colour, and a fringe of white hair. 'Tell Phred I'm very grateful but could he *please* stop sending me Helping Hands volunteers?' said the exasperated-sounding old lady. 'I don't need any help, thank you very much.'

'Are you sure there isn't some little job you need doing?' pleaded Nell, who was in danger of failing completely at this 'tailor-made' assignment. She wasn't even past the doorstep. 'Isn't there some wonky shelf I could fix? Or does your, er . . .' Nell peered at the healthy plant clambering up the front of the small house, took a guess and plunged on: 'Does your clematis need pruning?'

'If I had one, it might. But my honeysuckle is fine, thank you.' The blue eyes looked amused, but the door didn't open any wider.

'Perhaps I could cook you a nourishing meal?' suggested Nell, whose entire culinary repertoire relied on the word 'microwaveable'. She had to find a way of getting into this house. She was going to help this unhelpable woman if it killed her. Or possibly both of them. Inspiration struck. 'I could wash your hair?'

Now the eyes narrowed. 'I've been washing my own hair since the nineteen thirties. Do you,' she asked, 'need help washing *yours*?'

'Oh, I can wash it OK,' Nell assured her. 'It's just the blow-drying that makes me look like a refugee.'

The blue eyes crinkled. 'I wouldn't say that.' The old lady hesitated. 'I've just baked a sponge,' she continued pensively, as if mulling over a state secret. 'If you're determined to come in I suppose you could help me eat it.'

The door opened.

Maggie, her capacious chest covered with crumbs, handed Nell a mug of tea. 'I think I know what a "wanker" is, but tell me, my dear, is that the same as a "tosser"?' She paused. 'Are you all right with mugs? I find cups and saucers so fiddly. All that washing-up.' She reverted to her original subject. 'As for "knob-end" – is that an insult? Is it as bad as, say, "twat"?'

'Er . . .' Maggie didn't fit the frail template of Nell's imagination. She had expected small and skinny: she had got ample. Maggie was composed of circles, from her round pink cheeks to her sky blue eyes to her impressive bosom. She walked slowly and sat comfortably in her book-lined sitting room, which didn't, despite Tina's prophecy, smell of biscuits or cats. It smelt of vanilla sponge.

'And then there's "tosspot",' Maggie mused. 'Very colourful. But what can it mean?'

'I'm not sure,' mumbled Nell, uncomfortably.

Maggie had heard two boys arguing in the street, and was surprised at how much children's insults had changed since her days as a teacher. 'It was all "git" and "pigface" back then,' she'd said nostalgically. Now she changed tack, possibly aware that she was embarrassing her visitor. 'Been doing this long? Visiting broken-down old broads like me?'

'Oh, you're not . . . I haven't . . .'

'I'm teasing you, my love. More cake?'

By the time Nell and Maggie had finished the whole lot – with the prerequisite quota of we-shouldn't-reallys and just-one-more-little-slice-thens – Nell knew that Maggie's fiancé had been shot down during the war and she had never felt the same way about any other man; she knew that Maggie had retired from teaching twenty years ago and now she was devoted to *EastEnders* and *Coronation Street*, studying for (another) degree with the Open University, ordered her groceries over the phone and hardly ever went out.

Maggie knew that Nell was newly single, that she found her job unfulfilling, was nervous around her grandmother and craved her mother's attention; she knew that Nell sometimes got up in the middle of the night to eat Smash and that she was looking around for a place in the world where she felt truly comfortable.

So, as Nell waved goodbye happily to her new assignment and promised to call back in a few days, her new assignment knew considerably more about Nell than Nell did about her.

Phred was smirking again, but this time he was doing it out of doors. 'What do you mean what am I doing here?' he said. 'I live here.' He waved a hand airily in the direction of an untidy-looking house with ivy clambering up its front. 'Number thirteen. Unlucky for some, if you're bingo-minded. Maggie's neighbour.'

Nell had just clanged Maggie's garden gate shut when she'd spotted Phred, scarf akimbo, across the road, Clover's hand in his. Catching him in the wild had shocked her: he was still rumpled, still preoccupied, but a little less buttoned-up than when he was on HH duty. 'Oh. It's funny to see you out of context.'

'I don't live at Helping Hands, you know.' Phred seemed mildly insulted.

Nell knew it was bad strategy to mildly insult her boss while she was on a month's probation. 'Of course you don't!' She beamed. 'I bet you have a very exciting life! Where are you off to now, for instance?'

'We're buying tripe,' said Clover, loudly.

Phred frowned. 'She heard about tripe from somewhere and she can't stop going on about it. We're not really buying tripe. We're going to get some chops for our dinner. Honestly.' It seemed quite important to him that Nell believed him.

Nell smiled, and playfully flicked the end of Clover's flick-able nose. This went down well and resulted in a playful punch in the stomach for Nell. Quite a feisty punch for a seven-year-old of modest proportions.

'Hey! Don't hit the lady!' remonstrated Phred.

'I'm fine,' wheezed the lady, which prompted Clover to do it again.

'Clover.' There was an undertone to Phred's voice that the little girl obviously recognised. 'Be nice.' The punching stopped and she resumed trying to touch the tip of her nose with her tongue. 'How did it go with Maggie?'

'I think . . .' Nell sought for the right way to express herself. 'I think we're going to be friends.'

'You got in?'

'Of course,' said Nell, breezily.

'You're the fourth – no, hang on, the *fifth* volunteer I've sent in to Maggie. I was starting to feel like a First World War general, sending young soldiers off to be mown down. Nobody's ever got inside before.'

'She's really nice when you get chatting.' The hour and a half Nell had spent in the warm sitting room had zoomed by, and she'd only left because Maggie had some Open University coursework to finish. 'But, well . . . why was I there? The house is spick and span. She's in perfect health. In fact, I wish she'd look after me!'

'I told you – you're tailor-made for this assignment.' Phred smiled mysteriously which made Nell itch to thump him – if there was one thing she hated, it was a mysterious smile – but, luckily, he carried on: 'Maggie doesn't really need any practical help. I've been watching her over the past couple of years and she just seems to have given up. I never meet her out on the street any more and she doesn't have visitors. I think she's lonely, but far too proud to reach out. I'm fond of her.' He glanced down at Clover. 'She's always been very sweet to my little girl.'

'So you want me to . . . what exactly?' Nell was still puzzled.

'Be yourself. Make friends with her. Give her a stake in the world again. Think you can do that?'

'It'll be *very* easy to be Maggie's friend,' grinned Nell, surprised that that was all there was to it. She hadn't suspected Phred of being a matchmaker.

'Excellent.'

Nell preened herself as if the headmaster had noticed how shiny her shoes were.

Clover, who wasn't one for respecting boundaries, pulled at Nell's jacket. 'Are you coming to our food party?'

'She means dinner party,' Phred translated.

'No, chicken, I'm not.'

'Why?' Clover was quite cross. 'Why, Daddy?'

'Pickle, not everybody is coming to our food party.'

'But why?' She was scowling now. 'Why?'

'I'm not invited,' explained Nell.

'Please come.' Now Clover was about to cry. 'You're nice.'

Laughing artificially, in an aren't-kids-adorable way, Nell felt a bit embarrassed. 'Oh, I'm not that nice!' she said.

'Clover obviously thinks you are.' Phred didn't seem embarrassed at all. 'Come to think of it, there's no reason why you shouldn't come to our food party. Are you free on the twenty-fifth?'

'Yeah. Absolutely. Yes.' Nell felt on shaky ground. A social invitation from her manager opened up all sorts of opportunities for disaster. The only dinner parties Nell was familiar with ended up in a food fight as she snogged some man she had found repulsive before the wine-box kicked in. Instinct told her that dinner at Phred's would be more decorous. She suspected that his wife was a brainbox: would she expect Nell to discuss politics over the cheese? 'I'd love to,' she lied eloquently.

'Great. Well, you know where we are. The twenty-fifth. Seven thirty,' Phred said, in the tone he used to give her the Helping Hands assignments.

'Can't wait.' Nell turned away, then called over her shoulder, 'I don't eat tripe, though!'

'Tripe!' sang Clover, happily.

'Chops!' said Phred, vehemently.

The only thing that made Nell's ballotine of *foie gras* with Sauternes *jus* bearable was the knowledge that a fat little Cornish pasty was lolling about in the fridge for later. She had been alarmed when the greenish goo on her plate had been described by Claudette as celery emulsion, but apparently it was one of Carita's specialities. After a tentative taste Nell conceded that it was very good. But there was hardly any of it. Did Carita cook their dinners in pots and pans stolen from a doll's house?

As Nell greedily attacked the chocolate parfait that sat like a full stop on the big blank page of a plate, she consoled herself with a mental image of the full packet of Jaffa Cakes in the kitchen.

'Would you care for a few hands of poker?' asked Claudette, as Fergus served their after-dinner brandy in the ivory drawing room.

'Sure.' Nell had been looking forward to an orgy of bad Saturday-night television, but this seemed like a good opportunity to spend quality time with her grandmother.

Playing poker the Claudette way involved mother-of-pearl chips, Venetian tumblers of whisky and winning. Nell suspected her grandmother had X-ray vision: with those startling eyes it wasn't out of the question.

'How do you do it?' marvelled Nell, throwing down her hand in despair.

'You are utterly transparent, child. You must learn to cloak your emotions.'

Nell snorted. She'd never manage that.

'Please don't snort. Only Derby winners get away with that in polite society.'

'Sorry, Grand—' Nell winced under the skin-stripping power of the glare that came her way. 'Sorry, Claudette. I don't see much polite society, apart from you.'

Claudette shuffled the pack with the dexterity of a Vegas veteran. 'All that might be about to change. I've finalised the guest list for our cocktail party next Saturday. Every single young man with a name and a future will be here.' She dealt the cards efficiently. 'Hopefully a few dinner invitations will result. Then you might start to make the right sort of gentlemen friends.'

A faint warning bell sounded in a distant wing of Nell's brain. Next Saturday . . . Was there something else she had to do on that day? She didn't linger on the thought as the call of the Jaffa was now too strong to ignore. She needed an excuse to sneak off through the green baize door. 'Are you chilly, Claudette? Can I fetch you a . . .' Nell hesitated. What should she call those elegant things that Claudette draped about her shoulders? A wrap? A serape? A stole? A . . . big scarf thingy?

'Yes, please. You'll find a pashmina on my chiffonier.'

So they were pashminas. And there was one on her chiffonier. Whatever that was.

Nell hurtled into the kitchen and almost bumped into Fergus. 'Sorreee!' she sang, as she yanked open the cupboard door and reached up for the biscuit packet.

Fergus moved ostentatiously to the other side of the table to finish his coffee. He was in civvies.

'Nice togs, Fergus.' Nell approved: he looked almost handsome in his blazer and cords. If you liked 1940s stuff. 'Going somewhere special?'

'A concert.'

'On your own?' asked Nell, hyper-casual.

'With a friend.' Fergus dusted an imaginary speck from his spotless lapel.

'A . . . ladyfriend?' Nell ventured.

'An old friend.'

'An old ladyfriend?' Nell was a persistent interrogator. Crap, but persistent.

'Shall I decant those fancies on to a plate, Nell?'

'God, no! These fancies are going into my mouth before they have a chance to know what's hit them.' She peered into the packet. 'Hang on . . .' There were only two left. Nell's mental inventory of her junk-food store had all the precision her work at Morgan Theatrical Management lacked. There should have been five. She glanced slyly at Fergus, who was engrossed in arranging a handkerchief in his top pocket.

She tucked the packet under her arm and opened the fridge. Thankfully the pasty was there, unmolested. But the level in her Coke bottle had definitely fallen. She poured herself a glass, then surreptitiously marked the level with her thumbnail.

This was war.

Luckily Nell recognised the chiffonier – by the pashmina that lay on it. 'Sorry to disappoint you,' she told the bow-fronted piece of furniture, 'but in real life you're just a chest of drawers.'

It felt vaguely illicit to be in her grandmother's softly lit bedroom. She had never crossed the threshold before and padded over the velvety carpet like a trespasser. Claudette's elusive perfume hung in the air.

A photograph framed in ornate silver shared the chiffonier with the pashmina and Nell glanced at it. The face was young, male, handsome – and knocked the breath out of her.

'Daddy,' she whispered.

Philippe de Montrachet had been younger than Nell was now when he'd posed so cockily for the photographer. He stared out of the frame, amused and challenging, as if the firmness of his chin, the straightness of his nose and the size of his mother's bank balance gave him all the rights he'd ever need.

On Nell's first birthday Philippe had popped out to the corner shop and there must have been one hell of a queue because he still wasn't back. She only knew her father's face from blurred snaps she'd found in a shoebox under Patsy's bed. Daddy asleep on the sofa. Daddy posing like Superman in his seventies underpants. Daddy licking a dripping ice-cream on some forgotten bank holiday.

This image of him in the silver frame, she knew instinctively, was the most accurate: an audacious, beautiful young man so certain of his status that he'd forgotten to develop any strength of character to back it up.

When Claudette had turned her back on Philippe, he'd declared that he and his girl would live on love. Solidly working class, Patsy hadn't shared his confidence: the off-licence was unlikely to accept love in exchange for the Jack Daniel's he'd grown increasingly fond of. When having a baby turned out to be half the fun and twice the expense he'd anticipated, Philippe had taken that momentous trip for a pint of milk.

'Daddy,' Nell repeated, into eyes like her own.

Claudette arranged the pashmina about her shoulders with irreproachable elegance. The air of iron serenity she radiated was daunting, but Nell was about to ruffle it. She wanted to hear about her father.

'Who taught you to play poker like this?' she asked, as she relinquished another pile of chips.

'Your grandfather. We played for hours. We were very evenly matched.'

Claudette *never* mentioned her husband. Perhaps whisky and winning were loosening her up. Nell decided to risk a question that had intrigued her for a long time as a way of opening the subject of Philippe. 'Wasn't it unusual for a man to take his wife's name?'

'Not if his wife was a de Montrachet.' Claudette's eyes didn't stray from her cards.

Wistfully, artfully, Nell said, 'It's such a shame he didn't live to see his son.'

There was no tremor on that glacial brow.

Nell ploughed on: 'That's a lovely photo of Philippe in your bedroom.'

'He was a very handsome man.'

Was? 'I wonder where he is now.' Nell took an emboldening sip of the hundred-year-old whisky. It made the inside of her skull warm. Claudette didn't rise to the bait. She was skilled at all sorts of poker. 'Don't you ever wonder?'

'I do not. He made his choices.' Strange how Claudette managed to say brutal things without changing her conversational tone. It was surreal. 'One can only hope he didn't regret them.'

And one can infer that he probably did.

'Don't you ever daydream that you might see him again one day?' Unlike her grandmother, Nell couldn't keep the emotion out of her voice.

'I will never see Philippe again.'

That was chilling. But Claudette hadn't said that she never daydreamed about it.

Twelve

Nell was sitting on a kitchen chair her mother would have thrown on to a skip twenty years ago. They were in Eclectica, a hyper-funky new club that Tina and Marti had been among the first to join. The look was bordello-meets-kitsch-meets-media-people-with-too-much-disposable-income. Chandeliers dripped over Formica tables, and paintings-by-numbers lined the flock walls. 'Shouldn't Marti be here by now?' Nell had noticed the time on the cuckoo clock over their heads.

'He's not coming. Needs an early night. Big day's filming tomorrow.'

It would have been so easy to make a crack about how tiring it must be flogging musical toilet brushes, but the new, improved, *deep* Nell was above that sort of thing. She contented herself with raising an eyebrow.

'He works so hard,' said Tina, admiringly.

'Mmm.' The new Nell was struggling to hold her tongue. 'It's just you and me, then?'

'Yeah. Fancy some hot lesbo action?' suggested Tina, perking up the eavesdropping freelance script editor at the next table no end. 'We could eat here and then I might even let you take me to one of those lovely, lovely pubs you seem so keen on.'

'Let's eat here and see how we go.'

The amount of wine they consumed with their two courses dissuaded them from braving the mean streets of Soho. Instead they snuggled down on a leatherette sofa with their glasses. 'I can feel it coming,' began Tina, mysteriously.

'What, exactly?' asked Nell.

'Commitment. The M word.' Tina tried to tie down the smile that was bouncing all over her face.

'I'm assuming the M word is "marriage". Not "mince". Or "meningitis".'

'You asshume correctly,' said Tina grandly.

'Really?' Nell hadn't heard this kind of talk before. 'What makes you say so?'

'He's changing. He's softening up. He's admitting to himshelf that he needs me. He'sh taking me away shomewhere shpecial thish weekend.' She sat up straighter and leaned over at a perilous angle towards Nell to make her point. 'The schmuck loves me. He just doesn't know it because he'sh too . . .' Tina cast around for the right word. 'He'sh too . . .'

'Dimensional?' suggested Nell, pushing Tina back into a safer position among the cushions.

'Yesh.' Tina realised what she'd said: 'No! He'sh lovely, my Marti. And he lovesh me.'

The first statement was patently untrue, and the second was dubious: if he loved her so much, Nell thought, why wasn't he *nicer* to her? She looked at Tina's beautiful profile as she asked a waitress for another bottle. Her friend deserved so much better.

There was one unequivocal success that Nell could claim in her disordered life: Davina was popular with everybody at Morgan Theatrical Management. Only the women knew that Davina was a bloke and they exchanged many covert looks and smothered titters as they witnessed an outbreak of new shirts and improved hygiene among the male staff.

Len was particularly smitten. He had taken to stopping by Davina's desk, hands manfully on hips, to ask if she needed anything.

At this point Zoë usually muttered, 'Yeah. A vagina.'

It wasn't big and it wasn't clever, but Nell laughed every time. Davina laughed too, but discreetly. She was a reserved character, who didn't open her life to the gaze of her colleagues.

In awe of her beauty, and perversely fascinated by her ambiguous sexuality, the girls at Morgan were inclined to make a pet of her, and Davina was inclined to resist.

Only Dean remained immune. He was a one-crush guy and he was loyal to Nell. As he trundled his post-cart about he watched her from beneath the brim of his baseball cap, his face inscrutable with its dot-to-dot map of the world.

Good Heavens! was a tepid new sitcom about nuns, which had been designed as a vehicle for Louis's oldest client. The elderly actress was routinely described in the press as 'a national treasure' or '*grande dame*'. Chaperoning her for the recording of the first episode, Nell would have described her more accurately as 'a chain-smoking neurotic old bat who's only bearable once the industrial-strength Prozac kicks in'.

Having dealt with the national treasure's dressing-room tantrum about the tilt of her wimple, Nell didn't feel like joining the audience. She was in no mood to guffaw patiently through three, five, maybe more takes of tepid *double-entendres* about 'bad habits'. She was anxious: it had dawned on her that Annie's christening and her grandmother's cocktail party would take place on the same day. With luck she could make both – but luck was an unreliable ally, usually preferring to stay in and watch *Who Wants To Be A Millionaire?*.

Nell picked her way over the camera cables on the studio floor and let herself out into the corridor. Like Alice in TV Wonderland, she wandered along, peering through doors into vast, darkened studios haunted by ghosts of long-dead flops or smash hits. Production staff occasionally whizzed past, talking earnestly into walkie-talkies as if they were guiding down stricken jumbo jets instead of putting together telly programmes.

Ahead she saw an illuminated 'recording' sign. She waited until it went out, then pushed open the door and slipped in to see what was going on.

There was no audience and the small crew fussed round a

blindingly lit set, which consisted of chrome shelves. ShopAtHome! Nell recognised it instantly.

Marti sat behind a Perspex desk, having his nose powdered by a bored-looking girl.

'Take ten, Marti, while we set up the shot for the pets' karaoke machine,' barked an overweight man.

Marti stood, stretched, and saw Nell emerging from the darkness.

'Hello,' he said, surprised.

'Hello yourself.'

'This is one of my agent's staff,' said Marti, over-loudly, to people who weren't listening and didn't care. 'She's probably brought me something to sign. Have you brought me something to sign?'

'Oh, yes.' Nell spoke loudly and clearly too. 'I've brought you something to sign that's a matter of showbiz life or death.'

Marti glared at her, then ushered her into his dressing room. ShopAtHome obviously didn't believe in spoiling its presenters: Nell had been in more opulent Portaloos.

Paddy licked her hand from beneath the dressing-table. 'How's he been?' she couldn't resist asking, as Marti made them green tea in mugs with his face on them.

'Fine, thank you.' He sounded like a piqued fifties house-wife.

'I hear you're off somewhere special this weekend.'

Marti slammed the door hastily. 'Yes. It's a surprise.'

'Give me a clue!' begged Nell, with trademark nosiness.

Instead of replying, Marti asked anxiously, 'Tell me. Is this shirt too trendy?'

'No,' Nell answered, with absolute honesty. As far as she was aware yellow shirts with tartan collars had never been too trendy. Marti still dressed as if he was on children's TV. 'Is it somewhere wildly romantic?' she pressed, knowing Tina was smugly certain that the question would be popped on a balmy balcony.

Marti snorted. 'Teen and I got over all that romantic crap

a long time ago.' He was talking to his reflection, which was surrounded by lightbulbs. 'She knows the score,' he added, in a chilly voice.

Safely back in the bosom of the over-excited *Good Heavens!* audience, Nell had to admit that she hadn't seen much sign of burgeoning commitment in Marti.

A breakfast of thin toast with the crusts cut off was nicely augmented by a Yorkie. Another Jaffa Cake had gone missing but Nell had no time to scrutinise Fergus for crumbs. She adjusted the chic hat Claudette had pressed on her and set off for the christening.

A number-fourteen bus is no place to sport a spectacularly wide-brimmed hat, but Nell was too bound up in her thoughts to notice how much disruption the long navy feather was causing in the seats behind her.

Her first outing with Blair was looming and she felt like a factory hen that had discovered the date of its impending despatch with a blunt knife. Operation Beard's top-secret status had been compromised by Tina, who had told Zoë, who had told Jane From Accounts, who had told Jean, who had told Dean, who had told Len, who had let the side down by promptly forgetting about it and not telling anybody. Louis and Linda still believed that nobody knew, but Nell felt better in the knowledge that her colleagues wouldn't swallow the headlines when they came.

The other subject weighing heavily on Nell's overheated mind was the bulky envelope that had arrived in the post that morning at Hans Place.

The neat spinsterish handwriting was Gareth's. She hadn't been particularly excited to receive her accumulated post: a bank statement, enough circulars to paper a room, an offer from a credit-card company to fund her wildest dreams (how much might George Clooney charge for a night of love, anyway?) and a postcard with an indecipherable signature, informing her that somebody had eaten a bad prawn in Taormina. She'd rifled through the bundle for a note from Gareth but had been disappointed.

'He truly doesn't give a flying monkey's toss,' mused Nell, shaking her head and testing the nose of the turbanned man behind her beyond endurance. She didn't hear his explosive sneeze as she fantasised masochistically about Gareth and Miss X sitting up in bed at this very moment, laughing themselves into hernias at Saturday-morning television. *I* bought that duvet cover, she recalled angrily, feeling the searing injustice of it very keenly.

Georgina was 'grabbing a fag', as she put it, outside St Thomas's. 'Five more minutes and you'd have been late!' she admonished her elder half-sister, with all the confidence of a sixteen-year-old single mother.

'Sorry.' Nell kissed her cheek hesitantly. 'Where's little Annie?'

'Inside. They're all inside.' Georgina flicked the end of her cigarette towards the tombstones of Fulham's dear departed. 'Do I look all right? You're the classy one. What do you think?'

Yes: to her family, Nell, with her sarongs, her flip-flops and her history of ill-judged perms, was the classy one. 'You look gorgeous.' This wasn't the moment to discuss the compatibility of Lycra with the post-natal stomach, and if Georgina wanted to wear a halter-neck to her daughter's christening, so be it. 'New hairdo?'

'Like it?' Georgina patted the crimson crop nervously. 'I did it to show off me ears.'

'It certainly does that.'

The girls joined the rest of the family, who were clustered around the font. Surprisingly, the twins, peroxided and lean, were dressed the same. Identical outfits was a tradition they'd abandoned as soon as they'd acquired free will over their wardrobes, but today the effect of two unfeasibly handsome young men in sharp Italian suits was arresting.

Canvey, the younger heir to Ringo's millions, was uncomfortable in fancy waistcoat and his first long trousers. He tugged at his elasticated bow-tie with a chubby hand. When Nell bent down to kiss him he turned away his face with a gurn of kiddie disgust. She had to admit that despite his anti-social, possibly psychotic manner, Canvey had the family propensity to good looks. Her half-brothers and -sister, fuelled by cigarettes and takeaways, all exuded a wholesome bloom.

'Nice 'at!' laughed Ringo at pub volume, as Nell disappeared into the depths of one of his hugs. He'd added another belly to the collection.

'C'mere to me, love, till I kiss you,' cooed Patsy, folding her thin arms round her daughter and whispering into her ear, 'For Jaysus' sake, don't get too near the font. Canvey's after pissing in it.'

Glad of the warning, Nell squeezed her mum's slender frame, clad in the best that the local Oxfam had to offer, and stepped back. Patsy looked elegant and up to date in an emerald coat and dress that had experienced an entire other life before ending up in her wardrobe. Even Claudette might have been impressed, if she had deigned to take any notice, although the coat was a touch too big, a detail that made Nell smile and hurt just a bit, at the same time.

Patsy introduced the lanky bloke on her right, uneasy in what was obviously a new suit. 'This is Carl,' she beamed. He had a Hoxton Fin and a face peppered with craters. 'He's the godfather.'

'All right?' muttered Carl, shifting from foot to foot.

'Perhaps we might get started . . .' The milky-skinned priest didn't have the authority to control this particular christening.

Ringo did: 'Oi! Father's talking. Behave yourself, you buggers.' The chattering stopped and all eyes were on Father, weighed down by his embroidered robes.

'If Godmother could hold the baby . . .' He'd resorted to dot-dot-dots again.

John bounced the child awkwardly and held her out to Nell.

'Oh, no, not me, I'm not the godmother,' Nell whispered, in the low voice she reserved for churches and personal phone calls when Louis was around.

'Yes, you are, stupid,' insisted Georgina. 'Didn't those idiots tell you?' She glared at the twins, who shrank in their sharp suits. 'She's your goddaughter, Nell. Take her.'

So Nell took her. Warm and heavy, Annie was a happy boulder in her arms. Nell peered round her half-siblings. They were listening piously to the priest's shtick about sin and the devil, but Nell was oblivious to it. She was still taking in the massive compliment that Georgina had paid her.

The small family do expanded rapidly when they got back to the house. Neighbours and friends crowded into the tiny sitting room, obliterating the warring carpet and wallpaper, creating a wall of sound that Phil Spector would have been proud of.

Ringo took his duties as host very seriously. He had laid waste to the corner off-licence. He foisted a Snowball on Nell and kissed her wetly on the forehead. He was kissing everybody's head, regardless of sex or age, and soon would start crying. Sober, he was deeply sentimental; after three drinks, he achieved danger levels.

Foamy drink in one hand, the other tightly round Annie's plump middle, Nell negotiated a way through the throng. The tiny room was smoke-filled and noisy so she sought sanctuary in the kitchen. The modern units were all Ringo's handiwork, as was the conservatory, which was stuffed with bright plastic toys and baby paraphernalia. 'More is more' was his interior-design credo, so the pattern on the wallpaper didn't really match the pattern on the lino, which didn't really match the pattern on the blind. Nothing could really match the fluorescent dress that Georgina had changed into – she had presumably borrowed it from a thinner friend.

'Do you want your mummy?' asked Nell, into Annie's soft curls.

'No, she don't,' Mummy answered for her. Mummy was enjoying another fag. 'She likes you, Nell.' Georgina smiled approvingly.

'Well, I like her.'

Patsy bustled in and started to rip open economy bags of snacks. 'They're mental for cheese puffs in there,' she told them, then purred at her granddaughter, 'Aw, there's my little Annie.'

'Your little Anastasia Desdemona Liberty Fifi Arwen, you mean,' Nell corrected her. She had been right to suspect that Annie's simple name was too good to be true. The child's full, tonsil-torturing birthright had only emerged over the holy water. (Nell had wondered if water diluted by the urine of a Satanic five-year-old could still be considered holy, but it hadn't seemed the right moment to ask.)

'Well, would you look who's here?' Patsy gushed suddenly, with the sort of enthusiasm Michael Parkinson reserves for Billy Connolly. 'Carl! Will you have a cheese puff, Carl?'

Carl didn't mind if he did and scooped a handful.

Nell became acutely aware of a change in the conservatory atmosphere. Georgina was whistling innocently and Patsy's eyebrows were arching in a meaningful way. And Carl – well, Carl was staring brazenly at Nell. Or as much of her as he could see under her grandmother's hat.

Right. I get it, thought Nell, fighting an urge to fling both Annie and the Snowball at them then run out the back way. *They're setting me up.*

'All right?' Carl nodded. It seemed his favourite expression.

'Fine. Yup. Fine. Absolutely fine.' Nell was nodding too, sucking at her drink as if that would help.

Why was the world suddenly populated with spectacularly inept matchmakers? Carl was twenty at most, with the face of a Victorian urchin. The copious beer he'd consumed had not improved him. On the plus side he was, she guessed, *trendy*, but she'd never felt quite at home with trendy blokes. She'd always gone for rumpled ones, who went to their dad's hairdresser. They were no competition. 'So what do you do, Carl?' she asked dutifully.

'A bit of this.'

'And a bit of that?' she probed.

'Sometimes,' he conceded, once he'd thought about it. He popped a puff and seemed stuck for words.

'If you need knock-off scaffolding, he's your man,' offered Patsy, admiringly.

'I'll remember that.' Annie was getting heavy.

Another boy entered the kitchen. His reception was different from Carl's. 'Who the fuck invited you?' demanded Georgina.

Nell looked down at Annie and was relieved to discover that she was asleep. The latest arrival was her father: he was midway through a moustache-growing experiment that wasn't going to plan, painfully young and resembled a puppy expecting a kick.

'I wanted to see you both,' he mumbled.

'We don't want to see you. I'm a modern woman of today,' Georgina told him forcefully. 'I can look after Anastasia on my own, thank you very much. Why don't you get out of here and go and find *Cherelle*?'

Nell suspected that Cherelle was an old bone of contention between them and shifted uneasily: she loved watching soap operas, but she didn't relish living them.

'Now, now. He's always welcome here.' Patsy tried to pour oil on the troubled hormonal waters. 'Why don't you let him hold the baby for a while?'

'*No!*' Georgina was emphatic. She even put out her cigarette. 'He's not touching my kid. His hands have been all over that tart.'

'She's not a tart,' whined Annie's dad.

It might have been more diplomatic to deny that his hands had been all over her.

'She's a *tart*!' insisted Georgina, hands on sizeable hips. 'And you're a *nonce*!'

'Who's a nonce?' Ringo blocked the light as he came in from the hallway.

'He is, Dad. He's trying to take little Annie away from me.' Georgina burst into tears.

'Hang on, he only—' Nell tried to intervene, but was silenced by the dramatic appearance in the conservatory of various men, all connected in some way to one of Annie's parents.

'Out! Out! Quick!' Patsy ushered Nell through the back door into the tiny strip of garden. From deckchairs, the women and the baby watched the debate as it escalated. Patsy smarted at every smash. Nell cringed at every colourful insult that echoed through the afternoon air.

'Mum, should we call the police?' Nell was alarmed to see an old man in a tracksuit beat an even older man with a Fisher Price Activity Centre.

'No. They'll wear themselves out soon enough,' said Patsy, wearily. She was a veteran of these events.

Much later, when the last survivor had staggered off, Ringo opened a bottle of Malibu he'd found under the sofa while he was pressing a guest's face into the rug, and declared it was the best christening he'd ever been to.

Thirteen

Nell was speeding down the hallway, tugging off her hat, when her grandmother stepped out of the drawing room. 'So you've decided to come home. Do I need to tell you that your first guests are expected in ten minutes?'

'Yes, I know, Claudette, I'm so sorry.' Nell was gabbling. 'I'm crap, I really am. I mean I'm impolite, really, really impolite. But something happened and I couldn't leave and then—'

'Spare me the details.' Claudette's black chiffon shift shuddered with her. 'I can imagine what that family's social events entail. Please get changed as quickly as you can. You really should be on hand to greet your own guests.'

Your guests, Nell mentally corrected her grandmother. God, Claudette could be unbearable when she wore her snobbishness on her designer sleeve like that. Nell buried the uncomfortable knowledge that she herself had shuddered, Claudette-like, all through the christening and slammed the door of the Heliotrope Room.

There was no Pomagne at Claudette's party. There were no cheese puffs. There *was* somebody called Anastasia, but she was descended from Russian royalty.

By the time Nell, acceptable in a chocolate brown Dior cast-off, appeared nervously on the threshold, the party was in full swing. Claudette's guests obviously knew to be prompt.

Fergus kept the crystal glasses topped up with champagne, while Carita ensured that anybody who craved a salmon blini got one. The girls were glossy of hair and flat of shoe, with real pearls round their necks. The boys were in dinner jackets and bow-ties. Claudette's guests were young, but they might have been plucked straight out of the 1950s. This was old money, in all its stolid, steaming glory. An occasional high-pitched laugh punctured the polite buzz of forgettable small-talk – Nell couldn't imagine a fight breaking out in this drawing room over somebody called Cherelle.

In one respect, however, the Knightsbridge party and the one she'd left in Fulham were similar. 'My child,' Claudette swooped, 'you must meet Harry. He's the grandson of one of my oldest friends and very possibly the most eligible bachelor in London.'

Harry was *über*-posh, with floppy hair and a pristine DJ, but he was essentially just Carl mark 2. In answer to Nell's 'And what do you do, Harry?' he said, 'Oh, you know, bumming around until I go into Pa's firm. Travelling. Bit of modelling. The usual.' The accent was so cut-glass you could have served punch in it, but the sentiment was a reprise of Carl's 'A bit of this, a bit of that.'

Nell was displayed to two more Harrys, a Sebastian, and a smattering of honourables, some with surnames that could potentially fracture teeth if attempted without rehearsal. In a bid to conceal the real motive for the party, Claudette whisked her past a Jacinta, a Scheherezade, a Camilla. They were all delightful types, who told her her dress was lovely, asked intelligent questions about her job and laughed indulgently at her increasingly weak jokes, but Nell wished fervently that they would all put down their Kir and go home.

No lustful stirrings troubled her loins. This selection of men was all so hyper-clean. Sebastian, in particular, looked as if his willy smelt of Dettol. All the etiquette and diplomacy was having a strange effect on her: she had an urge to plonk some rap on the hi-fi and spray-paint 'The Queen smells' all over the walls. She missed Gareth, keenly and sharply. What wouldn't she have given to hear him belch all the stations on the Northern Line in their correct order? This party piece had usually earned him three days of stony silence when she was living with him, but now it represented a lost golden age.

At ten o'clock the room emptied, as if a silent signal had sounded: the Call of the Posh Wild. Decorous goodnights were said, and soon Claudette and Nell were alone in a room that was as tidy as a stage set. Such a civilised end to a party was novel for Nell: she was used to get-togethers that ended when the alcohol ran out or at daybreak, whichever came first.

When she imagined the karaoke session that Ringo would be leading right now, knee deep in post-christening carnage, she couldn't decide which scene she preferred. The apartment was silent, now that her grandmother had – with some irritation – turned off the music.

'I'm retiring,' announced Claudette, in a thin voice. 'I hope you had a pleasant evening, child.'

'It was lovely. Thank you for going to so much trouble for me.'

'It was no trouble, but do make sure you have a word with Fergus and Carita. They worked terribly hard.' She narrowed her glittering eyes. 'I didn't overhear you making any social engagements. I thought Tarquin might ask you to dinner. He asks *everybody* to dinner.'

'Everybody except me,' said Nell, jauntily.

'Goodnight.' Claudette escaped to her bedroom.

Nell, the high-society failure, flopped on to her bed in her couture frills. She wasn't posh enough for one side of her family and she was too posh for the other. However she looked at it, she was a fish out of Pomagne.

'Dig deep for Barry's shingles!' Linda started the week by rattling the Nescafé jar under Nell's nose.

Nell smuggled a token from the arcade on Brighton Pier awkwardly through the slit in the lid, and asked if the venue for her first date with Blair had been finalised.

'You're going to the Ivy. That's a restaurant.'

'I know it's a restaurant.' Nell tried to look on the bright side. 'I've always wanted to go there.'

'Let's hope it's worth breaking your diet for.' Linda turned away smartly.

'I'm not on a . . .' but she was talking to thin air.

The morning was sluggish. Louis was at home, sleeping off the aftermath of an epic row with Hildegard, triggered by a note she'd discovered during a routine pocket search. Somebody called Penny had eulogised his bedroom skills. It had taken fancy footwork, plus the promise of yet more vulgar jewellery, to convince her that Penny was a male TV producer and that 'orgasm' was Yiddish for 'contract'.

Nell had finished *Hello!* and *heat* and *OK!* and was busy making a necklace of paperclips when Gareth popped into the untidy attic of her mind. He worked from home on Mondays, she thought. He'd be at home right now, she thought. Probably, she thought, without the filthy harlot who had taken her place. This might be a good time for a friendly chat, she thought, and dialled the familiar number before she had a chance to reconsider.

Her face blank, Nell listened to her old phone ring in her old flat. Then, 'Hel-*lo*,' said Gareth.

Face still blank, she put down the receiver. There followed a long period of staring at it, trying to come up with a formula for turning back time.

'God, this is the food equivalent of having non-stop sex with Brad Pitt while all the girls you hated at school are forced to watch,' said Nell, with her mouth full.

'Really?' Disbelievingly, Tina eyed the Mario's Special – a sloppy chilli topped with plastic cheese.

'You'd think so too if your Sunday lunch had been an anchovy tartlet. Dinner was worse. It was a melon ball with a sliver of meat hiding under it, with seven – I counted them – green beans arranged artistically round the edge of the plate.'

'But surely you just stuffed yourself with Findus Savoury Pancakes afterwards?'

'I would have done if there had been any left.' Nell's tone was dark. It was one thing for Fergus to pilfer the occasional Jaffa Cake, quite another to leave a girl with an empty pancake box. 'Vengeance will be mine,' she muttered.

'Did you notice Linda's hair?' asked Tina. 'You could actually see the marks of the heated rollers in it.'

'Of course I did. How much did you put in Barry's collection?'

'Fifty p,' said Tina, mournfully. 'She was watching me like a hawk.'

'I did a bad thing.' Nell scraped clean the chipped bowl.

'Oh, we all know you put a funfair token in,' said Tina, with a regal wave of her hand.

'No, no, it's worse than that.' Nell winced. 'I rang Gareth and hung up.'

'You idiot.' Tina was shocked.

'I know.'

Tina slammed down her toastie in disgust.

'My fingers did it on their own. I was having an out-of-body experience.'

'Why did you ring him?'

'Just because.'

'Oh. I see.' Tina put her head on one side sarcastically.

'I wanted to hear his voice, I suppose,' admitted Nell, miserably. She felt like an abandoned dog in an RSPCA ad. Her head hung down. At least the dogs had the option of howling. A good howl up at Mario's Artex ceiling might make her feel better, she thought.

'What am I going to do with you?' Tina was using her disappointed voice, which Nell particularly disliked.

'You're going to have to take my brain out, scrub it and replace it.'

'Let's have dessert first.'

Tina had chosen the yellow gungy pie thing and Nell had

plumped for the pink gungy pie thing. Licking her spoon, she remembered that she wasn't the only one who'd had an eventful weekend. 'Hey! Your romantic surprise getaway! You haven't said where it was.'

'No.' Tina's tone might have told Nell to back off.

'Well?'

'Let's just say it wasn't quite as romantic as I'd hoped.'

'Where *was* it, woman?'

'It was . . .' Tina seemed to be in some sort of internal pain. 'It was a *Doctor Who* convention.'

Nell put down her spoon – this rarely happened.

'In Guildford.' Tina's voice cracked.

'Oh, my God. I'm so sorry.'

'I think we must have got our wires crossed.'

There was a silence until Nell picked up a menu, rolled it into a tube and held it sticking out from her nose. 'Ex-ter-minate!' she barked.

Tina shot her a look.

'Ex-ter-minate!' repeated Nell. Then, in the same voice, 'Will you marry me, Earthling?'

Tina saw the funny side. Eventually.

'What's in the tin?' asked Joy, nosily, as she tugged on a multicoloured afghan before braving the frosty night air.

'A cake.' Nell felt self-conscious. During a long, tedious Sunday with only a lah-di-dah OAP and a pompous, biscuit-stealing butler for company, baking a cake for the old man who had said it was his birthday soon had seemed like a good idea. Now, holding it in her hands, she wasn't so sure.

'You're so nice!' beamed Joy, and pulled on a bobble hat that perched precariously on the outer reaches of her Afro. She glanced over Nell's shoulder and asked suspiciously, 'Hey, boss man, what are you doing here? You're not on the rota.'

'Thought I'd look in.' Phred joined them. 'What's in the tin?'

Nell explained, bracing herself for one of his smirks.

Bernadette Strachan

'Right.' He was bemused. 'A cake. For Ted. It's a bit unusual. I don't know . . .'

'What don't you know?' demanded Nell, forgetting to be deferential and meek.

'It's not really what we're here for. Helping Hands is about practical support.'

Nell pursed her lips. She was tiring of his mantra.

Joy leaped in. 'Cakes are very practical. All those eggs and sugar. Highly nutritious.'

'And it's his birthday,' Nell reminded him. 'Everybody deserves a cake on their birthday.'

'I suppose so,' Phred conceded. 'Don't be disappointed if he's underwhelmed, though. He's been on the streets for decades. Sometimes little things that we take for granted confuse and depress men like Ted.'

Later, down in the dining hall, Nell said, 'He doesn't *look* depressed.'

Ted danced past them, a raggedy pair of underpants on his head, leading a meandering conga line and singing 'Happy Birthday To Me' as he handed out cubes of sponge.

Phred was gracious in defeat. 'You can look smug if you want to, you know.'

'I'm just glad he's happy.'

Phred gave her a sideways look.

Nell tried to look humble. It didn't suit her. She would have liked to punch the air and shout, 'I rock!' It was certainly a relief that the cake had delighted Ted, and hadn't just been a therapeutic way of passing some dead hours – because, once again, the main person she'd helped would have been herself.

Fourteen

Nell had decided that Fergus was lonely. He just had to be, she reasoned, eating alone in the kitchen every night after the dark, lively Carita had gone out with one of her immense circle of Italian friends.

So, she decided, he would welcome the sight of Nell, balancing the carefully laid tray he had just brought her, elbowing her way through the baize door, chirping, 'Fancy some company?'

It was arguable as to just who was lonely in this scenario. Possibly it was the dishevelled girl who had spent the midweek bus journey home from work fantasising morbidly about Gareth and double-jointed girls in the shower.

Politely, but with the level of enthusiasm people exhibit at the dentist's, Fergus laid a place for her beside his at the wooden table. There was no dropping of standards in here: Fergus used silver cutlery.

'What's that you're having?' asked Nell, curiously.

'Hotpot.'

'Hotpot! I love hotpot! Why don't Claudette and I ever get hotpot?'

'You do, Nell, but we call it *pot au feu*. Might I top up your water?'

'You're not on duty, Fergus. I'll do it myself.'

Silence fell, like one of Claudette's heavy silk curtains. Fergus didn't seem eager to chat.

'So . . .' Nell cast about for a topic he might find acceptable. 'Where's my grandmother tonight?'

'Madame is at a recital. Then she sups at Claridges.'

Repressing the urge to say, '*Oooooooh! Get Madame*,' in a

high-pitched camp voice, Nell contented herself with 'I've never been to Claridges.'

'I suspect they don't serve Pop-Tarts.' Fergus chewed stolidly.

'They don't serve them here since the last one went missing,' Nell said, meaningfully. More casually she asked, 'Are they your favourites? Or do you prefer Jaffa Cakes?' She'd had this cunning question up her sleeve for a while.

'I regret to say I have never tasted either.'

That was unbelievable. 'Never? You have literally *never* tasted a Jaffa Cake?' Had he been raised by wolves? 'You must have, Fergus.'

'I daresay you consider me woefully uncultured, but I have truly never experienced a Jaffa Cake.'

He was lying, she knew it. The swine was lying to cover his naked need for working-class confectionery. Any moment now and he'd change the subject, like the master criminal he was.

'Are you planning to stay with us for much longer, Nell?'

Defensively, Nell answered twitchily, 'I'll stay for as long as Claudette makes me welcome. If that's all right with you.'

'That's excellent news.' Fergus seemed to be attempting warmth. He hesitated before saying 'Madame has been very . . .' he struggled, then plumped for '. . . *content* since your arrival.'

Nell studied Fergus dubiously. He had told her, in a round-about way, that he was glad she was there, as he spooned hotpot into his face with his pinkie curled. 'That's nice,' she said, distrusting this new side to him.

'Madame's happiness is paramount.' Fergus rose from the table, taut as a furled umbrella.

Nell could tell he meant it. She looked at his straight back in his immaculate jacket as he put his plate into the dish-washer, and for the first time saw him as human. He even looked quite poignant. She'd stumbled on a little love story here in this swanky apartment: an old-fashioned one of duty and service.

Did Claudette appreciate him, she wondered. Did Claudette appreciate anybody?

Nell's investigation to discover who was filching the unwholesome food had stalled. With a limited cast of suspects – Fergus and Carita – she had expected results far quicker. Besides, she knew it was Fergus. His demeanour gave him away.

On Sunday morning Nell opened the door to the kitchen with a theatrical flourish, hoping to find him smeared with chocolate, but he didn't turn round from where he stood polishing something old and expensive at the worktop.

'*Madre del dio*!' squealed Carita, jumping a foot in the air at Nell's sudden appearance. 'What do you need, Nellie? Let me do it for you.' She tut-tutted away Nell's protest that she was old enough to get her own biscuits out of the cupboard. 'But I . . .' Nell could hardly explain that she wanted to count the Jaffa Cakes first, so she gave in to Carita's fussing and followed her down the hall. 'I haven't seen my grandmother all afternoon. Is she out, Carita?'

'No. Madame is in bed. It is good that you are here, Nellie,' Carita said emphatically, as she put the tray on a delicate side-table. She fixed Nell with her raisin-like black eyes, then swayed out.

Something was being relayed to her without words. Some significant message was being passed on. I'm too bloody shallow to grasp it, thought Nell, bitterly. Maybe chocolate would help her think. She picked up a Jaffa Cake, and smiled at the linen napkin Carita had wrapped round it.

There was something in its folds. A crackly envelope that had first been opened long ago. Nell knew it wasn't there by mistake. An old document fell on to her lap. Nell smoothed it out as the Jaffa Cake melted on her tongue.

She was looking at a decree nisi. Claudette wasn't a widow: she was a divorcée.

'More tomato sauce?' Maggie gestured as if she was about to lob the squeezy bottle from her armchair to Nell's.

'No, thanks. I don't want to flood my rissoles.' Nell had never had a rissole before. They were superb.

'Mash all right?'

'Perfect.' It wasn't made with olive oil or *fromage frais*: Maggie had used the top of the milk.

In the corner of the room Cary Grant traded wisecracks with Katharine Hepburn, both stunning in black and white. 'I think television actually *improves* the taste of food,' Nell declared.

'It depends.' Maggie spoke as if she had pondered this subject before. 'A good Cary Grant film can certainly improve your dinner, but I've had many a decent casserole ruined by *The Bill*.'

'Hmm. I s'pose.'

'Sometimes I prop up whatever I happen to be reading while I'm having my meal,' said Maggie. 'That biography of Disraeli's covered with gravy because I just couldn't put it down.'

Nell smiled. Maggie's tastes and interests were broad: she was fascinated by the whole world and everything in it. She had no snobbish hang-ups about what constituted culture: Maggie could lose herself gazing at a reproduction of a Manet print in an art book one moment, then switch on the television and get agitated about the latest goings-on in *Coronation Street*. She was the same with people. 'I take them as I find them,' she was fond of saying.

Maggie's inquisitiveness knew no bounds, yet her questions weren't simple nosiness. Nell could feel Maggie working her out, attempting to understand her. It felt good. It felt warm.

'So, this grandmother of yours, does she cook for you?'

'God, no!' Nell guffawed at the idea. 'She's only seen pictures of kitchens in books. She was brought up with servants.'

'I see.' Maggie digested this, along with her rissole. 'Does that make you feel a little . . . uncomfortable?'

'It makes me feel massively uncomfortable,' admitted Nell. 'My family is made up of two extremes – the salt of the earth and the hoity-toity.'

'You're somewhere in between, are you?'

'Yup.' Nell smacked her mash with the flat of her knife. 'Bang in the middle of no man's land.' She paused. 'I'm orphaned, really. That's how it feels.'

Maggie laid down her cutlery. Her light tone had evaporated. 'Nell, that's an awful thing to say.'

'I know.' Nell squirmed. 'But it's how I feel.' She chomped stolidly without looking directly at Maggie.

'Well, I *am* an orphan,' said Maggie gently. 'Oh, I know I'm a thousand years old and you don't think of orphans as being my age but, believe me, not a day passes without me remembering my mum and dad.' She glanced at Nell, as if to check that she was listening.

She was.

Maggie carried on: 'While people are still alive there's potential to improve your relationship with them. Maybe you're helping to orphan yourself.'

That was a strange remark. Nell thought about it as Cary Grant convinced Katharine Hepburn he was in love with her. As the credits rolled she jumped up and carried both trays out to the tiny kitchen.

'Don't wash up, dear. I know where everything goes. It's easier if I do it.' Maggie lumbered after her, rolling like a small galleon.

Nell tied Maggie's apron strings for her. 'What can I do while you're at the sink?' she asked. 'Do you need any shopping? Or can I dust the front room? Maybe it needs hoovering?'

'No. The shopping was delivered this morning and I've only just given the entire flat a good going-over.'

'Are you planning any redecorating?' Nell was beginning to sound desperate. 'I'm very good with a paintbrush.' She was there as a Helping Hands volunteer, but all she'd done so far was gulp down a delicious lunch and talk about herself. 'I'll do some gardening!'

Maggie snapped on her Marigolds. 'Is there anything you can't do?'

Nell thought it best to be honest with such a shrewd woman. 'Actually, I do my best, but I'm not much use at most things.'

Maggie smiled. 'Good,' she said unexpectedly. 'The world is full of useful people. We need a few more decorative ones, like you.'

Nell tried not to smile. She was decorative, was she?

Maggie threw her a tea-towel. 'Drying the dishes might salve your conscience.'

Somehow, as Nell wiped the floral plates and the dented saucepans, she found herself telling Maggie all about the disconcerting discovery she'd made in a linen napkin. 'So my grandmother's been lying to us all these years.'

Shaking her permed head, Maggie said quietly, 'I hope she has her reasons.'

'I could have a . . .' Nell faltered. 'I could have a granddad somewhere.'

Maggie held a sudsy glass up to the window and turned it in the weak sunlight. 'Going to look for him, are you?'

It felt good to be understood.

There were crossed wires at the penthouse. 'I'm *sure* I told Fergus I was eating out tonight.' Nell doubted herself as soon as she'd said it. 'Didn't I?'

Claudette looked at her reprovingly. 'I think Carita deserves an apology. She'd planned her special *fruits de mer* platter for you.'

Inwardly grateful that she wouldn't have to confront a mob

of crustaceans with only Claudette and a strangely shaped fork for protection, Nell hurried down to the kitchen. She apologised to Carita, who waved her plump hands about and said, 'Don't worry, darlink!' a lot.

'And, Carita, I wanted to say . . .' Nell glanced at Fergus's back as he placed pointless doilies on a tray. She knew he could hear through concrete. 'I wanted to say thank you.' She tried to inject a lot of meaning into her eyes. 'For the other day. That lovely biscuit you brought me.'

Carita winked broadly. 'Eet was my pleasurrrrrrre,' she purred, getting full value out of that R.

'I'll let you know how I get on with the erm, whole biscuit situation.' Nell, who was not spy material, scarpered as Fergus cocked his head, puzzled.

On the other side of that peeling front door was one of Nell's worst nightmares. A dinner party: a roomful of people you had never met before, would never meet again, but with whom you had to discuss house prices.

There was a distinct risk that Phred's friends would be the kind of freaks who enjoyed current affairs. Nell had no *bons mots* up her Miss Sixty sleeve, no pithy insights on foreign policy. She had only one joke: it was filthy and unfunny. Dinner parties shone merciless spotlights into the murky shallows of which Nell was so ashamed.

The front-door bell buzzed. Nell straightened up. It was like going to visit one of your teachers – not that she had ever even considered any such thing. Any minute now she'd meet Mrs Phred. Nell imagined a mixture of swot and Bohemian: Stephen Hawking in a peasant top.

This was all Clover's fault, she thought. Nell had a strong suspicion that Phred wouldn't have dreamed of inviting one of his volunteers to dinner if his daughter hadn't forced his hand. *Oh, God,* she realised, as the dim shadow beyond the door's dimpled glass grew and became recognisably Phred-shaped, *he expected me to say no.*

'Sorry. It's screwtop.' Nell thrust her bottle of wine at his chest. He was wearing faded jeans and a crumpled white shirt. 'I bought it by mistake. I mean, screwtop's crap, isn't it? But I was out of the shop and on the bus before I saw it. And I bet you're a bloody wine buff, aren't you?' She passed him and began to unwind her long, fluffy scarf. 'It's probably toxic.' Nerves were having their predictable effect on Nell's charm.

Bemused, Phred said, 'I'm sure it's fine. It all goes down the same way.'

Great. He's humouring me. Nell unbuttoned the duffel coat that had caused Claudette to make the sign of the cross. She looked about her. Inside, the house had none of the cottage feel of the exterior. White paint dominated, and the door handles and light switches were polished chrome.

A small figure hurtled down the hall, yelling, 'Coat! Coat!' Clover's fleecy pyjamas looked slightly out of place in her minimalist surroundings.

'Clover's just staying up long enough to say hello,' said Phred, firmly, then added, with emphasis, 'And then she's going to bed, aren't you, Pickle?'

'Shush, Daddy,' said Clover, imperiously, teetering on tiptoe to slide Nell's coat over a steel hook. She held out a hand to Nell and stamped a foot impatiently when it wasn't taken immediately.

'Looks like she wants to introduce you to the gang,' said Phred. He seemed awkward.

Maybe, thought Nell, he feels the strangeness of this situation as much as I do. They weren't meant to mingle socially, after all: he was predestined to be a boss and she was perfectly designed to be a thorn in his flesh. 'Right,' she said, with a fake smile to cover her apprehension. 'The gang.'

Dragged down the hall at warp speed, Nell lied to Clover in her best *Blue Peter* voice, 'I can't wait to meet your mummy.'

With one swipe of a Bugs Bunny slipper, Clover kicked open the kitchen door. 'My mummy's dead,' she said, with enviable clarity and volume.

Nell's smile fossilised, and the four people standing in the kitchen armed with nibbles and drinks stopped small-talking as if a switch had been thrown.

'She watches me from heaven,' Clover continued, the only person present not paralysed with embarrassment.

'Yes, she does,' ad-libbed Nell, hopelessly, wondering if it was acceptable dinner-party etiquette to scream and run.

Phred broke the mood. He came up behind Nell, swung Clover over his shoulder and said heartily, 'Mummy can watch you go to bed, you pest.' As Clover dangled, protesting, down his back he swiftly introduced everybody: 'That's Laura, and her husband Tom. That's Manda, and that's Dexter.' He turned down the hall, saying darkly, 'Watch him.'

Instinctively Nell knew that anybody Phred warned her against was going to be her favourite. 'Hello, Laura, Tom, Manda . . . *Dex*ter.'

'And she's Nell. Watch *her*,' advised Phred, as he reached the stairs.

Dexter, who was tall and trendily scruffy with eyes like cheap chocolate, offered to pour Nell a glass of her own wine.

'I'd rather have something drinkable,' confessed Nell.

Dexter laughed, and so did Tom, who had a lot of hair, a lot of beard and a gangly frame encased in ancient denim. 'You'll be lucky,' he said goofily.

Laura fitted Nell's paranoid template of a dinner-party guest. 'I think you'll find that the bottle we brought is passable,' she said languidly, jangling a selection of jade bracelets. The complex wrap dress she wore managed to be sexy without showing much flesh. 'I adore the wines of the New World, don't you?' Her face was beautiful – she looked as if she only ever had interesting thoughts. Deep thoughts.

It was a struggle for Nell not to dislike her instantly. 'As long as it's wet and gets me drunk,' she muttered.

Dexter handed her a very full goblet. 'Honesty. I admire that in a woman,' he said. 'Wet enough for you?'

They migrated to the sitting room, another spotless white and silvered space. Nell cradled her glass with paranoid care. She was terrified of inadvertently blotting the Arctic serenity, as if a dumb thought would leave skidmarks on the walls.

Manda was beside her on the sofa, closer than Nell would have liked. In a short time she had learned an enormous amount about Caesareans in general and even more about Manda's in particular.

Nell had zero interest in Caesareans but this hadn't registered with Manda, who seemed to have put together her outfit from a Dickensian dressing-up box. Despite the velvet, shawls, amber beads and eyes that were as wild as her hair, she was a sweet, nice person. A devastatingly boring sweet, nice person. 'My waters broke by the Pick'n'Mix!' she proclaimed dramatically. 'Can you imagine that?'

Nell couldn't, thank God. Silently Dexter refilled her glass.

Just as Manda was intoning, 'Slicing, slicing, slicing. That was *my body*, you know?' Phred put his head round the door.

'I'm going to make some noises in the kitchen. Dinner will be about ten minutes.'

Laura sprang up. 'I'll give you a hand.' She waved aside Phred's claims that he could manage. 'No, you can't. I know you. You *need* me,' she told him, like an indulgent nanny, and followed him out.

As Manda droned on, claiming the birth of her child felt as if the obstetrician was doing the washing up in her tummy, Nell noticed the momentary darkening of Tom's amiable expression.

*   *   *

Thankfully the food wasn't of the Marti I'm-a-man-but-hey-I-can-cook variety. A plain old roast was served at the kitchen table, with all the bits and bobs that go with it. Nell was oblivious to the conversation around her as she concentrated on getting the correct ratio of gravy to roast potato. She tuned back in to hear Laura say, in her confident way, 'Je-*sus*, Tom, spare us. We've heard your theory about how reality television's taking over the world a thousand times now.'

Grateful that the conversation had taken a turn into her kind of territory, Nell said, 'Oh, I love reality television, too! It's fantastic.'

A peculiar silence met her statement, not the enthusiastic babble she'd expected.

Tom had turned a bit pink. 'Actually, I . . .' he began uncomfortably.

Laura, who would never experience an uncomfortable moment if she lived for another five hundred years, said, with an air of rude disbelief, 'No, no! Tom thinks it's a bad thing. He certainly doesn't love it! He thinks it addles people's minds, turns us all into couch potatoes, appeals to the lowest common denominator. Don't you, Tom?'

'Wouldn't go that far, darling.' Tom concentrated on his plate of beef as if there was a diamond in it.

'Yes, you bloody would.' Laura cocked her head to one side and quizzed Nell: 'And yet you say you love it? Why? Do you feel it has some sort of anthropological merit?'

Oh, God. Nell was slap-bang in the middle of one of those dinner-party conversations that over-analyse the commonplace. She took a slug of wine while she tried to remember what anthropological meant.

The cavalry arrived in the shape of Dexter. 'Fuck anthropological merit,' he winked at Nell, 'I just like watching people with no teeth shout at each other.'

'Typical Dexter,' sighed Laura. 'Terrified of taking anything seriously.'

Dexter didn't seem insulted. He looked, as he had all night, handsome and happy. And familiar. Who did he remind her of? Nell wondered.

'Did I tell you about how my stitches went wrong?' Manda asked Nell urgently.

Dexter gasped. 'Don't tell me they put a zip in by mistake!'

Manda flicked him with her napkin. 'Oh, Dexter!' she said. 'It's obvious you've never had a Caesarean.'

'How do you know?' he demanded. 'These are the days of equal opportunity. Laura's got balls, why shouldn't I have a womb?'

Tom sniggered disloyally, then looked ashamed of himself, and coughed as he rearranged his face. 'The house is looking great,' he said hurriedly, obviously trying to get away from his wife's genitalia and choosing one of the top-ten dinner-party topics.

'Needs a woman's touch,' observed Laura.

A tiny muscle at the base of Phred's jaw pulsed. Nell hoped Laura had the good sense not to continue. In case she didn't, Nell asked, 'Is it my imagination or is that woman next door staring in at us?'

All necks craned. A scowling woman was indeed peering in at them through her kitchen window as she filled a kettle.

'Don't look at her,' begged Phred, 'or she'll—'

She stuck two fingers up at them.

'Or she'll do something like that.' Phred slumped back in his chair. 'Why couldn't Maggie live next door instead of that old . . .' he battled with himself and settled for '. . . individual. She'll put a note written in blood through the letterbox tomorrow, asking why we were gawping at her.'

'Tell her it's because she's so damn sexy', Dexter suggested. 'I love a bird in a stained candlewick dressing-gown meself.'

'Perhaps the poor thing's just lonely,' ventured Manda.

'Understandable if she is,' said Phred, quite unlike a community worker. 'She's a nightmare. She complains if Clover thinks too loudly and is always telling me I play my music too high.'

'You?' said Nell, in surprise.

'Yes, him,' said Dexter, who found it equally unlikely. 'My perfect brother. As if.'

'I have my moments,' Phred defended himself. 'Sometimes as late as, ooh, nine p.m. I've been known to throw some Manilow on to the turntable.' He saw Nell's face. 'Joke,' he confirmed. 'I prefer Neil Sedaka.' Her face didn't change. 'That was another joke.'

'Oh. Right.' Nell laughed. *That* was why Dexter had seemed so familiar, although she was amazed that he and Phred could be brothers. Dexter was flirtatious, wicked and handsome. Phred, of course, was staid, disciplined and not handsome.

A little voice, possibly the voice of the screwtop wine which they were currently wading through, whispered that she was wrong. Phred *was* handsome. Nell hadn't noticed it before, possibly because she had thought of him only as an authority figure. Here, in his own house, relaxed and chatting, he was really rather sexy.

'Gotta go to the loo,' she mumbled, and made for the door. She felt as if she'd been caught with her hand up a bishop's cassock. It wasn't right.

In the bathroom she splashed cold water on her face and stared at her pink cheeks in the mirror. It's been too long since you had sex, she diagnosed. Even Phred's starting to look good. She reminded herself that he was her boss, kind of. She needed his respect if she was to continue at Helping Hands and complete her self-rehabilitation. *I want to make a difference, I want to be a deep and worthwhile person.* Deep and worthwhile people didn't, as a rule, fancy the nearest bloke.

A rubber duck, covered with felt-tip scrawls, was staring at her from behind the bath taps. This room wasn't like downstairs: she was in the land that minimalism forgot.

The primrose bath and sink were ancient, and the toilet seat was lopsided. Sponge toys crowded the window-ledge, all smiling crazily as they awaited their next soaking. Phred's white and chrome masterplan hadn't reached this far.

It was much more inviting than the pristine tundra of the ground floor. Nell settled more comfortably on the loo. She glanced at her watch. Another two hours at most and she would be on her way home. She was actually looking forward to getting back to Claudette's. That's the effect Phred has on you, she mused. Handsome or not.

When she crept back down the plates had been cleared. Dexter pulled out her chair for her. 'I hope you left space for the *pièce de résistance*.'

'Phred's done one of his specialities for pudding.' Manda was holding up her spoon like an expectant toddler. 'You'll like this.'

So he was a closet foodie. Nell might have known. 'Oh, good,' she said, lukewarm.

'I can let you have the recipe if you like,' said Phred, as he put down an enormous dish in the middle of the table.

'It looks like . . . vanilla ice-cream with Revels mashed into it,' said Nell.

Dexter defended his brother's cuisine: 'It's *Wall's* ice-cream and they are, of course, all orange Revels.'

'The other flavours would ruin the subtle balance,' said Phred, gravely, as he dolloped out a big bowlful for Manda.

Laura toyed with her wooden necklace. 'Seriously? This is it?' she asked.

'With the compliments of the frankly crap chef.' Phred leaned over to serve Nell and said, 'This is what comes of living with a seven-year-old.'

Nell had seconds and she would have had thirds if there'd been any left. Thankfully the talk had moved on to various topics she could join in with fearlessly. 'Where did you have your first kiss?' Dexter wanted to know. Of course,

Laura's had been in Paris. Phred's, surprisingly, had been on the top deck of a bus. Nell had considered rewriting the truth, but had eventually confessed that it was by the meat counter in the Co-op. ('Weird, yet strangely arousing,' Phred mused.)

They talked about their favourite films, about whether Clover should be allowed to have the toy gun she was asking for, about why girls always went to the loo together in nightclubs. They were having fun, Nell admitted.

The woman next door banged on her window and shouted incoherently. They managed to make out 'Bastards' and 'Idiots' and something that sounded like 'Tories'.

'She's just jealous,' was Dexter's theory.

By the time the coffee percolator was schlurping, Laura had instigated another of her self-consciously sophisticated topics. 'Your house reflects your soul,' she asserted, 'and, Phred, I'm sorry, but your house is screaming out for a woman. And so are you, if you ask me.'

'But nobody did,' said Tom, from behind his beard, and remembered to add, 'darling.'

Dexter sat back in his chair, amused by Laura's persistence. 'Phred knows what he wants,' he said smoothly. 'He's married to his job and the only woman in his life is asleep upstairs dreaming about Winnie-the-Pooh.'

'Or world domination,' said Clover's proud daddy, and they all laughed.

Except Laura, who banged on: 'All this gleaming white paint and sterile steel.' She was as ardent as somebody on those late-night discussion programmes Nell sometimes flicked past when she was searching for a *Carry On*. 'What is it trying to say? That you're switched off emotionally? That you're driven by your head and not your heart?'

Nell looked at Phred with interest. That pulse was throbbing in his jaw again, and he seemed to be thinking hard before he answered. She hated to agree with Laura, whose rudeness was now bolstered by tipsiness, but the woman had a point. Ever since Nell had met Phred she'd been alienated by his cool, logical way of looking at the world and, to be honest, the sparse décor of his house reflected it.

But then she remembered something and, without thinking, she blurted out, 'But what about the duck?' She stumbled on, as everybody turned puzzled faces to her. Phred's face was unreadable. 'If his house reflects his soul, then we have to look at the whole house. What about the messy bathroom with a rubber duck who's covered with pen marks? Maybe that's . . .' she tapered off, painfully aware that she was now scarlet '. . . the real Phred.'

Dexter giggled, then covered his mouth apologetically

'I know what she means,' said Manda, gently and approvingly.

'That my brother's half man, half duck?' asked Dexter.

'No, no,' said Manda, wrapping a velvet layer more tightly around herself. 'She means that maybe the real Phred isn't as cool and analytical as he seems, that underneath he's as messy and human as the rest of us. I think she's right.'

Phred got up to pour the coffee. With his back to them, he said, 'If you remember, Laura, it wasn't my idea to decorate this house like this. She wanted it. It was what she'd always wanted, a modern white space. When she died we'd got as far as the landing.' He turned, his features composed. 'Actually, Clover and I have decided we're going to redecorate down here. Introduce a bit of colour. Throw a few cushions around. It's time.' That rhythm was still dancing on his jaw line. 'You're welcome to come back and psychoanalyse that, if you like.'

'I . . .' Laura was stuck for words.

Dexter saved her having to backtrack by shouting, 'Sexy from next door's back!' and pointing at the window.

'Ignore her,' said Phred, wearily.

'I can do better than that.' Dexter jumped on to his chair, sending his coffee cup flying, and crouched, backside to the window. 'Goodnight, darling!' he bellowed, and slipped his trousers and pants down just far enough to expose a tanned bottom, which he wiggled like a Chippendale desperate for a tip.

Nell glanced nervously at Phred, expecting him to be disapproving, even angry. But, no, he was shouting with laughter. As if she had been granted permission, Nell laughed too, and was still laughing when she tumbled into a cab an hour later.

Fifteen

'So, was it awful?' asked Tina, as they searched for nude photos of Jude Law on the web while Louis was at lunch.

'Eh?' asked Nell, understandably distracted. 'Oh, er, no, not really. It was quite nice in the end.'

'Really?' Tina sounded surprised. 'No, put in "Jude" and "nude",' she snapped. 'Not just "nude". We'll get every old sod if you don't narrow it down.'

'Sorry.' Nell squinted at the screen. She couldn't see Jude Law but she could see an awful lot of things she'd rather not. 'Oh, dear God!' she gasped. 'Look at that!'

'Switch it off!' yelped Tina.

'I can't. They keep popping back up,' squealed Nell, too panic-stricken to labour the obvious pun. 'Urrrgh, "Watch Alexei cum on his chest,"' she read, in horror-stricken tones.

'"Free hot lesbian movie"?' Tina was stabbing keys wildly. 'Make it stop. Christ – "Shaved and ready"! What do we do?'

Nell stood up. 'We do nothing. It's Linda's computer. We walk away.'

The two girls sidled off in the direction of the kitchenette, where Nell dissected her dinner party over a mint Options. 'Yeah, it was more fun than I thought it would be. There was one *awful* old bag there who kept trying to make us talk like grown-ups and obviously fancied the pants off Phred.'

'Who'd fancy Phred?' asked Tina, with a lot of feeling considering she'd never met him. 'He's the stuffed shirt, right?'

'Oh, God, yes,' said Nell. 'Yes. He is. Yes.' She nodded. 'Not fanciable at all,' she continued, hot under her borrowed Chanel collar. 'But his brother was there and he's a laugh, and this other woman was boring but nice and even Phred kind of unwound and was quite . . .' She had to admit it: 'Quite funny.'

A shout from Louis ripped through the office. 'Linda! Since when is it part of your duties as office manager to peruse *monstergaycocks.com*?'

That decree nisi was lying, like a dagger, in Nell's handbag, down among the bus tickets and the brittle corpses of Polo mints. Tina's summing-up of the situation had been succinct: 'What a cow your grandmother is!'

Nell had sucked her teeth. 'Teen . . .'

'Don't Teen me. She's been lying to you daily since you were born. If you ask me, you should move out immediately and—'

'Come and stay at yours. I know.'

Tina wasn't the right person to discuss this with. Much as she loved her, sometimes Nell had to accept that Tina was short on empathy.

Luckily she was big on other things, like good ideas. 'Let's go and put the little round paper bits out of the hole punch down Linda's umbrella!'

'You're a genius.'

'Today's the day!' Zoë was sadistically chipper.

'I know what day it is, thank you very much.' Nell picked up her messages. It was the day of the date. Make that The Date.

Linda ambushed her before Nell had reached her desk. 'I assume you're getting your hair done this afternoon.'

'I don't have time. Some of us have work to do,' said Nell, haughtily and inaccurately. 'We can't all sit around enjoying soft porn.'

'I told you that wasn't—' Linda stopped herself and took a deep breath. 'Fill this in by lunchtime.' She slapped a time-and-motion questionnaire on Nell's blotter. It was fifty-seven questions long. The first one was 'Exactly how many steps does it take for you to get to the lavatory? (State style of shoe worn.)' It didn't pay to mess with the office manager.

Nell's instinctive reaction to Phred's voice on the phone was to blurt, 'What? What have I done?' She reconsidered speedily. 'What haven't I done? Am I late for something?'

'That's a well-developed guilty conscience you have there,' said Phred. 'As far as I know you're in the clear.'

'Sorry. Can we start again? Thank you for the other evening.'

'You enjoyed yourself?' Phred sounded doubtful.

'Yes, I really did. It made a nice change.' There was no need to let him know how much she'd been dreading it.

'A change from what? Your hectic social life?'

'Believe me, I do *not* have a hectic social life. A typical night involves me, my grandmother, her butler and a chick-lit.' Nell felt she'd given too much away. Even though she'd been in his house, Phred was still more of a boss than a friend. Her bathroom musings on his handsomeness/sexiness/fanciability had been filed firmly under 'D' for 'Don't Even Go There'. 'So, like I said, it was a nice change.'

'We'll have to do it again. It made a nice change for me too.'

They had reached a conversational full stop. Nell set them off again: 'So, why did you call?'

'Oh. Yes. I thought you might like to know that Carol's been clean since your last visit. Do you want to babysit for her again next week? As you were so upset last time I thought it might be good for you to see her back on her feet.'

'I'd love to.' Nell quelled the memory of all those children iced with vomit. 'I've been thinking about her.'

'Not too much, I hope. I'd rather you didn't get over-involved in the cases.'

'Don't worry. Practical support only. I'll be completely professional.' Nell almost saluted.

'Good. Anything you want to talk about?'

For one mad moment Nell almost told him about her grandmother's divorce and her potential grandfather, but then it registered that Phred was, of course, talking about Helping Hands. 'Nope. Everything's fine.' She found herself wishing that she was a case rather than a volunteer, so that she could get Phred's opinion on her peculiar problem. She could trust him to give her a sensible overview; he might also give her a compassionate one.

'Good. It's Anita's birthday on your next soup night by the way. You know what that means.'

'A cake! I'll do her an extra special one.' Nell liked Anita, a thin girl with multi-layers of clothes and attitude.

'They've become a Helping Hands tradition already.' Phred paused. 'That's the sound of me eating Humble Pie, by the way.'

Nell smiled smugly. 'It's on my menu every day, if that's any consolation.'

After she had put down the phone, Nell felt that a corner had been turned in her relationship with the cold, daunting Phred. He was still pretty daunting, but certainly less cold. They were becoming friendly. That felt good. She hoped he thought so too.

'Please break my legs,' Nell begged.

'Shut up and keep still.' Tina was carefully piling Nell's hair into a casual knot that required a gazillion hairpins. They were in Reception, after hours.

'Break one leg if you don't feel you can do both.'

'Louis would make you go on this date if I ran over you with a steamroller, so stop moaning and hand me another hairpin.'

'Another? I won't be able to lift my head.'

'Finished. What do you think?'

Nell thought it was surprisingly nice, given the raw material. 'Thanks. I bet it's fallen down by the time I get to the restaurant. It always does. I've got sarcastic hair.' She sighed and stretched. Her temples hurt where the hairpins dug in. 'S'pose I'd better put on that sodding beaded dress.' How she hated it. She'd been having a recurring dream in which she made Elton John slip it on, then pushed him over a cliff.

'Not so fast.' Tina flourished a carrier-bag. 'This is what you're wearing tonight, Cinders.'

'But . . .' Nell peeped inside the bag. 'It's your—'

'Yes, it's my fantastic black jersey dress from Kookaï and you have to put it on straight away or I might change my mind and grab it back. Hurry!' Tina pushed her friend in the direction of the loo.

Genuinely touched, Nell looked at herself in the smeared mirror. The dress was the star turn of Tina's wardrobe. It had cost her a fortnight's wages and was only wheeled out on big occasions. It was so well cut that it forgave Nell for being two sizes bigger than its owner and transformed her bulges into curves. Nell looked good – not supermodel good, but definitely Nell Fitzgerald good. 'Far too good for that orange twat,' she informed the mirror.

The taxi deposited Nell at the door of the Ivy with Tina's fond last words ringing in her ears: 'Spill anything on that dress and I'll eat your liver.' Trying to look as if she went to swanky restaurants every day, Nell handed her best jacket to the cloakroom lady and smiled weakly at the maître d'. She had never met one of these exotic creatures before and was relieved that this one was English and nice.

The Ivy is the Rover's Return of showbusiness, feeding not just actors but writers, producers, directors, journalists – in short, all the wildlife of the media. The enormity of what she'd let herself in for struck Nell: 'I'm being thrown to the hyenas.'

In every media watering-hole there are tables to be discreet at and tables to be seen at. Blair, sweating exuberantly, was seated at a table that was most definitely one to be seen at. 'Yoo-hoo!' he yelled unnecessarily. 'OVER HERE!'

Nell took a deep breath, grinned and tried to look glad to see his damp features. Heads swivelled in their direction and, resisting the urge to tug her hem down, hoist her boobs up and punch Blair's face all at the same time, she perched opposite him. Then, smile rigor-tight, she hissed in the manner of a vaudeville ventriloquist, 'Should we, er . . . you know?'

'Should we what?' asked Blair, in a whisper only slightly quieter than a helicopter taking off.

Nell forced the word out: 'Kiss.'

'Ah. Right.' Blair gulped, and seemed to shrink beneath his weave. 'Let's do it, then.'

They both took a deep breath. 'Here we go.' Blair sounded like a Second World War pilot approaching Dresden. He leaned over the table, pursed his shaking lips into a vast O and bore down on Nell's tremulous pout.

It was a long kiss. It was a wet kiss. It was a kiss that Nell would remember long after others were forgotten. She would remember it chiefly for the brief debate that raged in her head: was it like kissing an old lady or was it like kissing a cod of dubious freshness? A mixture of both, she concluded, as Blair pulled away.

She sank back in her chair, reeling from the effects of his aftershave. At such close range it could kill.

The maître d' stood by their table. Possibly for the first time in his career he looked surprised. 'Enjoy your meal,' he exhorted, in a tone that suggested they already had.

'Eeeyuk.' Blair scoured his lips with his napkin. 'Hope we don't have to do that too often.'

Smiling hollowly, Nell groped for a conversation opener. 'You got here all right, then?'

'Yeah.'

Nell widened her smile. It was beginning to hurt. A furtive look round the room confirmed that many necks were craned, discreetly, in their direction. She could think of nothing to say. *Nothing.* She dredged the cruddy bottom of her mind but she had absolutely, resolutely, definitively nothing in common with the man opposite her, who was now fidgeting and looking about him with the air of a commuter waiting for an Intercity.

A gentle 'Ahem!' removed the immediate need for small-talk. The wine waiter was cradling a bottle like a newborn baby.

'Ooooh!' shrieked Blair, who could read a wine label at a hundred paces. 'Châteauneuf du Pape!' His eyes narrowed. 'We haven't ordered this.'

'No, sir. The gentleman in the corner sends it to you with his compliments.'

Blair and Nell followed the pointing finger to where Louis sat, waving a napkin and burping happily into his beard. The waiter continued, 'He asked me to wish you a very happy anniversary.'

'But it's not— Oooch.' A kitten heel can deliver a surprisingly mean kick. After a mutinous look at his lady-love Blair continued smoothly, 'How thoughtful.'

As he coaxed the cork from the bottle, the waiter enquired which anniversary they were celebrating.

'A year,' cooed Blair.

'A month,' offered Nell.

They regarded each other with panic. Nell cursed herself for not insisting they cook up a credible relationship history before going public. Blair was infamously hopeless at ad-libbing. All his hilarious asides on TV were prepared weeks in advance by chain-smoking script-writers in a windowless room at the BBC. She grabbed his manicured hand and held it to her chest, ignoring his alarm. 'We met a year ago but we've been together for a month,' she informed the waiter, and added huskily, 'Time means nothing to us. It feels like we've been together for ever.'

The waiter smiled indulgently, poured their wine and left them to each other.

Blair surveyed Nell thoughtfully over his glass. 'You're good,' he murmured admiringly. 'Damn good.'

'Ta very much.' Cockily Nell emptied her glass. She'd never tasted vintage wine before. If she had to endure Blair for an evening she might as well get drunk. Make that expensively drunk. She raised a full glass to Louis, who was mouthing something at her. She squinted, straining to understand . . . oh. Typical. He was saying, 'Take it easy. That's fucking vintage wine.' She took a giant gulp and saluted him with her glass.

Blair picked up his menu. 'Now, then. What shall we eat?' he pondered. 'I mustn't have meat – my colonic irrigator is overworked as it is. I suspect I caught a wheat allergy in the Maldives, so no pasta. Pulses spell flatulence. The fish sounds delicious, but my deputy astrologer has warned me to be wary of the sea until the next full moon.'

In an effort to lighten the tone, Nell said, 'I know just how you feel. My bin-men won't let me eat tomatoes, and my psychiatrist will have me sectioned if I so much as look at an oven chip.'

'Poor you,' muttered Blair, vaguely, without looking up. 'No oven chips. Fancy.'

This was going to be a very long evening.

With the help of a patient waiter, and only two calls to Blair's psychic, they had finally ordered a sumptuous array of food.

The dishes came at them in unrelenting waves. Nell ate as if she had recently been released from a high-security health farm and drained her glass like a good girl each time it was magically refilled.

Blair also hoovered up every delicacy set in front of him and matched his companion drink for drink, prefacing every slurp with 'Oh, I shouldn't. Maybe just a drop, then. It's so *ageing*.'

Every so often Nell placed her hand on Blair's, or straightened his tie, as lovers do. At one point she toyed with his hair – or attempted to. 'Not the hair, you fool,' he fizzed, as she tried to wrestle her fingers free. No part of Blair was quite as God had intended.

Conversation was stilted until Nell's inspired 'So how have you been, Blair?' as the hors d'oeuvres were placed in front of them. He didn't draw breath for two hours. Nell was furnished with a comprehensive list of all his ailments, from athlete's foot to a suspected (but never diagnosed) tumour the size of a cat, via the measles of his inner child.

It was then a conversational hop, skip and a jump to another of Blair's favourite themes: people who had done him wrong. These ranged from the Granada makeup girl who'd administered a life-threatening perm in 1987, to the floor manager who had ridiculed his microphone technique in front of the entire crew of *What's My Shoe Size?*. ('Never got past pilot stage. All those soap stars have corns, you know.')

Nell interjected the odd 'Really?' or 'You don't say!'. Her mind was free to stray. This was dangerous at the best of times, as Nell's mind was an intrepid traveller. Inevitably it wandered to Gareth and his whereabouts. The drunker she got, the more lovable her ex became. Half-way through the second bottle he was a smiling, happy, ironed individual in spotless underwear. This paragon was chatting up some other girl in a nice pub somewhere, while she was marooned with this tarnished idol.

Every so often Nell caught Louis's eye. He was evidently delighted with her. So delighted he sent over a congratulatory note. She opened it, struggled to focus and read, 'Don't think you can come in late tomorrow because you can't.' Nell rolled her eyes and poured another glass. She knew he didn't mean it.

A second note arrived. 'I mean it.'

'But I can't talk about me all night,' said Blair, as the liqueurs arrived. He grinned blindingly. '*You* talk about me for a while.'

Briefly – very briefly – she suspected him of making a little joke. She was saved from replying, with drunken honesty, 'Sure! You are the single most self-obsessed and tedious individual ever to blight the face of the earth and I can only presume you were fashioned from the leftovers after they'd made a proper person,' by the arrival of a very fat, very red-faced man. He snatched a chair from another table and sat down heavily opposite them.

'Mind if I join you?' slurred the newcomer, rhetorically, seeing no need to remove his cigar from between his dingy teeth as he spoke.

'Hi, Gerry!' beamed Blair, with nuclear-strength bonhomie. 'Nell, this is Gerry Hollywood, sweetheart.' He enunciated the endearment carefully. 'Gerry writes the gossip page for the *Oracle*.' He placed deep emphasis on this information. If he'd had a cape he'd have swirled it. 'He knows absolutely everything about absolutely everybody.'

'Not strictly true,' wheezed Gerry. 'I have no idea who this little angel is.' Puffing noxious cigar fumes all over her, he asked Nell, 'Who *are* you, love?' peering down her cleavage, checking out her legs and helping himself to a glass of wine at the same time.

Hollywood was a major player in the incestuous showbiz world, and Blair was sobered by his appearance at their table. He might not know Nelson Mandela from a bus driver but he could recognise all the tatty little characters of his own corner of the universe. Hollywood could make or break careers. 'I was going to call you, Gerry, honest. You can have the exclusive but we didn't want to go public too soon. This relationship means so much to me.' He reached across and took Nell's hand, rather as if it was a dead rodent he'd found floating in his bidet.

'So. What's the score?'

'It's . . .' Blair stumbled. 'It's love. The real thing. I want her to have my . . .' The tense pause was protracted.

He wants me to have his *what*? A drunken Nell stared wildly at him. His wig when he dies?

'Babies!' Blair pushed it out at last.

'Is that so?' Gerry's raddled old mug had seen it all before. He gave nothing away as he commented, 'Very touching. Going to introduce me, then?'

'May I present Nell Fitzgerald?' To his credit Blair remembered her surname, and even sounded proud.

Gerry plonked a tiny tape-recorder among the debris of the meal. 'Where'd you meet?' he asked brusquely, as if interrogating them for armed robbery.

'In my agent's office. She works there.'

'And, if I may be so bold, how old is the charming little thing?'

The charming little thing knew that Blair had no idea of the answer. She considered tapping his thigh twenty-eight times but Blair found inspiration and said coyly, 'Now, now. You know better than to ask that about a lady.'

'Ever the gent.' Hollywood sniggered, showering the table with ash.

'She brings out the best in me,' Blair motored smoothly on, his TV persona taking over. 'No more questions, you wicked old thing. We'll do lunch soon and you can have *everything*. Tonight we need our privacy.'

Hollywood tucked the tape-recorder away somewhere on his corpulent person. 'Interesting venue, Blair, for privacy.' He let the implication hang in the air, and turned to Nell, who jumped as his scarlet jowls waggled in her direction. 'Can I have one incy-wincy quote, darling? Tell me how you feel about Blair and I'll leave you two lovebirds in peace.'

'How do I feel about Blair?' This was important. Whatever she said tonight would be a headline tomorrow. She had to get this right. 'Gerry,' she said gravely, quelling a hiccup, 'I blove Lair.'

Sixteen

The tube was packed with people to whom hygiene was a quaint, old-fashioned notion. They scoffed at anti-perspirant, Listerine and natural fabrics. Nell, using tactics gleaned from watching Vietnam films, elbowed her way into a seat and hoped to get on calmly with her hangover, but the man looming over her, coughing on to the top of her head, obviously had other ideas.

Nell threw him a filthy look: a really good one, with spin on it. He coughed on. Filthy looks don't work underground: the tube bestows immunity.

For want of anything better to do she squinted at the newspaper of the man on her right. (Newspaper squinting, like smelling of sweat/coughing extravagantly/being deranged or so drunk you fall asleep and miss your stop, is a traditional tube pastime.) 'I BLOVE LAIR!' she read, in letters of flame.

Hollywood had printed her drunken babble. Nell's cheeks pulsed. 'I'll think about it later,' she instructed herself firmly. She stole a look at the paper of the commuter on her left. 'I BLOVE LAIR!' it shrieked at her. Jesus.

The man hanging over her stopped trying to cough up his oesophagus long enough to unfurl his paper. 'I BLOVE LAIR!' she read.

Nell was trapped. Doesn't anybody read the qualities any more? she thought angrily. Everywhere she looked she saw low-brow newspapers. Where was the *Independent*? Or the *Guardian*? Didn't these people *care* about unrest in the Middle East, how the stock market was doing, the latest upheaval in education? Handily forgetting that she only ever looked at cartoons and the astrologer, Nell cursed her low-brow fellow passengers.

The inky pages to either side of her attracted her gaze like magnets, however hard she tried to stare straight ahead at the groin of the coughing man. She really didn't want to look but – oh, cocking hell! There was a photograph. Nell clamped her eyes shut before it swam into focus. A lifetime of bad photos had taught her to sneak up on new ones with caution. At weddings or dinner parties or office nights out, Nell was always the one with her mouth hanging open when the flashbulb popped. Or her chin down. Or her eyes shut. Or a winning mixture of all three. When the film was developed there would be a throng of fresh, smiling faces with an overweight demon having a bad-hair day in their midst.

Nell vowed she would get through the day without seeing the photograph. She'd confront it when she felt able to. On her deathbed, perhaps.

Time was ticking by. She was five minutes to late. Nell beat her own record up the escalator at Leicester Square. For once she was glad to see the revolving doors of her building.

'Blovely day, isn't it?' warbled Zoë.

Making a mental note to kill her horribly as soon as she felt a little stronger, Nell stalked to her office, only to find Linda by the door.

'Linda,' mumbled Nell, folding herself into her chair. A smaller target is harder to hit.

'Or should that be Blinda?' Linda laughed musically at her own joke, then brandished the newspaper. 'You've read it, of course.'

'Actually, no.'

Whoops. Grave tactical error. Linda, who was more efficient than Napoleon at exploiting them, pounced. 'Let me read it to you, then.' She pulled up a chair and perched on it daintily.

'I'm rather busy.'

Linda looked hard at the unblemished surface of Nell's desk. 'I think you can make time,' she stated innocently. She cleared her throat and began to read. '"I blove Lair," says sozzled Nell, 29.'

('They got your age wrong,' said Linda, in an aside.

'I know.'

'You're thirty.'

'I'm twenty-eight.'

'Hmm.')

'Blair Taylor's famous smile,' she resumed reading, 'has been even wider recently and last night I discovered why. It's about five foot five, it's got auburn hair, it gazes devotedly at him and . . . it's a girl. The TV smoothie stunned fellow diners at a top West End eatery by openly canoodling with new lady Nell Fitzgerald. The pair toasted each other over and over – and over – again. Asked for a comment on the affair Ms Fitzgerald hiccuped and said, "I blove Lair," obviously intoxicated by his presence. The man himself has never looked happier and if all his new love's outfits are as abbreviated as the one she was sporting last night I can see why! The randy Romeo has promised me an exclusive on life with Nell, so watch this space.'

Linda lowered the paper and smiled into Nell's pink, tortured face. 'Pity about the photo. Still, they do say the camera adds ten pounds.'

Nell was attempting to look at the discarded photograph sideways. She still couldn't summon the nerve to meet it head on. 'I feel like I need to take a shower,' she said.

Jane From Accounts told Nell she looked very pretty in the paper. Jane From Accounts was wearing a tweed skirt so lumpy there might have been a family of rabbits living in it. Nell thanked her.

'Don't forget, the camera adds twenty pounds,' was the first thing Tina said, when they met up by the photocopier.

'I thought it was ten.'

'Yeah, well . . . How was it?'

'Ever had your toenails pulled out by giggling sadists?'

'Er, no.'

'Pity,' said Nell, with some feeling. 'Because then you'd know what it was like.'

'Jaysus, I nearly wet meself I was so excited. Why didn't you tell us? Are you going to marry him? What's his house like? I bet it's magnificent. Is it a showhome? Is it a mews? And there was I thinking he was a maryjane.'

'Mum!' Nell shoehorned herself into her mother's stream of consciousness. 'Of course I'm not going to marry him. I didn't tell you because it's all very casual. Much more casual than the journalist made it seem.' More lying. And Nell was disturbingly fluent at it.

'Will you be in *Hello!*?' Patsy was breathless. 'Can we come round if you are? I suppose you'll be having them breast implants any minute now.'

'How is everybody?' Nell attempted to drag her mother back to earth.

'Don't get me started. Annie's dad's been round, shouting about his rights. Ringo goes – I had to laugh – Ringo goes, "Rights? I'll show you your rights! I'll show you me right foot!" and he kicks him up the arse. Oh, it was priceless.'

Nell frowned. Weak humour and exuberant violence must be her family's favourite hobbies these days.

'The twins' career is going nicely.'

'What career?'

'Their modelling career, of course.'

Nell shook the phone. Had her mother just said the twins had a modelling career?

'They've been in *Homme* and *Arena* and, oh, all the posh ones. They're hogging the bathroom even more than usual, these days.'

Always playing catch-up with family news, Nell struggled to convince herself that her pleasure for her half-brothers outweighed her chagrin at being the last to know. 'I didn't know they were models,' she said sulkily.

'Did they not show you their portfolios? They're very photo-genical,' claimed Patsy, with some pride. 'Ringo always says they look like poofters but he thinks everybody looks like a poofter these days. He thought your fella was that way inclined!'

Louis was pleased with Nell, and smiled broadly at her all afternoon. This made her feel soiled and she was glad when the imaginary siren went off in her head at six o'clock.

'If you weren't still playing at helping the homeless we could go and get slaughtered.'

'Tina, I'm not playing. I serve food to people who don't have anything to eat. And, anyway, I wouldn't go and get slaughtered because . . .' Nell paused.

'See? We would.'

'No, we wouldn't.' Nell truly wasn't in the mood for a drink. Nor was she in the mood to go to Helping Hands, even though she had to. She was in the mood for a long bath and an even longer cry. Tina had listened sympathetically to her rant about how grubby she felt lying to her mother but Nell could tell she wouldn't understand about the feelings of invasion the newspaper headline had sparked in her: Tina would have *adored* being in the papers. As for how Nell felt about Gareth, Tina's tolerance on that subject had clearly been reached.

Edith's white hat was askew with the effort of preparing moussaka in a tin the size of a Mini Metro. 'Could you open the doors tonight, love?'

'Oh. OK.' Nell took the massive key Edith held out, and approached the double doors. 'Here they come.' She pulled back the rusty bolt, stuck the key into the lock and opened the doors. She felt slyly proud of herself and did it with a ceremonial flourish.

'Getoutoftheway', growled a dwarfish man, whose filthy hair stood up on end.

'Good evening, ladies and gentlemen,' said Nell, weakly, as the crowd sped past her to scoop up the trays.

'Good evening, love.' A tiny, unkempt sparrow of a woman flashed her a quick grin. 'I'm Bridie,' she said, importantly.

'All right?' A young girl with all her teeth smiled at Nell. She was delicately pretty, her slender frame swamped by the layers she wore to keep out the chill.

'Hi.' Nell noticed the beaded clips in the girl's dusty hair and smiled at the pride in her appearance they suggested. 'Moussaka tonight.'

'And?'

'And . . . more moussaka?' improvised Nell.

The girl frowned and passed on to the trays.

As Nell took up her serving spoon Phred materialised behind her. 'Oh, my God!' she squealed at his sudden appearance, then more calmly, 'Did you see me open the doors?'

'It's Anita's birthday,' he said, with emphasis, waiting for a reply.

He didn't get one, unless a baffled squint counted.

'She thought she was getting a cake.'

'Oh, my God,' Nell repeated. 'I totally forgot. It's been a mental couple of days.'

'Shame.' Phred wasn't looking her in the eye.

'I'll make one for her next week,' gabbled Nell.

'It won't be her birthday next week,' Phred pointed out, with maddening accuracy.

Nell sighed. What a moralistic terrier he could be. 'I'll apologise.' She gestured helplessly with a ladle. Why was Phred on her back over this? She thought they'd made some progress. 'I've been busy . . .'

'Well, yes, you have, if the papers are anything to go by.'

'You saw that.' Nell cringed.

A drunken voice said irritably from the other side of the counter, 'Can I have me dinner, please? I don't have to come here, you know. I could take my custom to another hostel.'

* * *

'They certainly like moussaka,' mused Edith, as she scraped out the last dollop. 'Funny I can cook it so well when I don't like it myself.'

'I'd eat anything on a cold night like this.' Ted was on his third helping.

'Charming.' Edith was proud of her cooking skills and often tried to tease a compliment out of her customers. 'Maybe next time I'll cook you *anything*.'

'Fine by me.' Ted was unembarrassed. And very difficult to fill up. 'Any more behind there? Any cake?'

'Can't we shut up about bloody cake?' Nell snapped, banging a plate into the huge dishwasher. 'I'm not a baker, you know, I'm a—'

'Celebrity's girlfriend?' Phred, who had a talent for turning up when Nell was exhibiting non-deep tendencies, finished off her sentence for her.

Dumbly, Nell stared at the dirty plates in her hands. 'Yup, that's me.' She sighed angrily. 'I am a celebrity's girlfriend.' She slammed in another plate.

'Are you going to be able to see Maggie this week?' asked Phred, in an offhand way, as he ticked boxes on one of his endless supply of clipboards.

Nell stopped punishing the crockery, straightened up and said sharply, 'Yes. Why wouldn't I?'

'Thought you might not have time. I mean, it's obviously demanding attending A-list parties with your famous friends.'

Nell forgot that this man was her manager, forgot that she strove at all times to impress him with her cool capability. 'Of course I have time for Maggie!' she snapped. As she resumed the plate-slamming thing, she added acerbically, 'And perhaps you might find the time to extract that stick from up your arse.'

You could have heard a pin drop. Nell closed her eyes, aware that, once again, she'd successfully located her self-destruct button.

Phred, being Phred, just walked away. Which made it worse, somehow.

*   *   *

It seemed appropriate to walk, rather than wait for the bus. Nell wanted to shiver with cold, she wanted to feel the damp pavements irritate her feet, she wanted to distract herself from the dismal soup of her thoughts, and to punish herself for being such a spectacular combination of rude and stupid.

Helping Hands was the only thing shoring up her rickety self-esteem – despite what the girls' mags say, Nell had never found that long baths and a new pair of shoes did much for this elusive part of her. Phred was the person who had given her a chance at Helping Hands and also the person she had advised *vis-à-vis* his arse-stick. It wasn't rainy enough for Nell: she would have preferred a monsoon.

The mansion block stood, hefty but elegant, right where she'd left it that morning. Nell had noticed that posh people don't pull their curtains: in the wet gloom, the illuminated windows of Hans Place glittered like one of Claudette's fancier necklaces. She fumbled for her key as she got nearer, cursing as she did every evening that she hadn't thought to place it carefully in her handbag's inner pocket. Down through the strata of gum-wrappers, bus tickets, elderly lip-glosses and leaky biros she delved.

There was a figure by the door. Nell made out the shape of a man, lurking. She had never witnessed somebody lurking before, but that was definitely what he was doing. She slowed her step, aware that even if Fergus heard her screams up in the penthouse he would probably only turn up the Vivaldi.

Then she realised. It was a paparazzo. Louis had warned her they might pounce. 'Look presentable at all times,' he had warned. Nell's hair hung down in snaky tendrils about a pale face, which sported an immovable frown. She dragged out an old smile that was hanging around from the days when she used such things, and quickened her step.

The figure moved into the jurisdiction of the porch light. 'Nell,' said Gareth.

'Holy moly,' said Nell.

*   *   *

The Up All Night café was as good as its word. Nell settled herself at a table while Gareth ordered exactly what she wanted without having to ask her. 'Get that down you,' he said hoarsely, as he put a mug of hot chocolate in front of her.

'Thank you very much.' Nell was stiff and formal even though she used to roll about naked with him.

'Why can't we talk at your grandmother's place?'

'She keeps traditional old-lady hours,' explained Nell. 'Besides, this is neutral territory. That's better, isn't it?'

'You're sure it's not because *he*'s up there?'

'Who's he when he's at home?' asked Nell, and licked off her whipped-cream moustache – it was not a good look for impressing one's recent ex. The penny dropped. 'You mean Blair?' she asked incredulously.

'Who else?' he said morosely.

Gareth's reappearance was sparking a landslide of emotions. Surprise, disbelief, uncertainty and raw excitement had all tumbled over Nell as they walked the two hundred yards to the café. Now she added hilarity to the list. He believed what he'd read in the paper.

'You're laughing?' Gareth was outraged. This wasn't unusual: Gareth could muster up outrage alone in a darkened room. 'You've broken my heart and now you're laughing at me!'

That stilled the giggles. Gareth's heart had never been mentioned in any of the conversations about their relationship that Nell had engineered. She felt strangely exhilarated, as if a breeze was whipping through her hair. With trepidation, she asked, 'Why have you come here?' She was a little afraid of the answer.

Gareth rubbed his big hands over his head, as if he was trying to press something out of his brain. 'I don't know. I just had to see you. I couldn't go on any longer.'

'Really? Truly?' Quelling an urge to get him to write it down and sign it for Tina's benefit, Nell bounced on her seat.

After all the trials of this long, horrible day, perhaps she was about to get a little reward. Gareth wanted her back. She stared at the froth on her chocolate. She wasn't about to prompt him. This had to be all his own work.

'Everything was OK until today.' Gareth's eyes were bloodshot. 'I was getting by fine without you.'

That stung. Silently Nell willed him not to ruin it. He had always ruined it, whenever he'd talked about his feelings for her. He could only talk about love if he rubbed it in the dirt first.

'But now . . .'

As Nell waited for him to spit it out, she trembled. She was on the brink of getting what she wanted.

If it really was what she wanted.

'Now the thought of you with him is driving me mad. When I saw you in the paper I wanted to . . .' Gareth scrunched up a defenceless paper napkin. 'I mean, him! Of all people. How could you?'

Obviously she couldn't, not even under anaesthetic, but if it took violent jealousy of a giant orange jessie to transform Gareth from macho to malleable, then so be it. She turned away, eyelids coyly lowered. She felt a prickle of guilt at deceiving him like this but it would be worth it for both of them in the end.

The newly voluble Gareth was carrying on: 'That photograph . . . You looked so . . . so . . .'

So what? So *what*? Nell wanted to scream at him, but she maintained her demure posture. So fat? So drunk?

'So beautiful,' Gareth concluded. 'So, so beautiful.'

It was now impossible to remain coy. Once, under the influence of a river of cider, Gareth had conceded that she was 'all-right looking'. He'd routinely told her she looked 'fine' when she asked him what he thought of a new outfit. He had never mentioned that he liked her hair, her eyes, her smile. It was one of the ways he'd starved her out of loving him.

He thought she was beautiful. She wanted to cry.

'I'd never seen you look like that. So sexy and glamorous.'

'Well, I did dress up now and then, you know,' she suggested gently.

'Not like that you didn't.'

'Well . . .'

'Trust me. I'd remember if you'd ever looked that good before. You were stunning in that photo.'

Nell knew she looked plastered in it. At last Gareth was viewing her through the goggles of love. 'I did dress up sometimes, though,' she persevered unwisely.

'Christ, can we drop that!' Gareth thumped the table, slopping her chocolate. 'I'm trying to tell you that you blew my mind. You were so glamorous and voluptuous. And no,' he added speedily, 'I don't mean fat, I mean voluptuous.' Obviously he had learned something from previous heated conversations. 'And I let you go. Just like that. That stunning girl in the paper was my bird and I let her go.'

They gazed at each other under the bald fluorescent light. Nell didn't feel exhilarated now, she felt deflated and disappointed. Gareth was offering her something she didn't want.

'I was a fool.'

Nell dropped her gaze from the need in his eyes. Through all the painful months of deterioration he'd never showed her his softer side. Now he thought she was beautiful because of a glammed-up photo in the paper: hadn't he thought she was beautiful when she was dashing around the flat in pyjamas with her hair in a scrunchie? Wasn't it all a bit late? And, if she was honest with herself, a bit suspect? He seemed to be telling her he wanted her back because she looked sexy. How damned shallow was that?

Wearily, Nell said 'You're not a fool, Gareth. You did the right thing in letting me go.' She stood up.

Gareth put his head on the table.

And let her go.

*　　　*　　　*

There was a new toaster in the Morgan Theatrical Management kitchenette. Davina was using her powers for good.

Jane From Accounts was impressed, cooing as her Pop-Tart popped in record time. 'I've been asking Louis for a new toaster for months. Davina just mentions it and here it is!'

Nell smiled. Jane From Accounts's persuasive powers (i.e. her breasts) weren't as irresistible as Davina's.

Fergus was every bit as painfully formal on the phone as he was face to face. 'I regret to inform you that Madame wishes to cancel her supper engagement with you this evening,' he intoned, in a voice straight from a Pathé newsreel. 'Madame has retired to her room due to an indisposition.'

'Hmm. Indisposition. Help me out here, Fergus. Has she got a cold or is her leg hanging off? I haven't a clue what that word's supposed to mean.'

'I feel confident that if Madame had wanted to be more graphic she would have been so.' A silent tut passed down the phone wire.

'OK, OK, sorry I asked.' Nell was now free to give in to Tina's pestering and go to the pictures with her. She had been bribed with as many hot dogs as she could eat. "Hope you've got your credit card on you, Teen,' she warned.

Zoë was invisible behind a massive arrangement of white roses. Unfortunately she was still audible. 'I don't care what she says, I reckon Nell must have shagged Blair for him to spend this much on flowers.'

Jane From Accounts, who was in the wrong place at the wrong time and had to listen to this unsavoury guesswork, tried to nod and shake her head at the same time. She could see what Zoë couldn't: Nell was leaning on the reception desk.

Nell said loudly, through the foliage, 'Did you ever hear the theory that men are more likely to send you flowers if you don't sleep with them, Zoë?'

'Yeah, right,' scoffed Zoë, who had never received so much

as a daisy, despite having slept with more men than Nell had had microwaveable dinners.

Jean, who was having a rest on the reception sofa with a copy of *Woman's Weekly*, theorised, 'That young man's fallen for you, Nell. I've always maintained there's no such thing as homosexiness.'

Nell staggered back to her office with the roses, closely followed by Tina. 'Blimey. Blair's got unexpectedly good taste in flowers. They must have cost a fortune.' She frowned. 'What is it? Why the face?'

Nell was looking at the card tucked among the stalks. 'They're not from Blair. They're from Ga—'

'Loos!' barked Tina.

Tina read the card and diagnosed an immediate course of action. 'Throw this away.' She underlined her command with a vicious pinch to one of Nell's soft bits.

'Yes, O Mistress of the Universe. And don't pinch me. Cow.'

'I will pinch you black and blue if it stops you getting back with Gareth.' And she did it again, to prove her resolve.

'Cow again.' Nell didn't need Tina's violent warnings. The card, now snuggling into a mattress of snotty tissues and discarded tampon wrappers, read 'To the beautiful girl in the photograph'. After years of togetherness Gareth had fallen for Nell after he had seen her with another man. All the sloppy mugs of tea she'd brought him in bed, all the kisses with which she'd brushed his nose as he slept, all the hours she'd shivered on touchlines pretending to understand rugby, even the warm hours they'd spent holding each other, hadn't done the trick.

Nell felt blank. Caring about Gareth had been futile, but being photographed with a celebrity had reeled him in.

All those years of struggling to get her hands on the prize and Gareth's love hadn't been worth the bother.

Saturday was a long time coming. 'Spoken to your folks this week?' Maggie asked, one eye on the last ham sandwich.

'My mum rang me. She saw that rubbish in the paper and wanted to ask me about it.'

'Of course. It was nothing to do with the fact that you're her daughter and she likes speaking to you.'

'That as well, I suppose,' agreed Nell, who was also distracted by that last flirtatious sarnie.

'About time you gave her a call, then,' Maggie prodded. 'Maybe you could suggest going round.'

'Why?' asked Nell.

'Do you need a reason? Wish I could go round and see my mum,' said Maggie. When Nell didn't answer she added softly, 'You mustn't orphan yourself, love.'

'I know, I know,' said Nell, sulkily.

Intuitively, Maggie changed the subject. Unfortunately to another uncomfortable one. 'Have you managed to confront your gran about your missing grandfather yet?'

'I'm too scared.'

'What can she do?'

Only somebody who had never met Claudette would ask that question. 'She could kill me with her manicured bare hands.'

'Seize the day, Nell. Best advice you'll ever get.' Maggie paused thoughtfully. 'Would you be a love and fetch me the phone directory from the hall?'

'If this is a ruse to get your hands on that sandwich . . .' warned Nell, as she winched herself out of the soft recesses of Maggie's ancient sofa.

'I just want to look somebody up,' said Maggie, with a coy half smile that peeled decades from her.

Nell returned with it. 'Here.' She tutted eloquently. The plate was empty.

As she passed number thirteen, Nell couldn't resist peeking in. She wished Phred could have heard Maggie's parting words to her: he would have put her at the top of the class and forgotten all his dull worries about Nell being too busy to visit her. She had washed up the tea-things and tidied the kitchen, then taken out the bin. She had said proudly to Maggie as she left, 'At least I managed to get a bit of housework done for you. I feel like a proper volunteer for once.'

'You do more than you know,' Maggie told her, as she popped a Bakewell Slice into Nell's bag.

Flushed with the warmth of having made a difference to somebody as special as Maggie, Nell had a spring in her step as she glanced through Phred's window and saw the sharp chrome edges of his sitting room winking in the spring sunshine.

Seventeen

Dreaded events come round much more quickly than happy ones: it seemed like no time at all before Nell was zipping herself in to the sparkly white dress for her second date with Blair.

Kiddifeed was the brainchild of a posse of double-barrelled it-girls, who had been so touched by the plight of starving African children that they simply had to throw a party for them. Nell had never understood how these events worked: whenever she'd thrown a party it had cost her money, not the other way round.

The luxury of the limo almost took her mind off how uncomfortable the dress was, and how absurd her position. However, even with its soft-as-butter white leather seats, its maple woodwork and its hi-tech sound system, it couldn't distract her from the rant Blair launched into as soon as he clambered in beside her.

'I mean, how dare he?' he fumed. 'How fucking dare he? Who does Louis think he is? Telling me – *me*, of all people – to try to be more masculine?'

'Outrageous,' murmured Nell. By now she knew that most of Blair's questions were rhetorical.

'What does he want? Should I drive a white van and carry a rolled-up copy of the *Daily Mirror*?' he blustered.

'You're getting all upset. Try to think of something else,' said Nell, soothingly. She didn't want him arriving at the gala in this state.

'All right. Sorry. I'm very passionate, comes of being a Leo. I won't say another word about it.' Blair punched the uphol-stery. 'But I'm *very* bloody masculine!'

'Yes, you certainly are,' reassured Nell. 'Nice French mani-cure, by the way.'

'Thanks.'

The blizzard of flashbulbs as they stepped out of the car left Nell with spots before her eyes. She hadn't expected so many photographers and she certainly hadn't expected them to be interested in pictures of *her*. Wobbling like a geisha in her long, tight skirt she teetered beside Blair, hanging on to him tightly.

Blair was amazingly natural, tilting his chin up as if spotting a good friend on a distant balcony and fixing a wide smile on his face. The barrage of 'Over here!' and 'Give us a smile!' was deafening and felt like an assault to Nell's ears, but Blair was used to it. As they went through the doors he whispered to her, 'Don't worry. They probably won't use any shots of us. There's a few film stars here tonight.'

The doors to the cavernous ballroom opened and they walked into a wall of sound. It was the cacophony of a roomful of small-talk floating to the gilded ceiling like bubbles.

Huge leopardskin pennants swooped from the rafters. One wall was covered with a massive illuminated map of an African country that Nell had never heard of. A platoon of unfeasibly long-legged girls, clad in shortie jerkins of the same leopardskin material, pounced on them. 'Welcome to Kiddifeed!' they grimaced, and Nell was handed a brochure bound, inevitably, in leopardskin.

'"Welcome to a spectacular night of African music and food in aid of the starving peoples of that troubled continent!"' she read. She felt a little shaky, as 'Hello!' and 'Darling!' ricocheted around her. Beside her, Blair had transformed smoothly from spitting misanthropist to party bunny. Swallowed up by the sea of celebrity, he was engulfed in kisses and bear hugs from his legions of close friends. 'Look at you! You've lost so much weight!' he cooed at an obese astrologer, than smooched a weathergirl.

Blair introduced Nell diligently to all and sundry. He even

managed to look proud as he said, over and over, 'And this is my Nell.'

A hundred times Nell squeaked, 'Hello,' and smiled mechanically. The rapacious self-confidence of the people she met had rendered her shy.

Help was at hand. Another of those giraffe-legged girls was proffering a tray of drinks. Nell grabbed one. 'No, don't go away.' Like a music-hall ventriloquist she spoke while she gulped it down, then grabbed another. It contained vodka, and not much else. Very nice, Nell thought.

'Thanks, but I couldn't.' Blair presumed the second drink was for him. 'Vodka shrinks my chakra.'

From the depths of the room a steel band struck up. 'We must have a boogie later on!' Blair threatened a breakfast-TV presenter, who was passing. Then he muttered to Nell, 'My sinuses are going to jump out of my face. Have you any ginseng on you?'

Nell gestured to her tiny evening bag (a fiver in a Topshop sale many moons ago) and informed him that, oddly enough, she had left the house without it. 'Aren't steel bands from the Caribbean?' she asked, puzzled.

'Yeah. No. Whatever.' Blair was too busy mouthing, '*Snogs later*,' across the room at a male model.

'Er, that's not *terribly* heterosexual behaviour,' Nell felt obliged to remind him.

'Oh, fuck heterosexuality. If it was any fun I wouldn't be gay,' huffed Blair, segueing seamlessly into 'Gerry Hollywood! Fancy meeting you here!'

'You know me,' leered Hollywood. 'A free drink and I'm anyone's.'

Not mine, thought Nell, who was no slouch with a free drink. 'Hello, Mr Hollywood,' she said, as sweetly as she could muster, then performed an impressive swoop and dip to snaffle two more vodkas from a passing tray. 'You look very smart.'

Dripping a Rorschach pattern of ash down his dated lapels,

he raised his eyebrows at her. 'And you look very glamorous, doesn't she, Blair, baby?'

'Gorgeous. Having trouble keeping my hands off her.' Blair forced it out: earlier he had told Nell she reminded him of his late mother.

'I bet.' Hollywood had a way of saying the simplest thing with a double edge. 'Ah, grub.' He grabbed a handful of sushi from a passing waitress. 'Healthy shit,' he enlightened them, through a mouthful of prawn.

'This is a benefit for the starving . . .' Nell was thinking aloud. 'And they have anorexic-looking girls handing round huge trays of food?'

'I know. Fabulous, isn't it?' Blair snaffled some organic tapas.

The look she gave him wasn't wasted on Hollywood, who said, 'You're in the wrong place if you have a functioning irony gland, love. Most of the people in this room couldn't point to Africa on the map.'

'But they can find their way to the Ivy blindfolded.'

Hollywood laughed, and lumbered away. Nell's irony gland absorbed the fact that she got on better with the malicious tub of lard than she did with her supposed fancy man.

The fancy man was now prodding his stomach and gurning. 'I feel something. Can you develop a hernia from eating tapas?'

By now Nell knew how to handle him. 'I have anti-tapas-herniatic medication on me. Would you like some?'

'Please, please,' begged Blair, and grabbed the ancient Tic-Tac Nell had extracted from the seam of her bag. 'This stuff is good. It's working already. What's in it?'

'Oil of evening squid-rose,' she answered fluently. 'And, of course, a touch of tittle juice.'

'Of course.' Blair nodded sagely. 'Oh, look! There's Su Pollard!'

Nell learned a lot over the next three hours. She learned that a six-foot-four man in a two-thousand-pound tuxedo can air-kiss forty-eight times, roar, 'I LOVE your new show!' thirteen times, attempt to look modest and fail forty-two times, and reassure a chat-show host that his (science-fiction-style) face-lift was undetectable once.

At Blair's side as he worked the room, Nell grinned until her teeth hurt and found herself embroiled in all sorts of conversations with people she had only ever seen on the television. She had a new respect for Blair: he made it look easy. He was well aware that almost everybody was sceptical about his new romance, but he was brazening it out with style. Perhaps there was more to Blair than she had suspected.

'Darling,' she heard him say, to a reality-show star, 'I don't need Jesus. I've got Liza Minnelli.'

And perhaps there wasn't.

High up on a balcony, Nell stared down at the gala. On the pretence of needing the ladies' she had slipped away to clear her head. It might have been the vodka, it might have been the weight of the dress or it might have been the strain of talking diets with minor celebrities, but her brain was turning to *papier-mâché*.

The strains of the steel band were further away up here, and she could hardly hear the barbershop quartet at the far end of the hall. Looking down at the tops of heads might have given her perspective, but she was finding it difficult to marshal her thoughts. Her grandmother's lie kept jostling to the front. How could you, Claudette? thought Nell, bitterly. She looked down at the hordes of people and felt very alone.

'Sorry I was so long.'

Blair hadn't noticed she'd gone. 'Nell, meet Angel.' Blair had a look on his face that Nell only wore when confronted by ice-cream. It was easy to see why. Angel looked as if he had indeed been sent direct from heaven. Thick dark curls framed a face so perfect and so sensual that no plastic surgeon could have hoped to emulate it.

'Hello,' she said, abashed by such beauty.

In a ludicrous Cockney falsetto that negated all his good looks, Angel chirruped, 'Boyno, bold.'

'Er . . .'

'That's Polari,' Blair told her, in a stage whisper that could have been heard in Belgium. 'You know,' he prompted her, when she still looked blank, 'the traditional gay language. He said, "Hello, darling." It's hilarious, isn't it?'

'Er, yes.'

'Nice drogle, bad caxton,' Angel continued, pouting with those perfect lips.

'But it's not very butch,' Nell reproved Blair.

Sighing deeply, as if cruelly deprived, Blair said wearily, 'No, it isn't. He said, "Good dress, bad wig," by the way. Angel, we'll have to catch up later.' He clocked Nell's disapproving look. 'I mean another time. I'm NTBH tonight. I will keep my promise, though, don't you worry. Vada you later.'

Angel melted into the crowd. 'Promise?' Nell was suspicious. 'And what does NTBH mean?'

'It means I'm Not To Be Had. At this rate I'll be NTBH until the cows come bleedin' well home. The promise was to model in the charity auction. I get asked all the time. It's not just the looks, I have natural poise,' asserted Blair. 'Are you having a nice time?'

Touched to be asked, Nell opened her mouth to reply, but was silenced by Blair's distracted 'Good. Good. Who the hell are *they*?'

Nell looked over to where two young, blond gods stood on a podium wearing little but gold loincloths and a lot of baby oil. 'That's John and Paul!' she breathed.

'You know those divine beings?' gasped Blair.

'I'm related, I mean, half related to them.' Nell was nonplussed. Why couldn't any of her relatives be trusted to do normal things? Why did they turn out to be world-class liars or stand about on podiums in their knickers?

'Introduce me,' ordered Blair, frothing at the mouth.

'OK,' said Nell, eager to find out what they were doing there. 'But try to be, you know . . .'

'Masculine. Yes, yes, I won't bugger them in front of Gerry Hollywood, don't worry.' Blair gave Nell a push and she led the way.

The situation became clear as they neared the dais. The twins were the 'faces' of the brand of vodka that was sponsoring the party. Massive posters bearing their unsmiling, razor-sharp images towered behind them as they handed out tiny bottles and the occasional kiss. Laughing and kidding about as unselfconsciously as if they were down the pub, John and Paul were a hit. Nell was probably the only woman within a hundred yards of them who didn't want to shred their loincloths.

John spotted her in the hormonal scrum and squatted, affording Blair a disquieting ringside view of his inner thigh. 'This your new boyfriend?' He smiled, showing off the whitest teeth ever to come out of Fulham.

'He's not—'

'I'm not—'

Blair and Nell spoke together, then stopped abruptly. 'Yes. Blair meet John,' she said resignedly.

'My mum loves you.'

'Why, thank you,' simpered Blair, like a southern belle.

'Hope you're looking after my big sis.'

'Half-sis,' corrected Nell. 'But never mind us. This is amazing! I'm so pleased for you.'

'It's a laugh,' said John, laconically. 'You coming to the wedding?'

'What wedding?' Nell's thin skin prickled. Another family event she had no idea about.

'Georgina's wedding.'

'Georgina's . . .' Nell shook her head to make sure her ears were working properly. 'She's marrying whatsisname, Annie's dad?'

'God, no.' This notion was ridiculous, judging by John's expression. 'His best mate. She owned up. The baby's his, after all.'

There was no answer to that. Her family were becoming a travelling *Jerry Springer Show*. 'Nobody told me,' she said weakly.

'I'm telling you now,' John pointed out reasonably. 'I'd better get back to prancing about like a ponce for money. See you later, OK, sis?'

'Yeah. Vada you later,' smiled Nell.

'Those boys are far too handsome to be straight,' opined Blair, with the decisive air of an expert.

'Sorry but they are.' Nell checked herself. 'Far as I know.'

'I may have to carry out a little research . . .' Blair smoothed an eyebrow.

'Not tonight you won't!' Nell steered him away from the podium. Looking after Blair was like trying to keep a skip of nuclear waste steady. He could tip at any time.

Rubbing shoulders with glamour models and soap stars at the front of the stage, Nell sweated anxiously into her expensive beaded apparel. She didn't like Blair being out of her sight. Anything could be happening backstage. She had torrid visions of a St John's Ambulanceman using a spatula to remove Blair's tongue from a male model.

If only it wasn't so hot, she thought. If only there wasn't such a crush. And if only I wasn't me. She would cheerfully have changed places with Ted or Bridie at that moment, as she scanned the room for the regional newsreader with bad breath who had taken a shine to her.

Her attention was drawn back to the stage as the fashion show began. Again, just how a fashion show raised money for the starving was a mystery, but she clapped along with the rest of the enthusiastic onlookers, praying that Blair wouldn't step out in a tutu.

Something vibrated against her hip. A text message had

been left on her mobile phone. With some difficulty in the crush, she retrieved it from her bag and peered down at the words 'Where are you? Phred.'

Nell's brain convulsed. She was due at Helping Hands tomorrow, wasn't she? She visualised her desk diary – and there it was, in neon on today's date: 'HH SOUP KITCHEN'.

'Shit! Shit! Shitty Shitsville!' she exploded, to the surprise of those pressing against her.

An announcement diverted her attention to the catwalk. 'And modelling the latest look for the urban cowboy . . . it's *Blair Taylor*!' A massive roar went up as Blair burst on to the stage, clad only in leather chaps, a Stetson and a lot of baby oil.

Nooooo, squealed Nell inwardly, willing her fake boyfriend not to turn round.

Blair spun and the crowd went truly wild. In a volley of flashguns, the naked Taylor behind was displayed to a hollering audience. It was every bit as orange as his face, and nicely pert. He was obviously very proud of it: Nell could have sworn it was smiling.

'Don't tell me off,' shouted Blair, when Nell got within ten yards of him backstage. 'It wasn't masculine but it was bloody good fun. Nobody noticed.'

'Nobody noticed?' Nell had no time to waste arguing. She thrust his coat at him. 'Blair, we've got to go.'

'I'm just beginning to enjoy myself,' whined Blair.

'I've got an emergency. I have to get away.' She saw the mutinous jut of his jaw. 'And you have to come with me. We're a couple, remember?'

With a theatrical sigh Blair followed, his happy bottom wriggling smugly under his clothes.

An unhappy Cinderella, Nell raced down the stairs of Helping Hands in her finery, holding the stiff material so that she could pick up some speed. She skidded to a halt down in the

Bernadette Strachan

kitchen, panting and shedding beads. A volley of wolf-whistles from stragglers finishing off their sausage casseroles almost drowned her question to Edith: 'Am I too late?'

'You know you are, dear,' answered Edith, mildly. There was a speck of gravy in one eyebrow. 'It's nearly midnight.'

'I know, I know, I know.' Nell wrung her hands. 'How did you manage?' She had never experienced such guilt, not even when she'd lied to the head nun about telling the younger children Jesus had been run over by a bus.

'We did all right,' Edith said calmly. 'Phred came in, as soon as he'd found somebody to look after Clover.'

The guilt cranked up a notch. Hot on the heels of her outburst the other evening, Nell had caused Phred to be dragged away from his daughter. 'Is he still here?' she whispered.

'Yup.' The voice was behind her.

Nell wished that Phred would invest in some shoes with hard soles. She rolled her eyes eloquently, rearranged her features into an expression of abject misery and turned to face him. 'I am so sorry,' she said, aware that even though she was sincere, she sounded fake.

Phred looked her up and down. 'Were you getting married?'

Nell counted to ten. 'No.' Inspiration hit. 'I was at a gala for the starving in Africa,' she said earnestly, as if this might win her some sorely needed Brownie points.

Phred's irony gland was, if anything, even healthier than Nell's. 'So you were helping to feed people, just not here? Perhaps the dinner queue should wear evening dress to get your attention.'

'I forgot,' said Nell, in a small voice. 'I got the day wrong.' She was disheartened by this return to the old, cold Phred, the pre-dinner-party model. They'd crossed a line, but now they were firmly back where they'd started. 'Everyone gets it wrong once in a while.'

'Nell, I'm really tired right now.' Nell's paranoia added the subtitles flashing across his cotton crew-neck – '*And it's all your fault.*' 'Why don't we talk about it when we have your review?' Phred smiled for real when he saw her face fall. 'Don't look so scared. I can't have you flogged.' He dragged a hand through his hair. 'Unfortunately.'

Jean was puzzled. 'In my day we were pleased when a gentleman sent us flowers,' she whispered to Len. She had just seen Nell drop-kick a basket of lilies across Reception.

Jane From Accounts had dived for her phial of Rescue Remedy and dropped some on to Nell's tongue. Nell, who thought homeopathy was evil, had to be restrained by Tina for her to achieve this.

'Isn't that much better?' asked Jane From Accounts, in the baby voice that made grown men long to strike her.

'Oh, yes,' said Nell, sarcastically. 'I feel like shit *and* I have the taste of rotting leather in my mouth.' She saw Jane From Accounts's face assume its pre-tears expression and said hastily, 'Actually, now you mention it, I'm tons better. Thank you – you've really helped.'

Tina sat Nell down at her desk with a Bounty. 'Eat,' she advised. 'Why don't you take Gareth's flowers to Helping Hands? That way you wouldn't have to look at them all day and the homeless would get some benefit from them.'

'I didn't think of that.' She looked slyly at Tina: was her friend showing an interest in her good-doing?

'Now. Do you feel strong enough to see the *Oracle*'s front page?' Tina continued.

At least there was no picture of herself to wince at. Nell's face had been eclipsed, so to speak, by a close-up of Blair's bare behind in the leather chaps.

Linda was looking sympathetic by the water-cooler.

Nell was looking terror-stricken by a filing cabinet. 'How angry is he?' she asked unwisely.

'Hmm. Do you remember when the post-boy caught fire in front of Sir David Attenborough?'

'God. Yes.' Nell quailed.

'He's much angrier than that,' said Linda, sombrely and with a great deal of satisfaction.

A roar, loud and leonine, ripped through the office. 'NE-ELL!'

'I'll tell him you're out,' Dean said desperately.

'No, no, don't do that.' Nell swallowed. 'I'll face him. Who is he, anyway?'

'That's the spirit!' said Linda, admiringly. 'All he can do is sack you without a reference and put the word out in the business that you're unemployable.' She patted Nell on the back. 'Go get 'im.'

'Picture the scene.' Louis was starting off calmly. 'There I sit, sipping my breakfast coffee, trying not to look at Hildegard in her négligé, and glancing over the morning papers. Aha, I think. Hopefully there will be a small picture of my most valuable client and my trusted employee out on the town. Hopefully it will underline the masculine nature of my client, as that is specifically what my trusted employee has been trusted to do. So I turn to the *Oracle*, to the *Sun*, to the *Daily Mirror*, and what do I see?'

Nell felt unable to neglect the pause for breath. 'You saw a picture of your most valuable client,' she said, as brightly as she could, 'enjoying himself in a slightly risqué outfit that was just a bit of fun?'

'I SAW HIS ARSE!' shrieked Louis. 'A FOOT HIGH!' His volume control seemed to have malfunctioned. 'HIS ARSE!' He punched the table. 'HIS ARSE, FOR CHRIST'S SAKE!'

'You can't blame me, Louis.' Nell was on shaky ground.

'No? Oh, I see. Who should I blame, then? The President of the United States? Winnie-the-Pooh? Of course it's your fucking fault,' snapped Louis. 'It's a débâcle. We'll have to exercise damage control.' His expression darkened. 'You'll have to marry him.'

*   *   *

The fateful picture was open on Nell's desk. 'Fancy' was felt-tipped on the right buttock and 'lunch?' on the left.

Yes, Nell did fancy lunch with Tina. She could ask her to be bridesmaid.

'You said no, I hope.'

Nell toyed with her skipload of spaghetti. 'I told him I'd daydreamed about a proposal many times but never quite like that one. He tried to persuade me by saying that I didn't have to go through with it, I just had to let him announce it.'

'You still said no, I hope.'

'Tina, of course I said no. Very loudly and in three languages to make sure. Don't you have *any* faith in me?'

'It's just that I know what you're like for giving in to people.'

'Whoa.' Nell held up her palm. 'Stop right there. This is shaping up to be a lecture and I don't need it. I am *not* going back to Gareth.'

'Sure?'

'Quite apart from anything else, the card with today's flowers read "My bum's better than his bum. Come back to me."'

'Silver-tongued bastard,' commented Tina. 'But if you do . . .'

'There's no need to threaten me with elaborate punishments, Teen. I'll admit, there was a moment when . . .' Nell rubbed her eyes, as if to wipe away the memory. 'But no, I don't want to be with Gareth.'

'All right, I'll shut up.' Tina looked away as she said, 'But Marti reckons you'll go back to him.'

Nell said nothing. Very loudly.

Eighteen

Hans Place was a Bermuda triangle of snacks. Jammie Dodgers were going AWOL and Pot Noodles were following them over the wall. A precious Curly Wurly had somehow escaped. And still Fergus eluded capture.

Carita was beefing up Nell's portions, but Nell was still starving. She thanked Carita for the extra slivers of veal and waited for her to bring up the subject of Claudette's divorce. Carita didn't allude to it, and didn't contrive to talk to Nell about anything other than food and her Latin opinion of Nell's behind: apparently it needed more fat on it.

One evening, after dinner as they sat together in the drawing room Nell decided that she would start opening conversational doorways for her grandmother to step through. Perhaps if she gave Claudette a chance to come clean about her divorce, the old lady would take it.

'Do you think there are more divorces these days than there used to be?' Nell had spent ages thinking up that transparent question.

'It's not a subject to which I care to apply myself. Surely it's the sort of thing your socially aware friends at Happy Hands could tell you.'

After a pause for the BBC news, Nell probed, 'Could we visit Granddad's grave some time?'

'The young are so morbid.'

At no point did Claudette fall to her bony knees and gasp, 'He's alive! I'm a liar!' She was far too cool an adversary for her emotion-driven granddaughter. Nell knew this, but it wasn't going to stop her trying. It took an awful lot to stop Nell trying.

*   *   *

The flat looked different from the last time she'd babysat. When Carol said, 'Sorry about the mess,' this time there was something to apologise for.

Crumbs and fluff were trodden into the thin carpets. A coffee-stain snaked across the sofa. A tray bearing a half-finished TV dinner lay on the sitting-room floor: tiny foot-prints in mashed potato led away from it. 'Would you like me to, you know, tidy around?' asked Nell.

'So it's a pigsty, is it?' Carol snapped, so suddenly that Nell jumped. 'Tell them!' She pointed at Hayley and Leonardo, who scarpered from the doorway when she pointed angrily in their direction. 'They're driving me bloody mad.' Carol dug in her handbag, muttering angrily, 'Where are me keys? *Where are me sodding*— Oh. Got them.' She looked belligerently at Nell. 'Are you going to stay? Or is it too dirty for you?' She pronounced the word 'dirty' with a poncy sneer.

'I'll stay.' Nell was stung. She was doing this woman a favour, after all. Surreptitiously, she studied Carol dragging on her parka as if it was trying to escape. She had read all the pamphlets at Helping Hands on drug-taking but couldn't spot any tell-tale signs. Carol wasn't behaving as if she was high: to be honest, she was behaving just like Nell would if she had three small children and no money and lived in this freezing, dangerous place.

Carol bawled through the bedroom door, 'I don't want any bloody trouble out of you lot while I'm out! D'you hear me?'

A subdued, 'Yes, Mum,' drifted out.

'What? *What?*' Carol rounded on Nell, evidently seeing something in her face that she didn't like. 'What are you looking at?'

'I'm not looking at anything!' Nell's temper flared. 'What's your problem, Carol? I'm only trying to help.'

Snorting, Carol left in a whirlwind of bad temper.

For some time after she'd gone, Nell twitched and paced the flat. She'd given up her evening to sit in this cheerless place and she didn't expect applause but it would have been nice not to be yelled at.

Hayley got up to go to the loo. As she passed Nell she said quietly, 'Mum gets a bit depressed.'

'I know, sweetheart. Everybody does,' said Nell, through the crack in the bathroom door. She reminded herself that she didn't have to like Carol. She just had to help her out.

Being shallow had been much more straightforward.

Nell's overheated brain had a lot to contend with, these days. If she wasn't worrying about her possible grandfather she was worrying about Gareth or about being sacked from Helping Hands or about the dubious honour of being Blair's squeeze or, if she had time, about what her hair thought it was doing.

Among all this cerebral debris, Maggie's odd observation about how Nell was helping to orphan herself bobbed up regularly. On her way to Maggie's one evening, Nell decided to act on this oblique advice. She would call Georgina to talk about the wedding, instead of waiting to be called while feeling grimly confident that it wouldn't happen.

'Welcome to the mad'ouse.' Ringo had answered the phone. 'Smelly Nellie!' he whooped, when he heard his stepdaughter's voice. 'How are you diddling?'

Nell was diddling even worse than usual but she told him she was fine and asked for Georgina. A little surprised, Ringo hollered for his daughter.

'And was Georgina glad you'd rung?' Maggie was wielding an impressive combination of teapot and sherry bottle in the soft lamplight of her front room.

'She was chuffed,' said Nell, happily. 'I've never called just to talk to her before.'

'And the wedding? What are the plans?'

'The date isn't set,' Nell admitted. 'Even though she's decided that the new boyfriend, Fabio, is Annie's real dad, he wants DNA tests before he commits.' She looked up from her lap to see how Maggie was taking this.

Maggie was taking it the way she took most things. 'If your family didn't exist,' she said, 'we'd have to make them up.'

'What's that on the arm of your chair?' Nell leaned over nosily. An A4 page with a list of names on it lay under Maggie's mug. About a third of the names had been crossed out.

'Just a little hobby.' Maggie tidied the piece of paper under her Open University folder sheepishly.

'Margaret,' chided Nell, 'are you keeping secrets from me?'

'Would I do a thing like that?' Maggie's lined face was innocent.

'I mean it.' Tina sounded very sure. 'You don't look any fatter. Except when you wear your jeans.'

Nell was wearing her jeans so this wasn't as comforting as it might have been. 'But all that chocolate has to go some-where. It can't just vaporise. I can practically hear it laughing in my thighs.'

Tina suggested the obvious.

'Oh, be serious! Give up chocolate? Some people . . .' She sighed.

They were dawdling along the dusky street, talking about everything and nothing. 'Where's Marti tonight?'

'Filming another of those adverts.' Tina grimaced. 'They're so embarrassing.'

'*Hideous!*' concurred Nell. 'Prancing about with a wad of notes encouraging people to consolidate all their loans into one big unmanageable one and sign away their house to boot. *So* embarrassing.'

From the frosty silence Nell ascertained that it was fine for Tina to rubbish Marti's commercials, but deeply *un*fine for Nell to do it. 'Although they are . . . very well lit,' she added weakly.

'And they pay phenomenally well.' Tina recovered at the thought of the cheque. 'I've been slowing down when we pass estate agents.'

'Why? He's got that amazing loft.'

'Yeah, but if we . . . you know . . . we'll need a family house. Garden and that.'

'Are you any nearer to . . . you know?'

'God yes.' Tina nodded energetically. 'Well, no.' Perhaps the memory of Guildford had returned. 'The thing is, I'm just waiting. I'm getting good at it.'

'Don't get too good at it,' Nell recommended.

'Any day now he'll wake up, turn to me and say, "Marry me, Teen." I know he will. And in the meantime I'll get on with waiting. It's not such a bad life: flat stomach, lots of sex, you.' She slipped an arm through Nell's.

Nell didn't think Tina's description of her life sounded all that fulfilling. She squeezed her friend's thin arm. There was no helping Tina with this whole Marti thing but she could be there for her when it fell apart. Or when Tina got tired of waiting, whichever came first.

They were at the steps of Helping Hands and Nell had a rush of inspiration: perhaps Tina was just waiting to be asked? Perhaps she was sensing an emptiness in her life, just as Nell had? Strenuously casual, she asked, 'Do you, like, want to come in?'

'Jesus no.' Tina shuddered. 'I'm off home to dig out my boxed set of *Sex and the City*.'

Nell watched her until she turned the corner, jaunty in her chic coat.

'Here I am. On the jolly old dot.' Nell was so eager to please she almost clicked her heels but common sense prevailed. She needed to survive this review.

'Ah. Yes. There you are . . .' Phred was distracted, his hair curling on to his forehead in dark commas. 'Right.' He put his knuckles to his temples. 'It's all gone a bit pear-shaped in here tonight. Look, can you man Reception for a bit? Joy's not feeling very well.'

Nell could hear her not feeling very well: the sounds of

extravagant vomiting were audible all over Reception. 'Sure. Of course. My absolute pleasure.'

Phred gave Nell a funny look and rushed off with a towel. Nell parked herself behind the desk. She'd watched Joy handle the night crowd, but this was the first time she'd had to do it by herself.

They looked different, these days: they weren't just a mass of unwashed faces any more. She could spot at a glance the aggressive characters whose only way of expressing themselves was with loud strings of four-letter words. She could pick out the vulnerable ones, who looked tough but whose eyes glistened with old, remembered pain. She could still smell the fear that floated above their heads but somehow it didn't repel her any more.

It might seem like stating the obvious, but Nell had learned that people weren't born homeless: a thousand different paths had brought them to the door of Helping Hands. It had magicked the crowd back into individuals.

One of those individuals was towering over her now. A Geordie, built along the lines of those brick shithouses we hear so much about, he roared, 'I'm sick of being pushed around! Let me away to my bed *now*, woman!'

Nell's voice came out an octave higher than usual. 'Nobody's trying to push you around, sir. The dormitories aren't open for another couple of hours.'

'Y'auld fishwife!' he shouted accusingly. 'Don't push us around! I'm sick of being pushed around!'

A theme was emerging, but the last thing Nell wanted to do was push this drunken mountain around. 'I can't let you go upstairs yet,' she said, and added a twitchy 'Sorry.'

The rest of that night's guests had shrunk away subtly from the gigantic troublemaker. They eyed him and Nell with a mixture of unease and excitement.

'I TOLD YOU, YOU—' shouted the man, but he got no further.

Phred appeared, and stepped round to the public side of the counter. 'Hey, hey, come on, keep it down. People are doing very difficult crosswords in that office.'

The onlookers giggled nervously. The Geordie didn't giggle: his scowl could have curdled milk.

'It's too early to go to bed. My seven-year-old's still up.' Phred was inching himself and the man towards the door. 'Why not come back for your dinner? It's burgers tonight.' Phred manoeuvred the glowering giant across the hall, through a parting Red Sea of tatty clothing. His voice was good-humoured but firm, with none of the please-sir-don't-kill-me overtones of Nell's.

'Let the girl do her job, mmm? We'll see you in the basement later for a burger.' They were by the exit now.

There was a low growl, then the man caved in, accepted the inevitable and left. He even said, 'Ta-da,' genially to his audience.

A spattering of applause followed Phred back to the desk. 'Shucks, it was nothing,' he said good-naturedly. 'You all right?' he asked Nell, quietly.

'I'm fine. And, erm, thanks.' She really was grateful. For a moment she had been genuinely frightened of the big lout. 'That was cool,' she said admiringly. 'But of course I could have had him if he'd started anything.'

A mental image seemed to amuse Phred. 'Joy's a bit better,' he said. 'Ready for our chat?'

Nell's stomach lurched, as if she was in a lift hurtling down twenty floors. 'Yes!' she said toothily, and followed him out through the double doors, passing a distinctly below-par Joy.

'Sit down.' Phred indicated the chair, as if Nell had never seen one before and might be uncertain how to use it. He repeated, 'Sit down, sit down,' like a man who was unsure how to start. The clean lines of his face were blurred by tiredness. Nell almost felt sorry for him, until she remembered that she was the one in the firing line, and felt sorry for herself instead.

'Shall I get us a coffee?' she suggested. This tactic always helped to distract Louis.

'No, thanks.' Phred wasn't as easily sidetracked as the bearded one. He shuffled the papers in front of him like a newsreader and began reluctantly, in that deep, soothing voice of his which grated on Nell's ears just now like sandpaper. 'Nell, do you remember when you first came to see us I warned you not to over-commit?'

Nodding hard, Nell felt nostalgic for the Geordie bloke. 'If this is about the other night—' she leaped in, alibis and excuses bristling at the ready.

'Hang on, hang on.' Phred held up a hand. 'It is and it isn't.' Unlike Louis, he evidently didn't enjoy this part of his job. He toyed with one of Clover's Barbies, which was lolling on his desk. Nell found herself transfixed by his large hands round Barbie's surreally slender figure. 'You know by now how difficult it is when we're understaffed. The service suffers. And the people who need us suffer. They deserve better than that.' He left a gap for Nell to say something.

She chose to say, 'Indeed they do,' like a spinster librarian.

Phred turned Barbie upside down, exposing gingham knickers. 'The thing is . . .'

Nell watched poor Barbie somersault while Phred marshalled what must have been uncomfortable thoughts. 'The thing is, Nell, you've been in the papers recently.' He spoke in a rush, unlike his usual measured delivery. 'Look, your private life is your own business and I wish you all the best with this TV-presenter bloke, I really do. I don't want to comment on that, it's nothing to do with me, it's none of my business but—' Phred took a much-needed breath. 'When it affects Helping Hands it becomes my business.'

Nell's head was bent, as if she was expecting a swipe. 'Yes, it does.'

'It looks to me as if you're trying to keep a foot in two very different worlds. One is about looking beautiful, making money, publicity, and the other is about . . .' he smoothed down Barbie's dress, searching for an illustration of what Helping Hands was about '. . . feeding people like Bridie and Ted, who aren't in the least photogenic and smell of God knows what. We want to make a difference to the lives of people who have nobody else to care about them. Nobody can do that *and* be an It-girl.'

'I'm not an It-girl!' squeaked Nell. It was unfair: she wasn't rich, she wasn't thin and she didn't own a teeny-tiny dog – there was no way she could be accused of It-girlhood. 'Things aren't quite how they seem . . .' She faltered. She daren't tell Phred the whole ludicrous background to her high-profile relationship with Blair: the resultant smirk might kill him.

She found it difficult to admit, even to herself, that in the midst of this important and harrowing interview she could be amazed and thrilled that Phred had described her as 'beautiful'.

'I think the two worlds are incompatible.' Phred looked directly at Nell for the first time. 'When they overlapped you chose your other life.' He hesitated, then said firmly, 'You can't pick up and drop volunteer work when you feel like it.'

'That's a bit harsh.'

'Is it? None of our other volunteers go to parties when they're supposed to be here.'

'It *was* in aid of the starving . . .' Oooooh, how Nell wished she hadn't said that.

'It was a *party*, Nell. I saw the pictures in the paper the next day. Your boyfriend took his knickers off.'

Nell sighed. She couldn't argue with him. 'I know, I know. And, meanwhile, you were handing out real food to real people. You were getting ladle elbow and I was getting drunk.'

'I wouldn't put it quite like that.' He sat Barbie decorously on a box file. 'Actually, yes, I would.' He almost smiled.

Nell almost smiled back.

'Nell, I expect an awful lot from you and I can't offer you anything in return, except hard work with difficult people in difficult situations for no money and certainly no glamour. And a bad-tempered bastard of a manager to boot.' He raised an eyebrow at her laconically.

'I wouldn't say that.' Nell raised an eyebrow back. 'Actually, yes, I would.'

Phred almost smiled again. 'Fitzgerald, you're so damn . . .'

Nell was keen to discover just what she was so damn, but Phred didn't finish.

'I have to be honest. I don't know whether I can rely on you or not. And if I can't rely on you, there's no point in your being a volunteer.' His eyebrows caterpillared themselves into a long worried line. 'Is there?'

'There is.' Nell found her voice and it was emphatic. 'There is a point, Phred. I know I've made mistakes but I've learned from them.' This was true. For Nell, it was also novel. 'Helping Hands matters to me.' She struggled to explain. 'I had no confidence when I started here. I thought I'd end up dropping a shelf on an old lady or I'd poison Bridie at soup night. But I've learned that I'm not a completely useless member of society. I can make a difference. I *have* made a difference to Maggie, Phred, you know I have.'

Phred nodded without hesitation. 'Yes, she's much happier. I even saw her in the corner shop the other day. But your personal growth isn't Helping Hands' business. We're here for *other* people – not for us. It's not free therapy.'

Nell flinched. 'I *can* help others and I want to. It really, really means something to me.' A jagged edge cracked her voice. A tear was being born and Nell had to speak quickly before it emerged. 'Helping Hands is so important to me. You need people who feel as passionately as I do. Don't chuck me out. Phred, please, you took a chance on me before, and now I need you to take another.'

Nell had finished. She was an expert at saying too much and was determined not to this time.

Phred was troubled. He seemed to study every corner and crevice of the room without catching Nell's eye. Finally he stood up, his tall frame towering over her, and said, 'Well, all right. But, Nell, you've got to promise me—'

Nell interrupted with a heartfelt 'Anything.'

'Next time your two lives compete, we win.'

*   *   *

That evening flew by. 'I could have ladled on for hours!' Nell declared, as she walked out through the darkened reception area with Phred and Edith. She was dizzy with relief, and anxious to show Phred how indispensable she was.

Phred slowed, looking around him in the gloomy half-light. 'Are these flowers something to do with you, Fitzgerald?'

'Yes,' said Nell, proudly. 'I donated them. They cheer the place up.'

'Oi, can we have less chat and more action?' Edith could be quite narky when she was tired. 'Get your keys out, Phred.'

'Sorry, sorry.' Phred opened the door speedily and Edith was away on greased furry ankle boots. He scanned the dark street. 'You called a cab, didn't you, Nell? I'll wait with you.'

'No need.'

Phred ignored her and locked the doors behind them. He sat down on the steps, long legs folded like a grasshopper's.

Nell lowered her well-upholstered derrière to join him. The nuns at her various Catholic schools had engendered in her a deep fear of piles and she approached all cold ledges with trepidation. 'That breeze is soft for April,' she said. 'It's as if the year is just starting to think about summer.'

Phred nodded.

They sat in silence. The rush of traffic from the underpass reached them as a feathery swish. 'How's Clover?' asked Nell. She was being cunning, leading up to something that had been on her mind.

'Very, very Cloverish.' Phred smiled an inward sort of smile.

'I'm really sorry for asking her about her mum the other night.' Even mentioning it was like ripping the plaster off a graze. 'I didn't know.'

'No reason why you should,' said Phred, evenly. 'Don't worry. We talk about her all the time. You didn't do Cloves any damage.'

A lonely church bell, probably hemmed in by tower blocks, let them know it was midnight.

Perhaps emboldened by the darkness, Nell ventured, 'It can't be easy.'

'It's not,' agreed Phred, after a moment or two of staring down the street. 'But it's not that hard either.' That inward smile again. 'Clover and I are a team. She just forgets who's the boss sometimes.'

'Right.' Nell nodded, then asked innocently, 'Who is the boss?'

'It certainly wasn't me this morning. She went to school dressed as Spiderman. Couldn't talk or threaten her out of it.' Phred tilted his head to one side. 'She's like her mother. I could never get the better of her either.'

Nell said nothing. She was curious, for a stew of reasons, about the late Mrs Phred but this was delicate territory and she didn't want to trample in with her conversational hobnail boots.

But Phred wasn't finished. 'She died when Clover was two. It was very sudden. A car crash. Clover was in the car.' He saw Nell's shock. 'Yes, I know. I nearly lost her too. But she was lucky. And I was.' Phred turned his bunch of keys in his gloved hand. They chinked coldly. 'I had to rethink my whole life overnight. That was when I took over here. Complete change of career. I was in the City before.'

'You? Never!' Nell imagined him in a suit. The vision was quite appealing.

'The old me made loads of money for loads of faceless investors and hardly ever saw his family. Kirstie was always begging me to slow down, help her decorate the new house instead of working all hours.' Phred screwed up his eyes. Maybe he was watching out for Nell's cab, but she guessed he was staring back down the years at his wife. 'All of a sudden I had no choice.'

'Any regrets?'

'About leaving the City?' Phred chuckled. 'God, no. Best thing I ever did. Best thing for the worst reason. We talk about her, keep her alive, go out and fly a kite on her birthday.

It's almost all right when Clover's with me, but after she's gone to bed, it can be . . .'

Nell tensed as she listened. Phred wasn't histrionic, or even emotional. His tone was light and without heat, but she could feel the ache of loss between them in the night air.

'I'd just assumed she'd always be here.' He smiled ruefully at her, his teeth white in the midnight dark. 'There are lots of things to miss.'

Balding tyres squealed. Kwikkie Kabs' finest had arrived. It seemed a cruel point at which to end their chat. Reluctantly, Nell stood up. 'Well, g'night.'

'Safe home.' Phred held open the door for her.

The driver, from the distant land where Kwikkie recruited all its staff, said, in his distinctive accent, "E's a gennulman.'

'Yeah, he is a gennulman,' agreed Nell.

Nineteen

Weeks passed, and the year succumbed to summer. It took only a few short weeks to persuade Londoners, even the lumpy ones who should have known better, into shorts and flip-flops. Tables appeared on pavements outside cafés and in the royal parks the price of a 99 had rocketed. Days were stretching, and the pink evenings beckoned everybody out of doors after the house-arrest of the long, damp spring.

Nell hadn't missed another night at the centre, and she had baked a cake for any birthday boys and girls. She babysat every week for Carol, who was still drug-free and bad-tempered. Her friendship with Maggie was growing with the year and they regularly ventured out on sedate jaunts. She dared to feel that she was really doing some good.

Every morning Nell determined to confront her grand-mother about the divorce and every evening found a different excuse not to.

The pleas from Gareth, who claimed to be subsisting on baked beans and masturbation, continued, as did Nell's reso-lution to ignore them.

About twice a month, she was rolled out in a gaudy dress to hold Blair's sticky hand in public. She was getting used to it and was blasé about the bad photographs and the Paco Rabanne headaches. No exposé of Blair's real proclivities had been published, so Louis's master-plan seemed to be working.

London was blossoming all around her, but up in her opulent penthouse growbag, Nell didn't bloom. There could be no romance, or even an ill-considered snog, for a professional beard.

Twenty

Dressed for cocktails on a yacht, Tina leaned on the tea-stained kitchenette worktop and expressed the opinion that she was too good for this place.

Len happily agreed with her. He was preparing a decaff coffee for Davina, but his slavish devotion to one lady didn't mean he couldn't be gallant to another. 'Elegance and charm combined,' he said, with a bow of his greased head.

'Do you mind, Len?' said Tina. 'We're trying to have a private conversation here.'

'Ah. Of course. I'm sorry, ladies. Silly me.' Dejected, Len returned to the fray of the accounts department.

'Poor Len,' ventured Jane From Accounts.

'Like I said – private.' Tina raised a waxed eyebrow at Jane From Accounts, who reacted in a very Jane From Accounts kind of way by repressing a tearful sniff and wobbling off at speed.

'If you're going to be a cow, pick on someone your own size,' said Nell, disapprovingly. 'Me, for instance.'

'I like you. You don't annoy the pants off me,' said Tina, generously.

'Gee thanks. What *is* the matter with you? You've been like – well, like Louis all week.' Nell cast a scholarly eye over the low-cal hot-chocolate sachet selection.

'Nothing's wrong with me. At least, nothing that chopping Marti into tiny bits wouldn't solve.'

'Oh?' This note of disloyalty was unusual.

'Why can't he say the word "*love*"?' Tina's sarcasm dissolved into a babyish whine. 'What's so hard about that? He spends all his time with me. I make him laugh. I'm good to him. I *know* he loves me, so what's the problem with saying it? He doesn't even sign his Christmas cards "with love".'

Nell, who already knew that miserable little detail, nodded ruefully. She stayed dumb, guessing there was more.

'Now he says he can't come to my sister's wedding.' This much-discussed event promised to make the average royal nuptials look like a 'do' in a scout hut. 'Right at the last minute! And he's well aware I'm a fucking bridesmaid!' Everybody within a ten mile radius was well aware of it too.

Tina was on the verge of tears, which was rare.

'Is it because of his paranoia again?'

'Yes,' spat Tina. 'He's scared somebody will spot him in the wedding photographs.'

'Somebody who?'

'*Exactly!*' yelled Tina, effectively re-scaring away Jane From Accounts, who had come to relaunch her assault on the kettle.

Nell could have throttled Marti for making Tina so unhappy but there were no surprises in his behaviour.

Linda was fresh from a spot-check on staff bags. Unfortunately, Jean had a good reason for the stapler in her purse, but Linda was glowing with the thrill of the chase. 'No floral tributes this week?' Her all-seeing eyes swept the office.

'No.' Nell was relieved. She had neatly trotted from wanting Gareth to want her to not wanting Gareth to want her to a dull mixture of pity and irritation.

'Let's hope Gareth wasn't your last chance at happiness.'

'Did you want anything, Linda? Only I'm busy.'

'So I see,' said Linda, closing the copy of the *Puzzler* that lay open on Nell's blotter. 'I'm collecting for a staff birthday.'

'Linda, you're collecting for *my* birthday.'

'Maybe you'll be a little more generous than usual, then.'

Nell was mesmerised by Claudette's skilful dissection of a grapefruit with a silver spoon so Claudette had to ask twice. 'I said, my dear, what would you like for your birthday?'

'What? Oh, nothing, Claudette. You've done enough for me in letting me stay. I don't need a present.'

'Nonsense. What would you like?'

That tone was familiar. Nell racked her brain. Gifts from her grandmother tended to be hyper-expensive and rather useless. She remembered the silver-gilt grape scissors she'd received on her sixth birthday. 'Em, hmm, well, aaaaah,' she said.

'If you don't mind I shan't be buying you any clothes. The Parisianisation is coming along rather slowly. I notice you're wearing those appalling clogs this morning.'

'They're Scholls, Claudette. They're actually very trendy.'

'Trendy they may be, but you make a noise like a bargee in them.'

'I've got it! I know what I'd like!'

Claudette cocked her head.

'A donation to Helping Hands.'

'Isn't that rather dull, dear? How about some jewellery? It's such a shame you have no pearls.'

'A donation would be fine.'

'Are you being deliberately tiresome, Eleanor? They'll probably spend it on heroin addicts or single mothers or some such modern irritant. I'm offering you anything you want.'

'And I want a donation to Helping Hands, Claudette. It would make me very happy and do a lot of good.'

'Good.' Claudette examined the word and found it wanting. 'Pah.'

Again, there were no flowers waiting for Nell that day. Perhaps Gareth's given up, she thought, with relief.

Mid-morning she dialled the penthouse's number. She had begun to think that if it would make her aged grandmother happy to buy her pearls, she should let her. Fergus answered, 'The de Montrachet residence,' as if it were a funeral parlour.

Picturing him in his frock coat with Wagon Wheel smears on his chin, Nell asked to speak to her grandmother.

'I'm afraid Madame is sleeping.'

'But it's not time for her nap.'

'I can only repeat that she is sleeping.'

'OK. Thanks.' Nell put down the phone, puzzled. Claudette *never* went back to bed: she believed that people who were still in their dressing-gowns after eight a.m. should be branded. Perhaps it was divine intervention: it would be much better for Claudette's karma if she made a donation instead of buying pearls.

Nell wondered if her grandmother believed in karma. If she did, she was playing Russian roulette with her soul.

'This came for you.' Without looking up from her astrology magazine, Zoë lobbed a cardboard tube at Nell's head as she passed through Reception.

'Did you get any qualifications for being a receptionist?' Nell rubbed her forehead and bent down to pick up the tube.

'No, I'm a natural. Oh, and somebody rang for you.' Zoë squinted at her curly handwriting on a dog-eared Post-it. 'About something.'

'Good. Glad we cleared that up.' Nell strolled back to her office, past Barry the security guard, who was gleefully demonstrating to Jean how he could disarm a terrorist with a shoehorn if he had to.

'Ooh! Fancy!' Jean was saying appreciatively.

Gareth hadn't given up: he'd just changed tack.

'What do you mean?' asked Tina, clearing a space on Mario's corner table for the big sheet of stiff paper Nell had handed her. 'A charter? What's that?'

'It's a list of things that Gareth is willing to do, and *not* do, if I'll agree to go back to him.' She sighed down at the double portion of crumble in front of her: that was Gareth's fault. She also blamed the whipped cream on him. There was an Aero in her handbag, which was down to him too.

'This . . . is . . . incredible.' Tina was scanning the list. 'He's

215

a grown man, for fuck's sake. Does he really think . . . ?'

'Yes, he really does. He really thinks I'm that shallow.'

'Or that stupid.'

Gareth had used an antique-style font on heavy parchment to word-process his charter. It read:

To put an end to this silly business, I, Gareth Hope, promise to abide by the following guidelines if Nell Fitzgerald will resume being my girlfriend.

I promise not to:

- Laugh at Nell when she cries at *Titanic*
- Leave bits of toenail in the bath
- Say 'curry' every time Nell asks me what I'd like for dinner
- Tape over *Will & Grace* with the Grand Prix
- Request that Nell pretend to be Carol Vorderman during the sacred sexual act.

Furthermore, I promise to:

- Put my pants in the laundry basket and not on the coffee-table
- Remember all birthdays and anniversaries
- Throw out my valuable *Loaded* and *Maxim* archives
- Remember to video *Will & Grace* for Nell
- Phone Nell if I am unavoidably trapped in a pub after work.

'He didn't *really* ask you to be pretend to be C—'

'Yes, he did, and I want you never to allude to it again.'

'Right.' Tina reread the document. 'It says so much about him.'

'And all of it bad. Why won't he give up?'

'The crap ones never do,' said Tina philosophically.

*   *   *

A massive poster for St Petersburg vodka dominated the end of Patsy's road. Nell looked up at her half-brothers, twelve feet high and airbrushed to daunting perfection.

It had been Maggie's idea for her to turn up at the family home unannounced. 'You don't need an invitation,' she'd chided Nell. 'Take the initiative. *Seize the day.*'

So there she was, ringing the doorbell even though she still had a key.

'No!' shouted Patsy with delight, when she opened the door. 'No! It's never! Come in, come in, come in, come in!'

Nell picked her way down the hall over a minefield of gaudy plastic balls, ducks, cubes, playmats and, finally, by the kitchen door, little Annie. She picked up her goddaughter and said, 'I hope it's OK dropping in like this. Were you busy?'

'Me, busy? Of course I am, love, but it's always a tonic to see your face.' She cleared a pile of clothes from a chair. 'I'm just doing the ironing.'

'For the whole of the United Kingdom?' Every available surface was covered with clothes.

'I hate that fecking Dolce and Gabbana,' complained Patsy, unexpectedly. 'The twins get given all sorts of fancy gear now and the cost of it would turn your hair white. I'm always scared I'll scorch it, or flatten a bit that should be left wrinkled.'

'The sooner they get a place of their own, the better, eh?'

'Ah, no. I like looking after them.' Patsy picked up the iron. 'You were the only one who fled the nest early, Nell.'

'Yeah.' Nell didn't know quite what to say to that. Annie filled the gap by shouting, 'Eggoo!' imperiously.

'Yes, darlin', eggoo,' cooed Patsy. 'Will we have a bit of lunch, Nell? I've a lovely giant sausage roll going begging.'

Over the giant sausage roll and token salad leaf, Nell told Patsy about the divorce papers she'd seen.

'No!' yelled Patsy, even louder than before. 'Ah, the auld cow. Sorry, Nell, but she is.' Meditatively, she said, 'Poor

Phil. Never knew he had a father.' She collected herself. 'No need to waste sympathy on him, though. He wasn't exactly the best daddy in the world.'

'Maybe,' suggested Nell timorously, 'he might have been better at it if he'd had one of his own.'

The two women, lost in their own thoughts about the man they shared, were silent for a while, until Nell spoke again: 'I was thinking of trying to find Claudette's husband. My granddad.'

A whirlwind of Dublin patois met this idea, culminating in 'She'll skin him alive in front of you. I wouldn't cross Claudette – she has Satan on her side.'

'Satan would be too much of a wuss to work with her. Shouldn't I at least try?'

'You've asked my advice and it's to steer clear. You must do what you want to, but that's my opinion.' She pressed an expensive lapel without looking at it. 'But having kids has made me philosophical. You'll do what you like in the end, I know. Now, sit there while I tell you about what happened down the DNA clinic. I don't think they'll have us back in a hurry.'

'It's only a test, but let's all try and react as if it's real,' said Linda, through her mini-megaphone, as the office fire alarm jangled.

'OK.' Nell cleared her throat and said, 'Help, help, we're all doomed,' half-heartedly as she headed for the lift with the other good folk of Morgan Theatrical Management.

'Where are you all going?' asked Linda, caustically. 'I sincerely hope you're not heading for the lifts because if the fire reaches the lift shaft it could plummet to the ground and maim you all before your bodies burn.'

'Do you get asked out much?' muttered Nell, as everybody turned for the stairs, like a herd of disgruntled cows. Jean turned slower than the others, on account of her hip. 'Linda, surely Jean can take the lift as it's only a test?' she asked discreetly, once she had caught up with Linda, whose court shoes carried her along at quite a clip.

'We either take it seriously or we don't. Your choice.' Linda was brusque. The yoke of being Fire Warden was a heavy one.

'I choose we don't take it seriously and send Jean down in the lift.' They were on the fourteenth floor.

Linda braked abruptly, causing a pile-up of staff behind them. 'I only said it was your choice because I thought you'd make the right one,' she said crisply. 'I am Fire Warden and if Jean goes in that lift it makes a mockery of my position.' She glared at Nell.

Nell, who had been out-glared only that morning by Fergus, wasn't about to lose again. 'I'm sure you could cope. Jean has a new hip.'

'I wish I had a new hip,' scoffed Linda.

'It doesn't matter. I don't mind.' Jean hobbled along on her two flat feet. 'Honest.'

'*We* mind, don't we?' Nell looked to the others for support. Zoë looked blank. Dean was listening to gangsta rap on his headphones. Jane From Accounts was crying.

'Let Jean go in the sodding lift, Linda, or we'll all hate you for ever,' Tina said nonchalantly.

Linda switched her glare to Tina, then something seemed to snap in her tense frame. She lifted the megaphone and shrieked, 'GO IN THE LIFT JEAN!' shaking from head to foot. 'GO ON!' she yelled, as Jean meekly hesitated. 'APPARENTLY YOU HAVE THE MOST IMPORTANT HIP IN THE WORLD SO GET IN THE LIFT!' She stormed off towards the stairs, still venting her rage through the megaphone. 'PLEASE DON'T LISTEN TO ME, ANYBODY! WHATEVER YOU DO DON'T LISTEN TO LINDA! SHE JUST WORKS NIGHT AND DAY TO HELP YOU ALL BUT DON'T WORRY ABOUT THAT. IN FACT, EVERYBODY GO IN THE LIFT!'

As they sheepishly trailed down fourteen flights behind the manic Linda in her noisy heels, little was said. Zoë had stuffed her fist into her mouth and Tina was exchanging surprised and, it has to be said, delighted looks with Nell. They could talk about this for months. No – years.

Outside, Linda stood apart from her colleagues with a stoic look on her face. 'We'll pay for this,' prophesied Barry, squinting into the sun under his peaked nylon cap.

'I'm so sorry.' Jean didn't relish her position in the eye of the storm.

'What have you got to be sorry about?' Nell draped an arm round her. 'We love you, Jeanie, that's why we didn't want you traipsing down the stairs.'

'Besides, we would have had to wait for you all the way down,' Tina murmured.

Nell gave her a shove and they moved away from the little crowd. 'You've had a secretive look on your mush all day. What gives, fashion girl?'

'Marti and I had a leetle talk last night . . .' Tina looked at her meaningfully.

'And? *And?*' Nell tugged her friend's arm excitedly.

'*And* he's booking two weeks in the Caribbean as I speak.' Tina looked historically smug. 'I am buying me a bikini like you have never seen.'

'Oh.' That development was a disappointment after the build-up. 'So it's all OK now?'

'What's all OK?'

'You and Marti. You were pretty upset the other day about—'

'Oh, me and Marti are always OK.' Tina batted that line of questioning right across the carpark. 'The *Caribbean*, Nell!'

'We can go back in now,' said Linda, through thin lips. 'Those of us who didn't die a horrible death in the lift, anyway.'

'She loves her work,' said Jean, indulgently.

The beaded dress was out on the town again, with Nell inserted in it.

'Opera?' Blair had said scornfully, when briefed about

their next date. 'Overdressed fat people shouting their heads off?'

Nell guessed that he got enough of that sort of thing at home and pointed out that it was a special benefit performance for a cancer organisation. 'Besides, Blairy, we don't have any choice.' She had taken to calling him Blairy in the hope that a nickname might endear him to her.

She gazed up at him with the requisite devotion as they stood in the foyer of the Royal Opera House and had to accept that nothing could endear Blair to her. The more she got to know him, the more she ached to get away from him. As for the way he felt about Nell – she was certain he wouldn't notice if she imploded.

Resplendent in black tie, Louis beetled through the crush. Davina, statuesque in flowing emerald green chiffon, followed him. 'My darlings!' Louis hugged and kissed them both with extravagant fondness. You would never have guessed that two hours earlier he had loudly described Nell as a useless wank-rag for forgetting to book his Indian head massage. 'How wonderful to see you!'

'Great look, Davina,' said Nell, enviously, admiring the happy marriage of Davina's killer form and a well-cut dress.

'Thank you.' Davina rearranged her chiffon stole artfully. 'Do you like the opera?'

'I'd rather make love to Bernard Manning,' admitted Nell, 'but I'm relying on these to get me through.' She rattled the large box of Maltesers she'd bullied Blair into buying for her. 'Is Louis looking after you?'

Davina bent down to whisper, 'A little *too* well.' She smiled conspiratorially at Nell. 'Unfortunately for him, I'm going to develop the most awful headache during the opera so I'll be unable to join him at his hotel for drinks afterwards.'

'What a shame.' Nell pulled a sad face. 'Can I watch when you tell him?'

Davina winked. She was a real asset to Morgan Theatrical Management.

A rank mixture of body odour and cigar smoke announced the arrival of Gerry Hollywood in their midst. 'How cosy. Blair and Nell with their Cupid.' He eyed Louis wryly. 'Got a quote for me?'

'What do you think? Should we tell him?' Louis looked at Nell and Blair, who stared idiotically back at him. He took this as encouragement. 'Gerry, don't be surprised if you hear the sound of wedding bells some time soon.'

A button popped on Blair's fancy waistcoat. Nell's stomach contracted to the size of a grape. Gamely they managed to retain their fixed smiles.

'We can trust you not to breathe a word?' Louis tried to put a short arm round Hollywood's vast back in an avuncular fashion.

'Who would I tell?'

'If it's not funny, why are you laughing?' asked Nell, reasonably.

Tina, who was bent double under the towel machine in the ladies', honking like a goose, squeezed out, 'Oh, it's not funny. Really it's not. I'm a horrible, horrible person for laughing. I'm sorry . . .'

'You're not a bit sorry.' Nell looked with anguish at the gossip page. '"Wedding Nells For Blair",' it screamed. The only people Hollywood had told were his millions of readers. 'I can't go on. I can't face the world. I'll take all my calls in here. Until I die.'

Zoë poked her head around the door. 'Your mum's on the phone.'

Nell groaned loud and deep. The toilet acoustics made it sound like a message from hell.

It took a while to persuade Patsy that the reporter had got it wrong. 'But it's in the paper!' she had insisted. 'It must be true!' Nell felt quite guilty scuppering her mother's plans for finding a fancy hat at Oxfam.

When Louis appeared at eleven o'clock, smiling and exchanging witty banter with his staff ('You're sacked, Dean! No, you're not! Ha-ha!'), Nell scowled blackly at him.

'Darling, darling, darling,' he chanted. 'Am I not a genius?'

'A genius?' That wasn't on the long list of adjectives Nell had been rehearsing since yesterday evening.

'Hollywood didn't even mention you in his column last week. This week you're the headline!'

'Louis, you're meddling with my life.' Nell's voice shook.

'Yes,' Louis agreed blithely. 'Isn't it fun? Oh, go on, darling, laugh. It's funny. Remember funny?'

'No. I don't remember anything before last night. Not only did I have to sit through three hours of Italian shouting, I had to come to terms with being engaged to – to—'

'A star, who happens to make us an obscene amount of money. Don't fuss, darling. It'll be all right. We'll announce the break-up at the end of the summer and that'll be that. I'll negotiate you a six-figure kiss'n'tell and send you somewhere hot for two weeks. I'll even pick up your mini-bar bill. I can't say fairer than that, can I?'

One of the tragedies of being Louis was that he genuinely couldn't.

Every dingy scrap of London grass becomes hot property the moment the sun comes out. Soho Square is only about forty yards across but when the surrounding offices belch out their workers at lunchtime most of them head for it. Tina and Nell picked their way through strewn bodies, searching for a tiny patch to colonise. 'It's like a radiation disaster,' complained Tina, holding aloft their ciabattas. 'Careful! There's a particularly fruity tramp coming up on the left.'

'Hi, Kev,' said Nell, to the grime-encrusted teenager stretched out as if he was on the sands of St Tropez.

'All right, Nellie.'

Tina shook her head in disbelief, then speeded up. She reached a tiny clearing just ahead of a pair of girls, who looked ready to put up a fight for it until Tina treated them to a full-on look and a 'Well?'

As they slunk away Nell said, 'There's no need to be like that. But I'm glad you are.' She knelt on the stubbly grass. 'Summer,' she sighed dreamily, and added, 'in London,' as she weeded out the cigarette ends and lolly sticks.

'Here.' Tina handed over Nell's lunch. 'How can you bear to have chicken *and* tuna *and* pastrami in the same sandwich? You could at least have asked them to hold the mayo.'

'The day I use the words "hold the mayo" is the day they can bury me.'

'It might also be the day they finally get you into a size ten.' Tina sniggered. 'You should really be dieting to get into your wedding dress.'

'Shut right up,' warned Nell. In a low voice she said, 'I think I just heard those people over there say Blair's name. Do you think they recognise me?'

'Who cares?'

'Me. Can we get this straight once and for all? I am not you. I don't want to be famous. I don't want to be recognised when I'm necking my lunch. I hate it.'

'It won't last for ever.' Tina lay back gingerly on the mangy grass. 'Sorry if I sound unsympathetic. I know how you must be feeling.'

'Liar.'

'Actually,' pondered Tina, '*nobody* knows how you must be feeling. You're possibly the first case in history of a girl who is artifically engaged to a bright orange quizmaster.' She paused. 'Imagine the kids.'

Nell had to laugh. 'Tiny satsuma-coloured babies. With mascara.'

'Do you know what I miss?' asked Tina, suddenly, from her prone position.

'No. What?'

'You.' Tina sat up again. 'We don't go out half as much as we used to. You're always at Helping Hands or Maggie's, or out with Blair, or tidying up somebody's garden or painting a community centre or something. We used to do things together in the old days before you were good.'

'We used to get pissed together.'

'So?' Tina was defensive. 'It was fun. Or is fun not allowed for goody-goodies like you?'

'Believe it or not, the things I do for Helping Hands are fun.' Nell chased a piece of tuna down her chin with her tongue.

Tutting, Tina dabbed her with a paper napkin. 'You're covered with mayo. How can painting a community centre in the arse end of nowhere be *fun*?'

'It was. Joy came, and Phred brought Clover, and we all got plastered with paint, and we sat and ate ice-cream on our break, and Clover sang songs for us. It was fun.' She smiled at the memory. 'And when we'd finished, the old people of Holborn – *not* the arse end of nowhere – had a new place to meet their friends.'

'Remind me to pick you up a halo at Prada.'

Nell didn't expect Tina to understand. For that reason she still rarely spoke about Helping Hands. She often doubted how effective her good-doing really was, but Tina was not the person to mull it over with. 'Don't bother. I'll wait until Topshop bring out a copy.'

When the sandwiches had been eaten, and Linda's new sundress had been remembered and laughed at, Tina asked, 'How do you go about volunteering?'

'Why?' asked Nell, suspiciously, anticipating a joke. They were both lying down now, squinting up at the square tile of sky that central London allows its inmates.

'I can't beat them,' said Tina, with resignation, 'so I might as well join them.'

'You?' Nell was incredulous.

'Aren't you pleased?' Tina asked peevishly.

Nell channelled Phred to her: 'It's quite a commitment.'

'I don't want to do as much as you.' Tina shuddered. 'Just the odd thing here and there.'

'It's very, erm, *real*.'

'I wasn't born in Harvey Nichols, you know,' bleated Tina. 'Look, just think of something for me to help with that you'll be doing too. I don't want to do anything on my own.'

It was a half-hearted way to volunteer and Nell could see that it was for dubious reasons. The sensible Phreddish response would have been to tell Tina so, but Nell had one of her brainwaves. Somehow experience had not taught her to be wary of these: they usually culminated in having to say elaborate sorrys to long queues of people. Nonetheless she suggested, 'You can help with the summer picnic!'

'That doesn't sound too gritty.'

'Every summer Helping Hands organises this big picnic in the park for the staff and any regulars who want to go. This year we're pairing up with Clover's school, so there'll be a pile of under-tens as well. Apparently Phred's suggested a barbecue, so we need people to help with that and hand out food and stuff. You could do that, couldn't you?'

'Will there be alcohol?'

'Oh, Teen, that's not really the attitude . . .'

'Sorry, sir. Won't do it again, sir.' Tina poked Nell in the ribs. 'Loosen up. Of course I can barbecue and hand out food. Count me in.'

A cloud drifted over the sun and everybody in the square shivered.

Twenty-one

'I'm going to look for him.'

One of the delicious things about Maggie was the way she always knew what Nell was talking about. 'Good. A man should know he has a granddaughter like you.' She handed Nell her straw bag as they stood on the doorstep. 'How will you go about it?'

Nell had no idea.

But Maggie did. 'Next time you come round, we'll make a start,' she said.

Another old lady. Another sofa. This evening there was no cosy chat over cracked mugs. Among the silks and satins of the drawing room, Claudette was teaching Nell how to play bridge. 'Such an asset for a young woman. You meet the most eligible men across a bridge table.'

It was pointless to explain that no bridge was played at the sort of parties Nell went to. She had once met a sexy guitarist on a Twister mat but the relationship had fizzled out before the other partygoers had disentangled them. 'Erm,' Nell said, over and over again, as she stared unseeingly at her cards. It was the night before the Helping Hands picnic and she really should have been making sandwiches. Claudette had insisted that Carita make them, which didn't seem fair to Nell.

Fergus inserted his liveried self into the drawing room. 'There is a gentleman at the door for you, Nell.'

Something about the way his usually impassive features were set alarmed Nell. 'Who?' she asked. Then added, 'Or is it whom?'

On this occasion Fergus was unconcerned with grammar. 'He says his name is Gareth.'

'Gawd,' mumbled Nell, and jumped up.

'Why don't we ask Fergus to show him in?' said Claudette, graciously.

'The young man appears to be intoxicated,' said Fergus, his nose lifted to a record height.

'Great. I'll deal with him, Claudette,' she promised, and raced down the hallway. She opened the heavy front door a chink, the chain still on. Even the sliver of Gareth she could see didn't bode well. He was wearing the rugby shirt and baggy shorts he slept in. Both items looked as if he'd worn them to roll in the park. A bottle of whisky stuck out of a pocket. Nell sighed. 'What are you doing here?' she hissed, somewhat redundantly. It was obvious what he was doing there: he was being pissed.

'Come back to me!' Gareth howled.

His voice reverberated in the marble hallway. Nell could imagine the stuck-up neighbours pressing their ears to their doors. 'You're embarrassing me,' she told him. 'Go home and sleep it off. I won't talk to you while you're like this.'

'Why not? Not good enough for you? Not *famous* enough?' Gareth wobbled as if he was on an invisible unicycle and attempted to force all fifteen stone of himself through the inch-wide opening. 'LET ME IN!' he roared.

Behind her, Fergus, unruffled, asked, 'Do you want me to call the police?'

'No, of course not. He wouldn't hurt a fly. He's just . . . noisy.' God, was Gareth noisy! He could bellow like a bull with piles. 'Ssh,' she whispered ineffectually. 'Please go home, Gareth.'

As an answer Gareth hurled himself against the door. The chain tautened, but held. Nell leaped back with a squeak. Gareth threw himself again, and the door creaked painfully.

'What *is* going on?' Claudette had joined them, her face a portrait of aristocratic alarm.

'Step back, Madame.' Fergus spoke to her with authority. 'I will deal with this.'

Nell backed away from the beleaguered door. Gareth continued to fling himself at it with loud grunts of fury. She felt so impotent. She'd never seen him like this before. 'Maybe,' she said reluctantly, 'we should call the police.'

'As I said, I'll deal with it. Stand back against the wall, if you please, ladies.' Fergus stepped forward and, as Gareth gathered himself for another lunge, opened the door wide.

Gareth hurtled over the threshold and flew down the hall at speed. He crashed into a dainty table, which collapsed under him. Only in cartoons do people get up after this sort of accident, but the Jack Daniel's in his bloodstream seemed to have given him a *Tom and Jerry*-style tolerance. He bounced up and galloped back up the hall towards Nell.

Fergus sighed and stood in front of her.

'No, Fergus! Get out of his way!' gabbled Nell, terror-stricken. One Gareth equalled three Ferguses and, besides, a life spent buttling doesn't prepare a man for a fight the way a life spent playing rugby does.

Gareth tore wildly up to where Fergus stood, statue-like. He raised his hands to push the butler out of the way and his unprotected chin met a perfect right hook delivered in a white glove. Gareth staggered a few feet back and dropped to the parquet.

'Good Lord, Fergus!' Even the elegantly languid Claudette was galvanised by this display. 'Where on earth did you learn to do that?'

'One picks these things up, Madame.' Fergus was flexing his fingers. A punch like that (to a chin like that) had to hurt the puncher as well as the punchee. 'If you would like to retire to the drawing room, ladies, I will dispose of this unwelcome guest.'

'I'll do it,' said Nell, hastily, from where she knelt over Gareth. Fergus just might put him down the waste-disposal if left to his own devices. She slapped Gareth's face ineffectually, and wobbled his fleshy jaw. She had seen people do this in films – all of Nell's first-aid skills were gleaned from films: she knew, for instance, that to calm down a screaming twenties flapper it was best to deliver a resounding slap across the chops with a firm 'You're hysterical, Daphne!'

Gareth wasn't responding with a dull grunt and an 'Uh? Where am I?' the way he was supposed to. He was out cold, taking great snoring breaths that reeked of whisky.

'Gareth?' she said. Then, 'Gareth!' more firmly. He didn't stir. 'We'll let him come to and then I'll take him home in a taxi.'

'I forbid it!' Claudette had sunk to a gilt chair. Her voice sounded thinner than normal, almost reedy. 'Do you hear me? You are not to leave this house with that hooligan.'

'This isn't how it seems, Claudette.' Nell scurried over to her grandmother and knelt in front of her. 'He's broken-hearted. He really wouldn't hurt me. I know what I'm doing, I promise. I'll be fine.'

Claudette wore a wretched look that Nell had never seen before. Her composed face had sagged and she looked her age. 'I can't fight you,' she said eventually. 'The young do what they want. That's how it is. Fergus . . .'

Without being asked, Fergus helped Claudette to her room. He threw a look of undeniable anger at Nell as he walked his mistress down the long hall.

'Look what you've done!' Nell dealt Gareth a gentle kick. He snored some more.

Nell had thought she'd seen the last of her old bedroom in the eaves. She staggered through the door, somehow supporting Gareth's bulk. They tangoed erratically to the bed and she let him drop on to it. 'Gnnurrh,' he said.

'And gnurrh to you too, mate,' muttered Nell.

She was incandescently angry with him. Silent until now, she let rip with a torrent of complaint as she paced the bedroom. 'What did you think you were doing, you useless lump?' During their relationship Nell had never shouted so loudly or so candidly at him, but she wasn't afraid of him now. Plus, he was unconscious. 'How bloody dare you put my grandmother, an old lady, through such a scare? She's taken to her bed 'cos of you. Fergus could have broken his hand. You'll have to pay for the table you smashed and I warn you it'll be pricey. And me? Do you ever think about how I might feel? Do you think I want a drunken buffoon banging on my door?'

Hands on hips, Nell stood over the messy bundle of dirty clothes she used to live with. 'And that taxi ride! Manhandling an ape like you on to the seat, then trying to stop you rolling off it all the way to Twickenham. And I had to help the taxi-driver get you to the front door. As for heaving you up the stairs – I don't think I'll ever be the same again.' She beat his head with a pillow. It was curiously satisfying. 'Why did you do it, you idiot? What part of no didn't you understand?'

Nell stopped. Gareth was fully awake now. He had put his arms over his head to protect himself from her onslaught and his muscular frame was quaking with sobs.

Nell wished she could take back the kick, the pillow and the abuse. 'Don't!' she begged, crawling alongside him on the bed. 'I don't want you to cry, Gareth.'

'Then come home,' he whispered, and folded her into his arms.

It was warm there. It always had been. It smelt too, but that didn't seem to matter. Suddenly Nell relaxed, as if all her bones were melting to jelly. She laid her head on his shoulder. It fitted, as it always had. She closed her eyes.

Six a.m. was rosy and sleepy. Nell came round slowly, feeling the bed shift as a newly showered Gareth crawled back into it. He took up his previous position, enfolding her in the circle of his arms. 'Feels good, doesn't it?' he asked gently.

'Yes.' One of Nell's afflictions was her incurable honesty.

Yes, it did feel good, but that wasn't the whole story. It also felt wrong. 'I have to go.'

'No, no, no. Stay.' He kissed her cheek. 'Stay, Nell.' He kissed the shoulder he'd exposed by tugging down the sleeve of her T-shirt. 'You're home.'

Home. Nell shut her eyes. She wasn't sure what that word meant to her any more. It wasn't Claudette's house. It wasn't Patsy's house. Once she had thought it was this awkwardly shaped room with this awkwardly shaped man.

Gareth was kissing her neck with a warm, open mouth. Unexpected messages were popping from her nerve endings that they liked it. Nell's body was overriding her mind and she let it. But she didn't open her eyes once.

There was an indecent spring in Gareth's step as he bounced off to the kitchen, leaving Nell mummified in the duvet.

When he returned with a mug of coffee she hadn't stirred. She held out her hand. 'Oh. Did you want one?' He clambered back into bed, unwrapping her as he did so. 'I'll get you one in a minute. Budge up, Big-bum, make some room.'

The portable at the end of the bed jumped into life and lit up Nell's pale face with the gaudy colours of Saturday-morning television.

Gareth tousled her hair so roughly her scalp hurt. 'It's like you've never been away.'

Twenty-two

As they waited for Phred to pick them up in the minibus, Nell and Maggie shared a fortifying sherry in Maggie's front room. 'You're sure you really want to come?' asked Nell, not for the first time. They'd made several short forays out into the big wide world together, but a whole afternoon at the annual picnic might be too much for an old lady who'd got used to staying indoors.

'Yes. Now, stop worrying and let me enjoy it.' Maggie looked slyly at Nell over her glass and returned to their earlier topic. 'So, you succumbed to his blandishments?'

'I succumbed. Boy, did I ever succumb,' said Nell. Gareth's blandishments had been both familiar and brand new. It had been so long since she'd made love with him – with anyone – that it had felt like returning to a place she'd holidayed in years before. The scenery brought back memories and the local dish was surprisingly nice. Unfortunately, the analogy had to be stretched to encompass the sad fact that the more Nell saw of the sights, the more she remembered why she'd burned her passport. 'It was a big mistake.'

'If you're going to make mistakes, make them big,' said Maggie, comfortably. 'Anybody can make one of those piffling mistakes. How did you leave things with the poor boy?'

Nell groaned. 'Dooooon't call him that!' She recalled the lustre of satisfaction all over Gareth's considerable body, the sleepy happiness on his face. 'I told him about the picnic. He kind of, sort of, somehow presumed that I'm going back to his after it . . .' Nell sighed. 'Can you kill yourself with sherry if you drink enough of it?'

'Probably.' Maggie poured another minuscule glassful. 'I

hope you're not leading him up the garden path, Nell.' If there was such a thing as a stern twinkle, Maggie was pulling it off.

'I didn't mean to,' whined Nell.

'And you an engaged woman . . .'

'Oh, don't, Maggie. I wish I could take last night back. At first it felt right for some reason. Like going home. I haven't really found my feet since I left him, you see.'

'Really?' Maggie looked as if she could comment, but she said nothing. She was watching Nell's face carefully.

'Really,' answered Nell, without giving it any thought. She was too busy wincing at the memories of earlier. Gareth's large hands had left ghostly marks on her. After the initial rush of desire his touch had triggered, she had tried to slow him down. Gareth had thundered on, pushing past her protests. She had remembered, too late, how lonely she felt in bed with Gareth. His orgasm was epic, hers synthetic.

A car horn tooted vulgarly in the street. Nell pulled the lace curtain aside. 'Oh. Dexter's driving.'

'Who's Dexter?' asked Maggie, stuffing sandwiches into a carrier-bag.

'Phred's brother.'

Maggie peered through the curtains, then reached for her bifocals. 'If I was sixty years younger . . .' She glanced slyly at her companion. 'Of course, dear, you *are* sixty years younger.'

The park was as much countryside as Nell could comfortably withstand. She relished the abundance of trees, flowers, lakes and the arching sky overhead, while appreciating the proximity of policemen, photo booths, chiropodists and all the many blessings of urban life. Nature was a good thing, she knew, but it was best nibbled at.

As she helped Edith and Dexter lay out the donated food on a long trestle table, she could see the wobbly outlines of cars snaking along in the heat of the distant road. Above her, camouflaged in the boughs of a massive oak, birds sang lustily. They seemed unaware of the dreadful wrong turning their lives had taken leaving them immured in the city instead of being as free as, well, a bird in the open countryside.

Below, at the bottom of a gentle slope, a game of rounders had broken out. Homeless people, volunteers and teachers from Clover's school had divided into two large, not very energetic teams. A lot more sprawling about than running was going on.

'Who brought these?' Edith held up a crustless cucumber sandwich so thin that the June sun shone straight through it.

'Me. Sorry.' Carita's idea of a sandwich differed from the average homeless person's. Or the average Nell's.

Dexter snatched it and swallowed it in one. 'Very nice,' he commented, as Edith hit him with a tea-towel. 'My contribution.' He upended a Sainsbury's bag.

'They're all BLTs,' said Nell, starting to unwrap them.

'I like BLTs,' Dexter explained, with the postscript of a quite unnecessary wink.

Is he flirting with me? thought Nell, arranging them in a pleasing pattern on a foil platter. She glanced at Dexter, who was balancing another of her thin sandwiches on his nose, with one eye on her to make sure she was witnessing this feat. *Yes. He bloody is*.

Nell patted her hair and wished she'd washed it. She was spoken for twice over at the moment but both those 'relationships' didn't merit the title.

Besides, she reminded herself as she lobbed a Wotsit in Dexter's direction, nobody ever died of flirting.

The Wotsit hit, Dexter fell over and dragged Nell on top of him when she went to help him up. That was how she came to be rolling about, giggling hysterically, in the grass with him when his brother blocked out the sun by standing over them.

'Good. Glad to see you two are getting on,' he said.

Nell jumped up as if she'd been caught behind the bike sheds. 'Just . . . testing the grass,' she offered.

'And it's OK, is it? asked Phred.

'It's top fucking notch.' Dexter remained stretched out.

'Glad I asked you to help, Dex. I can see you're going to be invaluable.' Phred kicked his brother gently and turned to Edith. 'When do you want me to light the barbecue?'

'You mean you haven't lit it yet?' The tea-towel scored another hit. 'It should be warmed up by now! I thought you said you were good at barbecuing?'

'I said I'd done it once.'

'That's not what you said,' persisted Edith, darkly.

'Oooh. Phred's in trouble,' said Nell, under her breath.

'Go and play rounders, Fitzgerald,' ordered Phred, fannying about with a very long firelighter by the coals.

Something about the way he was standing helplessly by the barbecue touched Nell. It was unusual to see the great St Phred confounded. She found herself staring at him, a little half-smile teetering on her face.

Phred glanced up and met her gaze. For some reason he seemed troubled by it. Then he wiped a hand over his face and said, mock-sternly, 'Take this woman away, Dexter. She seems to have nothing better to do than watch a grown man do battle with meat products.'

'Let's check out the game.' Dexter sprang to his feet and held out a hand to Nell.

She took it and was whisked down the hill.

'Careful!' shouted Phred after them. 'She's somebody else's, you know!'

Being a bloke, Dexter wanted to get involved with the *ad hoc* rounders. Being a Nell, Nell didn't. Instead she looked out for familiar faces. She couldn't see Tina – it was unlike her to be late.

Maggie's bottom overwhelmed the camping chair she had nabbed, but she seemed comfortable enough, sitting between Joy and Joy's boyfriend, an impressively dull bloke who wore socks with his sandals. He was talking non-stop, as dull people are inclined to do. He made an odd match for Joy, who was wearing a sundress so bright and so abbreviated that Phred's voice had risen an octave when he'd said, 'Hello,' to her earlier.

The heart makes incomprehensible choices. Nell smiled to herself. Then she recalled the choice her heart had made the evening before and blushed. It hadn't been her heart: a totally different part of her anatomy had made that stupid decision.

Bridie was stepping up to bat, neat and respectable in navy Chanel, courtesy of Claudette's bin. With impeccable white cuffs and collar, she looked like a Knightsbridge lady. Until you got closer and saw the twigs in her hair.

'We're dying of hunger!'

Clover and her schoolfriends had surrounded Nell, complaining piteously. Some were kids with Downs, others weren't, but they were all emitting the high-pitched squeal copyrighted to girls under ten. 'Twenty more minutes and then you can eat until you explode,' promised Nell. This pleased them, if the banshee squeals were anything to go by. As they galloped off, Nell spotted Hayley and Leonardo trailing after them. They were both dressed like Gap adverts, their blond hair shining in the sun. If they were there, then that meant . . . '*Carol!*' shouted Nell, waving to where her favourite crack addict sat cross-legged with Carly on a rug. She walked across and giggled at the slurping noise Carly was making as she drank her milk.

'I didn't know we had to, like, bring stuff. I didn't bring any sandwiches or that,' Carol said uncertainly.

'You didn't have to. There's plenty to go round.'

'Yeah I know but . . .' Most humans are sixty per cent water but Carol was sixty per cent pride. She looked glowingly well, and sexy, in her white cropped trousers and little vest. If only her expression lived up to her outfit: her mouth was turned down defiantly, despite the cherry-coloured gloss.

'Is it going OK?' asked Nell, inanely.

'You know,' answered Carol.

'Yeah,' said Nell, who didn't. 'See you at the sausages?'

Taken by surprise, Carol laughed.

Nell had spotted somebody else she wanted to see. Anita was sitting a little apart from the others, hunched in even more layers than usual despite the sunshine. She was sucking at a roll-up and rocking to and fro. Nell sprawled beside her. 'Hiya.'

'All right.' Anita continued to rock. She was pale.

Since the Night of the Cake, Nell had taken a special interest in her. Phred made it clear that he didn't like volunteers having favourites, but that kind of cold common sense gave Nell hives and she ignored it. 'What's new? Any luck with getting on the council list?'

'Blah blah fucking blah.' The tone was a slap in the face. 'Just listen to you – "Any luck with the council list,"' Anita mimicked her. 'What do you know?'

Hurt, Nell knew Anita was being a cow and bit her tongue – but that bitter tone wasn't the usual Anita. She lay back in the sun and could almost hear the blood travelling round her body. 'I suppose I don't know much, but I'm interested.'

'Happy to be of service,' spat Anita. 'At least I'm interesting.' She dragged the last ounce of life from the roll-up and flicked it away.

'Yeah.' Nell risked a joke. 'You're fascinating. Especially now.'

Anita flung her a sharp look but she unfolded herself and lay back beside Nell, exhaling heavily. 'I'm in the shit,' she said, in a small voice.

The story she told was dreary and timeless. Anita moved from hostel to hostel. Like Helping Hands, most places had a policy of letting people stay two or three nights and regulars passed each other like pawns on a big grubby chessboard.

A manager at one of the larger hostels had taken a special interest in Anita. He looked out for her, offered her a shoulder to cry on. She soon realised that it wasn't the only part of his anatomy on offer. 'I don't fancy him. He's *old*,' she said, gazing beseechingly at Nell. 'But now he's leaning on me.'

'To . . . ?' Nell didn't know how to put it.

Anita did. 'Shag him,' she said succinctly. 'He's putting it around that I'm a drunk and a junkie and I nick anything that's not nailed down. I'm getting turned away from places. I've had to sleep in Topshop's doorway a few times.'

'Oh, Anita,' murmured Nell.

'If I give in what does that make me?'

'You won't have to give in.'

Anita ignored her. 'What a life. What a fucking so-called life.'

'Anita,' Nell grabbed her arm, 'sex isn't currency. You only have sex when you want to.'

'*You* only have sex when you want to,' said Anita.

Gareth's face popped to the head of the queue in Nell's brain. She could have debated the point, but perhaps now wasn't the moment. This was a critical time for Anita. A roll of imaginary drums started in Nell's head. What she said and did now was important. She wasn't protecting some bloated star's career: this was about Anita's self-esteem. 'You'd better stay at Helping Hands tonight.'

'Can't. I've been there the past three nights. I've run out of places to go.' Anita pulled her knees up to her chin again. 'I can't face another night out of doors,' she whispered.

'You'll be safe tonight.' Nell stood up and brushed the grass off her jeans. It was reckless to make such a promise and she knew it. 'Trust me,' she heard herself say.

'Yeah.' Anita closed her eyes. 'Sure.'

Phred was concentrating on a host of chipolatas as if they were going to tell him something. They spat and he frowned. 'Do these look done to you?' he asked Edith – every twenty seconds.

As Nell foiled a commando raid on the table by two hunger-crazed seven-year-olds, she saw Tina crest the brow of a hillock. She stopped mid-hurl, with a child suspended in the air, to stare in disbelief at her friend.

Tina was sporting a hat too fancy for a *Hello!* wedding. It was broad, with trailing ribbons. It co-ordinated divinely with her floaty chiffon sundress and her dainty spike heels. It certainly didn't co-ordinate with the scowl etched into her sweaty face. Labouring down the slope, her progress impeded by the heels and the hamper she was dragging, she was doing the funniest of funny walks.

'Teen! You made it!'

'I'm overdressed,' Tina said flatly, with a marked absence of good humour.

'A bit.'

'You said it was a special occasion. A once-a-year thing. A garden party.'

'Oooooh, no,' Nell corrected her. 'I'm sure I didn't say garden party. Helping Hands wouldn't do garden parties. It's a hostel for the homeless, a community outreach project. It's *not*,' she looked Tina up and down 'Buckingham Palace.'

'I can see that.' Tina cast a narrow glance at her companions. Kev was standing up to bat, his magnificently filthy outfit accessorised with wraparound shades he'd found in a wheelie-bin. 'Fucking great.' She was clipping her words. This was a bad sign.

'It doesn't matter!' said Nell, brightly. 'You look gorgeous!'

She was seconded by a minuscule Irish man in a puzzling combination of spotlessly clean shorts and grime-encrusted vest. 'Cworrrrr!' he said enthusiastically, with a grab at Tina's bum.

'Hey!' Tina spun round but, with speed born of much practice, the little man was yards away, leaning nonchalantly against a tree.

'You learn to dodge him after a while.' Nell sighed inwardly at the greasy handprint on the back of Tina's dress. After a swift battle with her conscience, she moved on without mentioning it. 'Let's give the hamper to Edith. You didn't have to, you know.'

'Fortnum's!' Edith yelped when they reached her.

'I got it on Marti's card. If you don't want it . . .' Tina was at sea in this universe where people wore ragged clothes, didn't gush at the sight of expensive food and played rounders but *seemed happy all the same.*

'We want it, all right,' Edith assured her, as she unpacked, with incredulity, the *pâté de foie gras*, the Brie and the salmon. 'Ah.' She held up a bottle of Moët and Chandon. 'Oh dear.'

'We're booze-free, Teen.' Some of the Helping Hands regulars had a problem – to say the least – with alcohol. 'We stick to the soft stuff.'

'Whoopee,' said Tina tonelessly. 'Well, I'm here now. What do you want me to do?' She was eyeing Bridie. The old woman was covertly scooping Heinz potato salad into the silk-lined pocket of what Tina could plainly see was vintage Chanel.

Phred left the barbecue to look after itself for a while and introduced himself. From the width of his smile, Tina's unsuitable dress was no problem. 'It's really good of you to help out. Now, what can we get you doing?'

Nell gave Phred a narrow-eyed look. She could imagine his sarcasm if she'd turned up dressed like Lady Muck. And was he holding his stomach in?

'The kids!' suggested Edith, with feeling. 'For God's sake, get her to control those kids.'

An admiring gaggle of them had already gathered around her. 'Are you a princess?' asked Clover.

'No,' said Tina slowly. 'I'm just an idiot.'

Her short-arsed audience laughed. Tina didn't. The scowl was still there, along with a growing pinkness that didn't bode well.

Phred heard a noise that sounded like prawns exploding (it was exactly that) and dashed back to the barbecue.

'Look, why don't you sit down and catch your breath?' Nell said. 'I'll open the champers just for you.' She could practically smell her friend's uneasiness.

'I'm supposed to be helping, aren't I?' snapped Tina. 'And, besides, who would I sit with?'

Nell could have pointed out that there were plenty of nice friendly people there if she bothered to open her eyes and look past the outer wrapping, but she knew better than to use that approach when Tina was in this mood. 'I'll leave you with the kids, then.'

'You never said!' Tina exclaimed in a rush, then stopped to choose her words more carefully. 'You never said about Clover.'

'Never said what?'

'That she's ill,' hissed Tina.

'Guess what?' whispered Nell back. 'She isn't. She's a kid who happens to have Downs syndrome. It's a condition, not an illness.'

'Oh, whatever.' Tina angled herself away from the children for the sake of discretion. 'How do I, you know, talk to her and the others? Do they . . . understand me?'

'They'll understand you a lot better than Marti does.' Nell gave Tina a gentle shove in the small of the back. 'Get over yourself, Teen. They're seven-year-olds.'

Nell left Tina with Clover and her cohorts then joined Phred. 'You should put the chicken on now. It has to be cooked all the way through or everybody dies in agony.'

'I do know about salmonella.'

'You could do that corn-on-the-cob on the grill too.'

'I'm going to. Why do you think they're there?'

'My . . .' Nell stumbled. What *was* Gareth? She decided he was still her ex, despite evidence to the contrary. 'My ex was big on barbecues. I know a lot about them. In particular I know that you're at your most dangerous right now. Talking to a man while he's barbecuing is like tickling a gorilla with toothache. You shouldn't do it.'

'So why are you?' Phred turned over a tiny sausage as if it was a time bomb. 'Talking to me, I mean.'

'It's about Anita.' Nell zipped through the squalid story

without drawing breath. She hoped, just this once, to appeal successfully to Phred's heart. It was his head, she had decided, that was the problem. 'So I told her she could stay tonight,' she concluded, 'even though she's spent the last three evenings at Helping Hands.'

'You shouldn't have done that.' Phred was frowning, whether at Nell or at the burger on his spatula she couldn't tell. 'But she can.'

Nell did a virtual lap of honour in her head

'I can make a guess at who she's talking about,' said Phred, thoughtfully. 'Not the nicest man in the world. If I make a few calls I might be able to repair her reputation. I'll do my best.' Before Nell could block her ears he uttered that hateful phrase, 'No promises.'

'Oh, promise! Just this once! Promise!'

Phred ignored her. He was good at that: it didn't seem rude when he did it, just grown-up.

'And the council list?' Nell was aware she was pushing him.

'Sure. Fetch my magic wand from the car.' Phred's head was back in charge. 'The first wave of burnt shit is ready.' He sighed. 'Can you start calling everybody to the table?'

'Okey-dokey.' When Phred was being human and *nice* like this, Nell would do anything for him. Perhaps it only happened on Saturdays. *'It's ready!'* she yelled.

'Simple but effective,' said Phred, approvingly.

The rounders game broke up, despite Bridie's cries of 'It's my go! Bastards! Youse is all bastards!' She quietened down when Dexter put his arm round her shoulders and led her to the table.

Nell bounded over to lever Maggie out of her chair, bent down and kissed her forehead.

'What was that for?' asked Maggie.

'Nothing. Lots of things.' Nell couldn't have said, 'For giving me the confidence to tackle Phred properly and actually achieve something,' without blushing so she left it at that.

'I wish everybody could just be *happy*.' She watched Carol approach the barbecue with Carly in her arms. 'Not ecstatic, not blissful, just happy.' Anita hadn't moved from her spot on the ground.

'What a silly notion,' scoffed Maggie, unexpectedly. 'Unhappiness is part of life, Nell.'

'Yeah, I know, but—'

Maggie didn't want to let her finish. 'It's how you deal with it that counts. Relying on happiness to see you through is like relying on . . . on . . .' she searched for an analogy, '. . . on Bridie to win the rounders game. And if you're thinking about that Carol girl over there, I'd say she's coping very well. She looks like a survivor to me.'

'But surely life should be about more than just surviving?'

'Surviving comes first, then you can aim for happiness. And, you know,' Maggie puffed, as she laboured up the small slope, 'survival is preferable to the alternative.'

'Hurry up,' said Nell, taking her arm. 'All the sausages will be gone.'

'Can't have that!'

There was a Tina-shaped mound of small girls where Nell's best friend had once been. She grabbed the nearest child and pulled, revealing Tina in the foetal position. 'Come on, monsters. Get off her.'

'We're tickling her,' said a curly-haired gremlin with no front teeth.

'To death,' added Tina, staggering to her feet. 'This is dry-clean only,' she said, looking down at her dress.

'I'll pay for it,' Nell heard herself say, although she couldn't see why she should. 'I'll buy you a new one. I'll buy you a new hat as well but, please, *please*, Tina, lighten up.'

This was a mistake. 'Lighten up? *Lighten up?*' Tina's hands flew to her hips. 'I'm fucking fine, thank you very much. I'm here, aren't I, at a picnic with no booze and the *crème de la crème* of London's street-dwellers. What more do you want from me?'

Back-pedalling with the ease of a practised coward, Nell told her, 'I want you to sit down and enjoy the grub.' It was safest to team her up with Maggie: the woman could charm to degree standard. 'Come on. I want to introduce you to somebody special.'

'Saw you chatting away to that Phred character. Thought you didn't like him much from the way you talk about him. It looked ever so cosy.' Tina sounded snide rather than playfully insinuating. 'Funny how you never mentioned he was a looker.'

Nell didn't like the way that sounded. 'He's my boss and we were talking business,' she said curtly. And truthfully. 'I need his help with somebody.'

Tina rolled her eyes, but rearranged her face to say a polite 'Hello' to Maggie.

'Back in a min.' Nell hurried over to where Anita still sat on her own. 'Hey, I have news.' She squatted in front of her.

A twitch of an eyebrow was all that Anita contributed to the conversation. She was staring out over the park.

'You can stay at Helping Hands tonight. And Phred is going to make a few calls, try to put people right about you. How does that sound?' she prompted, when Anita offered only silence as a response.

'Great,' said Anita, with an effort. 'That's great. Thanks, Nell.' Her smile brought no colour to her grey cheeks.

'Things'll get better. You'll see.' Nell was stepping out of her jurisdiction. Being a volunteer community helper didn't mean you talked to people like a mother to a toddler. 'Honest. Can we have a *proper* smile now?'

Anita seemed unaware of Nell's jurisdiction, and managed a small one.

'That's better! Now, come on, before all of Phred's magnificent cuisine gets eaten.'

Mingling had never appealed to Nell. Flirting, certainly, but mingling? No. At parties she clung to whomever she'd come with, hunched over a loaded plate and embracing a bottle. She didn't care what perfect strangers did for a living, or how they'd got there, or how they knew the hostess. She didn't want to tell them where she lived and what she thought of the latest films.

At the picnic, however, she found herself doing the rounds effortlessly. She wanted to say hello to all the regulars and be introduced to those she didn't recognise. Claudette would be proud of me, she thought, as she made her way to where Maggie sat with Tina at a tiny folding table. 'Sorry I was so long.' She sank to the floor, eyeing the remnants on their plates. 'There really is nothing like a blackened burger.'

'Tell me about it.' Tina held up what looked like a souvenir of Pompeii on her plastic fork.

'I'll have it if you don't want it.' Nell deftly snatched the burnt offering. 'How are we getting on, ladies?' she asked.

'Lovely. Lovely.' Maggie didn't meet her eye. She was smoothing imaginary folds in her lap.

Tina's face was a masterly representation of boredom as she lounged in her chair, lips pursed and outstretched ankles crossed. One foot waggled with angry energy.

'The food's going down well,' said Maggie, with phoney brightness. She was a drowning woman grasping at conversational rope.

'Yes, yes, it is,' agreed Nell. She was still watching that foot.

'My contribution didn't,' Tina said crisply. 'I'd have brought Wimpys if I'd known.'

'It's the thought that counts.' Maggie gave up. Tina's bad mood had overwhelmed even her reserves of cheerfulness.

'Want to help me clear up?' Nell straightened up and held out a hand, giving Tina an opportunity to redeem herself.

Tina took the hand, and the opportunity. 'Why not?' she said, with the semblance of a smile.

*   *   *

'Can't we save it for the fairies?' Clover pressed.

What the fairies might want with sat-on sandwiches and gobbets of quiche, Nell wasn't sure. 'These big black plastic bags are special fairy delivery sacks,' she reassured Clover. 'We're going to leave them in a big oak tree and the fairies will collect them at midnight.'

Clover's eyes opened wide with awestruck astonishment, then she lost interest and wandered off. Nell had had boyfriends like that.

'After this is all over,' began Tina, sounding like a Tommy during the First World War, 'why don't we go somewhere and swig the champagne?'

'Can't.' Nell grimaced, aware she was disappointing Tina yet again. 'I said I'd take Maggie home.'

'Never mind,' said Tina, resignedly. She slung a full bag of rubbish on to the growing pile and stretched.

A hundred yards away Bridie was being allowed her moment of glory in the reprised rounders game. Dexter bowled gently at her. She swung the club and somehow hit the ball very hard indeed, more or less exactly in the direction of Tina's head. The ball met it with a resounding thump. The fancy hat turned out to be necessary after all. It was only the presence of overpriced straw that prevented a serious injury. As it was, Tina was merely knocked off balance. She screamed and staggered backwards for some distance, then fell full length on to the pile of bin-bags. A shower of leftovers erupted around her.

Later on Nell and Maggie would both agree that it had looked very, very funny. They would also hurriedly correct themselves: no, it wasn't funny at all, not in the least. She could have been badly hurt.

At the time, Nell stifled her giggles and said, 'Oh, my God, are you all right?'

Tina struggled to her feet and stood, teetering, in the rubbish pile. Most of the others weren't as successful as Nell at hiding their amusement. In fact, they thought it was hilarious. The children, connoisseurs of people falling over, thought it was one of the best falls they'd ever seen. The yoghurt pot stuck to Tina's hat made it extra special and they showed their appreciation by laughing loudly.

Tina snorted like a racehorse, while various half-eaten food items dripped off her. With a face as red as the tomato adorning her left breast, she stormed off, ankles twisting dangerously in the turf.

The crowd tailed her, contrite now. 'Let me help you clean up,' suggested Joy, with one of her smiles.

Maggie, puffing to keep up, said comfortingly, 'It's really not as bad as it seems, dear.'

Bridie was apologising and swearing, and Kevin was offering his opinion that they were all tossers for laughing at her. Nell offered to swap clothes.

Clover and her friends, however, still considered Tina's collapse to be a work of comic genius and looked as if they would never stop laughing.

Tina wheeled round. Her little knot of disciples stopped dead. *'Leave me alone!'* she shouted. 'You've had your fun. I'm going home.' She stomped on, a crisps bag impaled on her heel.

Nell was the only one behind her now, like a little tug-boat chasing a liner. 'Teen, let me help.'

'Help?' Tina halted suddenly again. 'Who do you think you are? What is it with you and helping people? Do you really think anyone's taken in by this stupid play-acting?' Tina pulled off her hat with a vicious tug. 'Surrounding yourself with smelly people, and backward people, and mad people, and no-hopers who can't even handle a picnic.'

'The last one's you, I take it.' Nell's reserves of patience were finally exhausted.

'Oooh, you make out you're so perfect these days,' Tina growled. 'No time to get pissed, no time to listen to me, but you're not doing so badly out of this do-gooding crap, are you? No,' she continued, nodding her head maniacally, 'you've got yourself a bloke out of it, haven't you? Funny that, when you're meant to be in it for others.'

'What bloke?' For a nanosecond Nell thought Tina knew about Gareth.

'That whatsisname with the funny spelling,' spat Tina. 'Mr Perfect, Nelson Mandela – Gandhi!' she continued wildly. 'You're very *friendly-wendly* considering you're not even supposed to like him! Boring, you said! Cold!'

'Will you keep your voice down?' hissed Nell, grabbing Tina's arm and manhandling her further away from flapping ears. 'I don't know what you're on about but I wish you'd shut up. Remind me to ask you to help out more often. You're a real pleasure to have around.'

'I suppose you'd rather hang out with beggars and old people and – and –' Tina dropped her voice to a rasping whisper '– *mongols!*'

'Go home! Go home right now!' Nell wavered somewhere between wanting to sob and wanting to gouge Tina's eyes out with her thumbs.

Tina opened and closed her mouth, then her face crumpled and she hobbled off.

She left her hat behind. Nell stamped on it.

'Psssst!'

'Psssst?' Nell queried Dexter, who was beckoning to her from behind a massive oak. 'Don't people only say that in cartoons?'

'No. I'm asking you to come over here and get pssst with me.' He held up Tina's champagne, then hid it again.

'Righty-ho.' Nell nipped over to join him. 'Only one glass. I'm on duty, kind of.'

'Only got one.' Dexter produced a pint glass. He winked at her as he filled it. 'Thought you might need it after your friend's little tantrum. You're trembling.'

'I'll be all right in a minute,' lied Nell, hopefully. She was feeling undone: like a present after a children's party, her ribbons were trailing everywhere. She hadn't known that Tina could be so selfish and unkind. It wasn't a nice thing to learn about your best friend.

One gulp of the champagne was enough. 'Oh, God, the bubbles. I'll keel over.' She pressed it back on Dexter. 'I'm too upset to drink. *That*'s never happened before.'

'I have a cure.' Smirking obviously ran in the family (perhaps there had been a great-great-grandmother who'd been a noted Victorian smirker), but Dexter's version was crooked. 'Want to know what it is?'

Uncertainly Nell said, 'I think so.' There was a wildness about Dexter that made her instinctively take one step towards him, then two steps back.

'*Rounders!*' He snatched her up, slung her over his shoulder and raced off with her.

Screaming and pounding on his back in the approved feminine manner, Nell was thrilled. She'd often worked up vivid fantasies about being rescued by the SAS, and they had felt rather like this. 'Put me down!' she ordered, hoping he wouldn't.

Breathless, her hair over her eyes, Nell was set on her feet roughly by Dexter, who handed her a bat as a ball whizzed her way. She smacked it away over everybody's heads to an admiring, 'Whooh!' and set off like a whippet for first base.

She tore home triumphantly to whistles and applause (with a bitter 'Cheating bastard!' from Bridie) and handed back the bat to Dexter. She felt a bit better, she had to admit.

Dexter removed his T-shirt to bat and all the women under thirty-five fell simultaneously silent. Nell parked herself between Maggie and Joy. 'Did you see me? Did you see? I got a round, or whatever they're called.' Nell wasn't the physical type: it was a revelation to her that running fast could make you feel good. She had thought only sofas, cake and snogging could do that.

Joy wasn't listening. She was looking at Dexter with glazed

eyes and saying, 'That boy can handle a bat.' He winked in their direction and even Maggie gave a low moan.

Why, thought Nell, can't Phred be more like his brother? Then she shook herself. It was nothing to do with her whether Phred was like his brother or not. She glanced over to where he was dismantling tables on his own.

Dexter laid himself, panting, on the grass at the ladies' feet.

Maggie threw a napkin at him. 'Cover up that manly chest, dear, would you? I'm terribly old and I don't get out much. It's giving me palpitations.'

'You and your brother aren't very alike, are you?' Unconsciously Joy echoed Nell. 'Apart from physically.'

'Me and bro?' Dexter squinted over at Phred. 'You mean he's the good one and I'm the wicked one? You'd be surprised, Joy. My brother has his moments.'

Nell looked at Phred through her fringe. He was concentrating hard on a table leg that wouldn't fold. He worked it out.

Noses sunburned and tummies full, the ragtag Helping Hands crew slumped in the minibus as it drove back to Camerton Street. The sun was making its excuses over London's rooftops and somebody had pulled out Clover's plug. She slumped, thumb in mouth, on her uncle's lap.

In the front seat conversation between Nell and Phred was stilted. She was suffering several varieties of embarrassment at once. She was fairly certain that he hadn't heard Tina's insulting description of Clover but he might have caught the bit about his Nelson Mandela-like qualities and their being 'friendly-wendly'. *Friendly-wendly!* thought Nell, contemptuously. We're not. We never could be. We've proved that. She looked at his strong, stern profile as he leaned on the wheel. Nice nose, she thought.

Then she realised that the strong, stern profile was talking to her. 'What? I was miles away.' Nell rubbed her eyes.

'I said, I hope you and your friend make it up.'

'Hmm,' said Nell, darkly.

'Not everybody can cope with Helping Hands the way you do. Cut her some slack.'

Phred's generosity towards Tina surprised Nell. She didn't feel generous just then. Despite her dark mood she smiled: Phred had slipped her a compliment. She glowed, and not just because of her sunburn. 'I was really shocked by her,' she said. The sleepy atmosphere in the coach and Phred's unexpected empathy made her want to talk to him about the whirlpool of ugly feelings that Tina had stirred up. Timidly, she carried on 'I—'

Dexter's voice cut in: 'Why don't we make a night of it after we've dropped everybody off, bro? Buy our Nell a cocktail or two?'

'I've got to get Clover to bed.' Sensible Phred was back. 'And Nell isn't our Nell. She's engaged, aren't you?' He didn't look at her but kept his gaze on the traffic.

'Are you?' Dexter sounded surprised.

'Kind of,' mumbled Nell.

'He's a lucky bloke,' Dexter told her, ruffling the back of her hair.

'Oh, he knows just how lucky he is,' Nell assured him.

Twenty-three

Patrolling the office in a new pleated skirt, Linda was spreading pain in her inimitable manner. 'Dean, I have a herbal remedy for acne if you're interested. Oh, Jean, petty cash is short by two pence. Can we investigate? Zoë, please get back to Reception. We don't pay you to annoy Nell.'

'I'm not annoying Nell,' said Zoë, placidly.

'Actually, you are, rather.' Nell put her right. She was running out of ways to withstand Zoë's expert battering about her chilliness with Tina. 'Scuttle back to Reception, why don't you, and write some illegible Post-its.'

'Not until you've told me why you two aren't talking.'

'Is there any topic that you would consider none of your business? The Queen's Fallopian tubes, for example?'

'Why aren't you talking to Tina?'

'Zoë, the phones are ringing. You are the keeper of said phones.'

'Why aren't you talking to Tina?'

'I *am* talking to Tina.'

'Why aren't you talking to Tina?'

'Because she let me down.' Nell surprised herself by phrasing it like that.

'OK.' Zoë nodded. This was evidently enough for the time being. 'I'll be back,' she warned, as she sauntered over to the pulsating switchboard.

Across the office, Tina's neat head was bent over her computer. Today Nell had received no emails from her, and they hadn't indulged in any puerile instant messaging. Nell had half expected an apology, but the only communication in her in-box was from a bewigged comedian client whining that he hadn't been paid for a *Celebrity Ready Steady Cook* in 1998.

Without Tina's input the working day dragged. Nell struggled to find satisfaction in her work: a call from a client in rehab complaining that there was no minibar didn't help.

Mid-afternoon an email arrived from Phred, asking if she could babysit for Carol the following evening. Nell started to compose a quick 'yes' to email back. She had reworded it eight times before she stopped to ask herself, 'What's the matter with me?' She bashed out 'Hi, Phred, yes, that's fine,' then stared at the screen. She backspaced decisively. She didn't want to put 'Hi' – too matey. But 'Dear' was too businesslike. 'Hello, Phred,' she started, then stared into mid-air for quite some time.

Nell wrote umpteen hundred emails each day, reeling them off automatically. Suddenly she was Virginia Woolf, fretting over each comma. 'What's the matter with me?' she asked herself again. But the question was rhetorical. The deep down part of Nell, the part that knew everything but hated to admit any of it, knew very well what was wrong with her.

Phred's opinion had always been important to her: after all, he was the man who held the key to her programme of de-shallowfication and he had to believe in her.

But. A 'but' was lurking. *That wasn't all*. Phred's opinion was important to her because she liked him. Nell's vocabulary reverted to schoolgirlisms at times of stress: she didn't just like him, she *liked* him liked him.

'Aw, shiiiiiiit.' She groaned. 'I *like* him like him.' It was true. A door unlocked in Nell's mind and the truth, blinking and unused to daylight, tumbled out. Tangled and crumpled, it looked rather like the contents of her wardrobe.

Why couldn't she *like* like Dexter? He looked similar to Phred, and on paper he was much more her type. He was thoughtless and fun and lived his life in pursuit of a good time. And there was a good chance he *like* liked her.

But he wasn't Phred.

'I like the way he talks to people, as if they're all the same. I like the way he is with his little girl. I like the way he listens to me. I like the way he gives me another chance when I mess up. I like the way he stands, straight and reliable, like a tree. I like his bum.' She paused. 'Oh, I really like his bum. And I like his eyes and the way they go slitty when he smiles. And I like how he walks. And I like the curls that just touch his neck . . .' Nell sighed. Her fingers slipped on the keypad and typed 'cneoiafs'.

This was beyond bad. Nell's heart had made some questionable choices in its time but it had excelled itself by singling out Phred. Even if she discounted his stuffiness, his coldness, his obvious distrust of her, there was the dead wife to compete with. And he was her boss, in a way.

And, oh, yes, the little matter of the gigantic gay fake fiancé and the ex who wouldn't stay exed.

'Phred. Fine. Will be there. Nell.' She pressed 'send' and scrabbled in a drawer for her emergency Twix. It was past its sell-by date. She ate it anyway.

'You sound like you've had a hard day,' cooed Gareth, in a new super-smooth voice. 'Come round here and let me kiss it better.'

Nell's day wouldn't be improved by application of Gareth's lips, yet she found herself heading for Twickenham like a sleep-walker. There was a horrible inevitability to getting back with Gareth: unless she had a cast-iron excuse she felt unable to resist going to his flat. In the absence of anything else in her life making sense, this reversion to the 'old days' was too simple to fight. She was a raindrop running down a wet trail on a window-pane.

'Take this.' Gareth handed her a large glass of reasonable wine and sat her at a candle-lit table. The cutlery was clean, the food was edible, and Gareth was taking the time to chew his mouthfuls.

'This tastes . . . like food,' said Nell, wonderingly.

'I thought it was about time I learned to cook,' said Gareth, as if it was the most natural thing in the world, as if he hadn't previously refused to heat beans in case it compromised his masculinity.

'You always said it was woman's work,' Nell reminded him, with narrowed eyes.

'I found cooking was soothing when . . . well, when you weren't here.'

Enough's enough, Nell wanted to shout. *Where's the hidden camera?* 'And here was I thinking you'd had another woman in.' Nell smiled weakly. She noticed the change in his face, like a cloud passing over the sea. 'Oh. You did.'

Nodding slowly, unable to meet her eye, Gareth confessed all. 'It was that girl with the perm from the off-licence. I just wanted to hurt you.' His voice was tinged with shame. 'It's not a perm, by the way. It's just like that,' he added.

'God. Really?' Nell was briefly distracted by this snippet, then said, 'It doesn't matter.'

'No, it doesn't, darling.' Gareth beamed with relief. 'You and I are all that matters. I knew you'd understand.' He helped himself to more meatballs.

The truth was that Nell was indifferent. She couldn't have cared less whether Gareth had mounted every woman, man, dog and postbox in a hundred-mile radius. Perversely she congratulated herself on having been right about the made bed. She would tell Tina tomorrow, she thought smugly, then remembered that she wasn't talking to Tina.

After dinner Gareth was in a nostalgic mood. Holding Nell as tightly as he used to hold his pint, he harked back to their early days. 'Remember the first night I stayed over?' he whispered, nuzzling her ear.

'Yup.' Nell tried to position her head so that he couldn't reach it, but in the boa constrictor grip of his arms this was impossible. 'You slept on the floor,' she reminded him hopefully.

'Well, kind of.' He laughed, and Nell remembered what had happened – and wondered now why she hadn't taken it as a bad omen.

A phenomenally drunken Gareth had missed the last train and asked, with a hopeful leer, if he could sleep at her flat. Nell had agreed, knowing that she had an extremely effective contraceptive: she had only applied fake tan as far as her knees so there was no way a new man was going to see her naked. 'The sofa-bed's in there,' she'd said, throwing a duvet at him and closing the sitting-room door behind her.

The next morning, dry of throat but virtuously unfiddled-with, Nell yawned her way in to wake him. She had discovered Gareth, fully clothed and fast asleep, even though he was kneeling on the floor with his face flattened against the sofa cushions. She had never seen anybody in such an awkward position.

When she woke him, his face was red, with a mixture of hangover and anger, and sweaty, from proximity to Dralon. 'This sofa-bed's a nightmare!' he fumed. 'I pushed and pulled it in all directions but it wouldn't unfold.'

'*That*'s the sofa-bed.' Nell had pointed to the sofa against the opposite wall.

'How we laughed.' Gareth smiled whimsically.

'Hmm.' Nell could only recall Gareth scowling, and striding off to fill her bathroom with toxic fumes.

'We've had some good times, me and you.'

'Yes.' They almost ran into double figures if you were loose in your interpretation of 'good', thought Nell. Her selective memory, so pro-Gareth when they had first split, was now editing out any happiness they had known together.

'Some couples fight all the time, but not us.'

'We gave that up after the first year,' agreed Nell. She had stopped bothering because it never got them anywhere: Gareth had simply bellowed over whatever she said.

'Pick a number and I'll tell you the lovely memory it represents.' Gareth tickled her when she hesitated. 'Go on! It's romantic!'

When Gareth tickled you, you knew you'd been tickled. Rubbing her armpit, Nell muttered, 'Three?'

'Ah. Three. Good number. That's our boat ride round Lyme Bay. You, me, the sea and the sky. What a day that was.'

'But you . . .'

'What, my love?'

'Doesn't matter.' Gareth had demanded his money back, towering over the scrawny West Country teenager at the ticket booth and shrieking that he hadn't come all the way from London to row a poxy boat with a poxy warped oar. 'I think I'd better get going.'

'Oh, no, you don't.' Gareth tightened his grip.

'I have to. I promised I'd be back tonight. Fergus locks the door at ten,' lied Nell, inventively.

'The sooner you move your stuff back the better.'

Too fast was Gareth's only speed. 'Let's see how things go,' suggested Nell, evasively, unwrapping him and pushing her feet back into her Scholls.

'Can I see you tomorrow?' Gareth was as ardent as any lover could wish.

'It's difficult . . .' Nell was backing away slowly. 'It's a long way and you can't come to Claudette's after what happened there and I have to be at Helping Hands and I have to go out with Blair and—'

'Blair!' Gareth's face surged with its old claret. 'Surely you're going to break it off with that – that—' He was lost for an analogy loathsome enough.

Nell blinked. She'd forgotten that he didn't know the truth about Blair. It was time to let him into the secret.

Gareth shook his head with disbelief. 'I'm going to have a quiet word with this Louis,' he muttered.

Dissuading him took another ten minutes, and wriggling out of sexual duties with a disabling concoction of headache, tummy-ache and earache took a further twenty. By the time Nell got back to Knightsbridge she was ready for the virginal perfumed haven of the Heliotrope Room.

*   *   *

Hayley was pointing her foot, like a ballerina. 'Do you like my new shoes?' she asked.

'They're *gorgeous*,' gushed Nell, as if the tiny Mary Janes were Manolos. She'd been dreading coming to Carol's, but the flat was clean and tranquil, and for once Carol wasn't behaving like a Jack Russell with PMT.

'You've had a wasted journey.' Carol explained that the NA meeting had been cancelled at the last minute. 'Fancy a nice hot cuppa?'

'No, I don't.' A plan popped, fully formed, into Nell's head. 'I fancy a change of scene. And so do you.'

A teenager from down the hall was persuaded, with the help of a tenner from Nell, to watch the children for a couple of hours. Carol was forced into a taxi ('But they cost a fortune! Can't we get the bus?') and soon she and Nell were tucked away in a softly lit corner of Eclectica.

'Cheers!' said Nell.

'Cheers,' echoed Carol, timorously, looking anxiously around her as she sipped her colourful but non-alcoholic cocktail. A plastic chandelier hung over the plum *chaise-longue* they were sitting on. 'This place is done up strange, isn't it?' she ventured.

'Very strange. Too trendy for its own good,' agreed Nell. 'It costs a lot for a room to look this cheap.'

Carol giggled. 'I haven't been out for a drink for . . .' She frowned. 'You know, I can't remember the last time, it's been so long.'

'That's what I thought,' said Nell. 'I suddenly realised that the only time we babysit for you is when you go to your NA meetings. I know they're essential but they're probably not a lot of fun.'

Carol rolled her eyes. 'No. They can be a bit much, some-times.'

'And we all need fun,' diagnosed Dr Fitzgerald.

'Me and the kids have fun.' Carol thought hard. 'Me and my old man used to have fun – before he got serious about crack.' She pushed peanuts about in a Moroccan glass dish on the table in front of them. 'He was different before. I know everybody hates him, but he wasn't always like he is now.'

'Nobody hates him,' clarified Nell. 'They hate the effect he has on you and the kids. That's different.'

Carol nodded. 'Sometimes I wish—'

Nell didn't let her finish. 'Stop,' she commanded. 'This conversation is veering into non-fun territory. Tonight you don't have an ex with a drug problem, tonight you're that other Carol. The one you used to be. OK?'

'OK!' Carol seemed to like the idea. Soon she was sprawled back on the *chaise-longue*, playing with her hair and listening to Nell's stories about her nights out with Blair. She had a wild, full-throttle laugh that set Nell off too. 'He never!' she shrieked.

'He did!' shrieked Nell. 'Right in front of Vanessa Feltz!'

They had some tapas and they managed to slop garlic potatoes on a cushion: it was a good night.

'Oh.' Nell stopped in mid-anecdote and plonked her glass down with a clatter.

'What's the matter?' asked Carol.

'Hadn't we better get back?' Nell showed Carol her watch.

'Yeah. S'pose.' Carol stood up and pulled her parka round her, surreptitiously following Nell's eyes. 'Do you know those people?' she asked, in an undertone.

'Yup.'

Tina and Marti had just arranged themselves on a two-seater across the room. Tina, in a brand new and very brief dress, was staring resolutely in the opposite direction, while Marti just looked flustered. Nell steered Carol past them without a word.

In the taxi Nell shook off the dark cloud. 'You remind me of my mum, Carol,' she said, without thinking.

'What's your mum like?' asked Carol, doubtfully.

'I mean . . .' Nell was sorry she'd opened her mouth '. . . when my mum was your age, she was in your position. She had a child but no man, and she had to look after herself. Seeing you makes me realise how hard my mum had to work to get through.'

'It's not that hard.' Carol smiled.

Nell knew that Carol had had to say that, and she knew it wasn't true. 'You inspire me,' she told her.

'Get off.' Carol was embarrassed. 'Me? How could I inspire anybody?'

'Because you've got a home and three happy children and you manage to do all that and fight an addiction as well.' Nell hoped she'd put that properly. 'Hayley was delighted with her new shoes.'

'Yeah.' Carol didn't look insulted. She looked tired and happy, like a girl who'd just had a damned good night out.

The taxi pulled up outside the looming tower block. 'Thanks. I really enjoyed myself.' Carol leaned over and kissed Nell's cheek shyly.

'Listen,' said Nell, impulsively, 'when you want to go out for some fun, call me and I'll babysit. Not just when you're going to meetings.'

'I don't know.' Carol looked unsure. 'What would Phred say?'

At a guess, Nell reckoned that Phred would say, 'Blah blah blah practical support only blah blah blah don't get too involved blah blah blah.' 'He doesn't have to know.' She winked.

Carol winked back, and slammed the taxi door. Watching her skip up the pitted concrete steps, Nell hugged herself, happy that she'd made it possible for Carol to step outside her problems and have an uncomplicated evening.

As the taxi carried her back to Knightsbridge, she reflected that Carol had done the same for her.

Davina wouldn't join in with the other girls' regular bitching sessions about Louis. 'Oh, he's harmless,' she always said, when the other girls asked how she put up with his leering.

'Willies are strange things to carry about – I know. They can make men behave in very odd ways.'

That week Louis's willy had been particularly wilful. He was badgering Davina to go away for the weekend. There was much talk of jewellery and expense accounts and spas. Behind his beard, Louis was looking troubled at the ineffectuality of his best moves. It was as if, mused Nell, Superman was trying to chat up a girl whose dress was made of kryptonite.

Both Tina and Nell had become close to the fascinating and beautiful Davina, but now that they were at loggerheads they had their chats with her separately. Davina didn't approve of this. 'You two should sort yourselves out. Good friends are hard to find.' She sounded as if she knew what she was talking about.

'I don't know if she ever was a good friend,' said Nell, sullenly.

Davina tutted. 'I watched the pair of you. I was quite envious. You two have obviously helped each other through a lot. Don't throw it away for the sake of your pride.'

If anybody was proud it was Tina, Nell decided defiantly. She reckoned that she was owed an apology. And not just a common or garden one: Nell wanted a full-on, baroque, surround-sound apology. Tina had insulted people who were dear to Nell, she'd embarrassed her and let her down. Every time Nell remembered the bored, snotty expression on Tina's face at the picnic it made her fizz with anger. No, there would be no truce in the Cold War until Tina did the decent thing and apologised.

Preferably on her knees.

Some sneaky thoughts about her best friend had been wandering uninvited across Nell's mind. Helping Hands and her struggles to inject some meaning into her life had opened up a rift between her and Tina, but now that rift was a chasm. Suddenly there was a whole raft of experiences and ideas that Nell was reluctant to share. Did she and Tina, she wondered guiltily, have much in common any more?

Had they ever? That was one of the more unsettling thoughts, which Nell tried to push away. Was their friendship based on shallow foundations? Even now that she was really annoyed with Tina and longed to disarrange her hypergroomed hair, she didn't want to confront that suspicion. She carried on ignoring her and pretending not to notice the Pronuptia catalogue that poked out of her bag.

Ostensibly Nell was at Maggie's to hang curtains. 'Oh, blow that,' said Maggie, sitting her down with a large mug of tea. 'If you remember, we've got a job to do.' She flourished the A4 list. 'I've written down all the J. Fairweathers in London on this piece of paper.'

'Blimey. There are loads of them.'

'But one of them is . . .'

'My granddad,' said Nell, quietly. 'Or *might* be.'

'Is,' said Maggie, firmly. 'I prefer to think positive.'

'Some of them are crossed out,' said Nell.

'They're the ones I've already called.'

'You've called them?' squeaked Nell. 'But what did you say? "Hello, are you my stupid friend's granddad?"'

'I said I was doing market research and asked if they'd ever lived in the Knightsbridge area.'

'Oh.' Nell smiled. 'Very clever.'

'They all said no,' Maggie told her, 'so I think it's time you got involved. You might bring us luck.'

'Oh, yes. I'm the modern equivalent of a four-leaf clover,' said Nell, bitterly.

'You've been lucky for me,' said Maggie, simply.

'But there are over twenty names left to do.'

'Somewhere urgent you have to go?' Maggie's schoolteacher past was showing.

'No, but—'

'No but you've got cold feet?'

'Freezing. Right up to my neck.'

'The best thing to do is jump straight in. I know how much

you want to find this man.' Maggie had witnessed a lot of hand-wringing from Nell about her strange family set-up, and understood her conflicted emotions. 'He might even be the first name on the list. Miracles happen.'

'Not to me,' scoffed Nell, settling back into a cushion and dialling. 'Any cake going?'

As Maggie lumbered back with a hefty slice of fortifying Madeira, Nell was just putting the phone down on her first 'market-research' call. 'Maggie,' she said, eyes wide. 'I think that was him.'

The battered old floorboards were obscured by dust sheets, and ladders were propped where workmen had left them. Reception at Helping Hands was receiving a long overdue facelift. Nell picked her way through to the kitchens over paint-pots and brushes. 'Is it another donation?' she asked Phred, who was tasting that evening's Irish stew as Edith stood over him anxiously.

'Yes. An unusually generous one.' Phred licked the spoon. 'That is a truly historic Irish stew, Edith. My compliments to the chef.'

Edith made a noise that signified happiness, and tried not to smile. 'No need for that,' she said.

It went down well with the customers, too. 'Thirds?' Phred said, to a tiny man who had wolfed down two heaped bowls already.

'Is there a law against it?' asked the flyweight, belligerently and stalked off with his refilled bowl, looking murderously over his shoulder at Phred.

'Charming,' said Phred to Nell, who was on custard duty.

'What?' she replied blankly.

'You're miles away this evening, Fitzgerald. Daydreaming about your fiancé?'

It was a much older man who was on Nell's mind. She said quietly, 'No. I never daydream about him.'

'Poor bloke.' Phred sounded so unconcerned that Nell was

stung. She wanted him to be jealous, to throw stew at the walls and beg her to sleep with him.

None of that was about to happen: Phred was smiling at Bridie as though he didn't have a care in the world.

Bridie was still in the Chanel castoff, although it didn't look much like its former self. A camouflage pattern of suspect stains marched across it, and one of the cuffs was tied in Bridie's hair. Nell could almost hear the garment begging to be taken back to Claudette's wardrobe.

'Custard!' Bridie yelped.

'On your Irish stew?' Nell tried to intimate that it was a bad idea.

'Custard! I've a right to me custard!'

'Yes. You have.' Nell dribbled a thin stream of custard on top of the main course. 'Enjoy.'

When the queue thinned and finally melted away, Phred made himself and Nell a cup of tea. She watched as he stirred in two sugars for her: he'd remembered how she took it, a feat that had eluded Gareth throughout the years they'd lived together. She wanted to put Phred right about Blair, but she didn't know how. As usual, this didn't stop her.

'He's not my fiancé, you know,' she said abruptly, as Phred handed her a mug.

'Really?' Phred was satisfyingly surprised. Nell didn't trust herself to work out whether or not he was pleased. 'The Press says different.'

'They don't know what they're talking about. He isn't my fiancé and he never will be. Not ever. No way. No, sir.' She'd never said, 'No, sir,' before and felt vaguely twat-like for having said it now.

She had a compulsion to tell Phred the real reason she was distracted. His brand of sensible sympathy would be welcome. However, long-lost grandfathers were the stuff of fiction and weren't easily shared. As for her feelings towards Phred himself . . . She contented herself with another clarifying 'Not now and never will be.'

'I think I get your drift.'

'There it is again,' said Nell, before she could stop herself.

'What? There's what again?' Phred looked behind him.

She'd started so she might as well continue. 'That smirk,' she said, after a deep breath. 'You're always doing it when you talk to me,' she hurried on, looking into the amber depths of her tea. 'Like I'm funny, or silly, or something . . .' She tailed off.

Phred said nothing. After a moment he said, 'Am I doing it now?'

'*Yes!*'

'What are you up to next Tuesday?' asked Patsy, phoning from what sounded like downtown Saigon but was actually her front room. Canvey and Annie were evidently trying to get at each other through her torso.

'Why?' Nell asked cagily, hoping for yet dreading some sort of family get-together to mark her birthday on the Monday.

'That's the day Annie's DNA results come out. We're having a little party. Just a couple of drinks and a few sausages on sticks. Oh, and Ringo's hiring a karaoke machine.' Patsy broke off to yell, '*Canvey! Don't put your niece in the fish tank!*' She returned, with a hopeful, 'You'll come, won't you?'

'Yes.' And you can give me my surprise birthday present, thought Nell, aware that even Clover was too old for such childish thoughts.

'And will Himself be with you?'

'Himself? Oh, Blair. No, he's got an extremely important and ungetoutable-of meeting that night.'

'Shame.' Patsy sounded crestfallen. 'I suppose we could change the date. No, that wouldn't work,' she concluded regretfully. 'We'll have to enjoy ourselves without him.'

'Yes,' agreed Nell. 'We must be brave.'

*   *   *

It was a long tube journey, right to the end of the line. Maggie's nose was stuck in a biography of Marilyn Monroe.

Nell had tried to dissuade her from making such a long trek, but she'd been determined. 'I'm coming with you and that's that,' she'd said, standing stoically in a matching dress and coat, a lopsided hat on her head. 'Just in case this grandfather of yours turns out to be a two-woman job.'

It was a squat modern block, square and neat. It had an anonymous air. It was where Jack Fairweather lived.

'It's that one. Number five. On the ground floor,' whispered Nell.

'Why are you whispering?' asked Maggie.

'I don't know,' said Nell. They were on the opposite pavement, studying the building. 'I'm scared.'

'I know,' said Maggie. She had been holding Nell's hand both literally and metaphorically. 'We can turn round right now and go back to the station.' She took Nell's chin between two fingers and tilted the scrunched face towards hers. 'Or we can cross the road and ring your grandfather's doorbell.'

The bell was answered promptly.

Jack Fairweather was tall, with a slight stoop. His balding head was the colour of a shell and his eyes were an arresting blue. Slender and long-limbed, he actually looked a little like Claudette. This shocked Nell and she was slow to answer his 'Yes?'

The accent was a flat London one, unlike her grandmother's refined vowels. Nell rattled off her script. 'Hello. You don't know me but I think we might be related. Can we come in and I'll try to explain?'

'No,' said Jack Fairweather, bluntly, and started to close the door.

Maggie spoke up: 'We only need a few minutes of your time. We're not selling anything. This young lady really needs to speak to you.'

The man frowned, wavered. He looked Nell in the eye.

'Well, all right. Come in. I'm just on my way out, mind, so make it snappy.'

It was very snappy. Five minutes later Nell and Maggie were heading for the station in silence. Their pace was funereal, partly because of Maggie's traditional 'bad legs' and partly because Nell felt like a balloon the day after a kids' party.

Finally, as they reached the platform, Nell said, 'Do you think it's karmic?'

'How do you mean?' Maggie scanned the tracks.

'The way my family are unerringly crap.'

'At least we know he definitely is your grandfather.'

'Oh, yes. I think that was made pretty clear when he described Claudette as a she-wolf who would eat her young.' Nell sighed. 'Do you think there would be any point in leaving him for a while and then . . . ?'

Maggie shook her wise old head sadly. 'You heard what he said. He shook the dust off his feet when he walked away from Claudette and he doesn't want anything to do with her . . . or hers.'

'And that means me.'

'I'm afraid it does.' Maggie sounded choked. 'Stupid, stupid old man,' she said. 'This is all my fault.'

The train drew up. They got on and Nell helped Maggie to a seat. 'No. Absolutely not. I don't want to hear that again. Got it?' she said vehemently, and wagged a finger sternly at her elderly friend.

'Got it,' said Maggie, dismally, and they sat without talking for the rest of the journey.

Twenty-four

No birthday should begin at seven a.m. with two immobile figures standing silently in the half-light at the foot of your bed, but Nell's did.

'Whassappnin? Whassamatter?' she garbled, jerking herself upright. The figures swam into focus: Claudette, groomed to perfection, and Fergus, in his most Ruritanian get-up.

'Madame thought you might care for breakfast in bed on this special day,' intoned Fergus. His eyes were cast stoically upwards.

Nell looked down and hastily rearranged the rather low-cut T-shirt she'd slept in. 'How lovely,' she said weakly, wishing they would go away. She was painfully aware that her hair was a Ken Dodd tribute.

Fergus handed her a silver tray, which Nell balanced somehow on the mountain range of her knees. She reached behind to pummel the pillow into shape and a rivulet of coffee snaked across the satin eiderdown. 'Oh, bugger!'

Claudette ignored the spill and the vulgarism, presumably having awarded her granddaughter a Get Out of Jail Free card for the day. 'Eat! Carita searched high and low for those truffles.'

Suddenly this was more like Nell's idea of a birthday. Chocolates for breakfast! She lifted the silver dome and was disappointed to see that the truffles in question were shavings of expensive fungus on her egg-white omelette. 'Delicious!' she fibbed, consoling herself with a mental image of an Egg McMuffin on the way to the office.

Claudette, Nell noted, had been a little heavy-handed with her makeup. It was more of a mask than an embellishment this morning. 'Your present won't be ready until this evening,' she was saying. 'There are cards from myself and Fergus on your tray, however.'

'Thank you.' Claudette's card was a tasteful reproduction of an old master; an anodyne vase of flowers graced the front of Fergus's. 'May the coming year bring you all you deserve,' he had written in his precise hand.

Men were on Nell's mind. They were giving her gyp. Not in the way they gave supermodels gyp, by asking them out too much and spending too much on diamonds. No, the gyp Nell was getting included being rejected by an unexpected grandfather, being wooed clumsily by an unwanted ex, and being ambushed by inappropriately sexy feelings for an authority figure who seemed to think she was funny.

Perhaps these problems contributed to Nell's difficulty in summoning the requisite enthusiasm for the office birthday gift. 'A foot spa!' she gushed limply. 'How I have always wanted one.'

The semicircle of staff was watching her intently. Any pallid diversion from the phones and computers was welcomed with the kind of interest the Second Coming might generate. 'Do you really like it?' asked Jean, anxiously.

'I'm in love with it,' Nell assured her, with the biggest smile she could muster. 'I'll use it every single night for the rest of my life.'

The foot spa was destined, of course, to lurk in the bottom of the wardrobe for a few months, until eventually Nell dug it out and smuggled it on to a neighbour's skip. This is the lot of all foot spas: it would be interesting to know what they did to deserve such ruinous karma.

Away from the knot of gift voyeurs, Tina read *Bride* magazine ostentatiously. She was dressed as Jackie O on an official visit to Paris. Languidly she sneaked a look at the ceremony going on ten yards from her desk. She caught Nell's eye and snapped her attention back to the page.

If Tina had been responsible for her present, Nell would have been saved the horror of the foot spa. This gift had Linda's fingerprints all over it. 'I suspect I've got you to thank for this, have I, you minx, you?'

'We-ell,' smiled Linda, modestly, twiddling the pussycat bow on her Terylene blouse, 'it does usually fall to me to bear the responsibility for these things.' She felt the need to share her motives for choosing a foot spa. 'Your poor feet in those Dr Scholls . . .' Everybody's eyes travelled down to Nell's little wooden shoes. 'They're so neglected. No excuse for ugly feet now!' She shook a finger that Nell longed to grab and bend right back to the wrist.

An important question was taxing Zoë: 'Are we having a piss-up after work?' she asked.

'Can't,' said Nell, regretfully.

'Are you off to your poor people?' prompted Jean, proudly.

'Well, I'm on duty at Helping Hands.'

A loud scoff travelled over to them from behind *Bride*.

'Tina, what are you doing over there?' Jean was phenomenally slow on the uptake. 'Come here and join us.'

'I'd better get back to my desk,' Nell said quickly. 'Louis is in a funny mood today.'

'That'll be Hildegard's menopause,' said Linda, sagely. 'It's not going well.' For somebody who prided herself on discretion she gave an awful lot away.

Blanching, Len excused himself and the little group dispersed. Nell managed not to look Tina's way as she lugged the foot spa to her desk. She would not be the first to crack. Just because she missed having her to talk to, to mull things over with and lean on, didn't mean she was going to be the one to hold out an olive branch.

She wondered if Tina was yearning to talk about the latest development in Marti's life. The years in the arid tundra of cable shopping were over: he and Paddy were signed up to present a twelve-part history of children's broadcasting. There was a big budget, good writers and a dedicated groomer for the dog. Nell could imagine what this news meant to Tina. She covertly looked over at that tidy head, bent implausibly over a spreadsheet.

'HAPPEE BIRTHDAAAAAAAY!' Blair's inane tones filled her office. He blocked the doorway, his post-enema energy throbbing in the room. 'A little giftette for my sweetheart.'

A small box plopped on to the table. Nell hadn't realised that Prada made wrapping paper. 'Blairy, you're too good to me.' She undressed the little package. 'A key-ring! That's super,' she said, with a beatific smile. She'd been subjecting Blair to a charm offensive. She doubted that he'd noticed.

'It's got the Prada logo on it. Nothing but the best for my girl.' Blair could now say this kind of thing without retching. 'Louis in?'

'Go through. He's expecting you.'

'Before I forget,' he said, out of the side of his mouth, and flung a small piece of paper on to her desk.

'Of course. The receipt.' Nell smiled. 'I'll reimburse you out of petty cash.' Blairy never let her down.

A plate of toast appeared on her blotter. 'Dean! My birthday toast. Brilliant.' It was a long time since Nell had mocked her baseball-capped admirer. He was the only man behaving well in her life.

'Happy birthday,' mumbled Dean, placing a CD by the plate.

'El Stupido? I haven't heard of them.'

'They're, like, my band.'

'I didn't know you . . . I'll listen to this as soon as I get home.' Nell grinned encouragingly. 'Do you write the songs?'

'Yeah.' Dean squirmed as if he was five years old. 'One of them . . .' he forced out '. . . is about you.' And then he was gone, leaving behind only the whiff of burning hormones.

Nell scanned the back of the CD, searching the titles with a smug look. Maybe 'Girl Of My Dreams' was about her?

Or possibly, and here she frowned, 'Fat But Pretty'? She put it down when she saw the final title was 'Nobody Likes You But Me'.

'Where am I?' Nell had always longed to use those words, having heard them so many times in bad movies, but this was the first situation that had merited them.

'Believe it or not, you're in Helping Hands.' Joy looked shell-shocked behind what used to be chipped Formica and was now a massive leather-topped desk with ornate scroll legs. 'Our mystery benefactor has very fancy taste.'

Oddly enough, the mystery benefactor had Claudette's taste. The high walls were no longer nicotine-stained and decorated with heroin-awareness posters. Hand-blocked yellow wallpaper covered the room, a warm backdrop for the oak benches with velvet upholstery. The floor was also oak, and here and there stood delicate occasional tables, their curved legs matching the design of Joy's desk.

So this was Nell's birthday present. Nell stood, sucking in her cheeks, in the centre of the room. A few puzzled folk looking for a warm bed were queuing at the new desk, obviously too awestruck to lean on it as they gave Joy their particulars in hushed tones.

Not for the first time, Nell's family had bamboozled her. On one level this was an act of amazing generosity. And why on earth shouldn't homeless people have some luxury in their lives? Who said they had to have severe, utilitarian surroundings? But – and this was a big but, picked out in neon – there were much more pressing needs crying out for the application of a wodge of cash than poshing up the reception area.

Once again, Claudette had been amazingly benevolent *but on her own terms*. Nell was truly grateful, and yet . . .

Phred had done his sneaking-up trick again. 'What do you think?' he asked, from a foot behind her, making her jump in the air and drop the foot spa, ironically, on her foot. 'There was a Persian rug but I had to move it. Imagine how it would look by the end of the evening.'

'It's very different.' Nell picked her words with care. 'Do you know who's responsible for it?'

'Nope. A solicitor approached me and said his client would pay for everything and be finished in forty-eight hours, but that their identity had to remain secret and we had to accept their décor. It's actually very nice, but . . .' Phred had to use that important little word as well. He squinted into the middle distance as he asked, with strained casualness, 'You wouldn't know anything about this, would you?'

'Me? No. God, no. As if. Of course not. Yes, I do. It was my grandmother.'

'Thought so.'

'Why?'

'It's . . .' This time Phred was choosing his words carefully. He gave in and smiled. 'It's crazy.' He hurriedly straightened his face. 'Am I smirking?'

'No, I would call that a common-or-garden smile,' said Nell, with the thoughtful air of a connoisseur. Although, she had to admit privately, it was a very beautiful, sincere and handsome common-or-garden smile. She shook herself mentally. 'What's on the menu tonight?'

'Edith's famous Chicken Chasseur. Who's tonight's cake for?' He pointed to the box she had balanced on top of the foot spa.

'Me.'

'Really? Well, happy birthday. You should have changed your shift. Surely your boyfriend wanted to celebrate with you?'

'He's working.' Working his tongue down the throat of an impressionable nineteen-year-old, probably. 'We have a very loose arrangement.'

'Right.' This was apparently more information than Phred needed. He paused and said, 'Right,' again, then left her in the opulence of Reception.

'Fuck me!' Bridie had stepped over the threshold, and was as unselfconscious as ever in expressing herself. 'Buckingham bleedin' Palace!'

Crowds have moods, just the way individuals do. Tonight a ripple of high spirits ran through the basement. Ted was calling Bridie 'Your Majesty', a young West Country boy played the national anthem on his mouth organ and everybody greeted the cake as if it was manna from heaven.

As she helped Phred to collect the spattered trays, Nell asked, 'What's got into everybody?'

'Who knows? They amaze me sometimes.' Phred ran his hand through his hair in the familiar way.

As somebody who became profoundly depressed if she missed *EastEnders*, Nell marvelled at the resilience of Helping Hands' customers. A thought struck her. 'I haven't seen Anita for a while. How's that going?'

Phred's face closed. 'Not so good. It's harder than I thought. A lot of lies have been spread. And you know yourself that Anita's a surly sort. She's made a few enemies without any outside help.'

'You'll keep trying, though?' badgered Nell.

Phred looked at her very directly, with a hint of admonishment. 'I told you I'd do my best and I will.' He ran boiling water over the trays. 'This isn't much of a birthday for you, is it? Surrounded by homeless people, Edith and a worn-out community worker like me.'

'You're not—' Nell stopped short of a compliment. She blushed, glad of the camouflaging steam. 'I'm enjoying myself.' It was true. Nell usually celebrated her birthday with an ocean of alcohol and a meal she wouldn't remember eating. Last year Gareth had given her the infamous Boots gift voucher ('But you're always in Boots!' he'd said, when she'd exhibited unmistakable signs of disappointment) and had walked away from her outside their local tapas bar. This year the prospect of celebrating without Tina had been chilling, but at Helping Hands she hadn't had an opportunity to dwell on it. 'See how committed I've become?' she asked Phred coyly.

'You don't have to impress me. It's that lot out there.'

Phred never co-operated: she'd left a mile-wide gap for him to putt a compliment through. It wouldn't kill him, thought Nell, to say, 'Mmm, nice commitment' or 'God, you commit like a train'. 'You've missed a bit.' She pointed to a stubborn dribble of Chasseur on a tray, and stuck out her tongue when he lowered his head over the sink.

Yawning, Nell climbed the stairs to the darkened reception area. She wanted to see how the new furnishings had fared. She flicked the lights on – now wrought-iron Portuguese jobbies instead of the old complexion-ruining fluorescents – and smiled, relieved. Then she looked a little more closely. There was a smear of what looked like blood on the oak floorboards. A cigarette had been stubbed out on the leather top of the antique desk. Somebody had scribbled 'Alison has crabs' on an oil painting.

The brocade blind was askew. As Nell righted it, she glanced through the window and saw Anita running up the outer steps from the basement. She bashed on the window and mouthed, 'Hang on!' then dashed out to catch up with her.

'Hiya.' Anita's demeanour was subdued, but it always was.

'Phred says he's still on the case,' said Nell, as reassuringly as she could.

'Yeah.' Anita zipped up her Puffa jacket, a garment totally at odds with the balmy June air.

'And you'll have a bed here, of course.'

'Oh, no, I won't. He told me this morning I couldn't stay any longer. There's been complaints or something.'

'What?' Nell couldn't believe her ears. 'So . . .' She was computing wildly. Anita was back to square one.

'I've got to go. Don't worry about me, Nell.' Anita laid a hand on her arm. 'I'm all right.' She sprinted off.

'But . . .' Nell watched her hopelessly. Where was Anita

going to sleep that night? 'Anita!' she yelled, but her quarry was gone into the London darkness. Nell stamped her foot in frustration, scanning the dark cul-de-sac. It seemed threatening. To Nell, homeless girls were always more vulnerable than the blokes. Without the chance of a hostel, Anita was doubly defenceless. Her options would dwindle until none was safe.

And Phred wouldn't let her stay at Helping Hands because of a few complaints. How, thought Nell, with crazed energy, had she ever deluded herself enough to fancy the man? He was like a computer. And just like every computer she'd ever used, he'd let her down at the worst possible moment.

Nell was keen to convert her thoughts into actions, to stomp back in and find Phred so that she could let him know exactly what she thought of him. She would use all the new swear words she had learned from the dinner queue, and the newly washed crockery as missiles.

'Happy birthday, darling!' said a voice thick with beer, from right behind her.

'Gareth.' She didn't turn round.

'Fancy a ruby?' the voice asked seductively.

Nell turned. 'Actually, I do.' Shrieking at Phred could wait. A girl can only do so much good on her birthday before she needs to be fed and, besides, what she had to say was important and Nell was starting to twig that her unrehearsed speeches created more problems than they solved. 'Gareth,' she said, putting her arm through his, 'lead me to the all-you-can-eat buffet.'

Twenty-five

'Len's not well,' reported Jane From Accounts, with an anxious face. 'Davina ruffled his hair so he's had to go for a lie-down. I'm doing him a bacon sandwich.' She looked happy to perform this modest task for Len, whose blood-pressure problems were common knowledge – Linda had access to the personnel files.

Jane From Accounts laid down her jotter on the Formica while she prepared Len's medicinal snack. Nell glanced at it as she turned the key in the padlock on Louis's coffee jar. Casually she pointed to the magazine photo Jane From Accounts had stuck to the front of her pad. 'Like them, do you?'

'The St Petersburg Twins? Oh, God, I *love* them! They're perfect, aren't they? Fabulous!' Jane From Accounts, who went on fewer dates than the Pope, was prone to wild crushes. The whole office had quaked with the violence of her longing during her Russell Crowe phase, although the reign of the big-eared boy behind the till at Mario's had been more disturbing. 'I mean, they're gorgeous and there's two of them! What could be better?'

Tempted to answer, 'Triplets? Quads?' Nell kept schtum. A little plot was hatching.

'Relax,' Nell instructed Marti, as the lift doors closed on them. 'My row with Tina is nothing to do with you.'

'No. Right.' Marti looked pained to be in such a small space with his girlfriend's estranged best friend. 'I don't understand what's going on, to tell you the truth.'

'It'll blow over,' said Nell, with more confidence than she felt. Every day the *froideur* dragged on made that less likely, she thought. She was still surprised at her own strength of purpose, and the doubts she was having about the damaged friendship, but didn't like to examine the possible consequences too closely. Life without Tina was unthinkable. Wasn't it?

Nell knew her duty to Marti as a Morgan Theatrical Management client. 'Congratulations on the new series. It sounds like it'll be fab.'

'I'm just glad those blinkered fools have given in and put me back where I belong.'

'Put you *and Paddy* back where you belong.'

'Yeah.' Marti stabbed the button for the ground floor violently. 'Bloody lift,' he said.

Clutching bottles of Bailey's and Tia Maria, Nell turned into her mother's road. The two beverages were a staple at a Fitzgerald soirée. Claudette had made it clear that Nell could always take whatever she needed from the wine rack in Knightsbridge, but it was pointless to bring vintage wine to a house that mixed everything together and drank the result from paper cups.

Nell was anticipating getting as drunk, if not drunker than, the proverbial skunk. Less of Tina in her life meant less boozing and she didn't dare drink in Gareth's company in case she woke up married.

And getting drunk was appealing because of the oblivion it promised. Nell was tired of turning things over in her mind. She wanted to bury for an evening the hardness on her so-called grandfather's face as he had told her point-blank that he wanted nothing to do with her. She wanted a respite from her complex feelings about Tina. She wanted to smother the growing hysteria about her resuscitated relationship with Gareth. She needed to block out the shame of her public alliance with Blair. And, most of all, she wanted to get off the roundabout of her feelings for Phred.

When he had been her married manager, an emotionless prig, he had occupied a neat Phred-shaped slot in her mind.

Since she had discovered he was a widower, and he had shown her glimpses of his more human side, he had elbowed his way out of the slot and cavorted messily through the ankle-deep debris of Nell's psyche.

At first, Anita's problem had prompted Phred's finest hour, and Nell had seen him in a different light. Suddenly it was permissible to notice the deep conker brown of his eyes. She had relaxed into laughing at his sardonic humour instead of rolling her eyes at it. In short, Phred had crossed a line: he wasn't an authority figure any more, he was something much warmer and sexier.

Then he'd had to ruin it all. Nell was disgusted by the way he had thrown Anita on to the streets again. It was a struggle to reconcile this heartlessness with her new, softer version of him. She could never snuggle up to a man who would treat a powerless person so shabbily. Helping Anita was well within his scope: it was just against his bloody rules.

So why did she find herself tracing the line of his lips in her memory as she fell asleep?

With all this going on in her overheated head, a nice pint of something rancid and green was just what she needed, and it was pressed into her hands by her mother when the front door opened.

'Take that before Ringo sees it. He's had enough.' Patsy pulled her daughter over the threshold. 'Oops. Sorry. Mind the boobs,' she apologised.

'Hello, Mum,' stuck in Nell's throat as she contemplated the gigantic plastic breasts her mother was sporting.

'Clever, aren't they? They do up round me neck and they look as if they're bursting out of a T-shirt.' Patsy twirled, keen to demonstrate the cunning design.

'They're a modern marvel.'

Patsy had never tasted an alcoholic drink. She didn't seem to need it. 'Go through. The DNA results are in so everybody's gone mad.'

Nell didn't know anybody else who had resorted to DNA

testing. It was the preserve of the very rich or the very poor who had access to daytime discussion programmes, as far as she knew. It was vaguely shameful and vaguely thrilling to have a half-sister who needed modern science to determine who was the father of her child.

The noise of raucous singing led Nell to the conservatory. The partygoers had spilled into the garden, where strains of *Sgt Pepper* filled the heavy air. She stepped over outstretched legs to the patch of grass where Georgina stood with Annie in her arms. Annie was arrayed in frills worthy of Louis XVI, and clapped excitedly at the sight of her godmother.

'Take her, will you?' Georgina handed over the baby.

'Hello, sweetie-pie,' said Nell, self-consciously, as she juggled baby and drink. 'So,' she began, shuffling to avoid an outbreak of dancing to her left, 'your new boyfriend accepts he's the dad now, I hope.'

'You what?' frowned Georgina. 'Oh. Right. No, you've got it all wrong, Nell. It turns out it was neither of them!' She couldn't suppress a giggle and an ooh-silly-me shrug of the shoulders.

Her half-sister, Nell reminded herself, was sixteen. 'Who was it, then?' she asked weakly.

'Probably the bloke who did next door's double-glazing.'

'Probably?'

'Definitely. Almost.'

'Almost?' Nell looked at the pink and white face of her goddaughter. Annie laughed uproariously. The baby seemed as unconcerned about the identity of her father as her mother was. 'So the wedding's off?'

Georgina found the question hilarious. 'Oi! Fabio! Nell's just asked if the wedding's off!' she shouted across the grass.

By the garden shed, Fabio bent double and shouted back, 'Too fucking right it is!' and raised his glass in salute.

'He's *here*?' Nell was dumbfounded. Could anything shake Georgina's *sangfroid*? She took everything in her stride. She was either bonkers or prime-minister material, and Nell didn't feel qualified to judge which.

'Course. He's all right. He's an all right bloke.'

To Nell he looked like a child in his baggy trousers and the statutory baseball cap. 'Will you be OK?' Nell examined Georgina for a chink of vulnerability. She was getting good at reading faces since she'd started the voluntary work but this one was tough to decipher.

'Eh?' The question baffled Georgina. 'Why shouldn't I? I didn't really want to get married anyway. I'm a modern, independent woman. Thanks to the DSS.' She leaned in to whisper, 'I've got me eye on Seb now. He's bloody stunning.'

Nell looked over at the bloody stunning Seb, a gangly black boy with a crop circle etched into his short hair. He was chatting to Fabio but sending covert glances Georgina's way. He looked as if he'd thrown aside his Tellytubbies to grow up too soon.

'I hope you're going to be, you know, *careful*,' said Nell.

'You make me scream!' Georgina's answer was neither illuminating nor reassuring.

It took a mere half-pint of whatever was in the glass to crank Nell's point of view round to match her family's. 'You must be very proud of her,' she said to Ringo, as they watched Georgina dirty-dancing with Seb.

'She's the apple of my eye.' Ringo wiped away a tear.

Another half-pint and Nell was dancing too. Seb had an older brother whose name she didn't catch. He had no job but spent a lot of time at the gym. It showed.

'Honest, I don't mind. I don't mind a bit. It doesn't bother me at all. Not even shlightingly.' Nell cradled her third pint of Fitzgerald's Special and told her twin half-brothers over and over again she didn't mind that they hadn't sent her a birthday card. 'I didn't even notice. It'sh a matter of shupreme indifference to me.' She burped. 'Honest.'

'Happy birthday.' John handed her a tiny parcel wrapped in metallic paper.

Bursting into flamboyant drunken tears, Nell thanked them a thousand times and tore open the paper to reveal a small bottle of Crabtree and Evelyn bath gel. 'Oh, God, it's STUNNING!' she shrieked, and fell off her chair.

John and Paul righted her and tried to arrange her on the stool so that she wouldn't fall off again. This proved to be difficult: her bones had dissolved. 'I love it,' she kept repeating. 'And I don't mind that Mum didn't buy me anything thish year, honest.'

'Oh, her,' smiled Paul. 'She's forgotten everybody's birthday since Canvey was born.'

'Not just mine?' squawked Nell, at what seemed to be the only volume available to her.

'No, silly, not just you.'

Nell was so happy to hear this that she fell asleep.

A hangover is a hangover is a hangover: linen sheets made no difference to Nell's suspicion that her body had been trampled by horses during the night. Carita sent in a ginseng infusion and Fergus, with a touch of sadism, suggested a raw egg in tomato juice. Nell bayed for a fry-up but Claudette forbade it. 'Your skin will thank me in twenty years' time,' she said.

'There's no way I'll live that long.' Nell was too wan to cry but she managed to phone the office.

'Morgan Theatrical Management.' Linda was on phone duty, covering for Zoë. 'Hmm, that does sound like a bad sore throat. You'd better spend the day in bed. Weren't you at a family party last night?'

'I put my head round the door,' croaked Nell.

'I see. I'll make sure that Louis knows what's going on.' Linda just loved to be cryptic. 'Look after yourself now.'

And you look after yourself too, thought Nell evilly, as she put the phone down. Don't walk under any falling anvils, for instance. Or accidentally stick your head in a mincer. Talking

to Linda had unnerved her, and she gathered all her strength
to crawl across the Aubusson and down the hall to the kitchen.

There were no Jaffa Cakes.

None.

'Nell, I'm your mother.'

'Uh-huh.'

'And you know I only want what's good for you.' This
was an unusual opener from Patsy, who believed in a strict
policy of non-intervention with her children.

'Uh-huh.' Why had her mother chosen the day of a blinding
hangover to come over maternal?

'I haven't been able to stop thinking about what you told
me last night.'

Mind racing, Nell wondered which of the several grisly
things going on in her life she might have spilled under the
influence.

'You know I was dead against you looking for your grandfather.' Patsy paused to take a deep breath and bellow,
'CANVEY! Do *not* microwave Annie!' It was early in the conversation for Patsy to execute her traditional swerve in attention, and she swerved right back. 'Nothing good ever came
out of that family. It's bad enough you're staying with
Claudette without chasing her ex-husband. Now he's upset
you and I could tell it's gone deep with you. You'll have to
forget about how he was with you and move on, love. I had
to, and I have. It's the only way.'

'But, Mum, you moved on to something else. I'm still
looking.' Nell had never before been so frank with her mother
about her state of mind. She listened to her breathing in the
pause that followed.

'Oh, Nell, I do worry about you.'

And, perversely, that was music to Nell's ears.

Louis called in the afternoon to check on her health. 'You're
skiving, aren't you?'

Too weak to argue, Nell answered, 'Yes.'

'Oh.' Her honesty had taken the wind out of Louis's sails. 'Just make sure you're presentable by seven when Blair picks you up. And look classy, if that's possible, darling. It's a gallery-opening on King's Road.'

It was three minutes past seven.

'Your young man is late,' commented Claudette, as she sat by the fireplace beneath the portrait of her. Both Claudettes wore the same supercilious, disapproving expression.

The ticking of the clock reverberated in Nell's head, disturbing the cotton wool it was packed with. 'You're not dressed for dinner, Claudette?' she queried. By this hour her grandmother was usually bejewelled and smelling gorgeous.

'I'm not dining tonight.' Claudette pulled her cashmere housecoat a little more tightly around herself.

'Not having your dinner?' If it was anybody else Nell would have felt her forehead. 'Are you feeling all right? Shall I stay in?'

Claudette appeared shocked. 'Whatever for?'

'To keep you company.'

A withering glance flew Nell's way. 'It is far too late to cancel your plans and the only reason I would need you to keep me company is if I were an invalid.' Those sparkling eyes were unwavering. 'Do I look like an invalid to you?'

'No, Claudette.'

The doorbell rang. Saved by the giant orange fool.

Fergus ushered Blair into the drawing room and Nell leaped to her feet, eager to make a quick getaway. She couldn't imagine what Claudette and her butler would make of a life-form like Blair.

'Nell, remember your manners. Perhaps Mr Taylor would like a cocktail,' her grandmother chided imperiously.

'Do you know?' said Blair, his head coquettishly to one side and his eyelashes working overtime. 'I could just go a Tom Collins.'

Looking daggers at him, Nell said meaningfully, 'Just a small one.'

'Fergus doesn't look like he knows the meaning of a small one.' Blair nudged Fergus and laughed loudly enough to rattle the chandelier.

Nell winced and watched Fergus for the inevitable expression of scorn. But he was laughing too.

Nell stared. She had never seen him laugh before. There was a tinkling sound behind her. Her grandmother was laughing too, one beringed hand over her mouth like a schoolgirl.

'You'll join us, won't you, you beautiful thing, you?' Blair urged Claudette.

Instead of shooting him in the eye, as Nell would have expected, Claudette nodded graciously and asked for a very small martini.

Immune to it, Nell was witnessing the full power of the charm that had earned Blair enough money to Botox the frown off Sweden.

'What lovely people! Your grandmother's a hoot! And that Fergus – what a guy!' said Blair, as they braved the phalanx of paparazzi in front of the gallery.

Nell nodded. It had been disturbing to watch Claudette laugh at *double-entendres*, like seeing the Prime Minister on the loo. Before she had dragged her 'young man' away from the penthouse Claudette had taken her to one side and said discreetly, 'I suggest you hang on to this one, my dear.'

'He's about as gay as you can be without exploding,' explained Nell, patiently.

'Homosexuality is no hurdle to a happy marriage,' said Claudette, with certainty. 'In fact, if one looks at the history of the British aristocracy one might conclude that it's vital.' She had glanced approvingly to where Blair was fingering Fergus's lapels. 'Furthermore, he is a cultured person. *Gareth* would never have taken you to an art gallery.'

Now, gazing around her at the artworks, Nell felt that this wasn't the sort of gallery Claudette had imagined. A life-size *papier-mâché* nude of a woman with a gigantic penis growing out of her forehead was entitled *Confusion*. You're telling me, thought Nell, and moved on to a Labrador made out of rubbish.

'What a load of old bollocks,' said Blair, smile glued in place.

'It's "symbolic of the growing ennui in modern-day society",' Nell read from the brochure. 'The Labrador costs eight thousand pounds.'

'They give them away for nothing at Battersea Dogs Home,' said her cultured date. He changed the subject abruptly. 'How old do I look to you?'

This was a booby-trap of a question. Nell's mind raced. She didn't know how old Blair was, so she couldn't undercut it by a few years. If she guessed *too* low he'd know she was indulging him. But if she guessed that he was older than he was there'd be *papier-mâché* all over the walls. 'Ooooh . . .' Nell stalled, hoping that some act of God might save her. 'Maybe, about, in the region of . . . thirty-three?'

'Really?' By the dazzling smile she was well under, but not *too* well under. 'This might surprise you but I'm thirty-nine. Seven,' he corrected himself hastily. 'No, no, I tell a lie, I'm thirty-five.'

From this Nell deduced he was somewhere in his early forties.

'It's time I settled down.'

Nell was startled.

'Oh, not with you, you silly cow.' Blair tutted at the thought. 'A cottage somewhere. Roses round the door. Somebody with tight buns baking a cake in the Aga . . .' He looked wistful. 'I can't do it while I'm in the closet, can I?'

'You could always . . . step out of the closet,' said Nell, encouragingly, aware that she wasn't toeing the Morgan party line.

Blair shrugged his shoulders with a hopeless expression. 'Could I? It's not that easy.'

'But it might be worth it,' pushed Nell.

'It might be . . . Nope, darling. I like my luxuries too much.' A real expression, one of doubt and even sadness, transformed his features for a moment. Then the permasmile returned and he posed for a picture beside a *papier-mâché* walrus on a ski, entitled *Frigid*.

Twenty-six

Yes, confirmed Joy, she'd definitely passed on Nell's message to Anita to get in touch. 'She only came in once last week.' Joy's omnipresent smile dimmed.

Knee-deep in used clothes, they were making up bundles for people sleeping rough. The idea was to package up one blanket, one jumper, and one coat, plus some smaller odds and ends. Despite Phred's instruction to remember that they weren't dealing with supermodels, both girls were instinctively trying to match things up. Everybody had a right to be co-ordinated, they agreed.

Clover was helping. She had been told to go through the huge piles of donated stuff on the floor of the dining hall and bring them all the socks she could find. This she did, detailing each one quite loudly. 'Here's a stripy one like my friend Lucy wears. Here's a blue one like old men wear.' She puzzled over one for a while, then decided, 'Here's a hard one like smelly monsters wear.' She rooted through the pile and came up with a fluffy sock. 'Here's a pretty one like my daddy's girlfriend wears.'

Joy and Nell looked at each other over the little girl's head. Nell suspected she might have gone ever so slightly pink. 'Daddy's girlfriend, Cloves?' she asked evenly.

'She doesn't sleep at our house every night.' Clover was matching up some holey pop-socks. 'She has princessy hair.'

This information had a strange effect on Nell. She wanted to shake Clover and shout, 'I've got nice hair too, you know!' Ashamed, she gave the child a hug instead, her lips pursed so tight they were sore.

'Go the Phred!' said Joy, much amused.

'Yeah.' Nell hugged Clover again. 'Go the Phred.'

Reeled in to Twickenham like a fish on a line, Nell climbed the stairs to her old flat. Tonight she had a speech rehearsed. It was long and it was probably very dull but it left no room for doubt: she was going to tell Gareth she didn't want to see him again.

One fake relationship was more than enough to cope with, particularly when Nell kept pulling at the leash in Phred's direction. Phred, a man proven to have a lump of metal where his heart should be, was now Nell's drug of choice. She had stopped fighting the daydreams about him, even though it felt forbidden, like daydreaming about Hitler. Or your gynaecologist. Or a bizarre mixture of both.

'He's pompous and he smirks and he won't lift a finger to help Anita,' she had reminded herself many times. 'And I want him,' she always concluded.

Of course, it didn't matter how much she wanted him. Phred was safely out of reach. To him she was just a volunteer, and an inadequate one at that. She wasn't princessy, like his *girlfriend*.

Nell found she couldn't say (or even think) that word without her lip curling at the corner, like Elvis.

'Gareth,' began Nell, as he opened the door to her.

'Don't say a word.' Gareth put his finger to her lips and led her into the sitting room.

The coal-effect fire was on, despite the soft warmth of the evening and that he had always roared, 'Do you think I'm made of money?' if she switched it on.

Beneath her feet, a trail of rose petals led to a new furry rug on which stood an ice bucket, containing a bottle of champagne.

Gareth took both her hands and pulled her down gently to kneel on it beside him. 'Firelight suits you,' he said softly.

That was the moment when Nell abandoned the moderate,

sane speech she'd rehearsed. She stood up. 'Do you really think this bullshit is what I want?' she spluttered. 'All I wanted, all through those years I spent with you, was a bit of respect. A bit of consideration. Some clue that you knew me for who I really was, that you *cared*.'

Gareth froze, kneeling, on the rug. He was staring at her as if she was speaking a foreign language.

'I mean, Gareth, rose fucking petals! Where has all this romance come from? It's too late.' She pushed away the arms that reached out to her and shouted hysterically, 'Will you listen to me for once? It's too late. I don't love you, and you're squeezing me to *death*!'

'No,' said Gareth disbelievingly. 'No, no, no.' He was trying to drag her down on to the new rug.

'Yes, yes, yes!' squealed Nell. She turned on her heel, unwilling to witness the inevitable blubbing and begging.

But Gareth didn't blub. He bellowed, 'Don't you dare walk out on me a second time, you ungrateful bitch!' The old Gareth was back. 'This rug cost me twenty-nine fucking nine!' he added, in a loud postscript.

'I'm not scared of you any more, Gareth.' Nell made for the door.

'You should be!' Gareth scrambled to get ahead of her.

'Don't touch me.'

The situation had escalated alarmingly. Nell and Gareth faced each other, both red in the face and breathing heavily. Nell had always backed down before they reached this stage. She wasn't backing down today. She was walking away, and they both knew it.

'I'm going to make you very sorry for this.' Gareth was snarling.

'You can try if you like.' The slamming of the front door sounded like a loud, triumphant, musical finale.

Jean looked puzzled. And disgusted. 'They're underpants, dear.' She drew back behind the photocopier. 'Worn underpants.'

'They're the nicest present that anybody has ever given me.' The sincerity in Jane From Accounts's voice made Jean grateful that she didn't spend Christmas at her place. 'Ooooooh!' Jane From Accounts crumpled the Calvin Kleins and buried her face in them.

'Oh, now, really – there's no need for that.' Jean hurried off.

Nell beamed. 'I don't know if they're John's or Paul's, but they definitely belong to one of them,' she told Jane From Accounts.

'I can't believe you're actually related to the St Petersburg twins.' Jane From Accounts was in a daze. 'They're so good-looking. Oh, I didn't mean . . .' She stopped in her tracks, pink and confused.

'I know what you didn't mean, don't worry. Carry on enjoying your underpants.' Nell could hear Zoë squawking her name.

She strolled out to Reception and stopped dead.

An elderly man, evidently in his best suit and holding a check cap between long, crooked fingers, stood by the desk.

'You've got a visitor,' said Zoë, unnecessarily.

'Will you see me?' asked Nell's grandfather.

She nodded.

Louis was having a day off so Nell led her visitor into his office. 'We'll have some privacy here,' she said shyly. 'Would you like to sit down?'

'I'll stand.' Jack Fairweather was formal. 'I'd like to apologise to you.'

'No—' Nell began compassionately.

'Please.' He held up a hand. He had a stern demeanour and an upright bearing. 'Let me finish.' He was evidently used to being obeyed. 'I apologise unreservedly for my rudeness and thoughtlessness. I should have exercised more self-control.' He let out a long sigh, as if exhausted by his short speech. 'A man would have to be a bloody fool not to welcome a lovely young lady like you as a granddaughter.'

'Granddaughter!' squeaked his granddaughter, who could allow herself to get used to the idea all over again.

'I only hope that you can find it in your heart to forgive me,' said Jack, gravely. He talked like a character in a Victorian melodrama. 'Can you?' he asked, apparently nervous of the reply.

'Yes! Yes!' cried Nell. 'You're absolutely and completely forgiven. In fact, you're over-forgiven!' She slapped her arms down at her sides, longing to bear-hug the awkward old man, but feeling that perhaps that kind of contact should wait. He was from a different generation, which took things slowly. 'I would have behaved exactly the same, I bet. A mad cow turning up out of nowhere, dragging up the past and expecting you to be glad about it. I do forgive you . . . Granddad,' she ended sheepishly, trying out the word for size.

'I'm very grateful.' A tear was glistening in the old man's eye.

That did it. Nell had waited a whole eight seconds. It was time for the hug. As she threw her arms round her stiff, surprised grandfather, she excused herself: she'd missed out on twenty-eight years of this.

'It's a big day at Morgan Theatrical Management today, innit?' Zoë had her feet up on the reception desk. 'Knickers. Granddads. It's got the lot.'

'Granddads?' asked Tina, as she sped past. 'Whose granddad?'

'Well, Nell's . . .' said Zoë, glancing over to where Nell was showing Jack round and pretending not to listen.

Tina broke step but carried on, clutching *Bride* magazine to her chest.

Bursting with her news and unable to share it with Tina, Nell rang Maggie as Jack waited by the lift. 'I have a granddad and he's *lovely*!' she gushed down the phone.

'I'm very glad he came to his senses.' Maggie was moved, Nell could tell. 'We did the right thing, going there.'

'We did. And you were the only one who encouraged me,' Nell reminded her.

Ignoring the compliment, Maggie said she had to go, a Fred Astaire film was coming on. 'Just a few other things for you to clear up now,' she said mysteriously. 'Then we can all relax.'

'You're sure you like Chinese?' Nell was anxious now that they were seated at a tiny table being served by a tiny waitress.

'Well, I've never had it,' confessed Jack, 'but I'm sure I'll like it.' He looked mildly uncomfortable. It occurred to Nell that he probably didn't go to restaurants much. Everything about this dignified man was ordinary. Reassuringly ordinary. How he could have been married to the hyper-sophisticated Claudette was a mystery.

'Will you order for me, Nell?' he whispered, having stared at the menu for a minute or two.

'Of course.' Nell purred like a cat at his need of her help. She turned to the waitress. 'My *granddad* will have chicken chow mein,' she said, smiling as if she had a whole banana in her mouth, 'and we'll have a bottle of the house white, please.'

Across the table, Jack sat up a little straighter. 'You drink, Nell?' he asked abruptly.

'A little.' Nell blinked with what she hoped was girlish innocence. 'A little at a time' might have been more honest: those sips added up to a veritable reservoir.

'I don't touch the stuff,' said Jack, eyes averted.

'Right. Fine. Scrub the wine,' she told the waitress. 'We'll have some mineral water, please.'

'Water?' Jack looked aghast. 'Do they not do tea?'

'Only green tea.' Nell felt adrift. She was desperate to please him. 'But we could ask for milk and sugar with it, if you like.'

'No, no, never mind. I'll have a nice glass of milk.'

The confused waitress left them to catch up with each other. The man opposite, Nell realised with a jolt, was a stranger. She'd daydreamed with her usual energy and created an entire personality for him. In her head, Jack was a perfect storybook granddad, always ready with a cuddle and an anecdote about whippets, perhaps, or the war. The flesh-and-blood version, perched uneasily on a spindly chair, was awkward and even a little shy. He had the air of somebody who spent a lot of time alone. Nell decided to draw him out, so she floated questions at him as he grimaced at his chow mein and did his manful best with it.

As Jack told her about his life – his little flat, his dog, his choir – Nell searched his face for a likeness to her own. The curl of his smile perhaps, or the way he gulped his words when he was getting ahead of himself. She could have stared at him all day.

'I want to hear about you,' he insisted. 'Are you married? Do I have any great-grandchildren I don't know about?'

It broke Nell's heart to hear the hope in his voice. 'Well, no and no. I do have a boyfriend, but it's complicated . . .' She didn't feel ready to explain Blair. 'The men in my life haven't been up to much, starting with my dad – oh, God, I'm sorry.' She bit her lip.

'No, go on.' Jack looked strained. 'Tell me all you can about him. I don't even know his name.' He put down his chopsticks and wiped his eyes with an arthritic hand. He coughed to collect himself, then leaned across to say, 'Do you mind if I ask the young lady for a knife and fork? I'll never get the food into my mouth with these sticks.'

Nell called the waitress, fighting the urge to tell her, 'Not only do I have a granddad, but I have one of those cute ones who can't handle new-fangled things like chopsticks.'

It didn't take long to share all Nell knew about Philippe. Jack listened in silence, then said scornfully, '*Philippe*. Typical. Claudette always did go for fancy names. What's wrong with plain old Philip?'

'Well, he's partly French so I suppose she wanted a French name for him.'

Jack put down his newly acquired knife and fork. 'Is she still peddling that twaddle?'

Gently, Nell defended her grandmother. 'She's proud of her family, Granddad. The de Montrachets do go back a long way.'

'Do they heck! They don't go back to last Wednesday. Claudette is about as French as a plate of jellied eels.'

'I don't understand.' Nell's universe tumbled on to its head. 'Claudette is a de Montrachet. Her – *my* – ancestors are Parisian aristocrats.'

'The name de Montrachet came from the label on a bottle of wine. Claudette's ancestors are from Glasgow. She was christened Ethel but . . .' Jack allowed himself a nostalgic smile at the memory '. . . I always called her Pinky.'

Nell was late back from lunch. She'd had to hear the strange story twice before she could take it in. Sitting shell-shocked at her desk, she took calls on automatic pilot as she mulled over what her grandfather had told her.

Pinky – as Nell was beginning to think of her – had been married to his employer. Jack was chauffeur to an immensely wealthy self-made man a few decades older than his beautiful young wife. 'Very unsure of herself,' Jack had said, remembering the twenty-year-old he had driven around town. 'Very shy. Self-conscious about her broad Glasgow accent.'

Nell had had to stop him there while she ordered more food. Such revelations called for calories. It transpired that Claudette was one of the nine children of a bricklayer. She had never been to school. She had hardly been beyond the end of her road before her husband-to-be had spotted her and made her his wife.

There had been elocution lessons and French lessons and deportment classes. Her new mentor had squired her round museums and art galleries. He'd encouraged her to read more than magazines about movie stars. She had blossomed into a polished, educated lady.

'Did you have an affair?' Nell asked hungrily.

'We certainly did not.' Jack looked reprovingly at his new granddaughter. 'We talked as I drove her around. We liked the same things. Underneath all her new sophistication she was still a fish-and-chips girl. I used to sneak her off to the East End when she craved a nice cockle. How I used to laugh at the sight of her in the back seat, picking up winkles on a pin, all done up in a mink stole.'

The romance that had ultimately led to Nell had only blossomed after the millionaire had keeled over and died one evening in their magnificent house. 'She became a very wealthy woman overnight.' All these years later Jack still seemed surprised when he said, 'I never thought she'd look twice at the likes of me, but she admitted she had feelings for me and I . . . I felt the same.'

'How romantic!' Nell had sighed.

'That's what I thought. But Pinky had plans.' Jack recalled how she had tried to get him to take elocution lessons. 'I wasn't having any of that rubbish,' he said vigorously, making Nell love him even more. 'We got married, and I believe to this day that we could have been happy if Pinky hadn't kept wanting more. She wanted to be accepted – it wasn't enough to be rich. She had to be upper class. She wanted to leave her roots behind.'

'How did that make you feel?' Nell had probed.

'It disgusted me,' said Jack, vehemently. 'And I let her know it. She came from a perfectly decent family. Poor as church mice, but good people. She cut herself off from them like *that*.' He made a chopping movement with his hand.

This sounded more like the Claudette Nell knew. In fact, the woman she recognised as her grandmother had developed from this part of her history. She had adopted the habits and tastes of the aristocracy, all the while inventing an impressively airtight past for herself. Her massive wealth had made it easy for her to fool the toffs she was so keen on, and soon she was an integral part of London Society.

'And you?' asked Nell, wondering how her grandfather, who felt out of place in a run-of-the-mill Chinese restaurant, would fare in a Belgravia drawing room.

Jack snorted. 'Those old biddies bored the pants off me. Talking about their good works and wearing outfits that cost more than a working man earned in a year.'

Uneasily aware that perhaps she was a modern version of those old biddies, Nell nodded sympathetically.

'I was sitting in the back of the car then, instead of in the driving seat. I don't mind telling you, love, I was bored witless. I never did work out what rich people did all day. Polish their vowels, I used to say.'

Nell giggled, and so did Jack.

'I wanted to get a job, but that didn't suit Pinky's plan. In fact, I was turning into a bit of an embarrassment all round. I can see it plain as the nose on my face now. I was the last remnant from the bad old days. At the time I couldn't work out why we argued all the time, but now I know that she was just setting the stage to ask me for a divorce.'

So many years had passed that her grandfather could speak about that time without being over-emotional, but Nell, spooning pineapple ice-cream furiously into her mouth, felt full of backdated outrage.

'She offered me a lot of money but I want you to know, girl, that I didn't take a penny off her. I did as she asked and stayed away. I went off and got a job up in Leeds and I was happy enough. Yes,' he said, in a tone obviously designed to convince himself, 'I was happy enough. I retired back down here, to the little flat you came to. It does for me and the dog.' He took a deep breath. 'If I'd known about Philippe . . .'

One day they would have the conversation about how different things might have been if Jack had known about his son, but not today. 'Oh, Granddad,' sighed Nell, her eyes swimming, 'we've wasted so many years.'

'Can we try and make up for them?' Jack sounded fearful of Nell's answer. 'I've found myself thinking these past few days of all the things we could do together. But a young lass like you must be busy. I reckon there's a queue of fellas at the door. Am I right?'

A queue of one, thought Nell ruefully. And he's wearing leather chaps. 'You're the main man in my life now, Granddad.' She gulped but the knot in her throat wouldn't shrink. She took Jack's gnarled hand in hers and squeezed it as if it was a lifebelt.

'Oh, Nell . . .'

When they could both speak again, Nell ordered coffee and asked, 'So this first husband, how come he was so rich? What did he do?'

'Ah.' Jack smiled. 'Here's the bit Pinky *really* wouldn't want you to know. His fortune was built on rubber foundation wear.' Nell looked blank so he expanded: 'Incontinence knickers.'

Twenty-seven

The plebeian food stocks were running low. On her way home from that unusual day at the office, Nell stopped at a 7/11 and returned to Hans Place clutching a carrier-bag that bulged with things that were bad for her.

On the steps she encountered Carita, glamorous in black ruffles, on her way out. 'I found him!' Nell blurted out. 'I found my granddad!'

There was no way to translate the rapid Italian this unleashed, but Nell got the gist of it. Covered with lipstick kisses she made her way up to the penthouse. One eye on Fergus, she refilled her cupboard. Ostentatiously she marked the level on the Coca-Cola bottle. 'Going anywhere nice on your night off?' she threw Fergus's way, with little hope of gaining information.

'I have no plans.'

'Where are you spending your summer holiday this year?' Nell resorted to the hairdressers' gambit.

'I have an aunt in Newquay.'

Nell gave up. She hoped that one day Fergus would slip up and say something along the lines of 'My body will be covered in honey that will be licked off by swans before I am ravished by various Tory ministers,' but he never did. The aunt in Newquay was the most salacious detail to date.

The phone rang. Fergus answered in his most supercilious tones and informed Lady Something-or-other that Madame was out at present.

When he replaced the receiver Nell said, 'You're a big fibber, Fergus. Madame is in the drawing room, large as life.'

'I am acting under instruction,' said Fergus, in his habitual over-formal manner.

Wondering why Claudette would turn down a call from a genuine ladyship, Nell sought her out. 'Are you feeling all right, Claudette?'

'What a tiresome question, and one you ask far too often,' answered Claudette, with irritation. 'Might we agree on this, child? When I don't "feel all right", as you put it, I'll let you know. Now,' she smiled, turning the page on her swingeing rudeness, 'a hand or two of poker?'

As she tried her best but still lost spectacularly, Nell carried on an internal conversation with herself. She was steeling herself to confront Claudette with the truth. Surely her grandmother knew that at some point the ludicrous façade would crumble? Perhaps she would greet the end of the game with resignation, even relief.

Some hope, chortled the more realistic portion of Nell's brain, which occasionally got a look-in during these dialogues.

There were so many layers to the stratum of deceit that had been carefully laid down over the years. The fake family history, the feigned lack of knowledge about the lives of ordinary people, the plans to Parisianise Nell, who didn't have a drop of French blood in her veins. Ironically, Nell felt much more comfortable knowing that she came from a large, jolly Glasgow family than she ever had believing she was from fancy French stock.

Nell looked at Claudette, whose cool eyes were scanning the cards. Diamonds at her ears and throat hinted at the immense wealth that underpinned this woman – this creation. This *fraud*.

And it's all thanks to people wetting themselves. It was hard not to smile, but Nell maintained her poker face.

A day or so later, as she came out of Maggie's front garden, Nell closed, opened and reclosed the wooden garden gate. Smugly she noted that it clicked shut with a satisfactory clunk. Earlier she had repaired it, with the help of a *Reader's Digest* DIY manual, Maggie's motley collection of old tools and only three oh-fucking-hells.

'Hiya!' Anita was on the pavement beside her.

Nell blinked, surprised to see her out of context. 'Anita! You look great.'

And she did. A broad smile was plastered across her face and she was in only one layer of clothing. Which was clean. 'I've got a job.' She was exuding enough positive energy to light Wales. 'And I love it. They're dead nice to me.'

'No! That's brilliant!' Nell was reeling at this about-turn in Anita's fortunes. It felt magical. 'I'm so pleased – I'm so pleased,' she repeated stupidly. 'But what are you doing in this neck of the woods?'

Anita hesitated, then said, 'You might as well know. I'm with Phred. Nobody's supposed to know.' She smiled secretively. 'He's so sweet to me, Nell. There's never been a man like him in my life before. And I love Clover – she's a doll. I never thought I'd say this but everything turns out for the best, doesn't it?'

'Ye-es.' Nell let this sink in. So Anita was the princess who didn't sleep there *every* night. She felt as if God had poured a big jug of iced water over her head.

It was stupid to be jealous. Very stupid. And mean. Didn't Anita deserve some kindness and happiness in her life? So what if she was with Phred? Sleeping with Phred . . .

Nell dug her nails into her palms.

There was no real need for Nell to be at Helping Hands that Friday lunchtime. She just found herself gravitating there. She paused at Mario's, scanning the place paranoically for Tina, to buy a bread truncheon. 'Fancy sharing this baguette?' She waved it at Joy.

'We'll eat it on the roof,' said Joy.

The metal steps were rusty and worn. Nell was uncomfortably close to Joy's behind as she climbed up after her. 'Not much headroom here,' she grumbled.

'It'll be worth it when you see the roof garden.'

Joy pushed open a hatch and brilliant sunlight streamed over them. They emerged, blinking like moles, on to the flat roof of Helping Hands.

'Roof garden' was pushing it a bit. True, there were two pots of wonky sunflowers up there, but if it hadn't been for the deckchair it would have been just a roof.

Phred was stretched out in the deckchair, head flung back. 'I thought I was the only one who knew about this place,' he said, in a voice that didn't sound too thrilled.

'Who do you think put the sunflowers out?' asked Joy, as she gave Nell a hand to clamber up.

'I suspected the fairies.' Phred stood up. 'Do you want a seat?'

'No, you stay put, you're all right,' said Nell, but Joy nipped over and sank gratefully on to the moth-eaten striped fabric.

'You're a gent.' She beamed up at him.

'I'm a mug. And aren't you on duty?'

'I do get a lunch-break, you know.'

'I spoil you.' Phred kicked the deckchair half-heartedly, but he smiled. He always smiled around Joy, Nell noticed. It was only Nell who inspired the smirks.

Phred came over to where she had settled herself, cross-legged. She was scanning the view, shading her eyes with one hand. 'All those roofs,' she murmured. 'All those lives. London is so full of people.'

'And they all have their stories.' Phred caught her mood. They stared at the jagged horizon in silence for a few moments. 'You're very quiet this afternoon, Fitzgerald. Is there something on your mind?'

Your eyes, thought Nell. Your hands. How I imagine your neck smells. 'Not really.'

'No problems? Nothing you want to run past me?'

Nell glanced at Joy. She seemed to be lost in a sunbathing trance, so Nell said quietly to Phred, 'There is something.' She leaned closer to him, smelling the clean citrus tang of him

and quelling the way it made her rude bits lurch. 'I *know*.'
She needed to get it out into the open. It was nagging at her,
like a hangnail.

'You know.' Phred's face was blank. 'Am I supposed to
know what you know?'

'About you and Anita.'

'Ah.' He was definitely embarrassed, Nell thought.

As well he bloody might be.

'I did ask her to keep it quiet,' he said. 'You can understand why I don't want it to get round.'

'Yeah, I can.' When she spoke again she sounded spinsterish and disapproving. 'I was very surprised.'

'So was I,' he said ruefully.

Nell noticed with disappointment that there wasn't a trace
of shame on his open face. 'Is it . . .' she plumped for a very
Phred word '. . . *advisable*?'

'It's the opposite of advisable,' Phred admitted, with a
galling smile. 'I thought you, of all people, would approve,
though.'

'Me? Why would I approve?' spluttered Nell.

'Well, at least it got the stick out of my arse, didn't it? I
let my heart rule my head for once.' Phred wasn't taking this
seriously. His heart had turned out to be as wild as Nell's
own. Something about Anita had inspired it to misbehave, to
go well beyond the limits of 'practical support'. Nell felt that
odious jealousy swarm over her again: why couldn't she have
been the one to make Phred break his own rules?

She stared at his firmly drawn profile against the electric
blue of the sky. Aware that she should answer him, she said
haltingly, 'Your arse is certainly free of sticks.'

She transferred her gaze to the rooftops again, knowing
she had no option but to slap Phred if she saw the smirk that
just had to be on his face.

It was lolly weather. Every afternoon Dean was sent out for
ice lollies and every afternoon he was roundly abused about

how much they'd melted. 'I can't help it. It's hot,' he would mutter, as he handed out sagging Mivvis.

'Didn't you get one for Tina?' asked Nell, discreetly, noticing that Dean hadn't bought a Fab. Strange that she should be looking after Tina's lolly needs yet not talking to her, but there you go: girls *are* strange.

'She's not in,' Jean interrupted. 'And she didn't call either, naughty girl. I expect she's got this twenty-four-hour virus that's going round.' Jean shook her head as she constructed a complicated barrier of tissues round the hand that held her lolly. 'Everything's a virus, these days. We used to just get colds.'

In the past, a Tinaless day at the office would have been a barren prospect, requiring a lorryload of chocolate. Nowadays, it was a relief, as Nell didn't have to avoid her. Going cold turkey from her best friend wasn't easy, but she still felt no desire to go back to the way things had been. It was no longer a case of needing an apology or an explanation, she felt that Tina and she had taken different turnings.

It was peculiar for Tina to stay at home without calling the office but Nell had no brain space to fret about her today: she was fretting instead about her bright idea. Well, it had seemed bright when she'd come up with it. On reflection, it had dimmed. Rather radically.

There was no way out, however. Her grandfather, although sceptical, had agreed to come to the penthouse tomorrow evening and try to resuscitate his long-dead relationship with Pinky.

The lolly dribbled on to her T-shirt. Nell tutted, then tried to re-create the pattern on her other breast. She was nothing if not resourceful.

Later, Nell tipped a pile of paint colour charts over Maggie's kitchen table. She was going to redecorate the sitting room, just like a real volunteer. Understandably both women were apprehensive at the prospect.

After half an hour or so of sifting through the tiny squares,

all outrageously titled – 'Baby Cheek Pink', 'Old Brick' –
Maggie swept them aside and plonked a bottle of sherry in
the middle of the table.

'What's this?' asked Nell.

'You've been staring at "Mouse's Back" for ten minutes
without even seeing it. You need some sherry and a talking-
to.' Maggie pulled out the stopper with a satisfying plop.

Nell accepted the sherry, but grumbled mutinously, 'Can
we skip the talking-to?'

'Tell him,' wheezed Maggie, as she flopped into the
armchair.

'Who's him? And what am I telling him?' asked Nell.

'Tell Phred how you feel.'

Nell just stared at her. 'You're a witch. I've never even
mentioned—'

Maggie interrupted. 'Never mentioned? You've banged on
about him since I met you, dear. First he was a prig with a
stick up his fundament. Then he was a struggling widower
heroically doing his best for his daughter. Then he was a
tyrant. Then he was all heart. Currently he's a heartless seducer,
taking advantage of homeless girls. But all along you've been
bonkers about him.'

'I have not!' protested Nell.

'Bonkers, bonkers, bonkers.'

'I admit that recently I've been thinking differently, *slightly*
differently about him.'

'You've just become even more bonkers about him than
you were before.'

'Honestly, Maggie, you're wrong.'

'Let's not waste any more time arguing,' said Maggie,
impatiently. 'Just promise me you'll tell him how you feel. I
wasn't always a lonely old lady, you know, with nobody to
call her own. It took some doing. I don't want you to make
the same mistakes. Tell him, Nell.'

'What's the point?' Nell dropped her protests. 'He's with
Anita now.'

'Little girls aren't reliable reporters. Maybe Anita's just a fling. Maybe he feels the same way about you as you do about him.'

'I'd know,' said Nell, gently.

'Would you?' Maggie asked, with sympathetic doubt. 'I've watched you worry about that family of yours and you're no expert at gauging people's feelings about you, dear.' She paused. 'You know what I'm going to say, don't you?'

'Seize the day?'

'I'm predictable, but it's good advice.'

'Maggie,' said Nell quietly, 'you do have somebody to call your own. You have me.'

'There you go again, my dear. Trying to be all things to all people. That's one of the reasons I love you.'

Friday was one of Claudette's 'good' evenings. They were getting rarer: she was often in bed before it was dark with a headache, having picked at the dinner Carita had prepared. Tonight she was wearing an elegant kaftan, shot through with silver thread that gleamed like her immaculate hair.

She really does look French, marvelled Nell, as she sat beside her on the sofa, covertly sneaking Chipstix out of her handbag. 'What are you reading?'

'The *Lady*.'

Not *Winkle Fanciers Monthly*, then. Nell had taken to making these sneaky jokes to herself. Never out loud, of course. She yawned. It was the end of a difficult week at work. Tina hadn't been in for two days running, triggering a litany of passive aggression from Linda. Nell wondered if perhaps she was avoiding her? But something was niggling at her about Tina's absence: it just wasn't like her to stay out and not ring up with a credible excuse. Miss Marple-like, Nell was having an intuitive flash that something wasn't right. But, sadly, she was Scooby Doo when it came to knowing how to follow up her intuition.

The doorbell interrupted these gloomy musings. Nell glanced

at the clock. He was on time. She wiped salty crumbs from her chin and sat up straight. Suddenly her courage evaporated. She looked nervously at the silver head bent over the magazine.

Fergus's soft tread down the hall resounded in Nell's head like gunshots. The door took an age to open. She heard him say, 'A Mr Jack Fairweather to see you, Madame.'

Claudette looked up slowly, as if a fog was clearing in her head. Blank amazement showed on her usually composed face. Instantly it was wiped away, and she said, in a voice devoid of any emotion whatsoever, 'I am not at home to Mr Jack Fairweather, Fergus.'

With a servile nod Fergus retreated, but now Nell sprang into action. 'Grandmother!' she gasped, using the forbidden name instinctively.

Claudette appraised her. 'This is your doing.' It wasn't quite a question.

'You have to see him.'

Fergus bridled at an order being given to his mistress and took a step back into the room.

Claudette stared at Nell. 'Very well. Fergus, show Mr Fairweather in.' She folded her magazine and took up her position under the portrait.

Nell watched the door.

It opened, and in came the now familiar and dear figure of her grandfather. Touched, she noted that he was wearing a new suit. He carried his cap in his gnarled hands.

'Hello there.' He addressed Claudette as if Nell wasn't in the room. His voice sounded different.

'Good evening.'

Oh, Gawd, thought Nell. Claudette was choosing to be at her most regal. She was holding her nose so high she could have scratched her name on the ceiling.

'Hello, Granddad.'

'Nell.' He nodded at her, then returned to Claudette. She had the effect on him that outside-loo lights have on moths. 'It's been a long time.'

'Too long, I fear, for any reunion now. I would prefer it if you left my home, Jack.'

Nell gasped. Claudette was as slender and as poisonous as a wasp. 'Don't you think—' she began unwisely.

'Don't *you* think, child? Don't you ever, ever think?' Claudette asked, with a control that was far scarier than rage.

'Claudette, I believe we have a son.' Jack was doggedly holding his ground, but his fingers were torturing the cap.

'*Had*,' said Claudette. 'His whereabouts are unknown. He's as dead to me . . .' she hesitated for only a moment, then said levelly '. . . as you are.'

For Nell, it was like watching a car crash in slow motion. She threw Claudette a pleading look, full of anguish, but her grandmother didn't notice it.

'I came here today willing to forget the past, Claudette,' said Jack, with an acidic undertone that startled Nell. 'But I can see you're still the same cold, hard, unyielding woman you were. Goodnight to you.' He stepped out into the hall and pushed past Fergus, who had been standing rather close to the door when it opened.

'Granddad, wait!' Nell shouted, then turned to Claudette: 'How could you speak to him like that?'

Claudette scoffed. 'Granddad!'

Nell caught up with Jack at the ornate lift. 'I can't believe . . .' she began breathlessly.

'I can,' said Jack, calmly. 'She washed her hands of me like she washed her hands of eight brothers and sisters. That woman has no heart.' The lift clanged to a halt. He seemed to be struggling with himself. Although Nell yearned for him to throw her a kind look, he kept his eyes down as he stepped in.

'Do we still have a date for Sunday?' she asked, as the doors drew together.

'Yes.' Jack's bowed head disappeared.

Tears were racing down Nell's face as she sloped back into the apartment. She wasn't sure if she was crying because of Claudette or for her. The soft thud of her grandmother's bedroom door informed her that, for Pinky, the subject was closed.

An ice age descended over Hans Place. Claudette kept to her room and Fergus's demeanour towards Nell suggested he knew all about her serial-killing hobby. It was so chilly that Nell was actually looking forward to her date with Blair.

On Saturday afternoon the clothing bundles that Nell and Joy had made up were handed out. Was it good or bad luck that threw Phred and Nell together for this task? Nell couldn't decide.

'Thank you,' whispered a boy, studying the worn blanket in his pack as if it was cashmere.

'That's all right,' said Nell, warmly. 'You look after yourself.' He had the skinny physique of a teenager, and the haunted eyes of an old man. 'Come back for your dinner tonight, won't you?'

Bridie, perhaps predictably, had a loud word or two to say about the coat she'd been allocated. 'I'll never get meself a man wearing this!' she complained, baring her remaining teeth in a snarl. 'I want something sexy!'

'Bridie,' soothed Nell, noting the Co-op bag into which Bridie had coquettishly tucked her hair, 'no coat is sexy enough for a woman like you. Let's be honest.'

'S'pose you're right,' agreed Bridie, patting the bag. 'You've either got it or you don't.'

'How true.' Nell assumed she was talking about lice.

The tilt of one girl's head as she joined the back of the shuffling queue reminded Nell unexpectedly of Tina: there was a haughtiness about her, despite her grubby T-shirt with the faded Mickey Mouse. For a moment, Nell felt the intuitive prickle that had troubled her at intervals over the past couple of days. She reminded herself that she was busy, that what she was doing was important, and swatted away the question mark that hung over Tina's time off.

When she wasn't handing out bulky packages, Nell studied Phred as if she was preparing to sit a GCSE on him. She saw him help a pregnant teenager into her new coat. She saw him listen, with a fascinated look on his face, to an endless tale from Ted that was about nothing and went nowhere.

Of course, it wasn't just his small kindnesses that she clocked: she also noted the pleasing way his bum behaved in his shorts. Phred's body was spare and toned, without any narcissistic gym contours. All the bits she could see were brown, and getting browner, which boded well for the bits she couldn't see.

And never would. She sighed and handed over another package.

'See you. Thanks for coming in on a Saturday. 'Preciate it.' Phred was jangling the keys like a jailer, dismissing Nell with the friendly nonchalance that had begun lately to bruise her. She wanted him to want her to stay. She wanted a lot of things, none of which were coming her way.

'Something's on my mind.' She had surprised herself: this wasn't rehearsed.

Phred stopped playing with the keys. 'You look very serious, Fitzgerald. Do you want to talk about it?'

No, I want to snog your features into the back of your head, you idiot, thought Nell. She was tired of the compassionate, caring, philanthropic Phred, she wanted the toned, tanned, crumpled-up-in-the-bedsheets Phred. 'It's about you and Anita . . .'

Nell saw him wince, and even dart a quick paranoid look behind him. She didn't like to see this honest man being so furtive. He looked like somebody with a lot to be ashamed of.

'What about Anita?' he asked, in an undertone. 'You haven't mentioned it to anybody, I hope?'

'Don't worry. Your secret's safe with me.' Nell heard the spite in her tone and took a deep breath.

Phred evidently heard it too: he frowned at her. 'What is it you want to say?' he asked her. She recognised that voice: it was the one he used with stroppy drunks who might or might not have wet themselves.

'Are you in love with her?'

Phred's dark eyebrows shot up into his hair. 'With Anita? In love with Anita?' He was – there was no other word for it – *goggling* at her. 'How on earth – oh, Fitzgerald. You've added two and two and made a thousand.'

As has already been pointed out, Nell wasn't much good at maths. She squinted at Phred. 'Have I? Clover told me about your girlfriend with the princessy hair. Anita stays with you and she's *bursting* with happiness. Doesn't that make five? I mean four,' she corrected herself hastily.

'Right, then.' Phred put down the keys, parked his bottom on the posh new reception desk and counted off some salient points on his fingers. 'One, seven-year-old girls are notoriously unreliable witnesses. Yesterday Clover was convinced that she'd seen all the Teletubbies go past in a Mini. Two, Anita has been staying in the *spare room* on the nights she can't find a bed anywhere else. Three, if you ask her, she'll tell you she's *bursting with happiness* because I helped her get a place on an apprentice scheme for welding. Yes, welding, I don't understand either, but it floats her boat. Four, and I think this is the most important point,' Phred gave her one of his trademark searching looks, 'what kind of person would it make me if I took advantage of Anita's situation to sleep with her, or even start a relationship with her? Don't you know me a little better than that?'

Nodding dumbly, Nell conceded defeat. She could hardly admit that rampant envy had fogged her judgement.

'So I'm cleared?'

'Yes.'

'But you still have to stay schtum, Nell. Anita shouldn't be staying in the spare room. I'm risking my job.'

'I won't say a word. To a living soul. My lips are sealed.

They'd have to kill me to get it out of me.' Nell oversold as usual. 'At the very least they'd have to beat me so I was unrecognisable.'

'Let's hope it doesn't come to that.'

Twenty-eight

Assiduously avoiding the Sunday papers, Nell made her way to Maggie's. The night before she had traipsed down another red carpet in another new dress, smiling, waving and trying not to scream when paparazzi congratulated her on her engagement. She'd been happy with the front of the dress, but as luck would have it she'd caught a glimpse of her rear view in the mirror before she'd left Hans Place. She'd looked like she was towing a small caravan.

By the time she got to Maggie's, Jack was already on a sofa, tea in hand. She'd been itching to introduce them properly. They were so important to her that she needed them to like each other.

''Lo there,' said Nell, sheepishly, unsure how to greet her grandfather after the débâcle of Friday evening.

'Hello . . . love.' Jack squeezed out the endearment with appealing self-consciousness. He smiled shyly.

'All right?' said Nell, sounding like Georgina on a date.

'Quite all right, thank you,' said Jack, sounding like a man of his age.

'Don't you people believe in hugs?' asked Maggie, impatiently, from the doorway.

With a giggle, Nell flew across the rug and threw her arms round him. His spine went rigid, but then he relaxed. 'Don't worry, love,' he said into her hair, as she squeezed his bony frame. 'I got over Pinky a long time ago. We won't let her spoil things again.'

'OK, OK,' said Nell, with a happy snivel. For the umpteenth time she wished that all this doing-good stuff came with a manual. It was so easy to plunge in with the best of intentions and end up causing pain and uproar. Her grandfather was being generous about the whole business, but she knew that if she'd had a window into his heart she would have seen fresh wounds there. 'And I'm—'

'No sorries in this house!' Maggie butted in briskly. 'Now, I never thought I'd say this but I'm out of cake. I'll just have to go and . . .' She tailed off, leaving a nice wide gap for Nell.

'I'll go.'

'Wonderful. I need a couple of other bits and pieces. I'll just get my list.' Maggie went into the kitchen, where much drawer-banging and tutting ensued.

'D'you like her?' whispered Nell, urgently.

'Thoroughly decent sort.'

Nell frowned. That wasn't effusive enough for her. Old people were so careful and polite in their praise. 'I've been daydreaming that you marry her,' she confessed.

'No offence, love, but I've always been partial to the Catherine Zeta Jones type. There's a girl who appreciates the older man.'

Clutching the list, Nell made for the parade of shops round the corner. Maggie assured her that the relevant ones would be open 'as the pagans have reclaimed Sundays'. She'd said this with some satisfaction: she was a pagan herself.

As she passed number thirteen, Nell took the sneakiest peek at the scuffed front door. It opened, as if by magic, and Phred and Clover tumbled out on to their path.

'Oh. Hello,' said Phred, nonplussed.

'Nellie!' screamed Clover, with Blair-like energy.

'Fancy meeting you here,' said Nell, and made a mental note to kick herself later. *Fancy meeting you here.* How original.

'I'm just off to get the papers,' Phred explained, as if Nell was a police officer.

'And I'm off to get . . .' Nell looked at the list in flowery, old-fashioned handwriting, '. . . a pint of molk, some iggs and a nice cock. Or so it says here.'

As he opened the gate, Phred said gravely, 'I hope the cock shop isn't shut.'

'Better not be. You know what Maggie's like for cock.' She paused, distaste on her face. 'Actually, we'll end that joke right there.'

Phred was wincing too. 'I'd like to, please.'

Clover gambolled on ahead, blowing about the pavement like a leaf. Behind her, Phred and Nell strolled at the exact speed laid down by law for going to the shops on Sundays in summer. Any slower and they'd have been going backwards.

A silence, one of those slightly uneasy ones, cloaked them despite the sunshine. Nell struggled to think of something to say, something that would make him laugh, impress him with her keen intelligence and render her sexually irresistible all at the same time. 'Turned out nice again,' she said.

'Yes. Although the forecast said there might be rain by two o'clock.' Phred caught her eye and winked. 'Fascinating, aren't we?'

Nell giggled, her hormones set on simmer by that wink. If I was a man, she mused, I'd only wink at women I fancied. It was hardly scientific, but it unnerved Nell enough to chase away even the mundanities she'd been coming up with.

Thankfully, Clover rushed back to them and grabbed their hands. 'Come *on!*' she wheedled. 'Why do grown-ups walk so slow?'

'We're enjoying each other's company if that's all right with you, Pickle,' said Phred. 'Grown-ups like to chat, just like you and your friends do.'

'You chat about boring things,' asserted Clover.

That was undeniable.

'I chat about clever things. Like cats,' Clover carried on.

'But do cats chat about you?' asked Nell, seriously.

This question stopped Clover in her tracks. 'I think so,' she said slowly.

Conversation picked up. By the time they'd wandered round the mini-mart and pointed out the misspelled price signs to each other, they had elevated the discussion from the weather to what board games they liked to play. Nell said, in amazement, 'I would never have taken you for a closet Cluedo fan.'

'Yeah, well, I've got a system,' said Phred, proudly.

'A Cluedo *system*?' This tickled her. She pulled a quizzical face. 'Did it take you long to come up with it?'

'I've been honing it for a number of years. But it bloody works,' he boasted.

'Where do you stand on Monopoly?' This was important.

'Life's too short?'

'That's *exactly* how I feel!' said Nell, triumphantly. 'You open up a Monopoly box and that's the evening gone.' She narrowed her eyes. 'Ker-plunk?'

'I'd rather Connect Four.'

'Uuurgh.' Nell couldn't approve.

'Pictionary?'

'Maybe, if there's no Operation on offer.'

'Clover has Operation,' said Phred. 'She beats me every time.'

Nell was liking this off-duty Phred with the low-brow leanings.

Meandering up and down the aisles they discovered a mutual weakness for Angel Delight. 'I'm very good at making it.' Nell was relaxed enough to allow herself a little boast. 'It's the wrist action.' She gave him a demonstration.

'I'm impressed,' said Phred.

'It's just practice,' simpered Nell.

They were by the chilled foods and Phred was picking things up and reading the labels keenly. 'I meant to do a roast chicken for Clover and me today, but I forgot the chicken.'

'Well, it's a fairly integral part of the meal,' commiserated Nell.

'She loves all this crappy packaged stuff.' Phred was learning all he could from the back of a Ginster's packet. 'I try not to give her too much fat or too many additives. I don't want her to be tubby 'cos it'll make her miserable when she's a teenager.' He hesitated, then slung the packet into the basket. 'One won't hurt. We'll have fresh fruit salad afterwards.'

He's so well balanced, thought Nell, aware that she was on the lower slopes of hero worship now. She admired the way he took care of his daughter with no partner to lean on, and she was moved by his efforts to let her have the things she liked without causing problems for her later on. Clover, she concluded, was a lucky kid.

Considering how long they spent in the mini-mart they didn't have much to show for it. Trailing around like school-girls, they had chattered away the best part of an hour. 'God, I'd better get back. Maggie will be desperate for her cock,' said Nell, startling the teenager behind the till.

'Ah. The papers.' Phred reached for the *Sunday Something-or-other*.

'Don't!' squealed Nell. She could see a sentence that began 'Inside – Blair's Babe' and she dreaded to think what rubbish they'd printed about her now. 'Promise me you won't read them until I'm out of earshot.' Nell had no desire to be around when Phred got a load of her bum in that frock.

'If you say so.' Phred folded them carefully and tucked them into the bottom of his carrier-bag. As they drifted out into the sun, he asked, 'Don't you like being in the papers?'

'Like it?' squawked Nell. 'I loathe it. It's so embarrassing. It's all made up anyway.' She wondered whether now was the moment to tell him the truth about her 'relationship'. She didn't dare. 'It won't last for ever. I'm not interesting enough.'

'Oh?' Phred sounded tantalisingly as if he might dispute that.

But he didn't, to Nell's disappointment.

They rambled down the street, talking comfortably about Helping Hands. Phred asked her if she had any fundraising ideas: 'I want to buy a minibus instead of having to hire one all the time. We need to find about seventeen thousand pounds and that's an awful lot of jumble sales. If you could put your thinking-cap on . . .'

Nell had never before been accused of owning one of those. She felt proud that Phred was involving her. 'I will. I'll think very hard about it,' she promised. 'Here's your house.'

Nell stood swinging her bag, unwilling to leave his side. She smiled goofily up at him. He smiled, less goofily, down at her. ''Bye, then,' he said. It didn't sound very final and his feet didn't move.

'See you.' Nell's feet weren't listening to her either.

'Yeah. See you,' said Phred, softly.

'Ta-ra,' said Nell.

Phred thought for a moment, then came up with '*Au revoir*,' still apparently reluctant to walk away.

Then his eyes widened and she caught his thought. At the same time they gasped, 'Clover!' and turned on their heels.

She was crouched down, lovingly stroking the coat of a small dachshund tethered outside the mini-mart. 'Can we keep him and call him Keith?' she shouted, as they approached her.

'I can't believe I forgot my own daughter,' mumbled Phred, shamefacedly.

I can't believe I made him forget his own daughter, thought Nell, with a touch of shameful pride.

Whispering so they didn't wake the snoring Jack, stretched out with a full tummy on the sofa, Nell told Maggie, 'I think there were sparks, if you know what I mean.'

'Of course I know what you mean. I might be antediluvian but I still watch Cary Grant films,' Maggie reminded her. 'Sparks, eh?'

'Small ones. But definite ones.' Nell was prone to great surges of over-confidence followed by crashing waves of self-doubt. 'I think. Oh, I don't know! If only he didn't think I was going out with Blair. If only I could be sure of how he felt, I could say something . . .'

'If only, if only,' murmured Maggie, placing a cushion under

Jack's head. 'You'll get as grey as me waiting until you're sure.'

In no hurry to return to the unwelcoming pair in Knightsbridge, Nell was still lolling about at Maggie's when darkness crept over London. She was deliciously tired, her bones sun-warmed and ready for bed. 'I'd better be off.' She kissed Maggie and let herself out.

As she made her way to the bus stop, the thought that had been nagging at her subconscious like fabric catching on a nail, broke free. 'What's Tina playing at?' She said it aloud, and didn't have an answer. There was no way that argumentative, confrontational Tina would take time off work just to avoid her: the very idea was daft. She thought back over the week. Tina had been absent for two days without phoning in. A low panic rolled over Nell, like a fog off the sea. This scenario smelt suspicious now that she was concentrating on it. Like Nell, Tina could never have been accused of having a fanatical work ethic, but neither was she stupid enough to annoy her boss.

Something didn't add up. 'Or am I adding two and two and getting a very large number again?' worried Nell. Another part of the puzzling equation revealed itself: Tina's first day off had been the day Marti was scheduled to start filming his new series. She had always suspected that any success for Marti would spell disaster for Tina . . .

She didn't waste any more time mulling but whipped out her phone. The potential for humiliation was high but she stabbed out Tina's number. It went straight to answerphone. As did the landline at the flat. She took a deep breath and tried Marti's mobile number. His outgoing message informed her that he was filming for another week.

Biting her lip, Nell absorbed this. Tina might have gone with him, but she would certainly have booked the time off. Besides, she reminded herself, Marti was too paranoid to allow Tina to go on location with him.

Nell's gut feeling couldn't be ignored any longer and she crossed the road to catch a bus in the other direction.

The concierge was grumbling as he turned the key in the door. 'I could lose my job for this.'

'Mr Goode meant to leave you a message to let me in. I *have* to water his bonsai or they'll die.' Nell injected this lacklustre lie with as much drama as she could muster. 'Think of it. Tiny dead trees all over the loft.' She glared at him. 'Their little branches rotting . . .' He broke. 'Thank you,' she said, and slipped quietly into the flat.

Nell tiptoed into the gigantic main room and peered about her. There had been no answer even when she'd leaned on the buzzer for a full minute, but she couldn't discount the possibility that Tina was here, perfectly healthy and about to be very annoyed with her. 'Tina?' she said tentatively, then, louder, 'Teen? Are you here? It's me.'

The big space smelt stuffy so Nell opened a window. Everything was perfect, just as Marti liked it. The dining-table held a single jade bowl. An orchid arched on a floating shelf.

She shivered. She felt drawn to and repelled by the sleeping area, hidden from view by a large sliding bamboo screen.

She reached out a hand to draw it back. It whispered open to reveal a crumpled bed with a figure half hanging out of it. The mound of empty Jack Daniel's bottles and the crumpled-up notes scattered around told her the whole story. 'Tina!' Nell heaved up her friend, whose eyes were closed and whose mouth was open, her hand trailing on the floor.

There was a dribble of vomit on Tina's chin. Her ashen forehead was plastered with greasy tendrils of hair.

'Oh, Tina!' Rising panic made Nell clumsy. She manhandled Tina into a sitting position, then set about slapping her face.

Tina didn't react. Remembering her made-for-TV movie first aid, Nell scrabbled about and found a small mirror, which she held up to her friend's mouth. Reassured that Tina was breathing when the little glass steamed up, she started slapping again. 'WAKE UP, YOU STUPID COW!' she bellowed, in her unique bedside manner.

With a snort and a gush of snot, Tina opened her eyes. Then she shut them and started to sob. 'Leave me alone,' she slurred. 'I want to die.'

'Well, you can't. Listen to me, Teen, have you taken any pills?' asked Nell, clearly.

'Nah.'

'Are you sure?'

'Nah.'

Nell dragged the unco-operative patient out of the bed and staggered with her to the sculptural washbasin that stood in the middle of the floor. As she splashed Tina with cold water, Nell interrogated her further until she was confident that only a lake of Jack Daniel's had been self-prescribed.

'I wanna die,' gurgled Tina, as Nell laid her on the floor and dragged her jeans up.

'It's going to be worse than that,' Nell promised her. 'We're going to Claudette's.'

In the calm of the Heliotrope Room, Tina seemed much more peaceful. The storm of tears had subsided and she was in a deep sleep under the satin quilt. Nell stroked her brow. She'd read about people doing this in books but had never actually brow-stroked before. A smile fluttered across Tina's face at the gentle pressure of her hand and Nell felt relieved.

Fergus had been surprisingly non-judgemental at the sight (and smell) of her friend. He had put a hot-water bottle into the bed (despite the warm night, Tina's teeth had been chattering) and laid out fresh towels and toiletries for her. At Claudette's request he had brought in a Dior nightdress and dressing-gown of pale aqua silk. As Nell had sponged Tina down and eased her into bed, he had lowered all the lamps so that the room felt like a haven.

Now it was just the two of them, two battered best friends

who hadn't had a decent conversation in weeks. Nell took the sleeping girl's hand. In the aftermath of so much activity she felt choked with emotion and had no idea how to express it. 'Oh, Teen,' she whispered.

As Tina slept on, Nell crept out to make a telephone call. At Helping Hands, Edith lifted the phone. 'Hello?' she said uncertainly. 'There's nobody on Reception. Could you call back, please?'

'It's me, Edith, Nell. Listen, I know it's short notice but there's been a real crisis and I can't come in tonight. Please make sure that Phred gets the message. I'm not skiving – there's a very good reason I can't do it.'

'Can't say I'm surprised.'

'Oh?' Nell was puzzled.

'I saw the papers.'

Nell groaned. So the pictures of her bum were *that* bad.

From her sentry post in a little velvet armchair, Nell kept watch over Tina. Feet up on the bed, she found it soothing to watch her sleep.

Disjointed snapshots of their past peppered her thoughts: the two of them hiding under a desk when Louis was on the warpath, finishing off each other's baguettes at Mario's, staggering along, crying with laughter at the end of chaotic evenings they would barely remember in the morning, the silly emails, the gossip, the dissection of relationships, the doling out of ignored advice, all to a constant backdrop of helpless giggling. 'I've laughed so much with you,' she said silently to Tina. It had been the chorus of her life ever since she'd met this poised, egotistical, bossy and loving bundle of energy.

That night Nell had a lot of time to think, as Tina snored off the after-effects of far too much Jack Daniel's. The girl in the bed had failings that were as broad as her virtues. Unable to summon up much sympathy for the world in general, Tina was generous to her friends. Nell, who was trying to widen the net of her compassion, had been shocked by Tina's self-ishness, but she reminded herself that she'd basked many times in the sunshine of Tina's warmth. This vigil by Tina's bedside was helping to replace some of the missing jigsaw pieces for which Nell had groped when she'd questioned what held her and Tina together. It wasn't one single big thing: their emotional glue was comprised of thousands of shared moments.

Tina's eyelids were twitching. She stirred, then opened her eyes. 'I've been very stupid, haven't I?' she croaked.

'No change there.' Nell crept out to rustle up a snack fit for an invalid.

'Oooh, tomato soup and white bread!' Tina tried to sound excited, but she still seemed like a cheaper, less powerful copy of her usual self.

When the bowl was empty, Nell asked, 'Do you want to tell me what happened?'

Tina closed her eyes tightly, scrunching them up against the memories. 'He's dumped me, of course,' she said drily. 'Wants a fresh start for his new series. Told me to be out by the time he got back from filming.' She opened her eyes, but kept them lowered. 'I'm so ashamed, Nell. You must think I'm an idiot.'

'What does it matter what I think of you? It's only me,' said Nell, comfortably. 'Was there a big scene? Have you spoken to him since?'

'He's screening his calls. He means it.' Tina gulped, then managed a twisted smile. 'It's over. I've just got to get used to it.'

'Mr Jack Daniel was supposed to help with that, was he?'

Hiding her face behind her hands, Tina groaned. 'Can you believe I actually wanted him to find me lying there, hopefully half dead? I thought it would make him sorry, make him see how much I loved him.'

The hyper-hygienic Marti would have seen only germs and emotional carnage. He would have run a mile if he'd found

Tina in that state, as they both knew. 'Not the best plan you've ever come up with.' Nell smiled.

'I'm sorry.' Tina was crying unashamedly now, tears gushing down on to her luxurious borrowed nightie. 'You poor thing, finding me like that.' She sobbed harder as Nell's arms went round her. 'Had I been sick?'

'Had you? The bed looked like you'd been sharing it with some Hell's Angels.'

'Oooooooooh,' howled Tina. 'I feel so humiliated.'

'I've seen far worse. You should see what happens at Helping Hands some nights.'

Tina pushed away Nell's arms and faced her. 'Listen, I really am sorry about that day. I've been replaying it in my head and I could shoot myself. That sodding hat. And making such a fuss about – well, everything. I'm sorry.'

'So you should be,' agreed Nell.

'I was really rude, and I'm so ashamed. Rude about a child, for God's sake! What was wrong with me?'

'I've been trying to work it out, but I'm sorry too. I didn't prepare you and then I didn't take enough care of you. No, don't interrupt, it's true. Let's both say sorry and put it away in the drawer marked "Crap Moments In Our Friendship".'

That wasn't supposed to make Tina cry again, but it did. 'I don't deserve you!' she wailed.

'Stop it! You'll start me off.' Nell pulled the covers up round Tina and tucked her arms in. 'I'll be right here all night.'

'OK.' The tears subsided and the tomato soup had its soporific effect. 'Blimey,' said Tina, drowsily, as sleep overwhelmed her again. 'This nightdress is Dior, isn't it?'

She was going to be fine.

'Claudette, I know I'm in your bad books but—'

'Why are you covered with dust?'

'It's flour. I'm baking a cake for—'

'One of your poor people. Very well. Was there something you wanted?'

'Is it all right if my—'

'Of course she can stay.' Claudette was slitting the throats of her post with an elegant silver letter-opener. 'Fergus and Carita will ensure she's comfortable while you are at work. Is she a drug addict?'

'Noooo! She's my friend. Her boyfriend's dumped her and—'

Seemingly unwilling to allow Nell the luxury of a whole sentence, Claudette said, 'Spare me the gruesome details. I cannot bear the grubby realities of the emotional lives of the young.'

No, thought Nell. Far simpler to pretend everybody's dead, isn't it?

'And you, child?' asked Claudette, looking up from her various engraved invitations. 'How are you? Is the charity work as fulfilling as you hoped?'

'Yes. It really, really is.' Nell was pink to be the focus of Claudette's attention without any badgering about her clothes or her hair. 'Thank you for asking.'

'Hmm. I was hoping you might have got it out of your system.'

Twenty-nine

'You're smiling at me.' Nell backed away suspiciously as Louis approached. 'Why? What's going on? What do you want?'

'I'm smiling at you because I'm delighted with you, you silly little thing.'

'This is weird. You didn't even swear just then.' Nell looked behind her to make sure nobody was covertly filming them.

'This latest piece in the papers is a masterpiece. You should have told me you were planning it. Well done, darling. If it wasn't against my religion I'd give you a pay rise.'

'I don't know what you're talking about, Louis.' Anything that made Louis so happy just had to be a disaster for Nell.

'Then scurry out to Reception on those strange Nordic clogs of yours and have a look at the Sunday papers. Linda's just pasting the cuttings into the scrapbook.'

'Awwwww!' Zoë was saying, looking at the page Linda had just handed her. 'In't she sweet, bless her?'

'How could I possibly be *sweet*?' asked Nell, tetchily, peering over Zoë's shoulder.

'Not you, obviously,' said Linda brightly, unscrewing the Copydex with a sado-masochistic flourish. 'That little girl. She's adorable.' She waited a heartbeat and added, 'Poor little thing.'

Clover was smiling up out of the smudged pages of a Sunday tabloid, her cheek squashed against Nell's in a wonky snapshot.

Nell went cold. She snatched the page out of Zoë's hands and gobbled up the whole story in one. It left her speechless.

'Oi. Don't crumple it up. It has to go in the bleeding book.'

Zoë took the cutting back from her and straightened it out. 'Are you all right?' she asked, as she took in the zombified look on Nell's face.

Like a vampire sniffing blood, Linda's senses heightened at signs of real distress. 'Oh *dear*, whatever's the matter?' she cooed.

Nell was paralysed. 'St Nell,' screamed the banner head-line that presided over two pages of illiterate rubbish about Nell and Helping Hands. The journalist was gushing, in baroque tabloidese, about how Blair's selfless girlfriend was no 'shallow good-time girl' but a 'saint' who devoted her spare time to helping people 'who don't have her advantages in life'. Apparently Nell 'didn't turn away when she met low-life vagrants like Bridie, a broken-down old alcoholic', or Ted, 'an unwashed old man'. She had an especially close relation-ship with 'Clover, a Downs tot', whom she spent 'hours patiently helping. Her only reward is the child's laughter.' There was even a quote from Nell, speaking like a Victorian philanthropist: 'I do my best to shed a little light into the deep, deep darkness of their lives.'

Numb, Nell sank on to the reception sofa. Like the layers of a particularly pungent onion, the repercussions of this article were unfolding rapidly in her mind.

'I think we should frame it,' said Linda.

Gareth's clumsy fingerprints were all over this. Nobody else had access to that snapshot and Nell had talked to him endlessly about the characters at Helping Hands in her attempts to distract him from sex. He was well aware of her fondness for Clover, and he also knew that she was desperate to prove herself to Phred. Nell remembered, with retrospec-tive bitterness, the loyal boyfriendly interest he had shown when she'd laid the photos out in front of him. She'd noticed at the time that one or two were missing, and guessed that she'd mislaid them at his place. No doubt, Gareth had simply picked them up and tucked them away safely, waiting for an opportunity to return them. Only later, after their raucous break-up, would he have realised what a marvellous weapon they were. The pain it was causing her was the best revenge he could have hoped for.

I wonder how much he made out of breaking my heart. Nell wasn't even angry. Perhaps one day she'd wake up out of this numbness, buy a cudgel and find Gareth, but for now more important people were on her mind.

As Nell dragged her steps towards Camerton Street, it was to the sunny photo of herself and Clover that her mind kept returning. Before today she had always smiled when Clover popped into her head, but now she ached. She had exposed a little innocent to the unwanted, misplaced sympathy of millions of people who had never met her. She wanted to beat her head on the scorching pavement, but she kept going, like a condemned man headed for the gallows.

From behind the antique desk, now studded with coffee-cup rings and bearing the scar of a well-aimed kick, Joy looked up with her trademark grin as the doors swung open. The smile froze, then died. 'Nell. I wasn't expecting you tonight.'

'I bet.' Nell approached the desk, her head held defiantly high. She'd worked out a little speech. 'Joy, I need you to know that I had absolutely nothing to do with that story in the papers.'

Looking sceptical, Joy nonetheless seemed inclined to listen. 'But how – why?' she spluttered.

'I was stitched up by an ex-boyfriend. I didn't even speak to a journalist. I wouldn't. You know that, don't you?'

Joy shrugged and couldn't come up with a proper answer.

Just then Phred pushed through the double doors behind the desk. 'Nell. Hi.' The lack of anger terrified her.

'Phred, I can explain—'

'No need.' He paused. 'Let's just draw a line under it, shall we? Perhaps you thought you were doing the right thing, but we don't need this kind of cheap publicity.' He tossed a rolled-up newspaper on to the desk.

'I didn't think that!' protested Nell. 'It was absolutely nothing to do with me!'

Phred's tone was disconcertingly sane. 'Nell, I took that photo myself, with your camera. We're all named. The only person who could have given them the photograph is you. No wonder you didn't want me to look at the papers while you were with me.'

'No, that was my bum. Obviously – I – You see, it's—' Nell's brain was short-circuiting in the face of the circumstantial evidence against her. She flailed about until Phred cut in.

He didn't raise his voice, but somehow turned up the heat under it: his controlled passion horrified Nell. 'How do you think it made Bridie and Ted feel to be described as low-life by somebody they trusted?' He stared at his feet for a long moment, but when he spoke again his emotions were under control once more. 'As for Clover . . . Well, Clover doesn't read the tabloids so she still thinks you're great.'

Nell wanted desperately to defend herself and make everything all right again, but somebody had Hoovered all the words out of the back of her brain.

'Look, I'm sorry.' His tone was calm. 'I should have trusted my instincts. The simplest way of putting it is, we're not compatible.'

Nell flinched.

'You and Helping Hands, that is,' he added hastily. Almost to himself, he carried on, 'Shit, I don't like saying this sort of thing but it would be better if you'd just go.'

'But I'm scheduled for soup—'

'We'll manage.' Phred was curt. He rocked on his heels while the silence in Reception thickened. He hesitated briefly, then turned and went back to his office.

Nell jumped as the door clicked shut. 'I've got a cake for Anita,' she said to Joy. 'But I probably don't need to leave it.' It was a long walk back to the entrance door. Nell's throat felt as if she was deep-sea diving without equipment.

'I'll take it.' Joy chased after her, in her platforms. She took the tin with a sigh, then cocked her head to one side and said quietly, 'Nell . . .'

'I know,' whispered Nell.

Joy peeked inside the tin. 'It's a funny shape.'

'It's supposed to be a blowtorch. To celebrate her welding job . . . ?'

'Ah. I see,' said Joy. After a pause she stuttered, 'It doesn't really . . . look like . . .'

'No, it doesn't.' Nell walked out into the velvety night air.

'I'm a pain in the arse, aren't I?' asked Tina, propped up on clean pillows in a fresh silk nightie, eating chocolates from a heart-shaped box.

'No.' Nell was glad of the distraction from her ugly thoughts. She had buried herself in looking after Tina, while a tiny voice she didn't like the sound of chided, 'See? You're not to be trusted, just like Phred said. You're not doing good at all, you're helping Tina to help yourself. Same as all your other assignments.' 'Feeling any better?'

'Loads. I'll go back to work tomorrow.' Tina pulled a face. 'Can't wait, as you can imagine. How I've missed the fragrant Linda.' She popped a violet cream into her mouth. 'And Jane From Accounts. And Len, ah, sexy Len.' She leaned back on her pillow and sighed romantically. 'Perhaps I'll go out with him next.'

'You'd make a beautiful couple.'

'What's on your mind, Nelliphant? We've been analysing me till the small hours all week, but we haven't talked about you. You're not missing Gareth, I hope.'

'If you suggest that ever again I'll devise some sort of punishment that involves a coach tour of the Mendips with Linda.' Nell took a deep breath. It was time to tell Tina about Gareth's revenge. Tina was strong enough to hear it and, surprisingly, Nell was strong enough to talk about it.

*　　*　　*

'Miss Tina', as Fergus insisted on calling her, was moving on. She had called up her old flatmates and they happened to have a room to spare. 'That's no surprise. It's overpriced, the walls are damp enough to count as a water feature, and they have weekly meetings to work out who owes who thirty-two pence for a pint of milk.' Tina zipped up her case with difficulty. 'Back to square one.'

'It's not such a bad square,' said Nell, philosophically. 'It can't be or we wouldn't keep revisiting it the way we do.'

Tina, who now knew about Nell's unrequited yearnings for Phred, pulled Nell's hair in a friendly way. 'Onwards and upwards. Or, at the very least, sideways, with nice shoes.' She stood up and put her hands on her hips. 'Christ. That's not much to show for thirty years on the planet, is it?'

That very thought had struck Nell when she'd gone to retrieve Tina's stuff from the loft apartment. It was mostly clothes, with a few haircare appliances.

'Teen,' Nell began tentatively, 'if you ever feel that bad again . . .'

'Don't worry. I'll talk to you. I won't do myself any damage.'

'Good.' Nell was relieved that the necessary exchange had been so easy and brief. 'I mean, if you really want to harm somebody, go and find Linda.'

'I'd need a mallet. She's made of Teflon.'

'You're being really brave,' said Nell, admiringly. She knew what it took to be so cheerful about moving back to a Camden basement.

'It's not bravery, it's pride. The Bible's not keen on it but sometimes it comes in very handy.' Tina loaded herself with bags like a Spanish donkey. 'Don't worry, I'm never going down like that again. And if I feel I might, I've got you to talk to this time.'

'I've got you a moving in, moving out, whatever, pressie.' Nell handed her a small tissue-wrapped package. 'It's recycled, to be honest. Blair gave it to me.'

'A Prada key-ring!' Tina was delighted. 'It's far too good for the key to that dump, but thank you – it's brilliant.'

'It's for the key to your fresh start,' said Nell, meaningfully.

'Aah.' Tina threw the little gift into the air, caught it and stowed it in her pocket. 'Listen, I know I've suggested this a gazillion times, but why not try and—'

'Explain to Phred?' Nell shook her head. 'I've told you, Teen, he was right. I *am* responsible for that story getting into the *Oracle*. If I wasn't taking part in this charade with Tan Boy, if I hadn't got mixed up with Gareth again, if, if, if . . . Helping Hands is better off without me.'

'Blimey, Nell, why don't you get off the cross? We need the wood.' She punched her arm lightly. 'Come on, help me to the taxi.'

Claudette was in the drawing room when Nell returned. 'I'll miss Tina. Such a well-dressed girl,' she said approvingly, and with the merest of sideways glances at Nell's shortie nightshirt. The old lady had apparently decided to make the whole incident with her ex-husband 'unhappen'. She never alluded to it and she had stopped being chilly with her granddaughter. 'I never did make much headway with your Parisianisation, did I, child?'

Glad that it was dismissed with a past tense, Nell was amazed nonetheless by Claudette's brazen ability to carry on with the fiction that there was anything remotely French about either of them. 'Game of poker?' she asked, with a cheeky look.

'What an excellent proposition.'

The evenings were long now that Nell had no Helping Hands commitments. She played a lot more poker with Claudette, and she had a lot more time to go out with Tina, which meant that she was often drunk. She was still a regular at Maggie's – that would never change. A little too late as ever, Nell had realised what Phred had meant when he'd described Maggie as her tailor-made assignment: Maggie's only real problem was loneliness, but she was far too proud to admit it. Phred had known that there was something about Nell that Maggie would take to: he'd known she'd make it over the doorstep. He had never shared Nell's delusions about her practical skills but his pairing up of her with Maggie allowed Nell to imagine that he'd seen some abstract virtues in her . . .

She often made the long tube journey to her grandfather's. It pleased and surprised her that she could help out with his house and garden. He had let things slide as his arthritis worsened, and now Nell was doing the odd jobs he'd neglected, civilising his untidy patch of garden. During her assignments her empty boasts on the Helping Hands application form had started to come true.

Babysitting for Carol had become a regular fixture in the diary, and she'd managed to strong-arm her into a couple more nights out as well. They had finally got past Carol's drug problem and wandered into more mundane territory, tending to focus on blokes and how crap they were.

Despite this alternative Helping Hands universe that Nell had set up, a game called I Wonder What Phred's Doing Right Now took up far too much of her time.

'We've got to forget them,' asserted Tina, draped over a leather banquette in yet another new club. 'And luckily they do a very good forgetting juice here.' She poured two brimming glasses of red wine.

'You handled it brilliantly when Marti came in for a meeting today,' said Nell, guiding her glass carefully to her eager lips.

'When *who* came in for a meeting? See? I told you this stuff was good.'

It was testament to Tina's strength of purpose that she could continue to work at Morgan Theatrical Management after the break-up. Marti had told her, with deep regret, that the only way to get over each other was to have no contact: 'So, no tear-stained letters, babe, or late-night phone calls,

OK?' Bringing him coffee while he discussed his career was permissible.

Even Nell had been shocked by how cold and uncaring Marti had been since he'd told Tina it was over. 'It's better for you if I just leave you to heal on your own,' he told her, with transparent self-interest. 'Oh, and I'll deny it if you go to the papers.'

So there was a lot for them both to forget as they sat side by side, waiting for London's finest to chat them up. London's finest that evening included a graphic designer in a Motorhead T-shirt ('It's ironic,' he assured them, as if they cared) and an advertising creative who bored them about his healthy lifestyle, unaware of the gritty white deposits clearly visible up his scarlet nostril – but at least they paid for two more bottles of forgetting juice.

Thirty

'It's early days, but we're very happy.' Jane From Accounts was in love, wiggling with pleasure in an ill-advised miniskirt.

'What's he like?' asked Nell, all agog as she carefully assembled a crisps sandwich in the kitchenette.

'You know him, actually,' said Jane From Accounts coyly.

'*Whaaaat?*' This was getting better and better. 'He doesn't work here?'

Jane From Accounts nodded, her face getting happier and pinker by the second.

In the corner Tina, who was under strict instructions to be nicer to Jane From Accounts, these days, lowered her head over her coffee.

'Come on, woman, put me out of my misery!' begged Nell.

'Well, he's very handsome and he's very funny and he's dead sexy!' Jane From Accounts giggled at her sauce.

Behind her Dean hove into view, carrying a refill for the water-dispenser. 'Is it . . . ?' Nell pointed at him behind his back.

Jane From Accounts shook her head vigorously.

Nell was relieved. She rather liked Dean being 'hers'.

'It's Barry,' said Jane From Accounts, her voice drenched with pride and disbelief.

Tina didn't lift her head but she made a muffled noise.

'Bar-ree?' Nell strung the word out while she came up with something positive to say about the man. 'Barry,' she repeated, still struggling. 'Barry the security guard Barry.' The same Barry who had given the temp a medieval sexual disease, she failed to add.

'Can you believe it?'

'No, I truly cannot.' Nell knew how much Tina would be enjoying this in her silent corner. 'He certainly knows how to treat a lady.'

Swooning, Jane From Accounts agreed that he did. 'He's so *manly*.'

There was a persistent rumour at Morgan Theatrical Management that he was a Nazi. It wasn't natural for a man of his age to be so fond of his truncheon. 'Do you have a lot in common?'

'Well, he likes to talk and I like to listen,' said Jane From Accounts. 'He told me all about machine-guns last night. They have a really fascinating history when you get right into it.'

'I can imagine.' Nell decided to get into training for the long hours of toilet-crying that she would be required to oversee at some point in the not too distant future.

Tina had slipped away. A sudden gust of Zoë's laughter meant she had reached the reception desk.

An evening spent with Claudette always ended early. Nell and her grandmother had watched a wildlife documentary, and Nell was now qualified to take gnus as her specialist subject on *Mastermind*. Back in her room by ten, she lay on top of the bedclothes in her Elvis T-shirt and tried to concentrate on her book. She didn't care, she realised, what became of the spunky heroine, and couldn't be bothered to read another hundred pages to find out. She threw the paperback across the room sulkily.

What, she wondered, had she done with her time *before* Helping Hands? Suddenly she seemed to have acres and acres of it. One speedy way to gobble it up was to drink. Then, she found, the next few hours took care of themselves.

Nell recognised this old cycle of boozing and hangovers, then some more boozing, followed by a hangover, alleviated by a little light boozing. She didn't welcome its return. Toppling back into her old habits meant that she'd wasted her time at

Helping Hands. She had gone to Camerton Street feeling shallow and useless: her experiences there had forced her to re-examine prejudices and develop skills.

Recently she had been re-examining the bottoms of wine-glasses and developing the skill of forgetting. But the memory of Phred was harder to shake than a hangover.

'I need something to look forward to,' she decided. Something more interesting and more emotionally nutritious than another night out drinking herself stupid.

And that was exactly what she told Tina the next evening, as they drank themselves stupid.

Maggie's advice not to make an orphan of herself had gone deep with Nell. She'd dropped the 'half' prefix with the twins and Georgina, and although she felt a bit self-conscious calling them her brothers and sister, she enjoyed it. She'd also shaken off her qualms about calling Patsy for a chat. Speaking to her regularly meant she didn't resent it when a Canvey-related incident stole her mother's attention.

'I've had an idea,' she told Patsy. 'How about a big lunch, everyone together at Hans Place, all the people I . . .' she hesitated, then used the little word she usually shied away from with her family. 'All the people I love. That's you lot, Claudette, Granddad, Maggie, Tina. Sort of like a summer version of Christmas.'

'What's brought this on?' asked Patsy.

'I thought it would be fun. I want something to look forward to, to plan.' That was true, but it wasn't the full-fat explanation. When Helping Hands had gone belly-up, Nell had been starting to realise (with Maggie's help) that she *did* have a place in the world, that she was part of a network of relationships and loyalties that meant something. It was harder to grasp without her voluntary work to define her: a lunch would help. 'Will you help me with the cooking?'

'I'll help with the defrosting,' laughed Patsy. 'Oh, Jaysus. Canvey's after dressing the cat as a priest. I'll have to go.

We're expecting Father Rooney round any minute and he takes offence terrible easy.'

After some research into which joints of meat didn't kill you if they weren't cooked properly, Nell was planning a menu.

'How about a nice gazpacho to start?' suggested Maggie.

'Cold soup!' This was treason to Nell. 'Soup should be thick, hot and taste of the tin,' she insisted. 'Egg mayonnaise?'

'Boring.' Maggie was dismissive. 'Jack, any ideas?'

'Eh? I was only resting my eyes.' Jack sat bolt upright on the sofa.

'How did Claudette take to the idea of him going along to lunch?' asked Maggie discreetly, when Jack was resting his eyes again.

'Or possibly smoked salmon and . . . something that goes with smoked salmon.'

Maggie laid down her pen. 'Tell her tonight,' she said firmly.

Claudette took up her position under the portrait and subjected Nell to a long, meaty stare.

Nell, shocking herself, stared back. Her knees were knocking but unless her grandmother could see through Topshop cheese-cloth she wasn't to know that.

Claudette toyed with one of the spectacular bits of bling on her long fingers. She quelled a sigh, and said, 'I'll countenance Patsy and her gypsy entourage, but that is as far as I'll go.'

'I've invited him now, Claudette. It's too late.' She felt like David to Claudette's Goliath, but the thought of disappointing her grandfather gave Nell the nerve to stand up to this formidable woman.

'You talk such nonsense, child. It's not as if you've issued engraved invitations and requested black tie. Simply arrange to see him another night.'

'It's not nonsense.' Nell was stung. 'I've just found a member of my close family whom I believed to be dead and I want him at my special lunch. Surely you can see that.'

The glitter of Claudette's eyes told Nell she had used the wrong tactic. 'I will not open my doors to that man.' She turned her back: it was like the slamming of an oak door.

'"That man" has a name,' said Nell, infuriated with the tears she couldn't keep out of her voice.

'The subject – the *tiresome* subject – is closed.' Claudette took her customary refuge in silence.

The hastily rearranged venue was looking good. Two of Maggie's tables had been pushed together and covered with a patched white cloth. Some of the plates were flowery and some were striped; a shortage of wine glasses meant that Nell was sipping her plonk from a mug; Ringo had volunteered to use a spoon for his main course, due to a cutlery crisis; it didn't resemble lunch at Claudette's one little bit.

A joint of beef, cooked to perfection despite Nell's involvement, was carved and waiting to be served. Jammed round Nell at the table on chairs, stools and a set of kitchen steps were Patsy, Ringo, John, Paul, Georgina, Annie, Canvey, Tina, Maggie and Jack. Elbow to elbow, they jostled for space good-humouredly.

For safety's sake, Nell had put Tina between the twins. It had been proved scientifically that a bored Tina was a dangerous Tina. She seemed far from bored as she looked from one perfect profile to the other. Canvey sat beside Jack, imitating the way the old man was tying his napkin round his neck. Maggie was trying to control the bundle of nylon frills that was Annie, while Ringo and Patsy held hands under the table as they had for the past twenty years.

Too busy to notice how much she was enjoying herself, Nell bustled about, making sure that everybody had a full glass of whatever they liked best.

'Make a toast, love!' Jack clinked his knife on his Woolworths plate for silence.

'Oh, no – nonono,' mewled Nell, as conversations screeched to a halt.

All except Georgina's, via her mobile. 'You was looking at her. It was doing my head in 'cos she's a slag, right?' She looked round the table and mouthed, 'Sorry,' then said into the phone, 'We'll have to sort this out later, but I promise you, you are *dead*, Seb.' She slammed the little handpiece shut.

'Er, thank you,' said Nell. She lifted her glass and tried to clear her head. This ramshackle gathering was probably more important to her than anybody at the table could guess and she wanted to express herself carefully. 'I had a special reason to get you all here today. It's not just to eat – although I hope you enjoy the beef – it's because I wanted to have everybody I love round one table. I wanted to be able to see everyone who's important in my life in one room. These past few months I've tried to change into a person I might like more and, to be honest, it's been more difficult than I expected. But, and it's a big but, I *have* learned what's important. So, this toast is to you all because you're important. You're home. You're my family.'

With a smattering of 'Aww!' and 'Lovely!', glasses were raised. Nell wasn't finished. She had a postscript, which might not be popular. 'But there's somebody missing from the table today, and I'd like to include her in our toast because she's been good to me and taken me in when I had nowhere to go. She was the first one to encourage me to do what I had to do. And she has her own demons to fight. To Claudette.'

Silence, apart from Annie's gurglings, met this. The guests looked at each other, not sure they'd heard right. 'To Claudette,' said Nell again.

'To Claudette.' Patsy raised her glass, and muttered, 'The auld feck,' before she sipped.

Jack and the rest followed suit, without much enthusiasm, but Maggie had a special proud smile for Nell.

'I don't like beef,' said John, loudly, and disappeared under a hail of thrown bread rolls.

Snoring bodies were splayed on the sofas, the television glowed quietly in its corner and whipped cream had been trodden into the carpet. 'Just like Christmas,' said Nell, approvingly, as she harvested dirty plates.

In the warm fug of the kitchen Maggie was elbow deep in suds, admiring Jack's way with a tea-towel.

'I'm very good at housework,' he was boasting. 'I've had to be. I've been a bachelor for over forty years.' He held up a glass to the light. 'If a job's worth doing, it's worth doing well.'

'Actually, if a job's worth doing, it's worth getting somebody else to do it,' Nell amended.

'I don't know of anybody who could have put up a shelf for my seedlings better than you did.'

'Aw, geddoff,' said Nell, coyly.

'Not more plates!' complained Maggie. 'Where did they come from? I don't own this many!'

'I'll finish the washing-up,' said Tina, coming in from the garden. 'Don't look at me like that,' she said to Nell. 'It's a one-time only offer. A bit like Halley's comet – you'll never see it again in your lifetime. Have a sit-down, Maggie.'

Not needing to be asked twice, Maggie went out to the peeling wooden bench that gave her a good view of next door's roses. 'Can almost see Phred's garden from here,' she said airily, as Nell joined her.

'Almost.' Such a sad word.

'Are we happy, girlie?' Maggie patted Nell's knee.

Nell nodded – it was a nod with reservations, but she didn't have to go into those right now as she savoured the last drops of her wine.

'I was terribly proud when you called me family,' said Maggie, leaning in close.

'Oh, I'm just glad I found you.' Nell didn't go any further

because she didn't trust her voice. She sucked her lips between her teeth and gave Maggie a speaking look.

'See? You *have* found your feet, haven't you?'

Another nod. More reservations. That garden a few doors down was on her mind.

Partly because she was so full of roast beef, partly because the night air was so sultry, Nell dallied on her way back to Hans Place from the bus stop. Her limbs felt lazy and a delicious tiredness was creeping over her. The day had been a success, there was no doubt about it. Accustomed to examining and re-examining anything she achieved until she found an inevitable flaw, tonight Nell was in self-congratulatory mood. The faces round the table had been happy, and if the operatic burps from her mother's lot were anything to go by, they were full too.

Now all I have to do is creep into bed without encountering Claudette and the day will have been perfect, thought Nell, as she turned the corner.

It's always a shock to see an ambulance anywhere near your door. It's so easy to panic and imagine that it's something to do with your family. Nell stopped dead when she realised with a jolt that the ambulance *was* at her door. Fergus was sobbing on the shoulder of a medic.

Not lazy any more, Nell sprinted the hundred yards and grabbed Fergus by his pristine lapels. 'Has she—'

'No.' Fergus, most un-Fergus-like, wiped his nose on his sleeve. 'But . . .'

'She will?'

He nodded and started to cry again.

Sitting in a ruthlessly lit hospital corridor on uncomfortable chairs and sipping undrinkable tea, Nell shivered despite Fergus's jacket round her shoulders. Things were moving too fast, she told herself. Her stylish, confident, all-too-alive grandmother couldn't be dying in a room off this migraine-bright hall.

'We've known for about six months.' Fergus was in control again, back straight, tone even. 'It's cancer.'

Nell supplied the gasp that the word always merited. She shuddered, and a wave of shame, as hot as the scalding tea she was cradling, engulfed her as she remembered how just an hour ago she'd been hoping to avoid Claudette. All those evenings when her grandmother had gone to bed early or avoided phone calls . . . *And I like to kid myself that I'm not shallow any more*, thought Nell, with a special bitterness she'd never felt before.

'Madame's had cancer before, but it's always responded to treatment. She's always recovered. This time it was different, inoperable. She chose not to have chemotherapy. She didn't want anybody to know. Madame is the bravest woman I have ever met.'

Very possibly, agreed Nell, silently. And the most foolish. 'And today she collapsed?' she whispered, both desperate and unwilling to know.

'I heard her fall and when I went to her bedroom she was on the floor.' Fergus squeezed his eyes as if to block out the memory. 'Madame's been unconscious ever since. I think it's the end,' he forced himself to say.

But it wasn't. An hour or two later Claudette's voice, thin and reedy but most emphatically hers, was announcing, '*I am going home!*'

'Claudette,' Nell cajoled her, holding her papery hand for the first time ever, 'the doctors are advising you to stay here. You'll get the best care in hospital.'

'*Look* at the colour of that wallpaper! It will kill me long before the cancer does,' insisted Claudette. 'I can hire round-the-clock nurses. Fergus and Carita know how to look after me. If they won't give me an ambulance I'll call a taxi. I am going home.' She looked steadily at her granddaughter. 'I'm going to die there, child. You understand that?'

Nell's first tear dropped. 'Yes,' she said shakily.

'No tears,' said Claudette, crisply but not unkindly. 'We all die. I'm lucky enough to have had some warning. So, no tears and no dark colours at the funeral. You look best in red. And do remember to put on some makeup.'

'Yes, Grandmother.' Nell smiled ruefully, then realised what she had called her and glanced at Claudette in alarm.

'And *certainly* no "Grandmother",' shuddered the tiny form in the bed.

The doctor, 'very handsome but sadly common', according to Claudette, took Nell to one side.

'There are hospices, you know,' he suggested in an undertone. 'It's a lot of responsibility, looking after a woman at this stage of the illness. We can help you find her a bed.'

Grateful for his concern, and impressed by his handsomeness, Nell thanked him. 'My grandmother's a strong-willed woman. And don't worry, I can look after her.'

And she could. She knew that now. She also knew that she wanted to.

Thirty-one

Linda was at Nell's office door in terrifying puff sleeves. 'So sorry to hear about your grandmother,' she said, in doomy tones quite at odds with the milkmaid outfit.

'Thanks.' Nell knew Linda too well to trust her sympathy. 'Anything else?'

'Yes. Blair's here,' Linda brightened, 'so if you could pop through to Louis's office for a meeting, that would be nice.'

'Actually I'm in the middle of some important correspondence.'

'So if you could pop through that would be nice.'

'I have to get this in the post by lunchtime.'

'*Pop,*' snarled Linda.

'Close the door, Nell,' said Linda.

'I did.' Nell pointed to the closed door.

'This is a top-secret meeting,' emphasised Linda.

'But I can't close the door any more than it already is,' said Nell. 'We're not MI5,' she muttered, as she sat on a wooden chair, thankful that Blair was already in the low-slung leather one.

'Shut up, ladies,' said Louis. 'We're here to review Operation Beard. We're all agreed that it's been a massive success?'

'Oh, *massive,*' asserted Blair.

'We-ell,' started Linda.

'You don't agree?' asked Louis testily.

'I thought some of the photographs were unfortunate. With hindsight, maybe we should have chosen a classier girlfriend for Blair.'

Nell was speechless.

Defence came from a surprising quarter. Blair said in his customary loud manner, 'Nell was quite magnificent. She looked great and she was funny and friendly and everybody loved her.'

'Thank you, Blair,' murmured Nell.

'Besides,' he went on, 'if I'd had a really good-looking girl-friend nobody would have believed it. I'm the guy next door, so I had to bang the girl next door, big bottom and all. No offence, darling.' He beamed.

'Of course not,' said Nell limply. 'But can we get over my bottom, please?'

'I'll never get over your bottom,' sniggered Louis, 'but we're here to discuss the next step.'

'Oh, please say we're going to split up!' begged Blair, his brown eyes like a puppy's. (A puppy with access to Harley Street, that is.)

'It's time.' Louis nodded.

Nell gave a long sigh of relief. The endless deceit was cancerous.

Louis lit a cigar. He gestured to Blair to take one.

'I might as well stick a bomb in my gob.' Blair was affronted. Happy to shovel cocaine up his amended nose, he was nevertheless vehemently anti-smoking.

'As you wish.' Louis snapped the box shut. 'Blair and Nell's little relationship has achieved exactly what we wanted it to. Blair's rather shaky heterosexual credentials have been validated. It's also encouraged some discretion on your part, Blair, which I hope will continue.'

Tutting loudly, Blair said sulkily, 'I suppose so.'

'I don't see the need to prolong the bearding. In fact, if we handle it properly, the split could generate more column inches than the rest of the affair put together.'

Blair had an idea. 'She could shoot me! She could go to prison!' He blazed with excitement beneath his orange camouflage.

'Er . . .' began Nell, when nobody leaped in to point out the flaws in the plan.

'Perhaps something a little less dramatic.' Louis was always diplomatic when handling artists.

'Please yourself.' Blair was huffy. 'I've got an astrological dermopeel at eleven, so if we could move things along . . .'

Linda reeled off a list of possible break-up scenarios she had prepared. 'One, Blair chucks Nell because she's been unfaithful. Two, Blair chucks Nell because she's a lesbian. Three, Blair chucks Nell because she's an alcoholic. Four, Blair chucks Nell because she's a drug addict. Five, Blair chucks Nell because she's an unfaithful alcoholic drug-addicted lesbian. Six, Blair chucks Nell because of her bottom.'

'Excuse me,' ventured Nell, 'why can't I chuck Blair?'

The other three laughed heartily at this, then ignored it.

'None of those is quite right,' mused Louis. 'How about this? Blair and Nell split because he's so devoted to his career that he can't give the relationship the time and attention it deserves.'

Surprised, Nell had to concede that Louis had come up with a reasonable proposition that reflected well on both of them.

'It's very dull.' Blair pulled a face. 'Can't we have a row? Can't I be unfaithful? I need an edge if I'm ever going to leave the blue rinses behind.'

Louis frowned at such heresy. 'Why on earth would you want to leave the blue rinses behind? They pay for your astrological dermopeels.'

'Just a tiny row? Can't I hit her?'

'No, you can't.' Louis wasn't being gallant, just a hardheaded businessman. 'The public will turn against you if you hit a woman. Even a woman like Nell.'

Nell was immune by now.

Blair gave in. 'All right. Pressure of work it is.'

'Cheer up, troops!' Louis grinned. 'One more date, then the deceit's all over.'

'Not for me it isn't,' muttered Blair.

Louis didn't hear him. 'One last big splash. We'll choose

an event in two or three weeks' time. Make sure you have a stunning outfit, Nell, so there'll be lots of pictures. The next morning we'll send out a press release about your sad but amicable split.'

Nell groaned inwardly.

'Christ, me peel!' This sufficed for a goodbye, and Blair raced from the room.

Louis stubbed out his cigar. 'Parting is such sweet sorrow.'

'May I talk to you?' asked Nell, and added, 'Alone,' as Linda lingered by the door.

'But—' began Linda.

'Out, out, out!' roared Louis, over her protests. 'What do you want, Funnyface?'

'Some time off.'

'No, seriously, darling, what do you want?'

Nell explained about her grandmother's condition. 'I want to help nurse her. I want to be there for her. And you owe me,' she said bravely, knowing that if Louis was in the right mood a certain defiance impressed him.

Luckily he was in the right mood. 'Oh, fuck it, darling, take a month. You deserve it for all that that orange madman has put you through. You've behaved with grace under pressure, and there's not many of us can say that.'

Unaccustomed to sincere praise, Nell stared at him.

'Get up. Fuck off. Go,' Louis encouraged her as she continued to sit there. 'Oh, darling,' he added, as she reached the door, 'I suppose we can rely on the old dear to die in a month, can we?'

The old dear was wearing a marabou-trimmed négligé that was worth Dean's annual salary. 'Wash those peasant hands of yours!' she shouted at the kind nurse, who was just leaving the bedroom. 'Now, Fergus, Nell, where were we?'

'The hymns, Madame.' Fergus, who had refused to sit down in his mistress's presence, was standing to scribble the details of her funeral with a gilt pen.

Not enjoying this *at all*, Nell squirmed on a pouffe. 'This is morbid, Claudette,' she ventured.

'Not at all.' The voice was thin and sometimes disappeared altogether when the morphine kicked in, but the determination was as steely as ever. 'If I leave it to you my coffin will disappear, no doubt, to the strains of Cliff Richardson, or some such hooligan.'

On her present form the old dear might just outlive them all.

There was an uneasy truce between Nell and Fergus. They had recognised in each other genuine concern for Claudette and trod more carefully round each other as they nursed her.

It wasn't always easy. Fergus was still Fergus and Nell was certainly still Nell. He was still making secret inroads into her food stash, and she was still sniggering at his pretensions.

Carita was finding Claudette's decline difficult to bear. Her soft Latin heart was touched. 'I deed my best,' she said tearfully to Nell. 'I knew that you would find your grandfather. I thought she should not be alone at the end. But she send him away . . .'

'She won't be alone. She's got us. We're here,' Nell reminded her.

Later that day Carita and Nell tenderly lifted Claudette out of bed and laid her on the sofa while they changed the sheets. During her time at Helping Hands Nell had helped various old ladies in this way. Essentially, Claudette was no different from a woman who lived in a tower block and slept on chainstore sheets: they both needed a gentle touch.

Before Helping Hands, she would have been all at sea when confronted with her grandmother's changed needs. She had a lot to thank the people there for, even if they did consider her the Antichrist. She pushed that thought to a dark corner of her mind that she intended never to visit again.

*   *   *

Miss Tina was a regular visitor to Hans Place. 'Well, I don't see you in the office any more,' she pointed out to Nell. She was also reluctant to spend too much time with her flatmates in case she caught the strange disease that had warped their brains. 'I don't want sleepless nights about the Hoovering rota. One of them did the weekly shopping and gave herself a migraine working out how much a fifth of a Dairylea triangle costs.'

The first thing Miss Tina always did when she arrived was to present herself to Claudette in the dimly lit boudoir, where her clothes and grooming were expertly appraised.

'Not tonight,' said Nell. 'It's been a bad day.'

'Don't,' said Tina, who was allergic to death. She threw herself on to Nell's bed. 'Did you know it's over a week since we went out and got sloshed?'

'Sorry.'

'I'd rather be here, to tell you the truth.'

'Yeah. Right.' Nell threw her a packet of Nik Naks.

'Honestly, I would. I am *so* fed up of being chatted up by arsewipes. And there's nowhere in town that's guaranteed arsewipe-free.'

'But how will you find your next bloke if you don't wade through the sea of arsewipes? Or at least get your toes wet?'

'He'll come along.' Tina didn't sound concerned.

'Don't tell me *you*'re ill,' said Nell. 'Could it be that you're enjoying not having a boyfriend?'

'I wouldn't go that far,' mused Tina. 'Let's just say that I don't want to repeat recent mistakes.'

'Is that how you see Marti – as a mistake?'

'Do we have to do this? I can't talk about him and make any sense.'

Nell backed off. 'You're OK, though, Teen? You'd tell me if you weren't?'

Tina nodded. 'In fact, I'd bore you to death.' She winced. 'Sorry.'

'It's all right, you can say the D-word.'

*   *   *

On Friday afternoons Nell went into the office to keep up with what was happening in the business. That was the theory: in reality it was an opportunity to catch up with the gossip.

'How's it going with Barry?' she asked Jane From Accounts trepidatiously.

It was a relief when joy flooded that round face. 'I've never been so happy! We're going away for the weekend!'

'*To the Fatherland*,' hissed Tina, out of Jane From Accounts's earshot.

'To the Isle of Wight. I've always wanted to go there but never dared,' she said.

On this particular Friday, Louis was brandishing a bottle of champagne. 'Gather round, my devoted little proles!' he roared. 'Help me toast the lovely Jean.'

Always glad to see a bottle of champagne, even the substandard stuff Louis kept for his staff, Nell held up a glass. She smiled encouragingly at Jean, who was looking mortified to be the centre of attention: presumably it was her birthday. She would never know what Nell had been through for her. As the cheap bubbles gasped in her glass, Nell remembered all the excruciating nights she had spent trussed up in evening gowns listening to Blair talk crap: it had all been to save Jean's job. Now, looking at Jean's pink flustered face behind glasses that were held together with a plaster, Nell knew it had been worth it.

'Let's have some hush. Your leader is speaking.' All faces turned towards Louis. 'Jean has been at this company for a very long time. When she first totted up a Morgan Theatrical Management ledger, dinosaurs roamed the earth. Well, much as we hate to lose her, it's time for Jean to go.' There was a gasp from his audience. 'Yes, Jean has decided to retire. We're sending her off to the knacker's yard.'

Jean frowned, then stared into her already flat champagne.

'Oh, laugh, you bastards!' shouted Louis. 'Here's to Jean!'

'Jean!' the little crowd echoed. Hugs were administered, tears were shed and Jean smiled at last.

Nell smiled too, but it was the stiff rictus smile of one who knows she's been had. She caught up with Louis as he galloped back to his lair. 'How long have you known?' she hissed.

'Jean's very proper. She gave me six months' notice, instead of the contractual three.' Louis seemed amused.

Nell didn't. 'So you knew when you blackmailed me?'

'Oh, darling,' Louis threw his arms round her, 'this job has to have *some* perks!'

Jack was half-way through the front door. He was arguing with Fergus. 'I know she's weak, but I mean to see her. I warn you, I'm not taking no for an answer.'

Outraged, Fergus was having difficulty keeping his temper. 'Madame is a very sick lady,' he hissed. 'Show some respect.'

'I've seen her throw up after stuffing her face with cockles and Guinness. I ran out of respect for Madame years ago.' Jack pushed past the younger man, who seemed reluctant to lay hands on him.

'Granddad! I don't know if it's a good idea. She's kind of feeble,' whispered Nell, as she caught up with Jack at Claudette's bedroom door.

'Shush, love.' He turned the handle and went in.

Just one look between Nell and Fergus was enough for them to understand each other perfectly. They stepped forward and leaned against the door, straining to hear what was going on inside the room.

Frustratingly they could hear only snatches of what Jack was saying. 'Hear me out, Pinky.' Then, 'You owe me this much.' More blah blah blah, and Jack said loudly and distinctly, 'I made a vow to look after you and some of us take our vows seriously.' Then, try as they might, they couldn't make out the rest of the conversation. When the door opened they had to spring back and look very interested in the dado rail. 'That's settled, then. I'll pop by to see you every day. Ta-ra, Pinky.'

A Valentino slipper whistled past his head. 'That's my girl.'

He laughed and came out, closing the door softly behind him. 'Feeble, you said,' he commented to Nell.

'That's the kitchen, sir. Sir, that's the kitchen.' Fergus trotted alongside as Jack headed for his turf.

'Yes. Sink. Cooker. Fridge,' said Jack, in an eerie echo of his granddaughter's assault on the same room months earlier. He held out his hand to greet Carita. 'I have a suggestion or two that might tempt Madame to eat something,' he said.

That evening Carita shed tears of joy when Madame managed to finish a tiny portion of *morue dans la pâte lisse et pommes frites*.

'Pinky always did enjoy a nice cod and chips,' said Jack, with satisfaction.

'It looks *terrible*.' Linda threw up her hands in despair.

'It looks a-fucking-mazing.' Tina shook her head in awe.

They were in a chi-chi boutique, and Nell was giving them a twirl in a racy little Julien MacDonald number.

Nell had begged Tina to help her buy the dress for the momentous final date. Louis, who had heard a rumour that Davina was in jodhpurs that day, was too busy scanning the outer office to take much notice. 'Yes, yes, whatever you want. Fuck off,' he'd grumbled.

Linda, however, hadn't got where she was today by giving in that easily and insisted she had to be present when the company credit card was used, due to Nell's past criminal tendency.

'*One* fucking taxi fare!' Nell flared up.

'One that we know about,' said Linda.

Nell shut up.

Now Nell was staring at herself in the mirror, wondering if it was a distorting one. 'But it's *beautiful* . . .' she gasped.

'It's too short. Look at your knees,' hissed Linda.

'Who's going to be looking at her knees when it makes her boobs do that?' Tina reached out and squeezed them. 'Sorry, I had to.'

Even Nell had to admit that her breasts looked damn fine. Without Tina she would never have dared to try on such an incredible dress. On the hanger it looked like a collection of big square gold beads clinging to some unfinished knitting, but on the body it magically arranged itself into the kind of thing Kylie Minogue wears to put out the milk. 'How come it's so flattering?' she asked, staring at the pert little bottom she had acquired.

'I keep telling you. That's what you pay for with *haute couture*. It's all in the cut.' Tina tweaked a shoulder strap.

'It's too flashy.' Linda looked pinched. She pulled out a trump card. 'And, of course, it's far too *young*.'

'For you, maybe,' said Tina, with a wide smile, 'but not for Nell.'

How Nell loved Tina. 'Shoes next,' she said.

Linda was down but not out. 'There won't be much left in the budget. Maybe enough for a pair of Laura Ashley-style pumps.'

Tina and Nell looked at each other. 'Davina,' they said in unison.

Davina, by deft use of her neckline and some casual fingering of a specially bought sausage roll, secured a sufficient increase in the budget for Nell and Tina to return with a pair of Jimmy Choos as well.

'Mum!'

'Where is she?' Patsy stood on the threshold, popping with energy.

'Claudette's in bed, resting. What are you doing here?' Nell was goggling at Patsy as if she was a mirage.

'I'm here to make me fecking peace with the auld cow. Now get out of me way before I change me mind.' Patsy barged down the hall. Her face was red, and she seemed close to tears. 'In here, is it?' She blundered into the darkened room and addressed the recumbent form on the bed before Nell could stop her. 'Listen to me, Claudette. I know you've never liked me. Well, it's mutual. You were a cow when I met you and you're a cow now. But I'm sorry you're suffering. I'm sorry that we never managed to patch things up. And I want to thank you from the bottom of my heart for taking in my Nell. God bless you.' Patsy finally took a breath. 'There. That's what I came to say.'

Outside the door, Nell threw her arms round Patsy. 'Oh, Mum!' she said. 'Am I your Nell?'

'Of course you're my Nell, darlin'.' Absentmindedly, Patsy kissed her daughter's forehead, unaware of how much the moment meant to her. 'Would you believe I bought a new coat to do that?' She dusted down her Etam trench.

'Well, you're going to have to do it again.' Nell grimaced. 'You just barged in on Carita's afternoon nap.'

Patsy looked devastated. Then she was all furious movement again. 'Ah, tell her I called,' she threw over her shoulder as she stomped out.

It was dusk, and Nell moved silently about Claudette's room, lighting lamps. She took away the tray, which still held most of the pie and eels Jack had gone out for, and settled down in a comfortable chair by the side of the bed.

Surprisingly, Nell liked these quiet times in her grandmother's bedroom. They were still and glowing, unlike any other hours in her day. She usually let Claudette lead, but tonight Nell had something to say. 'Claudette?'

'Yes.' The patient was sitting up, making barely a dent in the pillow. Her hair was carefully set, but her face was drawn.

'Why did you ask me to stay here?'

'Are you asking me if I wanted you here because I knew I was dying?'

'Sort of.'

'That was certainly part of it.' Claudette coughed, and Nell held a glass of water to her lips. 'I'm all right,' she reassured her, then returned to her answer. 'But that was only part of it. You needed a place to live. You're my granddaughter. And I like having you near me.'

It had taken imminent death to wring a compliment out of Claudette. Now Nell carried on, sticking to a formula she'd been working out in her head all day. 'I need you to hear me out. You won't want to, but I think you should.'

'I'm tired . . .' said Claudette.

'Hear me out,' said Nell, ruthlessly. 'Claudette, I know everything. Jack told me every last detail. Your eight brothers and sisters. Your name nicked off a bottle of wine. Your Glasgow accent. Your first husband. The rubber knickers . . .'

Claudette stared straight ahead. Her nostrils flared but she said nothing.

'The lies about my granddad. Bullying my mum. Abandoning my father. I know it all. I see you as you really are.' Nell was crying. 'And I love you. I really love you, Grandmother, and I'm going to miss you.'

There was a moment of complete stillness. Nell's heart sank. Had she gone too far again?

Claudette let out a small sigh. Her dry hand covered Nell's and they cried together.

'You deserve this.' Tina pushed a glass of champagne towards Davina. 'For selfless bravery in the cause of shoes.'

'It was nothing,' said Davina, modestly.

'That's not what I heard.' Nell handed her a menu. 'Apparently Dean saw the sausage-roll thing by accident and Zoë had to slap his face before he could speak again. Hence supper on me at this poncy paradise.'

'Keep your voice down!' threatened Tina. 'This is the hippest place on the face of the earth.'

They were sitting on a seagrass mat round a low red lacquered table. The champagne had been brought by a rather tired-looking waitress with chopsticks in her black wig. Turning Japanese was indeed the hippest place in town, but Nell would have swapped that knowledge for a nice soft seat with a back to it. 'I'm not having sushi,' she said, for possibly the eighteenth time since they'd sat down.

'Oh, shut up,' said Tina, who always ate what was fashionable. 'You can have a nice Japanese Welsh rarebit or something.'

It was good to have Davina to themselves. Over the rim of her champagne flute, Tina asked, 'Do you fancy men?'

'Well, I'm not changing sex to become a lesbian,' Davina pointed out. 'It's complicated.'

'I bet it is,' agreed Tina. 'When do you tell them the truth? When they're buying you a drink? When you're climbing into bed?'

On the other side of Davina, Nell winced. This was personal territory.

Davina seemed to think so too. 'It's complicated,' she repeated, and took a demure sip of her champagne.

Time, thought Nell, for a change of subject. 'Tina, I noticed Marti hanging over you like a vulture when I came in for my Friday session yesterday.' She laughed. 'Hope he wasn't trying to entice you back.'

'That's exactly what he was doing.'

'Oh dear!' sighed Davina.

'How? Not with marriage?' Nell knew that her friend was particularly vulnerable when that subject was bandied about. Even by Marti. Perhaps, worried Nell, *especially* by Marti.

'He said he'd made a mistake. He said he missed me. He said he'd never felt so bad in his whole life.' She threw a sideways look at the other two. 'Well, he didn't actually say that there and then. He said it when I'd followed him to the men's loos like he asked, and we were locked in a cubicle together.' She was starting to giggle at the memory. 'He made me crouch on the seat that so only one pair of feet was visible under the door.'

'That's not very romantic,' Davina pointed out.

'It gets better. He offered to set me up in a flat of my own. Fully furnished. And a car. He only left one thing out.'

'A dishwasher?' suggested Davina, whose glamorous exterior might be misleading.

'I know what he left out,' said Nell. 'He didn't say he loved you.'

'When I asked him he said, "Who knows what love means?"'

'What did you say?'

'I said I'd think about it. More champagne, ladies?' Tina clicked her fingers.

The waitress adjusted her wig, sighed and approached. Her kimono, Nell noticed, had a ketchup stain on it.

Thirty-two

It was three a.m. in the kitchen. The apartment was chilly. Two cups of Earl Grey sat cold and untasted in front of them. Nell rested her chin on her hands while Fergus cried unashamedly. She was dry-eyed, still in shock. Claudette had gone from their lives for ever.

In the bedroom Jack was dealing with the doctor. Somehow, Claudette's husband had managed to make it all the way from his flat to her bedside before she died. 'It was a last privilege,' he said to Nell.

Surrounded by love and care, it was possibly a better death than Claudette deserved. She'd wasted years of her own life, and the lives of others, in the pursuit of status. What a terrible, terrible shame: the thought rolled round in Nell's head like a stone in a washing-machine. In her lap lay the Bible that had always sat ostentatiously on Claudette's bedside table. The grainy feel of the old leather gave her a vague sense of comfort.

The whole apartment was altered by the lack of Claudette. Her body was still with them but her extraordinary, infuriating, unforgettable spirit had fled. Nell shivered as she sat back and looked round the kitchen. Even the ladles and wooden spoons in their jar seemed listless.

The only noise was the sound of Fergus's sobbing. Nell suspected that he would have pulled himself together by the time dawn broke, and be back to his erect, irreproachable self. For the moment, though, all rules were meaningless and they were united by their sadness.

The old, pre-Helping Hands Nell might not have been able to reach out to him, but these days she had no time for such self-consciousness. 'C'mere,' she whispered, and put her arms round Fergus.

He didn't pull away.

After the doctor had left, Jack asked if Nell would like some time alone with her grandmother. 'Oh, no,' Nell answered quickly. 'I don't need to see her.' She felt a prick of guilt, but she couldn't face the prospect. She had a lifetime's worth of memories to flick through whenever she wanted to remember her grandmother. 'Sorry.'

'Don't apologise, love,' said Jack. 'It's your decision to make.'

Jack was serious and thoughtful. He moved with a slow gravity, showing respect without any morbid overtones. Nell was glad he was there. She wondered – hoped – that towards the end Claudette had felt the same.

'Could you put this in her hands?' she asked softly. She handed him Claudette's Bible. 'She always kept it by her bedside. She didn't talk about religion or God much, but this was obviously important to her.'

Jack took it with a ceremonial air. Then he frowned. 'Feels light.'

'Does it?' Nell took it back. Her grandfather was right. It was *very* light. She opened it to find that the pages had been hollowed out so that it was now a box. Laughter mingled with Nell's first tears since her grandmother had died when she tipped it upside down and a flurry of Twix wrappers, crisp bags and Jaffa Cake crumbs fluttered to the floor.

There's a tide of goodwill after a death that can be comforting. Nell cherished the card from Tina that read, 'If you want to talk about it, even at three in the morning, I'm here,' and the little notelet from Maggie that advised, 'Remember her and she'll always be with you.' Perhaps Linda's 'One consolation is that black is so slimming' was less kindly meant, but at least Louis's 'Does this mean you can come back Monday?' made her laugh.

These days, Nell tried to be honest with herself, and so, after her grandmother's death, she found herself shining a spotlight on their relationship. It had been unique, complex, even loving in its own dysfunctional way. Towards the end, at a time that might have been unbearably grim, they had become truly close.

There was one fact Nell always returned to: Claudette had pushed her towards Helping Hands. Life with her hadn't always been comfortable but, despite the stonking lie that had lain at the heart of their relationship, it had been *real*.

And Nell was going to miss her.

Nell wore red to the funeral. Fergus showed his disapproval by lifting his nose every bit as high as his employer used to, but Nell ignored him. She was acting on direct instructions.

The vicar, who had known Claudette as a generous benefactor to his comfortable Knightsbridge church, droned on about what a spiritual inspiration she had been. Nell assumed he'd never peeked inside her Bible.

At the cemetery the titled old ladies of Claudette's vintage admired the extravagant floral displays. Circling like birds in their feathered hats, they pecked at the cards from the honourable this and the dowager that. One tribute puzzled them all. 'Must be a mistake,' they drawled in Sloanese, frowning at the commonplace carnations that spelt out 'PINKY' in letters a foot high.

Fergus and Nell were the last to leave the graveside. 'I know you took the heat for her,' said Nell, as they walked towards the gates.

'I don't understand.'

'About the food. That was very loyal.'

'I loved her,' said Fergus.

*   *   *

The sun slanted dazzlingly across Maggie's tiny garden, making the shed shimmer like a mirage. 'It's as good as St Tropez,' she said.

Nell, who had never been to St Tropez, said, 'It's better.'

Jack, who had been to St Tropez, said, 'It's nothing like bloody St Tropez.'

Nell accepted now that Maggie and Jack would never be married. She accepted that her grandfather, lovable though he undoubtedly was, sometimes annoyed Maggie so much that Maggie wanted to pull his cloth cap over his face and suffocate him. But she felt good being around them so they put up with each other for her sake.

Maggie's had seemed the obvious place to come after the funeral. She asked them about it but didn't linger on it. 'What was the sermon like?'

'Rubbish,' said Jack succinctly.

'The vicar said that Claudette was an inspiration and that we could all learn from her,' said Nell.

'See? Rubbish.'

Maggie, back pointedly to Jack, asked from her deckchair, 'And what do you think you learned from your grandmother, Nell?'

Nell surprised her companions by saying, 'A lot.' Claudette had tried to teach her granddaughter how to match her shoes to her handbag, but her legacy to Nell was 'She taught me how not to live my life.' She smiled, hesitant. 'That sounds disrespectful, but I don't mean it that way.'

It was a fairly negative memorial but Claudette's death had sharpened Nell's philosophy. At the Sunday-lunch table, she'd told the people around her that they were the truly important ingredient in her life. This simple fact was clearer than ever to her now; her grandmother would have dismissed it as useless sentiment. Nell tried haltingly to explain to Maggie who, instead of resting her eyes as Jack promptly did, listened with her usual care.

Maggie narrowed her eyes against the sun. Shielding her

face with one soft fleshy arm, she said, 'There was somebody missing from that table, wasn't there?'

Nell sighed.

'And he's only five gardens away.'

'If you're going to say, "Seize the day . . ."'

'That's exactly what I'm going to say.'

'Haven't you noticed, Maggie?' Nell gestured at the low sun. 'The day is almost over.'

'Almost. But not quite.'

Tina and Nell's rapprochement meant that Mario's had been reinstated as their lunchtime haunt. Nell was leering at the dessert selection like a dirty old man in a Girl Guides' changing room. 'Lemon meringue or pink moussey stuff?' she pondered.

'Neither,' advised Tina. 'What are you doing tonight? Do I know?'

'No.' Nell snatched up the lemon meringue *and* the pink concoction. She said, 'The solicitor's coming round to read the will.'

With a gasp, Tina wheeled to face Nell. 'The will! OhmyGod!' She put her hand over her mouth. 'You're going to be rich! You're going to be really rich! Really, *really* fucking rich!'

Nell's face darkened. 'Tina, shut up. And get a move on.' They were holding up the queue.

At their corner table Tina prattled on in the same vein: 'You're her only living relative. Well, the only one she admits to. Let's see . . . that flat alone must be worth over a million. And then there's all that art and all those antiques and the jewels . . .' She stopped, lost for words. 'You're going to be—'

'You said.'

'Rich!'

'Can we drop this?' Nell wasn't matching Tina's enthusiasm. In fact, she was decidedly morose. Tina, gushing like a geyser, didn't notice.

'Even if she leaves Fergus ten grand or twenty grand or a hundred grand you'll still be rich!'

'Jesus, Tina, could you stop using that word?' Nell pleaded.

'Why? It's one of the nicest words in the English language.'

'Tina, my grandmother has literally just been buried. I don't feel like dancing about in her jewellery just yet.' Nell pursed her lips. 'It just feels wrong to be . . . *whooping* about Claudette's money. After all, I don't think it brought her any real happiness.'

'I'd rather be unhappy in a tiara than unhappy without one,' muttered Tina, who was shameless when it came to wealth.

The truth was, it unnerved Nell. Did a millionairess still go to work on the tube? What kind of birthday presents would she buy? Would Tina want them to go to Monaco in their lunch-hour?

Tina waggled a fork. 'Oi. I don't want to hear that you've given it all to Helping Hands, all right?'

'Hardly. They'd probably throw it right back.' Nell didn't admit that this had crossed her mind. She shifted on her seat. Any mention of Helping Hands made her feel as if she had a stinging nettle down her knickers.

'Can I have Claudette's clothes?'

'Tina! Can't you wait until the bloody will is read?'

'Of course.' Tina looked contrite. 'But I can have her clothes, yeah?'

Nell didn't remember inviting her family to the reading of the will, but suddenly the elegantly appointed penthouse was overrun with them.

Annie was dribbling rusk on to a Chippendale sofa, while Canvey headed a ball against the handpainted silk wallpaper. Georgina, who was in charge of both children, ignored them as she stood flicking ash into an ancient Greek urn and asking Nell the price of everything. 'And that painting?'

'I don't know, Georgie.'

'And that statue thingy?'

'I really don't know.'

'What about that little bowl that Annie's rolling along the rug?'

'I don't know what it's worth but I don't think she should be playing with it.' Nell stooped to retrieve it but Fergus was there before her.

'It's Meissen, Miss,' he said icily, wresting it from tiny drool-covered fingers. 'The insurance value is two thousand pounds.'

'But it's tiny!' exclaimed Georgina. 'And it's minging.'

Noticing Fergus's pained look, Nell attempted to gain some control over her guests. 'Canvey, put the ball away. Georgie, could you pick Annie up? She keeps dribbling on things.'

'She *is* a baby, you know,' said Georgina, deeply insulted on her daughter's behalf.

From the hallway came the rhythmic stamp of feet. 'We came, we saw, we conga-ed!' sang Ringo lustily, as he led Patsy and the twins in a snaky line towards the drawing room. 'We came, we saw, we conga-ed.' They stopped, giggling and out of breath, as they crossed the threshold. 'You could hold a party in the hall,' he declared.

'This place is well cool.' John looked around approvingly. 'Can we borrow it when you own it?'

Aware that Fergus's ears were flapping like Dumbo's, Nell said evenly, 'Let's hear the will before we make any plans.'

Paul didn't want to wait. Surveying the drawing room with his ice blue eyes, he suggested, 'You want to get a plasma screen on that wall. It could slide out from behind a suede panel. Kind of James Bond meets Elvis.'

Stuffing a white-gloved hand into his mouth, Fergus left the room.

The solicitor had a dull voice and the beginning of the will made dull listening. Arrayed in gilt chairs behind Nell, her clan were restless. Like a music-festival audience who were only there for the headline band, they yawned through the necessary legalese and only perked up when bequests started being made. The local Conservative group got a few thousand, as did the church. Carita got a hefty lump sum plus some jewellery, and promptly burst into tears.

Nell leaned over to squeeze her hand, almost missing the words, 'And I leave the remainder of my estate in its entirety to . . .'

'Nell, listen! This is your bit!' hissed Patsy, behind her.

Nell, gulping, sat up straight to hear the solicitor clear his throat and repeat, 'I leave the remainder of my estate in its entirety to my loyal butler, Fergus Kincaid Duffy.'

It was the first time that Nell's family had ever been silent *en masse*. Even Annie's hiccups stopped.

The solicitor started to fold up his papers. Nell blinked, then turned to look at Fergus, who had insisted on standing up by the door.

The loyal butler was stunned, as if somebody had covertly entered the room and slapped his face with a sizeable haddock. His eyes met Nell's and he recovered sufficiently to nod at her.

Nell nodded back, without knowing why. She had never lost a fortune before and she wasn't sure how one behaved.

She turned to look at her mother, stepfather and siblings. 'Fish and chips, anyone?'

Tina couldn't believe it and repeated it, so loudly and so many times, that Nell eventually sent her an email asking her to shut up or find another job.

Despite the nonchalance she was cultivating, Nell found this development hard to digest. She didn't mind not having the money: it was the fact that Claudette had left her nothing at all. Not even a knick-knack. Had it been, she wondered, deliberately cruel? Should she read some kind of message into it? Should she construe it as payback from beyond the grave for exposing Claudette's secrets?

After a lot of mental tussling, Nell chose to believe that her grandmother had recognised the shift in Nell's priorities. Claudette had finally listened to Nell and accepted that, for her granddaughter, there were more important things in life than wealth. Perhaps the old lady had even understood at the last that her money had distorted her life, not enhanced it.

Yes, that was it.

And, of course, Nell *did* mind not having the money.

With scrupulous politeness, Fergus had insisted that Nell stay in Hans Place until she found somewhere else to live. She had accepted, even though it was disconcerting to see Fergus wandering about in John Lewis menswear instead of his uniform. She kept out of his way as much as she could.

'I feel like an illegal immigrant,' she moaned to Tina, as they sat sipping vodka in a Soho basement.

'There's only one thing for it. We've got to face facts.' Tina pulled an expression of deep sadness. 'We're going to have to share a flat.'

'Oh, no. That'd be awful. We'd have to sit up late drinking and talking,' moaned Nell.

'I know. And you can imagine how boring it's going to be at the weekends.' Tina sighed.

'And, worst of all, we'll have to share a taxi back from nights out like this.'

'It'll be hell. But, hey, we'll make the best of it.'

A moving date was set. When Nell told Fergus she was leaving to live with Tina good manners prevented him looking insanely relieved. 'Very well. As you wish,' he said, from the other side of the breakfast table.

These days, Carita was the only staff at Hans Place. She had agreed to stay on and look after Fergus. He seemed uneasy at being the master of the house, and sat awkwardly in a suit and tie first thing in the morning.

He'd told Nell generously she could choose anything she liked as a keepsake from the apartment. 'Might I suggest you take something that would be both a personal memento and somewhat valuable?' He hesitated, then said, with his habitual discreet language, 'It would be fitting for you to benefit monetarily in some way. After all, I think we both understand Madame's motives for the arrangements she made.'

'Do we?' Nell was still struggling with this begloved slap in the face from beyond the grave.

'Choose something, anything, and it's yours.'

'Hmm.' Nell had taken a long stroll round the penthouse, then told Fergus, 'I've made my choice.'

'I suspect I know what it is.' Fergus was allowing himself one of his rare smiles. It didn't suit his haughty face. 'The portrait?'

'God, no!' Nell would have no use for the large, fussily framed oil painting of her grandmother in all her *haute couture* regalia that dominated one end of the drawing room. 'I'd like the satin bedspread from the Heliotrope Room, if that's all right with you.'

Evidently puzzled, Fergus said of course it was.

Sensing he needed an explanation, Nell said, 'I don't need a painting to remind me of Claudette. She's pretty unforgettable. I just like the bedspread. It kept me warm and cosy at a time when I needed to feel that way.'

'I just presumed you would prefer a family piece,' murmured Fergus, who still spoke at butlering levels even though he was now a civilian.

'Ah. *Family*. Madame was quite wrong about families, you know.' This was sacrilege, and Fergus's expression told her so, but Nell barged on: 'Blood isn't thicker than water. Love's thicker than everything. My family is much bigger than the people I'm related to. I know that now. It includes all sorts.' Daringly, she nudged him. 'Even you, Fergus.'

Fergus straightened his tie and carried on reading his *Times*.

Another bottle of Louis's bad champagne was being opened. *Plip*, it muttered as Dean wrestled out the cork.

'Hurray!' said the little crowd round the reception desk, as animatedly as they could.

'To Jane and Barry!' Louis held aloft a plastic cup. 'Congratulations and may all your troubles, etcetera, etcetera,' He drained the cup. 'Right. I've got to go meet my wife and buy her something expensive.' He shook hands heartily with Jane From Accounts and her uniformed fiancé. 'If you're half as happy as Hildegard and I, you're two deeply unlucky bastards. 'Bye.'

'When's the big day?' asked Nell, squeezing her cup tight to stop herself yelling, 'DON'T DO IT! HE'S A MONSTER!' into Jane From Accounts's face.

'We don't like long engagements,' said Jane From Accounts, her cheeks shining pinkly and the red hearts dangling from her ear-lobes flashing on and off.

'Christmas time, maybe.' Barry took his job seriously and had refused alcohol. He was sipping sports Lucozade as he stood stiff in brown nylon. Under his peaked hat his eyes were alert for crowd trouble. If Jean should choose this moment to go berserk with an Uzi, Barry would be ready to handle it.

'Barry says it's going to be the wedding of the decade,' simpered Jane From Accounts.

'I'm sure it will,' said Tina, now fully trained in Being Nice to Jane From Accounts. 'It'll be like Charles and Diana all over again.'

Nell gave her the tiniest kick. Sometimes Tina tended to overdo it.

'Only we'll stay together for ever, won't we, Barrypops?' Jane From Accounts looked up devotedly through the two feet of empty space that separated her head from Barry's.

'You're going nowhere,' he said, with rather more menace than romance.

Linda counted on her fingers. 'Five months. Doesn't give you much time to slim into a wedding dress.' She smiled reassuringly, like a cosy mass murderer. 'Still, they do lots of nice designs with dropped waists.'

Gallantly, Len stepped in. 'She'll look a right bobby-dazzler in white,' he asserted, then ruined the compliment by saying generously, 'Anyway, I prefer a lass with a bit of flesh on her bones. That Kate Moss doesn't get my vote.' His smile was less broad these days, as he was running in new dentures.

Nell was looking over the heads of the little gathering. She was thinking of Phred. Maybe it was only because they were celebrating something (allegedly) romantic, but she had to admit it had been happening a lot. Romantic things made her think of Phred; unromantic things made her think of Phred; small dogs made her think of Phred; commercials for loo-cleaner made her think of Phred. Almost everything, in fact, turned her thoughts his way.

'Why don't you just live together?' asked Zoë, bluntly. 'I'm never getting married. It's only a piece of paper, after all.'

Barry disagreed. In a very loud voice. 'It's a legal procedure,' he barked. 'It's binding.'

'Awww,' said Jane From Accounts, in her special baby voice. 'Isn't he lovely?'

Jean, enjoying her last staff get-together before she toddled off for good in her droopy American tan tights, put her usual positive spin on events. 'I think it's marvellous to see two young people willing to stand up and commit themselves to each other,' she said graciously.

Barry put his arm round Jane From Accounts. 'Well, me mum's getting on and I can hardly do me own ironing, can I?' He laughed heartily at this *bon mot*. His fiancée forced out a titter.

Zoë stared open-mouthed at them. Unhampered by traditional notions of politeness, her face always illustrated what others only thought. Luckily the switchboard bleeped before she could verbalise and thereby inflict possible emotional scars on Jane From Accounts. 'Sorry, it's a work call.' She grimaced at Tina. 'Marti Goode. I'll put him through to your desk.'

'No,' said Tina, a flash of evil flitting across her features. 'Put him on speakerphone. And shush, everybody.'

Everybody obediently shushed, burying their noses in their champagne with a touch of resentment at being forced to listen to a business call during precious in-office alcohol consumption. 'Marti, hi. What can I do for you?' said Tina, in the hyper-casual voice he'd trained her to use with him at work.

'Can we be overheard? There's a funny echo on this line,' Marti whispered urgently.

'It's just a fault. Is this about your contract? Do you need me to fax you another copy?'

'This is about us. I need an answer from you. It's affecting my work.'

One or two heads bobbed up. Linda's antennae began to whir. This sounded interesting.

Tina said sweetly, 'An answer to what?'

Impatiently, Marti said, 'You know what! What we discussed last night. Tina, I need you back in my life. I've seen the perfect flat for you. And I know how you feel about soft-top VWs. How about a fluorescent pink one? And Bali next month?'

Zoë put her hand over her mouth in delighted surprise. This was gossip of the finest vintage, magnificent and priceless, and it was happening live at her reception desk.

'I don't know, Marti.' Tina feigned girlish indecision. 'I mean, we've been sleeping together for three years but I don't feel we've got anywhere. Why would things be different this time?'

Jean had to sit down suddenly on the chair that Dean quick-wittedly thrust under her.

'It just will be. Trust me.' He swallowed hard, and pushed out, *'Darling.'*

Zoë stuck her head under the desk and shook silently.

Tina asked, 'Do you love me, Marti?'

'Keep your voice down!' he hissed in panic. 'That witch Linda's probably on patrol!'

With great self-restraint, nobody reacted to that, although

the keen-eyed might have seen Linda's buttocks clench beneath her pleats. Zoë, under her desk, became totally, eerily still.

Marti returned to his silky, reasonable voice: 'Love's just a word, Tina.'

Jane From Accounts held Barry closer to her and he, in turn, jutted out his chin still further. Jean shook her lavender head sadly.

'And it'll all be out in the open?'

Nell watched her friend intently. This was pure malice. Tina's really seen through him, she thought, with relief. Nell, soft-hearted as ever, couldn't help feeling sorry for him. But not sorry enough to stop this deliciously wicked scenario.

'You've got to give me time,' Marti wheedled.

The little crowd looked at each other, pulling wry faces. 'He's had plenty of time,' their expressions seemed to say.

'Marti, I need to have some kind of assurance that you won't kick me out again at a moment's notice.'

Zoë's head reappeared above the desk. She'd stopped laughing. 'He's a git,' she scribbled on a Post-it and everybody nodded. Except Jean, who had left her reading glasses in the stationery cupboard.

Tina laboured the point. 'Can we get it out in the open or not?'

'Oh, Teen, it's not important. We've got each other – why does it matter who else knows? It's about you and me, no one else.'

'But I want people to know. I've chosen to be with you for all this time and it's part of who I am. I want the people I work with to know about us, Marti.'

'I know . . . and, believe me, I understand, but it's difficult. If life was as simple as that we'd all be happy. You know this crazy world we live in – surrounded by showbiz insincerity, people in it for themselves. They don't care about the real stuff and we don't need them. We can have our own special life, away from it all – just the two of us. It's you and me against the world, Teen. Just us, yeah?'

Marti's disembodied question hung in the air, dangling above the heads of his unsuspected audience. They watched Tina keenly, willing her to give the right answer. Tina twirled her cup as she looked at their expectant faces. 'Marti,' she said warmly, 'fuck off.'

A storm of applause and cheering burst out.

The paranoid splutters of 'Who's there? Who's listening?' were cut off as Zoë flicked the switch.

Thirty-three

A silence, dense and thick as snowfall in a forest, fell between them. They had both run the predictable gamut of reactions when the lift broke down: Blair had scrabbled at the point where the doors met, bleating like a trapped animal, while Nell had pressed all the buttons over and over again. After that they had reassured each other that they'd be rescued in a few minutes. Then they had harangued the lift-makers. Then they'd stared disbelievingly at their watches every thirty seconds. Then silence had broken out.

It was particularly cruel to be trapped with your least favourite gay man on the one night of your entire life when you knew you looked gorgeous, mused Nell, as she settled down on the rubber floor. The dress had worked its magic again when she'd slipped it on at Hans Place. It had hoisted her boobs, subdued her bottom and somehow achieved the effect of a thousand sit-ups on her tummy.

She looked down at her gold Jimmy Choos, the only Jimmy Choos she would ever wear. They had unravelled an extra yard of leg she hadn't known she had. The cheeky up-do by Tina's hairdresser had slimmed her face and the few tendrils trailing down on to her shoulders teased her bare skin and made her feel sexy, flirtatious.

Nell glanced across at Blair, who was mopping his sweating brow anxiously. A fat lot of good being sexy and flirtatious would do her in present company. Even Fergus had been impressed. She had noticed his impassiveness flounder as she'd flounced down the hall on her way out. For a nanosecond his eyes had widened, and for once Nell knew it was for a good reason.

Not a single photographer had witnessed her triumph over the ravages of a thousand Mars Bars and late nights. They were, apparently, all marshalled round the lift doors high on the roof garden of this 'sparkling nite spot', waiting for the A-, B- and Z-listers to be disgorged into a party celebrating the launch of a new alcopop.

Nell was a rose unsmelt. She might have been wearing a boiler-suit for all the notice Blair took of her appearance. He had been preoccupied from the moment she'd climbed into the limo beside him, but she had refrained from asking what the matter was. Tonight was to be their last night before the press release announcing their split and she already knew quite enough about him, thank you very much.

Nell looked at her watch again. A whole minute had passed since the last time she'd done this, and almost an hour had since the lift had juddered to a halt.

The silence was thickening to soup.

'How have your stools been?' A reliable conversational standby, this usually unleashed a good half-hour of self-analysis from Blair.

'Fine, thanks,' he said curtly, and resumed studying his shoes.

'And did your inner child manage to get over his bed-wetting?'

'Yes.' Blair was giving one-word answers to medical questions. Nell wondered if he might, for once, actually be ill.

Another minute passed.

Blair spoke suddenly, in a ragged voice: 'I hate the quiet,' he said 'I won't allow it at home. I always have the radio on. And the TV. Or I'm on the phone.' He threw his useless mobile petulantly on to the floor. 'If God had meant me to be quiet he wouldn't have given me a contract with Carlton.' He stabbed at the panel of buttons. 'There must be something we can do.'

'We just need to be patient,' advised Nell, quelling an urge to jump up and kick the doors.

'I'm too rich to be patient. I tell my microwave to hurry up.' Blair paced like a caged lion. Well, a caged spaniel. He stopped abruptly and asked urgently, 'Do you think this is God talking to us? Telling us to slow down, take a good look at ourselves?'

How like Blair, Nell thought, to assume that the Lord of Creation, the Architect of the Universe, would take time out from His busy day to stop a lift just so that one overpaid TV presenter, held together by the neat seams of various plastic surgeons, would take stock of himself. 'Maybe,' she murmured. 'Or maybe the lift technician's on a fag break.'

'This is why I dread the quiet,' confessed Blair, as if to himself. 'It makes me think.' He dabbed at his brow again, leaving a pale streak on his forehead. 'It's not good for me. I like action.' He made a motion with his hand like a shark moving through water. 'Oh, I wish I could remember me mantra.'

It occurred to Nell that there was something different about him. It was his voice. The campness had seeped out of it. He sounded more like a regular person, less like a performer. Risking a real question for the first time, Nell asked, 'Why don't you like thinking about yourself? You're very successful. A lot of people would kill to swap places with you.'

'*Professionally*, yes. I'm at the top of the tree. I'm gifted and handsome and adored.' Blair was admirably unencumbered by modesty. 'But I took a wrong turn a while back and now . . .' He grappled with the metaphor. He wasn't used to them. 'Now I'm trapped in the high grass, or something, and I don't know how to get back on to the . . . you know . . . the right path.'

'Are you talking about . . .' Nell trailed off. It was so easy to affront Blair, and despite their fake romance she was still an underling whose job depended on him.

'Yes, yes, I'm talking about being in the closet,' snapped Blair. He slumped, eyes shut and a frown across that famous face. Suddenly his brown eyes snapped wide and bright, he stood up straight and opened his lungs to bellow, 'I'M GAY!'

The noise echoed in the tiny enclosed space.

Blair, grinning, looked down into Nell's startled face. 'Christ, that felt good.'

Catching his mood, Nell jumped to her feet. 'YOU'RE GAY!' she yelled at him.

'I'M A HOMO!' shrieked Blair, throwing his arms in the air.

'YOU'RE A BENDER!' Nell was laughing riotously now.

'I'M A WUSS!' Blair was laughing too. It was robust and real, unlike the hooting noises he usually made.

'YOU'RE A WOOLLY WOOFTER!'

'I'M AS BENT AS A NINE-BOB NOTE!'

'YOU'RE CAMP AS A ROW OF TENTS!'

'I'M A SHOEBOX SHORT OF JOHN INMAN!'

'AND YOU'RE PROUD OF IT!'

'YES, I FUCKING AM!'

Their explosion of laughter and energy died down. Blair wiped his eyes, his hysterical laughter fading naturally.

Nell's laughter, however, had segued seamlessly into gulping sobs. 'I'm sorry,' she spluttered, through a waterfall of tears. 'I don't know what's wrong. I can't seem to *controoooooool* myself.' She was howling now.

'Oh, my Gawd.' Blair backed away, then crept towards her and patted her back timidly, as if she might explode. 'There there,' he said ineffectually. 'What's brought this on? I thought I was the one revving up for a nervous breakdown, not you.' He sounded slightly peeved.

'I'm sorry,' she insisted, in the time-honoured way of hysterical cryers everywhere. 'I'll be all right in a minute.'

'You don't look like you will,' said Blair, eyeing her dubiously.

'I will. I promise.' Nell struggled to contain the tears, feeling acutely sorry for Blair. Being trapped in a broken lift was bad enough, without her flooding it with oestrogen.

'You take as long as you like.' This invitation was distinctly insincere. He patted her again gingerly, as if testing a found body for signs of life, and repeated, 'There there.'

'It's just that I've taken a wrong turning too,' squealed Nell, making Blair jump back. Her voice had ascended swiftly to a pitch so high that dogs could have heard it streets away. 'I tried to improve myself and I tried to live a better life and I tried to be of some use but it's all collapsed and even my dead grandmother hates me and I cock everything up and I might as well give in and become a nun.' She followed this up with a long, possibly unique noise that was both cough and yelp, and attempted to clean her nose area with the back of her hand.

Looking horrified, Blair found his handkerchief and offered it to her. He watched for a while as she sobbed and apologised and apologised and sobbed, then narrowed his eyes to say, 'There's a man in this.'

It stopped her crying, but only so that she could turn on him angrily and say, 'Why does there always have to be a man involved? This is about me – *me*!' She jerked a thumb at herself. 'It's not about a man.'

'Oh, come on, love. That much bogey? Of course there's a man.'

'He thinks I'm horri*buuuuuuul*.' The sobbing was back.

'But you're not, are you? You're a little sweetie,' said Blair, in a matter-of-fact way.

'Am I?' Nell looked up from the honking nose-blow she was executing into his laundered hankie. 'He thinks I'm a bad person.'

'Put him straight.' Blair seemed unwilling to accept any complications. 'Just tell him. Don't dress it up. Say, "I want you, matey".' He sighed. 'God knows, I wish I'd been honest in my life. I wouldn't be sitting here, unable to cope with a few minutes' silence, if I'd lived the way I wanted to.' Blair slid down the wall of the lift and put his head on his knees.

Barely sniffling now, Nell sank down beside him, listening.

'I could be in a committed relationship now, with some wonderful man.' Blair looked into the middle distance. 'Or at the very least be drinking champagne out of a teenager's navel.' He gave a gentle, wry smile, unlike his usual high-calibre grins. 'You know, I had it all worked out when I walked into Louis's office the other day. I was going to tell him that when you and I stopped our silly charade I was going to come out. I'd finally do it. Stand up and tell the world.' He looked questioningly at Nell. 'The public would accept me, wouldn't they?'

Nell pondered for a moment. 'I think so. I think they know already and we're just treating them like they're stupid. They'd probably love you even more for being truthful with them. And you know what?' She patted the hankie back into his pocket. 'If they didn't, it'd be their loss.'

Blair peered down distastefully at his pocket. 'You're right. I know you're right. But I let Louis win again.' He poked her arm. 'Don't make my mistakes. If you've got something to say, you damn well say it, Nell. Find this bloke and tell him how you feel. In fact, tell him tonight. Fuck this stupid party. I want to go home anyway – all this honesty crap has worn me out. Take this opportunity and go to him.'

The lift shuddered. Deep below them the lift shaft groaned. 'Will you?' Blair's tone was urgent. As if he really cared.

Nell's chest constricted. She felt like a boxer about to go into the ring. She nodded, and a cold shiver tumbled down her backbone.

The lift started to travel downwards. They both stood up. Blair smoothed his hair and Nell rubbed under her smudged eyes with her fingers. Suddenly shy after the intimacy of the last few minutes, they avoided each other's gaze. There didn't seem to be anything else to say.

The lift stopped and the doors slid open. The vulgar cacophony of a hundred baying photographers, all eager to get a shot of the lovebirds who'd been stuck in the lift for an hour, burst over their heads as flashlights popped like fireworks.

Nell slipped off her shoes.

'Go, girl,' whispered Blair, with what sounded like pride.

She turned to him, drew back her hand and slapped his orange face resoundingly. 'How could you?' she screamed, taking care to enunciate carefully. 'Next time a girl falls in love with you, tell her you're gay first.'

Reeling from the slap, Blair's mouth dropped open. A ripple of hysteria ran through the photographers and the lightning storm of flashbulbs redoubled. Blair winked and Nell took off, out of the lift, through the scrum of paparazzi and down the dark street.

Nell's bare feet didn't register the debris of the pavements. She didn't notice the looks passers-by were giving the banshee dressed in gold. She didn't even notice that it was pouring with rain and her up-do was a half-way-down-do. Something had been kick-started during that one window of genuine communication with Blair and she was a woman on a mission.

In her head Nell could hear Maggie repeating doggedly, 'Seize the day.' She ran faster, taking corners at an angle and scattering disgruntled bus queues in her wake. She leaped over an upturned rubbish bin. Now she was two streets away from Helping Hands.

The lights were green. Nell zigzagged through the moving traffic. She raced down Camerton Street and took the steps down to the basement two at a time, only halting when she crashed through the doors of the dining-hall.

One door clanged back against the radiator. The line of people holding trays turned, startled, towards her.

Phred and Edith were doling out the dish of the day. Like the dinner queue, they gawped as she stood in the doorway.

Nell was breathing heavily, like a racehorse after the Grand National. Her gold dress was dripping raindrops on to the scuffed lino. Only one Jimmy Choo remained in her grasp. She leaned heavily on a table, suddenly aware of how far and fast she had run.

'Phred, I'm sorry,' she gasped, and bent over. 'I'm really,

really sorry. You don't know how sorry I am.' She straightened up. 'And, besides, I didn't even do it. So you're a bastard.'

Phred put his ladle down and stepped to the front of the counter. The homeless people, thrilled to be part of this scene, parted to make way for him.

'Yes, actually, you're a complete . . . bastard.' Nell warmed to this new train of thought. 'You decided I was guilty of betraying everybody and you never gave me a chance to defend myself. You just threw me out like a used – like a used – sausage. Yes, you heard – a used sausage,' she said, in a testy aside to a couple of tramps who were murmuring criticisms. 'So I'm crap at analogies – sue me.' She returned her focus to Phred, who was maddeningly passive in the face of this onslaught. She recognised this look: she'd seen it when he was calming the guy who'd threatened her all those weeks ago. 'And don't think you can treat me like a drunk Geordie,' she yelled, to the bafflement of everybody else in the room. 'I did my best and so what if my best wasn't good enough for you and your precious Helping Hands? I was getting somewhere. It *meant* something to me. And I did make a difference to a few people, I know I did.'

'She bakes a lovely cake.' A timid voice from the back of the room defended her.

'That's right.' One or two others joined in, muttering, 'Yes, that's true,' and 'A little too much vanilla for me.'

Nell soldiered on from her puddle by the door: 'I didn't sell that story. The quotes were made up. Somebody stole that photo of Clover and me. It was precious. I wouldn't embarrass Cloves like that. I wouldn't do that to you. I would never hurt you. Because . . .' She faltered.

A very deep, drunken male voice said confidently from under one of the tables, 'She's going to say she loves him.'

'Yes, I am, if you'll bloody let me,' snapped Nell. She looked straight at Phred. 'I know what you think of me and you probably hoped you'd never see me again, but love can be one-sided – it doesn't make it any less valid. Whether you want me or not I want you. So there. I love you, Phred.' She dropped her remaining Jimmy Choo and suddenly felt tiny as she stared at him, shivering, all the fight drained out of her.

Phred stood immobile, his face giving nothing away. He walked slowly towards her, peeling off his jumper. 'Arms up,' he ordered, when he reached her. She put them up obediently and he slid his jumper down over them. 'I can't let you get cold because people might think I don't love you, too.' He folded her into his warm arms. 'And you're much nicer than a drunk Geordie,' he told her, as they had their first kiss in front of an approving audience that smelt strongly of Special Brew.

'Thank you,' he whispered, into her wet hair. 'Thank you for coming back to me.'

Epilogue

Nell had heard the phrase 'great sex' a zillion times. Topless models who have one-night stands with footballers always claim to have had it; lads' magazines devote columns to it; problem pages are full of worried individuals wondering how to achieve it. She had never known what it meant, but had vaguely assumed that it must involve padded handcuffs and lots of yelping.

Now she knew. It meant having sex with Phred. 'That's one of the nicest things that's ever happened to me,' she whispered to him, as they lay in rumpled sheets by the open window. Birds were singing co-operatively as she stretched her toes like a contented cat.

'That's a very Nellish way of putting it.' Phred kissed the end of her nose and lingered there for a while, nibbling gently, until he pulled himself away with a sigh. 'I really don't feel up to explaining the birds and bees to Clover at this juncture so we'd better get up.' He put his head to one side.

'I love it when you do that!' squealed Nell.

He smirked.

'And I love it when you do that!' she squealed again.

He rolled his eyes.

'And I love it when you do that!'

It took them a long time to get down to breakfast.

They were referred to as 'Nell's lunches', and they were becoming a tradition. They were always on Sunday, and they involved friends, family and far too much food.

Nell was proud of this, but had some misgivings. For one thing, each lunch was a lot of work – even though Maggie bought, cooked and served the joint. For another thing, loving the people round the table didn't stop her wanting to shoot them occasionally.

For instance, Jack was a kind and lovable old gent, but he'd managed to argue with practically everybody. He got on very well with Canvey, but their kinship might have been based on the fact that Canvey had also argued with everybody. He had begun to talk about Philippe more often, and there was a glint in his eye when he did. Nell suspected she might be required to turn detective again soon: the idea both thrilled and terrified her.

Then there was Ringo's shaky grasp of political correctness. His amusing tales of how funny 'birds' were when they were all premenstrual went down like a cup of cold sick with Tina, who was prone to bouts of terminal scowling if she wasn't seated between the twins.

On this particular Sunday, Clover was crying noisily under the table, having just made the connection between what was lying on her plate and fluffy baa-lambs. Clover's father was deep in his girlfriend's bad books due in part to having underpraised the cooked breakfast she had risen at the crack of eleven to prepare, and due in part to his unwise confession that he had always rather fancied Kate Winslet.

Clover's Uncle Dexter, his handsome face showing the ravages of a hangover, was assiduously helping Carol to fill her plate. He was managing, Nell noticed, to ladle sprouts sexily. Now that Nell had spent time with Dexter she knew that he was on flirt mode at all times: his teasing pursuit of her had been nothing personal. She'd moved on from feeling miffed – with some effort – and now found herself smiling as she watched Carol ignore his seductive vegetable technique. Carol was far more interested in sternly eyeballing Leonardo and the girls, who had a tiny table of their own and seemed to be planning a gravy-throwing game.

Georgina and the twins were having a noisy disagreement about whether her current beau was a 'nonce' or not. She was certain that he wasn't, but the twins had detected nonce-like qualities.

Out in the kitchen, Nell and Maggie were dividing up a jam roly-poly. 'Give me strength,' muttered Nell, as she heard John and Paul start to chant, 'Nonce! Nonce!' over the sound of Georgina screaming in frustration.

'Do you ever think back to the days when you used to say you were orphaned?' whispered Maggie, as she took a dented pan of custard off the heat.

'Yes. With great nostalgia,' said Nell, grimly.

Maggie laughed. 'I don't know about blood being thicker than water. I reckon your custard's thicker than anything.' She poured a generous glop over each untidy serving. 'This binds us together, love, doesn't it?' She gave Nell a squeeze. 'We're all Nell's family, these days.'

'Oh, Maggie,' said Nell, emotionally, but was silenced from going any further by Maggie's application of a spoonful of roly-poly.

As they carried through trays groaning with calories, fat and fun, Nell asked suspiciously, 'What's going on?' Everybody was huddled together down one end of the messy table, hunched over something.

'It's the *Oracle*,' said Phred, with one of his smirks. 'Look at the front page.'

He held it up so that Nell could read the shrieking headline. 'BLAIR'S PLAYBOY PAL'. Beneath it was a close-up of Blair Taylor enjoying a lingering kiss with a handsome, dark-haired man.

'OH, MY GOD!' Nell dropped the roly-poly. Who would have thought Fergus was so photogenic?

THE RELUCTANT LANDLADY

BERNADETTE STRACHAN

Actress Evie Crump *seems* to have it all: glamorous job, beautiful man, and now – thanks to an unexpected inheritance – a lovely big house.

In reality, Crump isn't the name-in-lights to get Hollywood producers banging on her door; the man is her best friend Bing – more likely to borrow her kinky knickers than buy them for her; the house is a rambling ruin complete with lodgers from hell.

Then Evie gets her big break – in a dog food commercial. Suddenly she has two roles to play: leading lady to her gorgeous leading man, and reluctant landlady in the real-life soap opera of 18 Kemp Street – where the plot is about to thicken . . .

'Bernadette Strachan has ticked all the boxes for her debut novel . . . True love and a happy-ever-after ending? Well, that would be telling' *Heat*

HODDER